All In Glory

Web site:
http://www.ElisabethLee.com

Facebook:
http://www.facebook.com/pages/
Elisabeth-Lee/35316901242

All In Glory

A Carlyle Hudson Mystery

Elisabeth Lee

ISBN-13: 978-0-9839238-4-8

Publisher: Affinity Resources, LLC
Denver, Colorado

Also By Elisabeth Lee

For Glory
Flashes of Glory
All In Glory

For Aja

—inspiration for Glory, who taught me about sniffing under doors. Even now she can still mix it up.

1

It wasn't like a vow of chastity or anything; I just needed time away from the game. I'd been playing cards for so long in so many casinos, I lost touch with myself. Playing poker is just a job with a set of rules and expectations. The rules make sense; the expectations annoy me. As did the faces with their tics and tells, night after night. I'd look at the cards in my hand and wonder if this was a life. It was depressing, not to care if I'd win or lose. Ironically, I won. A lot. But it felt like dying. My dealer friend, Ann Marie, suggested a December break, a time out, to get my edge back. I took her advice. Besides, as my aunt, Loretta, pointed out, chastity is unhealthy for women of a certain age.

No sooner than I had left my house I was forced to park near the old steam engine in the park. I'd forgotten that the Lawrence Christmas Parade was in full horse today, literally. Massachusetts Street, the old-fashioned Main Street of downtown Lawrence, Kansas was closed from 7th Street to 13th, potential shoppers mobbing the sidewalks.

The Lawrence Christmas Parade is a 30-year-old event that feels like it's been around for a hundred years. The Parade is the only exclusively horse-centered parade in the Midwest, and it takes place regardless of weather, except if there is excessive ice, which is considered a danger to the horses. Two-footed participants are on their own. Farms, ranches, and organizations like the Nicodemus Buffalo Soldiers Association try to outdo each other with authentic coaches and wooden vehicles, costumes, and holiday trappings. Pride of place goes to Santa hanging off the back of a stagecoach at the rear of the parade. He waves onlookers home, or off to more shopping and lunch.

Outside on the brick sidewalk, I looked around at the late morning shopping scene. The Christmas season was in full swing, with decorated lampposts, holiday banners, and small, twinkling lights festooned everywhere. There were people in Santa hats, pushing strollers, negotiating their shopping bags around each other, and the occasional knot of carolers, but they're like mimes, as far as I'm concerned. It always feels like there's more than one. I gritted my teeth and turned north, heading up the street, looking for coffee or a jewelry store, any excuse to pop indoors out of the cold. Maybe I'd find a warm jacket somewhere. My ass was definitely freezing.

A hefty Santa stood in front of a new shop across the street that might do. It had cheery SALE! signs plastered across the glass. Crossing in the middle of the street, between a buckboard stacked with hay bales, pulled by two draft horses wearing Santa hats and a small buggy driven by a lady in Victorian garb. Her white pony wore an evergreen garland. I felt someone quickly cut ahead of me on the left. Gray hair sticking out over his ears, shorter than me, Santa hat. That's all I had time to register before the guy reached the other sidewalk and drew a classic western six-gun, the kind they carried in those 50s black and white movies, from a holster on his leg.

I was in the middle of Mass Street, between slowly moving horses. Didn't really have a choice, I told myself, had to move forward. So I ran, right behind the gun-packing Santa.

"Aw shit!" the hefty Santa shouted. He ducked into an alley, but instead of running away, hefty Santa turned his face to the wall and cowered. Was he whimpering? The gun-packing Santa walked up and clocked hefty Santa on the side of the head. At least he didn't shoot him. Mr. Hefty sagged to the ground and six-gun Santa stepped back and started kicking and cursing at him.

"Cut that out!" I yelled, shoving the guy, who had no idea anyone was behind him. The man made a sharp, startled noise, grabbed the Santa hat off his head, and ran north, up the street.

I knelt down next to Santa's victim to see if he was still with us. Well, I couldn't just stand there looking at the poor guy. Fortunately, Hefty was still breathing, doing a little groaning and moaning, too. Unfortunately, he didn't seem entirely conscious and the side of his head was bleeding. A small crowd of silent people gathered around us.

"Hey!" I pulled on the coat of a nearby woman. "Call 911, would you? We don't want to be here all day!" She pulled out her phone and got with it. I stuck my cold hands under my arms and continued to kneel by the stricken Santa. A pair of brown cowboy boots pulled up beside me. I looked up to find familiar, crinkly eyes and moustache beneath the customary Stetson.

"I didn't lay a finger on him!" I yelled up at MacDonald George.

2

I stood up, shrugged my blue satchel back over my shoulder, looked up at Mac and stepped into a hug. Not a quick, hello hug, something larger, more capacious, and close. Glued together close, right there on the street.

He stepped back first, breaking me out of my trance. "Nice hat." His hands still on my shoulders. I whipped the old beret off my head and shook my hair back.

"No it's not! It's a relic!" I was sure there was a line right across my forehead from pulling the hat too tight. I was pretty sure the old beret made me look like my mother. Her hat.

MacDonald George, just by standing there, made it hard for me to think. More than the physical appeal of dark eyes, broad shoulders, long legs, deep voice—OK, the physical appeal was considerable—but *more* than that, we had a history that confused me. And here he was, dressed almost exactly as he was when we met—leather jacket, wool scarf, leather gloves, Stetson—bringing that history up again, just by standing there. Bastard. His smile told me he was probably reading my mind, feeling pretty good about the lines on the page of that history. If he didn't look good enough to eat, I'd hate him.

As it was, I didn't know what I felt. Not true. I did know what I felt, I just didn't want to feel it. Any other woman standing there in the street with this good looking man looking at her that way would say I was crazy. Most of me would agree.

I was saved from any more chagrin and internal rambling by the arrival of the ambulance and police. A retired detective, Mac knew all of them and introduced me so that I could identify myself and give a statement about how the guy in the Santa hat came to lie bleeding on the sidewalk. I pulled the beret back on to keep from freezing.

"Coffee?" Mac asked, after I'd done my civic duty. I nodded numbly and he steered me to a coffee shop a few doors away. The Mug roasted their own beans, which made it a popular place. But they could have set dancing bears on fire for all I cared, I was that cold.

"If you unclench your teeth, you'll warm up faster," Mac advised me, putting a mug into my hands. I took a sip. Soymilk. The man remembered everything. I stretched my jaw tentatively. It was indeed clenched.

Mac sat across from me at a small square table near a paneled wall in the small coffee shop, well out of the draft from the door. Stetson balanced on crossed legs as of old, gloves on the table, Mac loosened his scarf and watched me drink my coffee. I found his innate self-assurance and ease anywhere he happened to be profoundly irritating.

"Better?"

I drained the mug, removed the evil beret, and ran a hand through my hair, hoping to bring the silver mess of it into some kind of order. "Yes, thanks. How've you been?" MacDonald George smiled, not even bothering to shake his head.

"I seem to be a magnet for random scenes of violence whenever I come to town. That's what you're thinking, isn't it. Well, I just got here yesterday, Mac. I didn't make it happen. I don't even know those guys." I was rambling, possibly working myself up into a rant. Couldn't figure out how to shut myself up. "I just walked right into it. Bam! Santa's going down!" I smacked my hand on the table, startling a rumpled, sour-faced man in tweed reading the paper at the table next to us. Mac reached forward and placed a calming hand over mine.

I took a deep breath and regarded the hand. It was gorgeous, just like the rest of him. Long fingers, firm rather than slender. A large, capable hand that did pretty much anything it wanted and did it well. I loved Mac's hands, and remembered things about them.

"It's OK," he said.

What was OK? Memories? Mixed feelings? Bleeding Santa?

"Sorry." Gave myself a quick, mental shake. "Guess I'm not feeling like myself." I gave him a rueful smile and squirmed around, uncomfortable with such a blatant truth. I started gathering up hat and gloves.

"You look good, Lyle." The words and the voice pulled me to his eyes. I found myself suddenly sitting very still, waiting.

"You, too, Mac, as always." I paused, flirting with him. "In fact, you just keep looking better each time I see you."

Nothing. Silence from the man. Clearly, MacDonald George was not in the mood to flirt back. Eyes on mine, he scooted his chair closer, so I could feel his breath as he spoke quietly into my ear.

"Lyle. I don't know what to do about you. But I want you to know I'm working on figuring it out, so take care."

"Take care? Like you're challenging me to a duel?"

Mac chuckled but continued with his point. "I'm seeing a therapist…"

"What?" I drew back in surprise. "Dating?"

"Yes. No. I was. I'm not. It's all kinda complicated." He pulled me back toward him.

"It's driving me crazy, being attracted to a woman who's never there, wanting you, only you, instead of some other woman nearby who might want to stick around." His voice had a raspy edge to it that made me shiver. He turned my face and kissed me full on, then let me go.

"Oh." The feel of his moustache left me at a loss for words. "I'm sorry."

Mac stood up, taking the Stetson off the table and putting it on his head, swept the gloves up, too. Nodded at me. "You will be." He turned and left the coffee shop, leaving me sitting there with the empty mugs. No more Mr. Nice Guy with polite manners. I licked my lips thoughtfully and smiled.

3

Why Kansas? Why not San Francisco where I had my own place, where winter was lush and green and smelled of eucalyptus trees, where the ocean danced with light. That's what Chas wanted to know. But Chas had a new love and wasn't really listening, was probably examining his blond hair for signs of gray in the mirror as we talked on the phone. The Heartland at Christmas, was I crazy? I could end up in a ditch at the side of the road, in a high-cholesterol sugar coma, he warned me. "Lyle, do not," he scolded, "let them put antlers on your dog." Point taken.

As it turns out, it wasn't antlers for the dog, and the body in the ditch at the side of the road wasn't mine. She was somebody else, strangled and left there.

It wasn't so much a choice to return to Lawrence as it was a default position, like folding your cards when you have no hand. I have a love-hate relationship with the place. I know it well; I'd grown up there. But even then it never felt like home.

Could have been I was lying to myself, afraid to admit that I belonged anywhere. Belonging means relationships; relationships mean expectations, obligations. To which I was allergic. Except for the house. It I loved.

I inherited the house a couple years back, when my mother died. A classic Victorian on a quiet street in an Old West Lawrence neighborhood, a place of brick sidewalks and tall trees, a few hitching posts still left, where people once tied horses. I loved the wraparound porch, the dark wood floors, the banister, the spacious rooms, the fireplaces. Louise's furnishings were still there. When I cooked, I used her pots. Drank coffee from her mugs. She was still there, in the paintings and the chairs, the towels and dishes. I hadn't made a dent in the house, hadn't really tried to.

When I was out of town, which was most of the time, Crista Banks looked after the house, taking in the odd roommate from time to time. Everyone had to be OK with my sudden, unannounced arrivals and departures. So far things had worked out. I liked Crista's youthful creativity, her Gothic princess style. She liked living in the top of the house and looking out over the trees, in the room I'd had when I was young. We both liked the independence the arrangement gave us.

Winters tend to be windy and dry in eastern Kansas, not at all the snowy postcards people imagine. This year it was bitter cold. People stayed indoors and piled on the heavy sweaters. I hadn't brought much clothing with me from Las Vegas, certainly no hefty sweaters, so I was rummaging through closets, looking to see what was there, muttering under my breath about freezing my ass off.

Glory enjoyed the activity and trotted beside me from, room to room, her toes clicking delicately on the polished wood floors, her stubby white tail wagging as I opened drawers and pulled stuff out, looking for anything that would help me stay warm.

I inherited the dog along with the house. A smooth-haired fox terrier, Glory has the lean lines of a whippet or a pointer, sleek muscle made for running. Black ears, black mask across the eyes, black nose, the rest of her pure white. Glory was always checking my eyes to see what I was thinking, hoping it would involve words like WALK, BALL, or FOOD. In that order.

I'd have to find something for Glory to wear, too. She wasn't built for cold weather and wasn't used to it, having spent most of her time recently in a warmer climate and hotel rooms. Louise had knit the dog a sweater, but I had no idea where it was. It could have been thrown out, it was so ugly. When she wore it, Glory looked like a hairball with legs.

"No antlers, Glory. Not gonna happen."

During my quest for warmth-producing garments, I'd come across storage spaces filled with Christmas decorations and ornaments, some of them quite old, remnants of my mother's childhood. One box held a leather rope of sleigh bells that shivered with sound as I lifted it. The bells gleamed, but the leather looked worn and cracked. I'd have to bring it downstairs and rub some lanolin into it. I smiled. Louise would like that.

I looped the heavy bells over one shoulder and bunched the pile of sweaters under my chin, so I could see where I was going. My plan was to drop off the sweaters on the second floor then take the rope of bells down to the kitchen. Things didn't go exactly as planned.

I did make it down to the second floor, but as I turned to walk down the hall to my room, a small, dark shape skittered past my feet and raced ahead of me. Someone yelled "shit!" behind me. Glory scrambled for purchase on the smooth floor and took off after the furry shape, barking joyously, bloodlust in her voice. There was a thudding of bare feet, a collision of bells, sweaters flying, bodies falling, people and dog yelling and cursing. Something screamed.

Caitlin, couch-surfer and guest-in-residence, sprawled across Glory's back, her hands on the dog's jaws, trying to free whatever it was the dog had in her teeth. Glory's growl shifted into high gear, her eyes rolling murderously. Not good. I crawled over to Caitlin and piled on top of the heap of girl and dog, putting one hand firmly on each neck. Caitlin growled at me, momentarily silencing Glory and shifting the focus of the dog's attention.

"Let me do it," I said gently and wriggled closer to Glory, my hands replacing Caitlin's on the dog's muzzle. Caitlin backed away, giving me room to move. Placing the other hand on the brown, yucky thing in the dog's mouth, I bent my head so my face was touching its wet fur. I inhaled deeply and blew a sharp breath straight up the dog's nose. Glory hates that. She opened her jaws immediately, releasing the limp creature into my hand, proceeding to sneeze furiously and scramble to her feet for more sneezing.

I stood up, wiping dog slobber and wet fur with one hand, handing the ball of fur to Caitlin with the other.

"Dammit, Caitlin. It's a rat." Not a question. Not a small rat, either, judging by the length of naked rat tail. "It better be dead," I added.

"Better not!" Caitlin said, shaking the disgusting mess and looking for signs of life. "Miss B. will only eat them if they're alive."

"Then you'd better hurry up and throw it in her cage while it's still warm." I pointed back down the hall to her room.

"Yeah. Maybe she's hungry and won't notice."

Miss B. was Brunhilde, Caitlin's boa constrictor. Caitlin herself was a snake-wearing, tiny young woman of cherubic countenance and aggressive attitude. She prided herself on living off the grid, tolerated no fools and took no prisoners, especially if animal rights were involved. The rat was an exception, its sole function in life to be snake chow. I had no real interest in how that was working out.

Pushing possible snake-and-rat scenarios out of my mind, I retrieved the sweaters and the loop of sleigh bells and headed down the hall. Glory removed her nose from the bottom of Caitlin's door and followed me.

The room used to be my mother's. Now, painted a pale yellow, it was arranged more as a sitting room with a bed in it. You could build a case that I'd spent too much time in hotel rooms, but the set up worked for me. It felt friendly, no particular demand to get to bed and get to sleep.

Glory jumped into a chair by a window and stood looking out at bare branches and a cold, gray day, her eyes scanning the sidewalk below for something to bark at.

Placing the bells and sweaters on the bed, I went and sat beside her, turning her pointed muzzle toward me to check for rat bites. No marks. Regulation dog breath. I ran my hands over her silky black ears and got a brief lick. The dog turned and settled herself beside me with a contented grunt.

I disliked thoughtful, quiet moments like this, the opportunity to just sit and think about life. But what the hell. I was here now. If I was lucky, there wouldn't be feelings and I could just get on with it. Figure out what *it* was. Fortunately, the moment didn't last.

Shoving the dog off of me, I decided to examine the sweaters. Most of them were crap—too old, wrong color, unshapely, whatever. I piled them on the floor to go out or to Goodwill. Probably a lot of stuff in the house could go with them. There was an orange merino that would work, though. I pulled it on and checked it out in the mirror.

Not bad. The sweater was warm and appealed to my anti-Christmas spirit. The color went well with the silver hair, too. I smiled, accentuating the characteristic Hudson architecture of my face. We all had it, my three aunts and I, the cheeky lines beside the mouth that made you want to smile with them. I'd found it handy when playing poker. One or two people said it was scary. The smile in the mirror widened.

Leaving the bells for later, I collected my blue leather satchel and various pieces of outerwear and left the house, telling Glory it was too cold, she'd have to stay home. She could sulk if she wanted to, but I wasn't going to change my mind, it was just too cold.

Environmental guilt reminded me that I could easily walk down to Massachusetts Street, called Mass Street by the locals. But environmental guilt would not have to carry stuff back to the house, or deal with the cold. I wanted the option to change my mind about where I went. And I loved the heated seats in my new car.

I've grown to like new cars and this car is hot. As in sexy, not stolen. I don't steal cars. I win them at cards or buy them outright.

It was sheer elegance that sold me on the Benz. That and a boatload of cash from a streak of outrageous success at the card table. Huge amount of money, just crying for a special purchase.

With 510 horsepower, the CL Class Coupe 600 has a bi-turbo V-12 engine and can go from 0 to 60 in 4.5 seconds, the distinguished salesman said. Really? My eyebrows rose over my impenetrable sunglasses. Why would I need all that? You never know; his white teeth glimmered through a mahogany tan.

It was a hell of a test drive, out of Vegas onto empty roads where I did indeed punch it, screaming well past 90 mph. The man figured it was safer not to distract a woman at such speed, so he wisely kept his mouth shut. The car purred, I purred, the salesman purred, sensing the cards were all his and he would sweep the table without lifting a finger.

He was right.

I refused to sit through all the paperwork and said I'd be back the next day, when I'd sign what I had to sign and the car would have to be delivered to me at the Kansas City airport. Oh yes, and I'd pay cash.

There was a bit of a kerfuffle over that one, but I told the manager No Cash, No Deal. They worked it out. She's a beautiful car: iridium silver, black leather interior with burl walnut trim. Black and silver look so good on me.

4

After Mac departed I pulled the old beret of Louise's down over my ears, adjusted my scarf and gloves, and scanned the other side of the street, looking for a boutique or clothing store. It was stupid to be walking around in this cold without a jacket.

A group of four college kids in Santa hats and blue Kansas University sweatshirts bounded onto the sidewalk in front of me, hands shoved into jeans pockets. To keep the pants up, no doubt. They'd just dodged between and around cars, leaping across the crowded street, laughing and joking and talking in that loud way kids have, defining their space with sound.

I pushed through them and stepped into a doorway on my left, desperate for warmth. It was a jewelry store, with cloisonné frogs and mistletoe in the window. Not a Santa or a Mac in sight. I felt safe.

It was one of those shops that had opted to keep as much of the original Nineteenth Century detailing as possible—pressed metal ceiling, wooden floors, brick walls. Jewelry was displayed inside glass top tables and apothecary shelves, handmade stuff by local artists blended in with high-end pieces and more affordable, imported, ethnic items. There were pre-made settings for rings and trays of loose stones. In this place you could invent your own jewelry. I liked the ambience. My hands were thawing out, too.

The only customer in the shop, I browsed for a while, thinking of my aunts, savoring the warmth of the shop. I had my nose literally pressed up against a case of bracelets and small carvings, when I felt the creak of floorboards as someone moved toward me from the back of the shop.

"Here, let me help you with that." A hand reached forward with a key and unlocked the case. Then the woman stood back unobtrusively, giving me tacit permission to explore.

I was no exception to the magic chemistry between women and jewelry cases, and I leaned in with wonder, picking up bracelets and turning them over in my hands, feeling the weight, watching the play of light on amethyst or topaz. It was like Ali Baba's cave, only better.

The woman stepped close beside me and reached up to a higher shelf. "Here, look at these." She held out two small carvings, one in each hand, a malachite bear and a small white cat. I lifted my gaze, inquiring.

"Ivory. Chinese, I think. You don't see these anymore." A quiet voice, gentle smile. I looked at her as she handed me the white cat.

"You don't know me, do you," she asked. More of a statement.

"Sorry, no." We stood there, just looking at each other. No particular pressure, giving it time. She was about my height and weight, about my age. Hair a warm brown—dyed—shoulder length, no gray. Blue eyes, clear gaze. Stunning cat's eye earrings.

"High school?" I was grasping at straws. But in Kansas, all relationships went back to high school, so it was a safe bet. She smiled, reading me.

"Wait." Now that I'd said it, the high school part of my brain kicked in, a part of my brain I didn't use too much and tried to avoid, along with all things Kansan. The brain skipped into overdrive.

"You…were an art student. Painter?"

The woman nodded. "Andressa Keach."

"Lyle Hudson," I said, shaking her hand.

"Carlyle. Yes, I know," she replied. "You were into books, and in the drama club."

"Right. I'm afraid I can't remember much else," I said.

"Not a problem. It was a long time ago. What do you think of the cat?"

I looked at the tiny carving I held in my hand. The color of cream, the ivory cat curled around itself, lithe rather than cuddly, pointed ears a perfect curve of a neck, a suggestion of hipbone.

"It's lovely," I murmured. "Luce would love it."

"Yes, she would!" Andressa Keach laughed.

"You know her?" Stupid question. Despite its size, just shy of 90,000, Lawrence was basically a small town. I felt like an idiot.

"Hard not to." Another smile.

I purchased the cat and we chatted a bit as she wrapped it and wrote up the slip. Andressa had taken over the shop from her parents, who were getting on in years. I told her about my travails and irritations with Hyacinth, my mother's bridal shop, now mine. She commiserated with a rueful smile. We agreed to get together over coffee or a drink sometime soon. There was a mutual appreciation between us, so I knew we would. We exchanged cell numbers.

Back outside on the sidewalk, ivory cat tucked safely in my blue satchel, I could almost hear Louise's voice, happy that her difficult daughter Carlyle had a new friend.

It didn't take me long to find a winter coat in the store plastered with SALE signs. I needed something that covered my knees, to keep in as much warmth as possible. I settled on a faux shearling with a hood. Black. Right price, wrong color. I look good in black; it offsets the silver hair. However, Glory is mostly white; her tiny little hook-like hairs dig in and don't let go. Too bad. I wore the coat out of the store.

Walking back down Mass Street toward my car, I noted yet more Santa hats. Maybe someone was giving them away. Or perhaps the hat was all that was left of Santa these days. Hardly anyone bothered with the full regalia of beard, boots, and shiny black belt cinching a rotund, red and white clad belly. Salvation Army volunteers were mostly replaced by paid donation collectors who waved candy canes instead of ringing a bell. No more Ho, ho, ho's, either.

Catching sight of my reflection in a passing window, I blinked. Not bad. The coat was doing wonders for my hair. But not great. The woman in the window had shadows under her eyes, as if she hadn't been sleeping. She looked like something was eating at her, but before I could think what that might be, she looked away.

I walked along the sidewalk, enjoying the warmth of the coat. I could duck back through the sporting goods place to get to the car or walk the length of the block and take 9th Street. I felt like walking but my stomach told me it was time for lunch. And I needed to give Glory a quick out.

The parade had ended. My fellow pedestrians split off, turning right to stay on Mass Street, or stopping to cross 9th and head south, looking for more shopping, or lunch. I felt like a lone bird leaving the flock. Pleased with the image, I took a few long strides, and then a car pulled into the bus stop on my left. It was a ratty old mastodon of a station wagon in need of a new muffler. I stopped and watched as the passenger door flew open and my aunt Loretta bounded onto the curb.

"Lyle! You're here!" She grabbed me in a viselike hug, giving me a smooch and turning to yell at the driver of the car. "Vern, I told you it was Lyle!"

Loretta's Santa hat, perched precariously above her curly, white ponytail, slipped over her eyes. Squashing the hat with one hand, she held onto me with the other. We were grinning hugely.

"Nice hat, Santa,' I said, giving Loretta a kiss.

"You, too! Lord, girl, you look just like your mother! Vern! Doesn't she look just like Louise?" Vern nodded, chuckling behind the steering wheel.

Loretta used a lot of decibels, indoor and out. It was a miracle the man still had his hearing.

"So," Loretta turned back to me, still talking, still holding on. "How long will you be here? Where've you been keeping yourself? Been shopping? Hey, is that a new coat? Did you get my Christmas present yet?" Each question punctuated by the fluffy bouncing ball at the tip of the red hat.

I'm staying for a while. Ta da!"

Loretta rolled her eyes. "You and *a while* are not usually such good pals. Excuse me for asking! And I'm not seeing any reassuring shopping bags, neither." Her bright eyes squinted at me suspiciously, making me laugh.

"My satchel works just fine in that department," I teased, taking a step back.

"Huh! Any present small enough to fit in there'd be pretty puny!"

The car made a strangled tooting sound and we looked over to see Vern jerking a thumb at the bus coming up behind him. They were all wearing Santa hats, Loretta, Vern, and the bus driver. I shook my head.

Loretta dashed back to the car and turned before getting in. "No cameo appearances, Lyle! We want to see your face! In person!"

I saluted her order, turning it into a wave as the car rumbled slowly into traffic. I gave a final wave to the patient bus driver, who waved back and smiled. Then I ducked through a low hedge to cross the park and find my car.

A parking patrol officer in a Santa hat was cheerfully slipping a ticket onto a windshield. I met her eye and smiled. Surprised, she smiled back and returned to her vehicle. Go, Santa.

At the Mercedes, I found a piece of brown paper under the wiper. It looked like a piece of grocery bag. CALL ME written in black felt pen. The hell I would. I folded the scrap of paper and put it in my new coat pocket as I got in the car.

5

I could hear Glory dancing around as I unlocked the kitchen door. She was a one-dog welcoming committee, absurdly, joyously delighted that I had come back to her, wagging her tail so hard that her rear legs skipped off the ground. I wondered if all dogs manifested this manic intensity, or if it was a terrier thing, or simply particular to Glory. Whatever it was, it was contagious and I never failed to feel ridiculously happy to see her.

I knelt down to rub the dog's neck and to let her lick my face, laughing and ducking my head to avoid the worst of it. Mid-lick, Glory stopped and noticed the coat, sniffing shoulders and sleeves, looking to see what it was and where I'd been.

I quickly stood up, but not quick enough to avoid the dusting of white dog hair. Not expecting to have much effect, I brushed the sleeves briskly. Dog hair slid smoothly from the suede-like material. I broke out in a grin.

"Very cool, " I told the dog. "I really like this coat."

Letting Glory out back for a quick *biological,* I put the magic coat away and came back to the kitchen to rustle up some lunch—chips, ham and cheese sandwich, and a cup of Earl Grey tea. Munching the sandwich, I let Glory back inside, noting that the day had turned gray. I'd have to check my computer and see what the weather was up to.

Weather may be a universal interest of people, but in the Midwest it was a conversational staple, a form of social glue that gave people something to talk about and a way to understand each other. If you didn't know what the weather was up to, or about to do, in Lawrence, Kansas, you were little better than the village idiot. Me, I just wanted to know if I'd have time to walk the dog.

OK, that was a lie. I tend to lie, do it a lot. Not just around poker and tricks like projecting false tells, either. Lying was a way of protecting my privacy. It made me feel tough, in control. It was a defense against social gooey-ness, a way of keeping my distance. Lately I'd been learning about the consequences of lying to myself. I was avoiding the truth about why I'd come home. As for the weather, I know its importance in local conversation, and I was practicing, boning up on regional social skills I knew I lacked.

I moved my tea and sandwich to the kitchen table and tried to eat like a normal person instead of pacing around the room. Once I was still, Glory flopped down at my feet, under the table. Caitlin had left a note by the salt and pepper shakers: *Sorry about the rat. Later. C.* Looping, curling, girlish handwriting. I'd have expected something jagged, maybe smaller. That she wrote the note at all surprised me. I sipped my tea.

The small, ivory cat I bought for Luce sat on the table in front of me, alongside my cell. In the gray light from the kitchen window, it glowed softly, a catlike pearl of a carving. I wondered how old it was, touched by its quiet beauty. It was something complete in itself, like Luce herself. She'd love the cat. I wondered if I could wait until Christmas to give it to her.

"You'd better," I chided myself. "And you'd better still be here."

I put the dishes in the sink and headed for the library, cell phone and pad of paper in hand, Glory beside me. The house felt chilly, even with the orange sweater. I'd build a fire, take the edge off the cold.

The library was a room just off the kitchen and got more use than the formal parlor at the front of the house. It had a leather couch and ottoman, two large leather chairs, fireplace. Books on the shelves gave the room its name. Fewer books, now that Louise's paperbacks were gone, but paperbacks don't age well; I was OK with my decision to get rid of them.

The small fire started easily. I had stacked the wood in the grate and had a set up ready to go. As I crumpled newspaper and fiddled with matches, I wondered about the two Santas this morning. Who were they? Why did the guy with the gun hit the other guy instead of shooting him? I reviewed the scene of the cringing man and his attacker. There was as much sorrow as anger present, I thought. The whole scene felt sad. The fire caught and I had no answers, maybe never would. I thought of giving Greta Danielson a call and asking a few questions.

Not that she'd want to hear from me. As far as Greta was concerned, I was a pain in the ass, always getting myself into situations and causing problems. And she didn't like my gun. Not at all. What Greta didn't know was that I now had two of them, Louise's gun, a classic, heavy Lady Wesson now residing at my place in San Francisco, and my own, a Taurus 22PLY conceal carry pistol. Blue steel and hardly any barrel, this super lightweight .22 carried nicely in my bra holster. And, I'd been taking lessons, though drawing and aiming without taking my bra down to my waist was still problematical. What officer Danielson didn't know couldn't hurt her.

I sat on the couch, the dog beside me, and watched the flames. Glory started to doze. I still hadn't found her sweater. Time to make that list: *Find sweater. Christmas decorations (?) Call Luce. Call AK. Do not call Mac. Ever.* Irritated with myself, I stood up and tossed the paper in the fire, used the poker and added another piece of wood. Idiot.

Back on the couch, Glory snoozing again, I picked up the cell.

"Hi, Luce. What? Nothing's wrong, I'm fine. Just calling to...OK, OK. Can we just have a normal talk, please? Thank you. Ah, you spoke to Loretta. Well, she had to jump out of a moving vehicle and grab me on the street, didn't she? I am not avoiding you. Hold on." I stuck my arm out, holding the phone away, and took a deep breath.

"I'm back. Yes, obviously." I glared at the phone, thinking about hanging up on her, but experience had taught me that would just make things worse. "Luce! Stop bitching at me, I need a favor." Silence. I never needed a favor. She might have gone into shock. I spoke into the silence.

"I'd like to borrow a jacket or something outdoorsy, kicking around stuff to wear while I'm here. Yes, like that. Yes, it does sound like I'll really be here for a while. Like I said...No. No need, Luce. I'll stop by your place. Really, I'm just going out. Glory's scratching at the door, I've got to take her for a walk." I looked at the sleeping dog sprawled on the leather couch beside me. "OK, see you in a bit." I closed the phone.

"C'mon, Glory. Might as well avoid getting caught in the more obvious lies."

It was a short walk, the afternoon growing grayer and colder, the skinny dog without a sweater. I was warm enough in the black coat, but I felt overdressed,

way too fancy. Most of the houses had tasteful
Christmas decorations, suited to the Victorian
architecture—evergreen garlands on porch railings, holly
wreaths with red ribbons on doors, electric candles in
upstairs windows. If it ever snowed, the street would
look great.

I didn't know any of the neighbors, even with my
comings and goings since Louise's death. Schnauzer
Man lived somewhere up the block, I knew. I'd met
him last time Glory and I were in town and she'd
attacked his dog, a giant schnauzer named Margot.
Glory now had a rap sheet with Animal Control. I did
not want to go through that again. The guy's name was
Shore or something.

Coming back from the walk, we went around the
side of the house so I could dispose of Glory's *prize* in a
trashcan. Luce's yellow Chevy truck appeared in the
alley and stopped by the garage. Glory and I waited on
the steps up to the kitchen.

"That was fast," I said as Luce pushed through the
wooden gate into the backyard. She smiled at me. "Let
her off the leash, Lyle, so she doesn't hurt herself."
Glory was yipping and whining, dying to greet my aunt.
I willingly complied.

"Oh, you're lovely, yes you are," Luce told the
ecstatic dog.

"Is that a backpack?" Either that or a small car slung
over her shoulder. "You camp?"

"Well, not in this weather, no. But some people do
like to get outdoors, Lyle, and I'm one of them." She
did not call my attention to assumptions about people
her age, in their seventies, nor did she remind me that
not everybody spent their time in dark rooms playing
poker. She didn't have to. I was all right there in her
eyes.

Inside, we were hanging up coats in the hall closet when the front door opened and Caitlin let herself in, balancing a plain cardboard box on one hip. Her angelic face was rosy with the cold.

"Stay," I ordered Glory, who went rigid but did not budge from beside me. The dog eyed the box and the girl eyed the dog.

"She's not going to come after me, right?" Caitlin asked.

"No," I replied. "But if that thing gets loose in my house, I'll kill it myself."

"Right," Caitlin nodded and headed up the stairs. Apparently the earlier dead rat had not met with Brunhilde's approval. The box held live food.

"Hey, Miz Hudson," Caitlin greeted Luce.

"Good to see you, Caitlin," my aunt replied, then turned to raise an eyebrow in my direction.

"Rat. For Brunhilde," I said.

"Ah." Luce made a small shuddering movement, a mirror of my own. "OK, come take a look at these clothes." She lugged the backpack into the library. I turned on the lights and went over to build up the fire, which had settled down into embers.

Whatever was in the backpack would fit, as all Hudson women, apart from Loretta who'd put on a few pounds, were the same size. Luce pulled out a hefty, durable fleece jacket in pale green, the exact color of *her* eyes, and a trim zip-up jacket of shiny black material, insulated, "for jogging if you're up to it," Luce grinned. There were assorted corduroy and flannel shirts, a pair of leggings, and "yoga wear."

"Yoga?" I asked, incredulous. A sinking feeling attached itself to my stomach. I checked the room for a quick exit only to find Luce standing squarely in front of me, blocking my path. She'd known me since I was born and knew all my habits. Just as I knew her right back and gave up my futile thoughts of escape. I switched my brain over to poker mode. We silently placed our invisible cards on the table. Time to ante up.

"Yes, yoga." A simple statement accompanied by a serene smile. Aunt Luce was a walking advertisement for the benefits of yoga, which she had practiced for decades. An entire generation of women revered her. Look at Caitlin's quiet respect on the stairs when we both wanted to get into it about the rat. Look at Crista Banks who thought Luce was right up there with Buddha, Mother Teresa, and Michelle Obama.

"Hey, Luce, have you seen Crista?"

"Do not try to change the subject, Lyle. You're not..."

"Getting any younger. Got it," I said, completing the thought.

"Exactly," Luce nodded. "Crista's been staying at the bridal shop, working on some Christmas thing with Nola. We had tea the other day, and she said that although she appreciates Caitlin and all, the snake bothered her, gave her bad dreams. She's thinking of spending Christmas with her mother. Come to yoga with me, Lyle. Just one class. Give it a try." She sat down on the large ottoman and took a strategic breath.

"You're not afraid, are you?" A catlike smile spread across her face, lighting up her eyes, activating the entire network of charming smile lines and superior mental attitude.

"Dammit, Luce." I sank back in the couch, making the leather creak. I leaned my head back and closed my eyes. Game over, Luce takes the pot.

"It'll help you sort out your feelings about poker," she encouraged me, "and other things."

"What feelings about poker, what other things?"

"Well, you seem to be here for an extended stay. Last time I looked there were no casinos in Lawrence."

"There are casinos in Kansas City," I pouted.

"Been there?"

"Well, no. Not yet." I didn't care to remind her that I only just got into town.

"Planning to go?" Silence. "Didn't think so. I assumed you were brooding about it. That, and you haven't been getting out much. Seems to me like you're holing up, hiding out, or whatever."

I sighed and sat up, ran my hands through my hair, trying not to feel desperate. "You're right, Luce. I have been isolating myself. I came here," avoiding the word *home*, "because I needed to get away from poker for a time." I let the sentence fade and gazed at the few flames left flickering in the fireplace. "I need a rest."

"Have you," Luce asked, "been resting?" Her quiet, concerned tone made me laugh.

"Yes, I'll go with you to yoga, Luce. Let me put these things away. You can help me dig out some Christmas decorations, too, and I'll tell you about a bad man in a Santa hat down on Mass Street today."

6

"I started when I was about your age," Luce said. "It's important to retain flexibility, stay limber as one ages." My aunt's voice had that irritating, cheery edge to it that went back as far as I could remember. A reasonable tone reserved for an unreasonable child.

"It's OK, Luce. I get it." Reassuring her right back.

"It's good for balance, circulation, bone density." Luce loved lists, the litany of evidence as irresistible as a pile of poker chips when you're thinking of going all in. She had to be stopped.

"Luce, enough. Look, I'm even driving us there. Not tied up in the trunk of the car." I refrained from mentioning the spongy feel of the sports bra I was wearing and the nagging worry about having ugly feet.

Luce let out a deep, cleansing breath and turned to smile at me. "So you are." I could see her eyes twinkling at me out of the corner of my eye.

"Park in the lot across on New Hampshire street, Lyle. The yoga studio is right up 7th. There won't be any spaces open on Mass Street, anyway."

"Not when it's this cold," I agreed with her.

When the weather turned cold, wet, snowy, or whatever, people turned mulish and hunkered down in their cars, cruising the streets for a parking place close to their destination, convinced, despite the endless circling, needless expenditure of gas, and line after line of immobile vehicles, that the ideal parking spot would open up for them. It was exactly the same mentality of people who played the slots. Might as well roll your window down and throw your money into the street.

I locked the car and Luce handed me a rolled yoga mat and water bottle. We ducked our heads against the wind and trudged up 7th Street. It was five p.m. and visions of Happy Hour danced in my head. The Union Brewery was just around the corner.

Luce opened a door with clanking Tibetan cowbells and held it for me. I gave her a thin-lipped smile and headed up the stairs. We chucked jackets and outerwear onto an ancient maroon couch that looked like it had sat in the same place since the 1950's. It was beyond sagging and had become one with the floor. I stuck my socks into my shoes and stood looking down at my feet as if I'd never seen them before. Naked, alien, white things.

"Your feet are fine." Luce laid a gentle hand on my back. "Let's go." She walked over to a small wooden table and placed a five into a ceramic bowl. The studio ran on a donation system, she explained. Luce did a lot of yoga, so the five made sense. I felt this was more of a one shot deal for me, so I dropped Ulysses S. Grant on top of her Lincoln.

"Hare Krishna, " I muttered. "Let's see you wrap some serenity around that."

I turned to see Luce standing in the dimly lit studio, talking quietly with a young woman wearing a tank top and yoga pants. I rolled my mat out on the floor, next to Luce's and padded over to them, trying not to look down at my feet.

"Lyle, this is Deirdre, our instructor."

The tiny woman took my hand and smiled up at me. "Sure, and it's lovely ta meetcha." Irish yoga, why not.

"Namasté," I responded lamely. I could feel my feet emit a pale, alien glow.

"Luce here talls me it's yer farst tame at yo-ga?"

"Yes," I nodded. "I did aikido a while back. No yoga."

"Ach, ye'll be fine! Just listen to yer body, go yer own pace."

"Thanks."

People started arriving around us, snapping out their mats like towels, settling onto the smooth wooden floor like swans onto a familiar pond. Guess that made me the frog. Luce brought over a couple of folded, woven blankets and placed them near the wall, by our water bottles. "For Shavasana," she said. Right.

Deirdre set up the yoga music on her iPod, then sat in a half lotus on her mat, a small notebook beside her, hands on knees, eyes half closed. Tuning in her Kundalini, or whatever.

From our vantage point at the back of the room, I surveyed the class, a mix of college age kids and 30-somethings, like Deirdre. Luce and I were clearly the senior members. Fifteen people, two men. Brave souls, I thought to myself.

Deirdre started with a series of cleansing breaths, relaxing neck and shoulder exercises, her soft, Irish voice going on about connecting to the rhythm of the Universe, capital U. I practiced my *invisible smile* and felt pretty good, in spite of my feet.

Long about the third sun salutation, that smile was a distant memory. I was panting like a labrador retriever. Mountain Pose, dive into Forward Fold, half lift, fold, Downward Facing Dog, Reverse Swan, into Warrior Two, tail bone in, front knee no more than 90-degree angle, breathe. No stopping. One pose flowed into another. Supposedly. Mostly I felt lost, trying to find parts of my body flying around in space. My feet kept scaring the hell out of me. Open my eyes and there they were, staring at me. I learned that you can pant upside down. Downward Facing Dog is a *resting pose*. My ass.

Beside me, Luce was practically humming along with the Krishna Das music, some waltz-like version of a Hare Krishna chant, her palms flat on the floor, head practically touching her knees. I hated her.

I think I slipped in and out of consciousness, totally losing track of time. I had to fight the temptation to grab my shoes and get the hell out of there. But I gritted my teeth and stuck it out. Giving up would have meant I lose, and I don't like to lose.

Shavasana sort of snuck up on me. Also known as Corpse Pose, it's a little bit of heaven on earth. Lying stretched out under that woven blanket, breathing in the fragrance of geranium oil that Deirdre dotted on my forehead (to seal in the benefits, as she put it), I felt happy just to be alive. I think my whole body was grateful it was no longer moving. Namasté, baby.

The floating feeling lasted until I went to get my shoes and saw that President Grant was no longer in the donation bowl with his pals. I whipped my head around to X-ray people's heads, and caught a little sweetie ducking away from me as she zipped up a blue hoodie.

I walked over, grabbed her little blonde ponytail with my left hand and swung her around to face me. Possibly there was steam coming out of the top of my head, but it was guilt that kept her from meeting my eyes even as she tried to push me away. Big mistake. I yanked the ponytail hard, popping her chin up and dug into her jeans pockets with my right hand. I knew I'd found General Grant without even looking at him. Miss Sweetie twisted away and ran down the stairs into the street, Tibetan cowbells clashing after her. It was over in a matter of seconds, neither one of us saying a word.

The few remaining students vanished, leaving me, Luce, and Deirdre standing next to the ancient couch.

"Oy appreciate yer sense of justice, Lyle," Deirdre said, "but if the choild is in need...Holy Crap!" Her eyes fell on the number 50 on the corner of the bill as I returned it to the bowl.

"Maybe you need a piggy bank or a box where people can't see who's donating what. Eliminate temptation."

"Oy take yer point," Deirdre smiled ruefully at me," but people need to be responsible fer their chices so they can grow in awareness, don't ye tink?"

I laughed, stepping into my shoes, taking my jacket from Luce and shrugging into it. "Oh, I think choices were made tonight. That little girl made her choice, and I made mine."

Deirdre and Luce exchanged a silent, yogic look. The Irish instructor cleared her throat.

"Yes, well. Thank you for yer donation," she said quietly.

"You're welcome," I smiled at her. "Good night."

On the way back down the hill to the car, I hummed and took a little skip in the cold night air.

"You know, Luce, yoga's more interesting than I thought it would be."

"You won't get to beat the crap out of somebody every night, Lyle," Luce said drily.

"Probably not," I admitted. "But a girl can hope." I really did feel at peace with the Universe.

7

"Ugh. What's next, gangs of Santas terrorizing the good citizens of Lawrence?" Chas found the incident on Massachusetts Street disturbing. I could see him rolling his green eyes, standing on his deck in San Francisco, the city spread out below. Compared to Kansas, San Francisco was a delight at this time of year, luxuriant and green, weather an almost constant 70 degrees.

Chas was my good friend and neighbor and I missed him, missed his blond good looks and ironic humor. He also drove me crazy with his teasing, so I wasn't too disappointed when he declined my invitation to Christmas in the Heartland and opted to stay in Oz, as he called San Francisco, with his current boyfriend, Trig.

"As in Trigger?" I asked.

"Hm," he mused. "Palominos are not my type, so...No. I blame it on Daddy, who's a math professor. Trig insists it's a family name and they just pinned it on this helpless baby. No wonder he's gay," Chas laughed. "And not at all helpless, I might add."

"Cool." I meant it. I was glad to hear Chas purring with happiness. When he was not involved with anyone, he tended to take me on as a perpetual renovation project. Way too much focus on make-up and clothing.

"So, is it love?" I asked.

"Possibly, my dear. I like to think of it as infatuation with privileges. How about you?"

"Beg pardon?"

"Have you taken up with Tall Man now that you're back in town?" Tall Man was his name for Mac. Chas said that if I was anywhere near the man I was at risk for TMS, Tall Man Syndrome, a form of temporary insanity. I wasn't finding it funny at the moment.

"Not really, Chas. I…"

"Oooh! Resisting each other! How delicious. Darling, is one of you a vampire? We could write a book, create a TV series, make gobs of money! That would make it perfect!"

"Now that you mention it, I have been feeling a bit undead since I've been home." Humoring Chas was the only way to make him stop.

"Poor sweetie."

I had told Chas about the sleeplessness but did not go into, or even risk mentioning, my time-out from poker. For Chas, poker was glamorous, part of my identity. To give it up, even briefly, meant walking away from myself. He'd jump on a plane immediately and fly to my rescue with a basket of Xanax. Nah. It made more sense to be a vampire. I looked great in black, even Chas said so. Vampires never wear Santa hats.

" Lyle. Lyle, come back to the mother ship, darling. You wandered away again. All I hear is breathing. Are you OK?"

"Entertaining thoughts about life as a vampire. It has possibilities."

"You do look fabulous in black."

"I know! You're reading my mind!"

"Not that hard to do, really, darling, in spite of your dark arts."

"Dark what?"

"Never mind. What about the snake? Vampires and boa constrictors seem a bit much, even for the Midwest."

"The snake stays. So does Caitlin." Housing Caitlin and Brunhilde when they needed a place to stay was a form of civic duty for me. Society needs eccentrics and misfits and other sorts who live off the grid, outside the usual networks and routines. We need to be reminded that at some deep level we're all oddballs. And that's OK. Necessary, in fact. I can be quite passionate about it.

Chas sighed. "I don't know, Lyle. Girls with snakes. It's so uber-Freudian, wouldn't you say?"

"No, I would not. Sometimes a snake is just a snake, Chas."

"Is not!"

"Is too!"

The conversation ended with snorting and other forms of juvenile behavior. As with most friendships, talking with Chas, going through the same ridiculous routines cheered me up. Here it was, full daylight, and I was in the mood to get out into the world of the living, undead no more.

I called Andressa Keach and asked if she'd like to meet for a drink after work. Pleased to hear from me, she said she'd be delighted. Done. I added it to my mental list for the day that included a stop at Hyacinth and taking another stroll downtown. I still needed presents for the L&L's and Uncle Vern.

Over the years, the Hudson family custom of gifts slowly evolved from its original incarnation as a rugby scrum of random stuff and white elephants. No longer did Hudson women torment each other with the *Angel of Glory*, a glass statuette that revolved on a gilt pedestal and played an unrecognizable yet very loud tune. If you could watch your victim unwrap that particular present with a straight face, you could grow up to be a very successful poker player. I wondered if that hideous little statue was where Glory got her name. Nobody knows. We never got around to asking Louise, so now it was one more family mystery.

These days, we were more discerning and considerate, giving each other one well-chosen gift. Not that I'd been around for many Christmases. I suspected the *Angel of Glory* was about to make a historic appearance.

Meanwhile, before I left the house I had to stretch out. I had allowed myself to be talked into a series of yoga classes with Luce. Her logic for continuing exploration of the benefits of yoga was impeccable, but it was the symphony of aching muscles that hit me after the first lesson that was the real persuader. My secret plan was to stretch every day, practice the poses, and impress Luce with my natural dexterity. My hands had yet to reach my toes in a single Forward Fold. Downward Facing Dog was not even close to becoming a place of rest.

Glory loved yoga. It looked like play to her. Not as much fun as a tennis ball, but highly entertaining. She invented her own poses—Playful Puppy, Lie Down and Pant with Tongue Extended, and Butt Sniff.

The only place in the house where there was enough room to lay out a yoga mat and make a complete fool of myself was the old-fashioned parlor at the front of the house. I pushed the two large, chintz-covered chairs against the wall and went to work, ignoring the large bay window that opened to the porch and faced the street. I told myself that if anyone looked in, they'd think I was cleaning house, or training my dog to do party tricks that involved leaping into the air.

After I finished with the real yoga, I picked up a tennis ball and improvised, inspired by Glory. Warrior Two now had a switch-the-ball component added to the lunge that she loved. It looked a lot like juggling. She also liked Shavasana, the final resting posture, and would stretch out beside me on the floor.

As chance would have it, we were well into Shavasana when Caitlin walked down the hall, ready to go out. Uncharacteristically, Glory did not move. I could feel her small tail tapping the rug as she lay beside me.

"Lyle? Are you guys OK?" Animals had full personhood in Caitlin's book. Glory was every bit as much a *guy* as I was.

"We're fine," I said, not opening my eyes. "Shavasana, the ultimate yoga posture," I explained.

"Ultimate? Dude!" I heard thumps as various belongings hit the floor. Two more thumps, Caitlin's Doc Martens. She padded over to us and stretched out next to the dog. Caitlin took a deep breath and let it out slowly. Silence enveloped us. We all fell sound asleep.

I woke up with dog breath in my face. Opened my eyes as Caitlin pulled the dog over to her and scratched behind Glory's ears. She sat cross-legged beside me on the floor. I wondered idly if I could move.

"Were we out long?" I asked groggily.

"Nah. Maybe fifteen minutes." Caitlin was guessing. She never wore a watch, didn't really care about time. People like her created their own time.

"Shivasana," Caitlin nodded her head, thinking about it, an eyebrow piercing winked in the gray daylight. "Very cool. You and Glory into yoga now, Lyle?" she asked.

"Only if I can get up off this floor. It's freezing in here. Aren't you cold?" I groaned and rolled over, sitting up slowly.

"Nah, I'm good. You guys good, too?" She really meant me, but was being diplomatic. "I'm heading out." Caitlin re-donned her outerwear and backpack, waved, and was out the door, clomping down the stairs in her boots.

I stood up and did a last stretch, then padded to the kitchen to find out what time it was in the real world, drink some water, and boost the heat. Glory needed a visit to the back yard, and I needed a shower. The dog followed me around the house as I puttered around and got dressed to go out. We kept eyeing each other.

"You read me like a book, don't you," I told the dog. "Allow me to confirm your suspicions. I'm going out and you're staying here."

We were in the library where I was looking for my blue satchel, the leather saddlebag that was my version of Caitlin's backpack. Glory hopped into my corner of the brown leather couch and curled herself into the smallest dog in the world, looking pathetic. Message understood. I grabbed the satchel and left the room, pausing by the small mirror near the hall closet. Silver hair brushed back off my shoulders, small diamond studs winking at my ears. A small indulgence, compared to the Benz. Chas would approve, I thought. Black cashmere sweater, black cords, black shoes. Practically a uniform when I was playing poker. Right now, I wanted only to stay warm. I grabbed the black shearling coat and headed for the door.

Not Mass Street this time. I wanted to be as far away from Santa hats as possible. Instead, I headed for the side streets near downtown, seeking out the glassworks I'd remembered when I was thinking of a present for Lenore, one half of the infamous L&L's.

It was still there, in a small stone building that had once been a stable. Open for business, the small black sign on the door read. I parked the Mercedes around the corner where I found a big enough space and walked back and went in, making the shop bell ring.

Blissfully warm from the heat of two kilns, the place was dusty and dark, illuminated by daylight coming through the large display window where various items created jeweled patterns of light on the cement floor.

Two other people were in the shop with me, one a well-dressed woman placing an order, the other a man with sandy hair and beard, a bandage on his left hand, writing it down. I nodded at them, opened my coat, and gazed around.

Anyone who liked poking around in a garage would love this place. It had its own kind of order, with an eye to storage rather than marketing and display. Old iron tools hung from overhead beams. Shelving was the cinder block and pine board variety . Everything wore a light coating of dust, but there were soft cloths on the shelves, so that if a vase or a plate interested you, you could dust it off, feel the weight of it in your hands as you held it up to the daylight coming in the window to examine its color and find the inner qualities of the blown glass. It felt a lot like visiting an aquarium when you were a kid. A hand-blown paperweight could be an entire world. I was enchanted.

I found a small vase of cobalt blue glass and walked to the window with it, turning it in the polishing cloth, removing dust.

"Heavier than it looks, isn't it?" I said to the man behind the counter, admiring the way the deep blue held the light.

"That's because of the skirt, the second layer of glass, at the base," he said, referring to the drapery of clear glass overlapping the blue. It formed the base of the vase, and a piece of it ran up the side, a stylized ripple in the shape of a wave.

"Reminds me of water," I said.

"Meant to. Glass is liquid, after all," he added. "Only slower moving." His tone conveyed his appreciation of the particular property of glass.

"It's beautiful." I brought the vase over to the counter.

"Thank you." The man wrapped the vase in a wad of paper.

"What happened to your hand?" I asked. It was a pretty sizeable bandage, hard to ignore.

"Occupational hazard," he said, and held out the right arm for me to inspect as well. Below the elbow where flannel sleeves were rolled up, his arms were crisscrossed with scars.

"Doesn't matter the pads and masks you wear. You blow glass, you're gonna get burnt. The rods get hot, the glass is bubbling. You get tired, lose your focus for an instant? Immediate consequences."

"Guess that means you love what you do," I said, nodding at the bandage. "Accepting the consequences."

"You bet I do!" He grinned. "It's exciting, challenging, you know? Glass is so beautiful." He patted the bandage unconsciously. "Usually I close the shop when I'm working. If a school group comes in for a lesson, the kids have to stand behind that rail." He gestured at the kiln area behind him.

"Probably a good idea." The man's enthusiasm was engaging. I could have stayed and asked him more about glass blowing. But a couple of folks walked in the door and started browsing, so I tucked the wrapped vase under my arm and left, wishing him a happy holiday, hoping he'd make a few more sales.

After the warmth of the glassworks, the cold air hit me hard. I ducked my chin and booked it to the car. The package was too large and too heavy for the satchel, so I stashed it on the floor behind the driver's seat, where it was all but invisible. On the way back downtown to my meeting with Andressa, I thought about the glass artist and his scars, the fierce joy he found in his work, the powerful feelings. Maybe I'd go back and talk to him some more. I realized I didn't even know his name.

The light was fading fast. Too late to stop by Hyacinth, I told myself, might as well head on over to the Union Brewery for Happy Hour.

A popular watering hole, the Brewery was filling up fast, standing room only at the bar. A mix of business folks leaving work early, college kids celebrating the end of classes or just starting the bar scene early, and other folks coming to meet up with friends. I unbuttoned the coat and waited for Andressa. The place seemed a bit noisy for a get-to-know-you conversation.

"You waiting for me?" A beery voice, burly guy, knowing he was going to get shut down but looking to entertain his friends. He might as well have had JERK written across his forehead.

"No. I'm not." I gave my voice a sharp edge and looked at him with arched brows.

"Are you sure?" He gave me a goofy grin and stepped closer.

"Look," I said, clearly and patiently, "The line's OK, only a little lame, you know? But I'd lose the hat. Santa doesn't get out much and he certainly doesn't hang out in bars. Not the image you want to go for."

His friends roared and pounded the beefy guy on the back, apologizing to me for their friend and laughing at him in a good-natured way.

I was having more misgivings about the place when my cell rang, buzzing in my hand. I'd been on the point of calling Andressa, but she called me first. She was running late and would be there in ten minutes. No problem. I suggested Reed's further down the street, this place was too loud for me. She agreed. I closed the phone and walked outside, past the group of guys and their beery friend.

"So long, heartbreaker!" he called after me. I made the L sign, for loser, against my forehead, and turned away. A wave of laughter followed my exit.

"She nailed you, dude!" one guy crowed, thumping on his pathetic friend.

Reed's was only a block away, but the walk was chilly, little grits of ice falling in gusts. The stuff made a hissing sound, like sand, as it hit the holiday banners on the lampposts. Heartbreaker. Wasn't that a song? I summoned my inner Pat Benatar and hustled up the street.

I took three steps up and opened the door to Reed's, which at one time had been a bank. Some of the original furnishings remained, like the marble floor and vaults in the basement which now served as restroom with very secure doors, but the rest of Reed's reminded me of San Francisco—art on the walls, deco light fixtures, open kitchen. I nodded at the hostess, refused an offer to take my coat, and made a sharp left into the bar.

The dating scene hadn't started yet, which was a relief. I grabbed a chair at the end of the long, paneled bar, draped the coat across the back, and hopped up. The muted lights and quiet conversations made it clear that Reed's was a place for grown-ups. No rowdy voices here. But it was early, I reminded myself. The bar scene could get loud later. I ordered a scotch and soda from the bartender and looked around.

A couple sat at a nearby table, an assortment of loners sat at the bar. At the far end a knot of waiters stood chatting, waiting for drink orders to take into the restaurant. Business started to pick up. Still no Andressa. I sipped my drink and took in the buzz of conversation, which was mostly about the weather. The gritty stuff falling outside was unexpected, took everyone by surprise. The sidewalk was turning slippery, people said.

I caught sight of Andressa at the back of the crowd, unwrapping a red scarf, shaking out her hair. She waved me over, pointing at the restaurant. I nodded and left my place at the bar. People parted amiably as I pushed through.

"Sorry to be so late," she said, brushing last bits of moisture from her hair. "I had to stop at home and then come back." The jewelry store was right across the street. I had wondered.

"Long story," she said, answering my unspoken question. "Let's grab a table in the back. It'll be easier to talk."

We were seated at a table for two by the open kitchen, away from the draft of the constantly open door. No cold air seeping in from windows. The restaurant was busy, with people passing by, but quiet enough. I told Andressa I appreciated the warmth.

"Me, too," she said. The words were followed by a yawn. "Excuse me, Lyle. Long day. Perhaps I should start with coffee," she laughed.

"Shall we order something to eat?"

"You go ahead. I've already eaten." I must have given her a blank look, making Andressa laugh again.

"I wanted to see Carl, my husband, and had a bite to eat before I came to meet you. He's in a wheelchair. Car accident years ago." She was condensing a lot of history into small bits, avoiding lengthy explanations. "The kitchen is old, hard to get around in." She smiled as the waitress poured our water.

I smiled back and ordered bruschetta, a house salad, and a glass of chardonnay. Andressa asked for coffee.

"Carl Keach?" I asked, not placing the name at high school.

Andressa shook her head. "Glasser. We met at KU, married right out of college. He's into computer information systems, now. Works mostly at home. Hey, this is hard, you know?" She meant putting an entire life into a few sentences for a person you hardly know.

I gave her a worried look and nodded, agreeing. "It really is. I've been dreading my turn. Besides, I'm an inveterate liar." That cracked her up

"Well, I already know a good deal about you, Lyle."

"You do?"

She nodded. "Even apart from high school. You grew up here, have family in this town. Everybody knows everything, Lyle. People talk!" I must've looked horrified.

"Have a sip of wine. It's OK," she said.

"Crap," I muttered, and drank my wine. "I find that totally alarming."

Andressa laughed out loud, then covered her mouth with one hand, attempting to smother her giggles. Clearly, the woman was having a good time. I thought of a husband at home in a wheelchair and decided that it was OK with me. Many people found me entertaining, after all.

"So," I said, "what do you know, O Well-informed One?"

"I know you live in San Francisco, play big time poker in Las Vegas and other dubious places, that you own Hyacinth, which you inherited from you mom, along with her dog, and," she flicked her blue eyes toward a point somewhere behind me, "I've heard a theory or two about that."

I looked over my shoulder to see MacDonald George taking long strides in our direction. At first, his eyes were on Andressa, then they shifted to me. I did not say "Crap."

We both looked up when he reached the table. The man really was tall.

"Good to see you out, Andressa," His voice, usually warm, held a note of wariness, but he put a smile on it and added, "Miss Lyle behaving herself?" Miss Who? Mac was putting on an act, and not for my benefit.

"So far, " Andressa said lightly, tossing her chestnut hair.

They appeared to be talking about me, but there was clearly another subject on the table. I felt oddly like a dud card, not in play in this hand. My existential angst pulled up a chair and sat beside me. Then I felt Mac's eyes on me. Crap. I must be unusually readable tonight, I thought. I composed my face into a semblance of a good-natured smile and gazed up at him. Mac gazed back, the handsome devil.

"In that case, let's not tempt the fates," he smiled. And took more long strides back the way he came.

I turned back in my seat and took a long swallow from the glass of water.

"You're funny," Andressa said.

"It wasn't funny for me," I replied.

"Oh, I think it was. Admit it, you were glad to see Mac."

"Was not!" I laughed in spite of myself and ordered another glass of wine. Andressa asked for one, too.

"He came over to talk to *you*, Andressa."

"But his eyes were on *you*, Lyle." She paused for emphasis. "The whole time."

Our wine arrived and we thanked the waitress. There was a quiet moment as we raised our glasses and took a sip.

"So, what's up?" she asked, still interested in Mac and me.

"Oh, nothing," I said in a light voice. "Just war."

"Lucky you." Thankfully, she dropped the subject. I didn't want to think about who might be winning.

A few other people stopped by to speak to Andressa, or waved to her across the room from distant tables.

"Visibility is its own reward," she commented drily, paraphrasing the proverb about virtue.

"Highly overrated."

"Exactly."

*

I paid the check and thanked her for coming out on a cold, sleety night. As we put our coats on, someone bumped my elbow and stopped to apologize. An aging academic in a damp tweed jacket, looking bedraggled and pale, he was rubbing at his hands with what had been a white handkerchief.

"Sorry. Oh, hello!" He said, turning his head and seeing Andressa.

"Hello, Richard," she answered, not terribly pleased to see him as he was to see her. She did her duty and introduced us. "Lyle Hudson, Dr. Richard Cassaday. Richard, Lyle." He had the kind of face that made me want to go Dr. to Dr. with him, but I don't usually mention my own Ph.D. Too much baggage, too much explaining, too much bad attitude on my part. Why antagonize the man just because I didn't like his face?

"Um, hello." He bobbed his head at me awkwardly. "Please forgive me if I don't shake your hand," he continued, rubbing with the ruined handkerchief. "Had to change a tire in this vile weather. Need to wash up." He split a thin smile between the two of us and scurried away, heading to the vaults downstairs.

"Creep?" I asked her.

"Total."

"You know, I think I saw him earlier today. Same tweed jacket." Andressa wrinkled her nose in distaste.

We were on our way out the door, so I didn't go into the incident of the two Santa hat guys. Which meant that I wouldn't have to mention Mac again, either. I cheered right up and followed Andressa Keach outside.

"Great evening," she said. "I really enjoyed getting to know you, Lyle. I hope you stay in Lawrence for a while. Stay in touch, OK?"

"Back at you, Andressa. You've got my number. Good night."

She hurried to catch the light at the corner, right outside Reed's, and I turned right, heading back up the street, feeling out the slippery pavement.

"Lyle, wait up!"

I stopped and turned, putting my back to the wind and sleet, and waited for MacDonald George to reach me. The gritty ice crunched under his boots.

"Mac. You are out in this vile weather, looking for a goodnight kiss, aren't you?" I pushed the hood back off my hair and looked at him.

"I was thinking of walking you to your car," he said.

"No." I pulled on the pockets of his leather jacket and tugged him into a shop doorway, out of the sleeting wind. "You want that kiss."

8

It was a great kiss, worthy of its own movie, a kiss from a Russian novel (it was snowing) or *Romeo and Juliet*, one of those kisses that created its own reality, some place tropical and hot. I couldn't believe Mac wouldn't come home with me.

"No? Just like that, NO?" I panted, trying to catch my breath.

"It's not that I don't want to, I do," he said, "but it's not a good idea, Lyle."

"Feels OK to me! What's the problem?" I stepped out of his arms and tried to get a grip on myself. The feeling I had inside at the table with Andressa came rushing back, a hole wanting to swallow me. I couldn't believe how sharp Mac's rejection felt. "Seems to me you were OK with it a minute ago."

"More than OK and you know it, he said hoarsely. The problem would be tomorrow when you woke up and got angry with me for taking advantage of you." He pulled me back in and kissed my hair. "You know I'm right," he whispered.

"Boo you." I gave him a half-hearted slug to the ribs. "Is this part of your evil plan to make me sorry?"

"Not tonight, no. If anything, I'm the one who's sorry."

"Apology accepted." I closed my eyes and leaned against him in the shop doorway.

"Besides, I have to get home to Jesse. I didn't plan on staying out late. This is turning into an ice storm. Got to go, now. So, let's get you to your car and see if you're drivable."

Jesse was MacDonald's ageing Irish setter, one of the few dogs on the planet Glory could tolerate. I might have issues with Mac, but I couldn't fault him for loving his dog.

We left the shelter of the doorway and headed out into the sleet and wind. A few minutes later we were at the car and I beeped it open.

"I guess the temporary plates would've led me to you eventually," Mac said. "No one else in Lawrence owns a car like this."

"Impulse buy. The Infiniti was fun. I like the CL600 even better. Need a ride?" I smiled up at MacDonald George, in spite of the ice stinging my face.

He kissed me. Another really good one. "Better not."

"Guess not." I got in the car. "Good night, Mac."

"Night, Lyle." He walked away and I sat there, warming up the car, watching the ice slowly melt on the windshield.

*

I opened my eyes and winced at the bright light of day. Glory wagged her tail, under the covers at my feet. The bed was warm, the house quiet. I called the dog, freeing my feet, and laughed as she dropped to the floor and bounced right back in bed, ready to play.

"Out? You need out?"

Glory zoomed over to the bedroom door while I pulled on a pair of wool socks and grabbed my robe. Downstairs, I let her out the kitchen door and stood there, back against the doorjamb, squinting at the bright sun gleaming on ice-coated branches. The rooftops, fences, and dry, scruffy grass all seemed encased in glass. Not too serious an ice storm, then. No broken trees or downed power lines. Glory trotted briskly up the stairs and past me into the warm house.

I closed the door and put water on. When it boiled, I'd have to make up my mind whether it would be tea or coffee. My mind was preoccupied with last night.

"I don't know, Glory, the man would not come home with me. I must be losing my touch." I yawned, wondering what the world was coming to and held my hair out of my face with one hand while leaning down and putting a bowl of kibble on the floor. It was in this inglorious position that I heard a sharp knocking at the door and turned to see Mac's face looking in the window at me.

"It's open!" As I stood up and blew strands of silver hair out of my eyes, Mac walked in with two containers of coffee on a cardboard tray in one hand and a paper bag under his arm.

"Coffee and bagels," he said, grinning at me as Glory leapt around him in joy. "You can eat in the car. Get dressed, woman! It's gorgeous out there and it won't last long." He set the coffee and bagels on the table and sat down to pet the dog.

"Go on, Lyle. Glory can come, too."

"Well sure, fine," I said, turning off the stove. "If the dog can come then everything's peachy."

He walked over and gave me a firm kiss, turned me around by the shoulders, and pushed me out of my own kitchen. "Don't be difficult. Git."

Git, my ass. Well, OK, maybe I did hustle up the stairs. Maybe the world wasn't going to hell, after all.

Maybe I still had it. The man certainly was full of surprises.

Mac started with a tour of the neighborhood, driving the Mustang slowly so we could admire the canopy of icy branches refracting sunlight. Munching happily on an onion bagel with cream cheese, sipping coffee, I took in the sights, pointing out a group of children sliding down the ice-slick sidewalk on their butts, no sled necessary this morning, laughing and bumping into each other as they slid. People stood in their yards or out by their cars, talking to neighbors and pointing at ice-draped power lines and heavy branches bending too low to be safe. Folks were smiling, though. The storm had passed with little damage, leaving behind a delicate beauty, a world transformed. Everyone felt it.

I reached behind me to give Glory my last bite of bagel, which she took gently with her front teeth and popped into the air, catching it on the way down and swallowing after a couple swift chews. I laughed and turned back around in my seat to find Mac looking at me, making those nice lines at the corners of his eyes. It was a warm, tender look, and I definitely liked it.

I sighed with contentment. "This is great, Mac. Thank you."

"It certainly is," he replied. "You're welcome." I find it interesting how a few conventional words can convey a whole unspoken level of conversation.

"Want to go take a look at the river?" he asked. "We could go north of the interstate, out by the railroad tracks, see what's there."

"Won't the road still be too icy?"

"If there's too much ice, we'll turn back."

"OK, Mac," I grinned. "Let's check it out!"

I loved that stretch of the Kansas River. It took some doing to get there, even when the roads were dry, and once you crossed the second set of train tracks, the pavement ended, turning into a dirt track with deep ruts. I doubted we'd get there, but it was worth a try. We might see bald eagles, foxes, or an eight-point stag leaping from the brush to cross sandbars and make his way to the other side of the river.

Our eyes watering from the constant dazzle of sun on ice, we took out our sunglasses, sighing in relief once they were on. The sky opened up as we left town and drove out into empty farmland, fields of coffee-dark earth glazed and sparkling under pure turquoise.

We passed a small lake, no more than a pond, really, where a few ducks were swimming around in a small circle of unfrozen water at its center. Farmhouses sat well back from the road. The Mustang crunched ice in the rutted road as we drove along. I kept an eye out for deer, but the car was the only moving thing out here. Everything seemed stuck to the landscape.

I was sharing my impressions of the passing scene with Mac when we rounded a wide curve in the road. Up ahead, where the dirt road began, two police cars blocked the road, red and blue lights flashing silently. One cop stood talking into a hand-held communication device. The shoulders of the second man were visible at the top of the deep ditch that ran along the side of the road.

"Maybe someone went off the road," I ventured.

"Could be," Mac said. "Whatever it is, we're not getting by."

Mac had to drive close to the two police cars in order to find enough space to turn around. The cop with the radio recognized Mac—or maybe it was the car—and waved. He walked over when Mac had the Mustang turned around and bent down to say hello when Mac rolled the window down.

"Mac," the man said calmly in greeting.

"Drew," Mac nodded. "This is Lyle Hudson. We're out ice-viewing."

Drew nodded at me and smiled briefly, as if looking at ice on trees made perfect sense. But, I realized, to anyone who'd grown up here it did.

"Got a car off the road down there?" Mac asked.

"This could have been a dangerous curve last night, with the storm, but, no, that's not it." The cop's serious tone told us he wished it were that simple.

The other cop, presumably the driver of vehicle two, climbed back up the bank, waving an arm wildly as he momentarily lost his balance in the icy brush of the ditch. In the waving hand he held a bright red hat with a fuzzy white pompom. He could tell we'd all seen it, so there was no sense in hiding it behind his back.

"Something bad happen to Santa?" I asked Mac. He signaled a low *be quiet* with his right hand, down by the gear shift, his eyes on the two officers, figuring out as much as he could before we were sent away.

"Matt!" Drew called out. "Is that evidence? You know not to disturb a crime scene!"

"Don't know what made me pick it up." The young cop looked at the bedraggled item in his hand and the looked back toward the ditch. "She just..." He shook his head.

"Wait by your unit, would you, man?" Drew turned and faced Mac. Didn't have to say a word. Mac nodded and put the Mustang in gear.

His eyes were still in the rearview mirror long after we rounded the curve and headed back to town.

There's a body down there," he said. "I'd bet my life on it." His words changed the icy landscape into something much colder.

On the way back into town, Mac pulled the car off the road onto a sandy patch of land near the small lake with the ducks. I was sorry to miss the visit to the river but sorrier still that the sign on Mac's forehead said, *we need to talk.*

He turned off the engine and we sat in silence for a moment, looking out at the sparkling scene. The ducks paddled in their small circle of water at the center of the ice, the sky was high and bright.

"What do you think happened back there, Mac?"

"We'll find out soon enough," he said.

"The police hadn't been there long, I think. Looked like they're still taking it in," I said.

"Protecting the scene." Mac looked at me and then over at the ducks.

I nodded. "How do you think they found out, knew to go there?"

"People see things, Lyle. Even out here. Could've been a hunter called it in, or somebody going by, like us."

"Oh." I didn't like the way he said *us.* "Hey, Mac? Do you know anything about those two guys on Mass Street, the Santa hat guys, that attack?"

He shook his head, knowing I was stalling. "Not much. They're brothers and business partners. You know, I think they might be related to your neighbor, Martin Shore." Mac searched his memory and then let it go. "Anyway, the brothers had a shop down town until quite recently. Lost the business, financial misdealings of some kind. One blamed the other; they can't get over it."

"Financial misdealings? What does that mean?"

"It could mean a lot of things. Mostly what it says is the person talking to me was being cautious. The gossip is that the poor man was being stalked by his brother, verbally abused, roughed up. He won't press charges, though. He feels too guilty. The family is torn up about it." Mac shifted in his seat and looked directly at me.

"That's all I know. Anything else?"

"No. Just curious."

The car windows were fogging up. Glory danced around on the back seat, signaling her desire to get the hell out of the car, please.

"Guess she needs some exercise," Mac said.

"Wait!" Before he could open his door, I pulled a ratty old tennis ball out of the satchel and showed it to Glory, who proceeded to writhe in delight.

"Ball control," I explained. "Voice control doesn't always work, but the ball never fails to hold her attention." The dog was obsessed.

We had the country road, the lake and ducks, to ourselves. I threw the ball a few times, and Mac threw it farther. Glory was in dog heaven, ignoring the water and the ducks, blind to a couple of deer that approached the far end of the lake, looking for a drink. When she was through playing, Glory carried the ball in her mouth and investigated smells in the frozen weeds. Mac and I leaned on an old fence, watching the dog, standing close. He reached out and pulled me to him, arms coming round my back, his chin on my head.

"What is it, Lyle? What do you need?"

"Oh, crap." I turned away but he pulled me back so my back was against him and we were both facing out. Not looking at him helped, but there were those arms. I leaned back, felt his breathing, and relaxed into the embrace.

"What I need, Mac, is to figure myself out." I paused and he waited for me to continue. "Not once and for all. That's not going to happen." I felt his chest move against my back. The man was laughing.

"Yeah, well. Ha ha." He gave me a hug, get on with it.

"I'm tired. No, that's not it. More a feeling pointless, purposeless, dull, blah, empty. I took a break from poker because it felt pointless, too. I didn't care whether I won or lost, and that scared me. So, I'm on hiatus, for now. But there's nothing to replace it. I still feel empty. Not a good quality in a girlfriend," I laughed. Besides, I'm too old to be a girlfriend. What a stupid word." I turned and looked up at him.

"It sounds like ennui," he said.

"Excuse me?"

"Ennui, weariness with the world."

"I know what the word means, Mac! What's your point?"

"Now, don't go getting all riled up. You use anger as a defense against feeling. Just listen."

"You have been talking to a therapist, haven't you? So, the two of you have me all figured out?" Yep, I was mad.

"Hardly. I have, as you'd say, my own crap to work on. Minefields, married women to avoid." He smiled but I could feel him struggle to stay patient with me. Since he was upset, too, I started to feel better.

"OK. I'm listening."

"Good. All I was going to say is that this feeling you have," he was avoiding the e-word, "is painful."

"Damn straight. It sucks! I hate it! I don't know what I'll *do*, who I'd be, without poker. If I had to stay here for the rest of my life, I'd kill myself!"

"Really?"

"I don't know! Maybe not. But I can't see it, living here til the edge of doom."

"Fair enough. But maybe there's something between never and the-rest-of-your life. Something that included me." My jaw definitely dropped.

"You crazy man. What the hell do you see in me?"

"Damned if I know, Lyle. I must be demented."

"Must be. OK. I'm frozen, Glory's frozen, and she's eyeing the paint of your Mustang. Let's go." Mac let me go and watched me let the dog into the car, but he stayed by the fence.

"What?" I called to him.

Silence. Hands in pockets. Tall man studying his boots, not knowing what to do about me.

"Included, OK? I'll buy you the t-shirt!"

A wise man, Mac did not smile, did not make eye contact with the crazy woman standing by his car. He shoved off the fence and walked over, long strides, looking good. Mac rescued the Stetson from Glory's dancing feet, put it on his head, and got behind the wheel.

"Those little white hairs stick to anything, don't they," he said, philosophically.

"They do. Sorry about the hat." He nodded and turned the key in the ignition.

"It's too cold for her," I said and was hit with a sudden inspiration. I pulled out my cell phone. "Maybe the L&L's will have an idea!"

Mac laughed out loud. "God help us."

9

The L&L's, my twin aunts, were at Loretta's house, a customary state of affairs since they not only enjoyed each other's company but were often engaged in various if sometimes dubious entrepreneurial enterprises. My aunts were nothing if not adventurous.

Loretta was the loud, rambunctious one, while Lenore was more subdued and ladylike. Of course, even a herd of buffalo would seem subdued next to Loretta. And Lenore had a contrary streak that could rise to the surface and make her behave in uncharacteristic ways, as when she took up the cause of Kenneth Bennett, a homeless, lightning-struck man accused of shooting an unscrupulous real estate developer and burning him in his car. You never knew what would be up with the L&L's, and it paid to keep an eye on them. That was Luce's job.

But Luce was nowhere in evidence when we arrived at Loretta's spacious, ranch-style house west of town. Which meant that the twins had been left to their own devices. The air was rich with the fragrance of vanilla, sugar, and cinnamon.

"C'mere, you skinny little bitch!" Loretta's voice boomed from the kitchen, where Glory had trotted as Mac and I hung up our coats. Loretta emerged from the kitchen red-faced, apron-clad, with a delirious Glory cradled in her arms.

"Fresh sticky buns, you two! Get 'em while they're hot!"

Mac grinned and gave Loretta a quick peck on the cheek and then glided past her into the kitchen.

"Why, MacDonald George, how good to see you!" I heard Lenore's voice sing out, a little louder than usual.

"She's trying to set me a good example," Loretta whispered, during our ritual hug. "She hates it when I call Glory a bitch! I tell her I'm just trying to be accurate!"

Loretta laughed heartily and brushed dog hair off her red and white HO HO HO apron. She pushed me into the kitchen ahead of her, over to a pan of golden, gooey sticky buns cooling on the stove. I waved helplessly at Lenore, who stood by the sink, drying her hands on a dishtowel.

She wore a bright blue oxford shirt, an industrial baker's apron slung around her trim hips, and blue jeans. No Christmas red for Lenore, she was a proud supporter of Advent blue.

"Here's a plate for that bun, Lyle. Keep that melted sugar from getting all over you."

Mac was licking his fingers, practically purring.

"And give this towel to Mac, please, he's getting all sticky," Lenore added.

"Well, damn!" Loretta said. "Wouldn't that be a crying shame, a handsome man all covered with sugar!"

Coffee was poured and we sat around Lenore's oak table, chatting about the ice storm, and catching up on the news.

I told her about driving out to look at ice with Mac, being turned back by two cops on the road. Loretta already knew. A KU student had been strangled and left in a ditch. The jungle drums of Lawrence, spreading breaking news, I thought.

"That batch over there has pecans, Mac. Want to try one?" Loretta asked.

"Why all the baking, ladies?" Mac declined the offer with a sad shake of the head, hands raised in surrender. "You have enough for—well, I don't know what. Looks like a lot of sticky buns, though!"

"We're getting last minute stuff done for the Faire," Lenore started to explain.

"That's fair with an E. The organizers think people will spend more money if it's spelled fancy." Loretta said. "It's just too precious for me."

"We're taking a three-pronged approach this year," she continued, sitting forward in her chair like General Patton in a curly white ponytail and Santa apron.

"One is the secret Hudson sticky bun recipe. We'll show those pastry snobs a thing or two! Two is the more traditional Christmas herbal line." She pointed to a stack of cardboard boxes standing by the French windows that led to the back deck.

"That would be mulling spices, lavender and sage potpourri, and here, look at this." Lenore walked over to a box and pulled out a tiny, woven wreath made of lavender stalks and decorated with a small sprig of holly. "A limited supply. They should go fast."

"It's lovely," I said. It really was a miniature work of art. I marveled at my aunts' ingenuity and creativity. "What's behind Door Number Three?" I asked warily.

The sisters shared a conspiratorial glance. "Something new!" they said simultaneously.

"Have some coffee," Loretta commanded. "I'll show you." She started to head toward a back room.

"Before you go, and before I forget to ask, this cold weather is too hard on Glory. I can't find that coat mom knitted for her, the one that looked like a hairball? Any ideas? I really don't want to buy her a dorky coat at a pet store."

"Got just the ticket! Come on, girl!" Loretta started down the hall, the dog trotting after her.

"She is so fond of Glory, Lyle. You know that, don't you?" Lenore said. "Loretta has devoted herself to this little project," she reached over and patted my hand. "So, just be appreciative of all that love," she added. "And don't panic." It sounded like a warning.

Immediately I started to panic. What was Loretta doing to my dog?

"Ta Da!" Loretta burst into the kitchen and pointed to the hallway behind her, awaiting Glory's entrance. Which took a while.

We could hear the tap tap tap of reluctant dog feet on hardwood floor, and the faint ringing of—jingle bells?

"Come on, Glory! Get on out here!" Loretta clapped her hands, summoning the dog.

"Loretta Hudson. You did not put antlers on my dog!" I stood up, indignant.

"Hell, no! Now, sit back down. Here, girl!" The hallway went silent.

"It's OK, Glory. Come to me, come on," I called my dog, silently promising her a hug, no matter what she looked like.

"There, see?" Loretta said as Glory slunk through the doorway, head down in abject doggy shame, "Santa!"

The little red hat, held on with an elastic strap, drooped over her muzzle, big white pom-pom blocking one eye. The red velveteen coat, if you could call it that, had a flared skirt that covered Glory's rear end. The outfit had a shiny black belt trimmed in jingle bells, fluffy white trim at the sleeves, where her front legs went through, and around the hood at her neck. It must have snaps underneath, I thought. It was so hideous it was almost beautiful. Looking at Glory, my beloved dog, in that monstrosity was too much. I couldn't breathe, much less speak.

A couple things happened when Glory made her entrance: Mac passed hot coffee through his nose, literally, and jumped up, coughing and gasping. My Aunt Lenore made a strangled whining noise, trying not to laugh. When the laugh got away from her, she put a dishtowel on her head, hiding her face, and gave in to some loud, unladylike guffaws. And me? I burst into tears. Loud, wailing tears, the kind that squirt out of your eyes when you are four or five years old.

Loretta stood immobile as a statue, leaning against the counter. She looked around at the pandemonium in the kitchen, and at the depressed dog lying flat out on the floor.

"Well, hell! I think she looks pretty!"

Lenore rose from her chair, towel still on her head, and bolted from the room, careening off the doorframe. MacDonald crashed over to the sink and tried to clear his nasal passages of coffee, attempting to breathe and laugh at the same time. I let out a wail that would've made Lucille Ball proud.

When the crisis passed, I hugged my Aunt Loretta and thanked her for all her love and hard work on Glory's behalf.

"But there is no way in hell she will ever wear that thing again. I could have it framed, though. You know, like a family heirloom?"

"Not even Christmas Eve?" Loretta pleaded.

"Not even if you put a gun to my head."

Loretta drooped in her chair, a picture of dejection.

"OK!" I said, cheerfully, "What's in the box? Show us the third prong of your attack for the Faire!"

"Just remember, Lyle, not everybody is like you in your lack of holiday enthusiasm," Lenore cautioned me. "Here it is. Go ahead, Loretta."

Loretta dived into the box and came up with, "Pet wear!" she announced proudly.

"Are those...?" I hesitated to ask.

"Elf ears! You can turn your pet into a genuine Santa's helper! They come with a detachable hat, see? Velcro makes it safe and easy," she explained.

I banged my head on the oak table and Mac patted me on the back. I could feel Glory trembling on the floor by my feet.

"Wait! There's more!" Lenore joined in gleefully, and I suspect spitefully as well. Hudson women were experts at tormenting each other, always on the lookout for a fresh opportunity. "Show her, Loretta."

Needing no further encouragement, Loretta pulled out an array of pet outfits and decorations my aunts had been making since the summer. There were: catnip reindeer, antler sets, with and without lights, for pets of all sizes, little Santa hats and booties galore. In addition to regular Santa costumes, there were tiny Santa capes for gerbils and iguanas. Visions of pet misery danced in my head. I wracked my brain for something to say. Something nice and at least in the vicinity of sincere. I cleared my throat.

"It's genius, aunts, all of it." They regarded me skeptically. "No, really. People who love...that stuff...will love it. You've worked hard in putting it together, I can see. I hope it sells. Good luck tomorrow." There. Sincere. My poker face kicked in when I needed it.

"Thank you, dear," Lenore said. "I hope you stop by our booth tomorrow.

"Looking forward to it," Mac grinned.

"You bet," I nodded agreeably. But I was not going near the mulling spices. Once bitten, and all that. Not too long ago I tried one of their herbal teas that happened to have some hallucinogenic side effects.

"Excellent!" Loretta was her cheery self again.

"So." I needed to change the subject before I gagged. Mac continued smiling and refused to make eye contact. "Where's Vern? What's he up to?"

"Oh," Loretta said, "He's at a men's drumming retreat out by Lone Star Lake. Three days, I believe."

"You're kidding me, right?"

Loretta drew back in her chair and put her hands on her hips authoritatively. "Yes, honey, I am! Thoroughly and righteously jerking your San Francisco chain!" She laughed and slapped her knees. "Nah, Vern's out with the boys, looking to do some ice fishing. They've got all the gear, but I suspect it's an excuse to engage in some unsupervised drinking." She laughed some more. "Drumming! Vern wouldn't know a drum if he stepped on one!" Loretta cut MacDonald a green-eyed smile, daring him to say anything.

"Don't look at me," Mac said calmly. "I'd rather drink than drum any day."

"Yeah!" Loretta cracked up. "I've seen your bumper sticker: Don't Drink and Drum!" I sat and waited while they had their own little yuk fest.

"And what are *you* up to, Missy? Luce says you're doing yoga these days. I said Like Hell. If it's true, I'm figuring you've got a bad case of existential angst. So, how's it going?"

I stared at Loretta, speechless. Mac excused himself and left the room. Men often do that when two women go eyeball to eyeball. Or maybe it was just when Hudson women went there.

"Honey, I'm old, not ignorant! I went to college, back in the day. I got a mind! I have a certain life experience and understanding of the human spirit. "Sides, you're not exactly hard to read. Why those poker boys don't clean your clock, I'll never know!"

"Loretta, ease off, now," Lenore said. "Don't you listen to her, Lyle. You are inscrutable, all Hudson women are," she said reassuringly.

"Oh, hell, Lenore. Lyle should ease up on herself! It's perfectly normal, sugar. Existential crap hits a lot of folks, especially at this time of year. Miss Lenore here's been a bit down in the mouth, too, if truth be told. Yes, you have!" she told her twin.

Lenore huffed at her and left the room to find Mac.

"And Luce is doing so much yoga, she'll wear a hole in her mat if she's not careful! Edgy is what she is. Don't mean to gossip, niece, but it's probably a lack of sex," Loretta whispered.

"What about William?" I referred to Luce's longtime companion.

"Haven't seen him for a while. I didn't care to have my head bit off, so I didn't ask. Do *you* feel brave enough to ask her? Thought not. Wait and see, I say. Time will tell."

Nothing like platitude in the face of uncertainty, I thought. I wasn't brave enough to say *that* aloud, either.

MacDonald came into the kitchen, Stetson in hand, ready to go.

"Are you sure you won't stay for lunch?" Lenore asked.

"I think not. Those sticky buns left no room for any more food. Do you need any help getting all this stuff to the Faire?" I gestured to the piles of pet gear and boxes jumbled about.

"No, Luce is loaning us her truck. It'll only take one trip to get there," Lenore said.

We returned to the topic of the day a dead college student so unexpected in our fair city, which led to speculation about the economic impact on the Faire.

"Ha! That'll be the day!" Loretta proclaimed.

"See you there?" Lenore asked as we left.

*

"Would you like to come in?" I asked Mac when we reached the house. "For a drink of water? You could go on rat patrol with Glory and me. Or maybe you'd like to see my fine etchings."

Etchings it was. Really hot ones, clothes all over the floor, sweaty-type etchings. Twice, thank you very much.

10

At some point the Christmas Fair became the Holiday Faire, a more politically correct and inclusive nomenclature. It didn't matter what you called it, if you were in Lawrence, Kansas at this time of year, you went. It was like the summer Farmers' Market, only condensed into three days, and best of all it was indoors, gave people the opportunity to get out of the house and socialize, some place that was neither a bar nor a forty-five minute drive to the nearest mall.

Additionally, you had a better chance of getting into the Faire than you did with KU sporting events, where tickets were hard to come by, practically hereditary. Parking was a problem, but people dropped off the older folks and children at the door and schlepped in from whatever space they could find or improvise. Located east of town, off Route 10, it took a car to get there, so the place was mobbed with vehicles.

Like the Farmers' Market, the Faire was a jumble of booths and concessions. Same folks, different crafts and goods. The meandering aisles were crowded with shoppers but easy to negotiate because strollers were parked at the door. Children walked or were carried. The pace was slow, but safe—no fear of collision with a stroller driver on a cell phone.

Mac and I arrived early, as the L&L's had recommended. We drifted with flow of holiday shoppers, looking around and getting our bearings in the massive barn, the first of three on the grounds. I recognized the bison/emu meat guy selling from a battered white cooler. Farmers' wives sold jars of honey and cranberry preserves, Mennonite ladies in their delicate bonnets sold pies and breads. There were stands of wreaths and Christmas trees against one wall, the fragrance of pine blending with cinnamon, mulling spices, and coffee. The air had a distinctly steamy feel to it.

We stopped by a table selling raffle tickets for a hayride at a local farm. "In this weather?" I asked the woman with the red roll of tickets. She laughed at my skeptical eyebrows. "Oh, yes. We pile people up with blankets, put bells on the horses. It sounds lovely, doesn't it? And we have thermoses full of hot chocolate and hot apple cider. Folks love it!"

MacDonald plunked his money on the table before I could even get a good eye roll going. He grinned at me and put the tickets in his pocket. The woman thanked him and we moved away.

"Wait, wait. Before you start." Mac held up a hand. "It's a chance, not a guarantee."

I nodded reasonably, pretending to think it over. If my luck held and worked *for* me, I wouldn't have to go, right? I considered the odds and thought of buying tickets to give to random people who might be more agreeable to the hayride opportunity than myself.

"Hey, Mac? I need to step outside for a minute. I'm overheating in here." The air in the barn felt hot and sticky. We agreed to meet up in barn number two. I stepped out a side door and took a breath of cold air.

No smokers—I had the doorway to myself. Barn number two loomed ahead of me on the right, a stream of people entering the main door on the left side of the building. The crowd was dotted with Santa hats.

Beyond them, I could see a split rail fence behind which stood remnants of a corn maze, grayed stalks listing at odd angles. I didn't automatically register the mess as a corn maze, I'm not that Kansan anymore. If I ever was. A faded sign with what was once Halloween-orange letters gave me a clue.

Hunching my shoulders against the cold, I continued to take slow breaths of air. I am an indoor person, I reminded myself, a woman who periodically spends long hours inside dark casinos full of annoying noises and far more people than this. What was my problem? Not the hayride tickets, surely. No, it was a larger, older, nagging dread. I did not want to go back into the goddam din of cheeriness.

The line of people crossing from barn number one to barn number two thinned out and left the path empty for a while. I looked up at the clouds piling overhead and then down at the weathered maze. Something caught my drifting gaze. Was it a person? A dog? Was someone looking at me? I took a step forward to take a closer look when a sudden crowd began crossing between barns again. My cell phone buzzed in my pocket. Keeping my eyes on whatever it was through the moving line of people, I fumbled under my coat and pulled out the phone. Chas. Looking up again, I found I'd lost my target. "Call you back." Put the phone back in my pocket and headed for the maze, quickening my pace.

*

"What do mean, why?" I said to Mac later while we were waiting for the police to arrive and do their crime scene thing with the body. "I was curious."

Curiosity had carried me through the people moving between installments of the Faire, across a patch of gravel to the fence and faded sign. What was it I had seen? A dark shape, a sudden movement against the stationary mass of corn stalks that formed the outside wall of the corn maze.

I had entered a low, wooden gate to my left and looked around. A frozen mud path, the entrance to the maze, led off to my right. To the left, an open space spread to the far side of barn number one, with parked cars in the distance beyond a stand of Douglas firs. Nothing moved. The emptiness of the place resonated with my sense of ennui, as Mac called it.

I crunched along the gravel at the maze entrance and turned to face the way I had come. Sounds of conversation from people who were mostly watching their feet, dealing with packages, keeping track of children. No one looked my way, not once. They could have been on a separate planet. Gaps occurred between groups of people moving between barns.

During one of the gaps, I looked over to where I had been standing before. The side door of the barn would have seemed like a frame if anyone had been watching me, waiting to see if I'd go back inside or head across to the path. If a person had been crouching here at the entrance to the maze, and not a dog, they might have wondered if I could see them.

Who would care, I wondered, some kid paranoid about getting caught smoking pot in the maze? Abandoned corn mazes were notorious hangouts for all sorts of clandestine shenanigans. I checked the ground at my feet. Hard and frozen, no footprints there. The shadows of the entrance curved around to the right, inviting me in. Why not?

Like all such mazes, this one was open to the sky, so the whole thing was in moldy stages of dilapidation. Hay bales that used to support walls had canted and spilled; sheaves of gray corn stalks tilted in crazy directions, leaned against each other, and occasionally stood up straight, as originally intended. The place smelled damp and musty. No bright orange pumpkins, now; no children playing and getting lost in the crisp leaves of dried stalks. All is forgotten, order replaced by disorder, then rot. How quickly the rot sets in. Even so, I preferred being here among the wreckage to the sugary din across the way. Maybe not such a good thing, Lyle. Fragile, shredded blades of leaf moved in a stray gust of wind. There were rustlings along the ground, possibly mice, or rabbits, or rats. I made a mental note to tell Caitlin. I was smiling at that thought when my cell rang again.

"You know I hate it when you hang up on me," Chas said.

"Hey, sorry. I thought I saw something."

"Saw what? Where? What are you doing," Chas said suspiciously.

"Um, I am, I was, at the Holiday Faire with Mac…" I decided to leave out the part about the claustrophobia and creeping dread. "And now I'm outside. In a ruined corn maze."

" A what maze?"

"Corn. Maze. Left over from Halloween. They don't take them down, just let them decompose and plow 'em under in the spring. I think. Don't really remember."

"Get out of there at once," Chas said in his I'm-talking-to-an-idiot voice.

"What?"

"You heard me. Out, as in what is wrong with you, Lyle?"

"Oh, crap," I said, interrupting before he could get started.

"I beg your pardon?"

"Chas, I think I just stepped on a dead body. Looks dead, anyway." I had been picking my way through wads of hay, lifting my feet over clumps of fallow corn stalks. I wasn't really watching where I was going as I spoke into the phone, just following the turns of what was left of moldy walls, one of which was crumpled flat in front of me, a man in a dark coat sprawled on top of it. My foot had landed on the left arm. My eyes stuck to the hand, thin and fine boned. Small man, small hand, I mused. Now even smaller. Lifeless....

"Dead?" Chas's voice squeaked, recalling me to the real world.

"Body." I took a few steps back and placed my hands on my knees. Utter silence. I put the phone back to my ear and stood up again, making a kind of gasping noise.

"Get Tall Man," Chas said. "Better yet, call him and tell him where you are. Do it now, Lyle. Call me back."

*

Mac told me not to move, but I took a few more steps back. I hugged myself, and started counting in my head, a slow, soothing string of numbers to forestall thinking and postpone the how-the-hell-did-you-do-this that wanted to replace the numbers. I got to two hundred by the time MacDonald arrived. Pretty quick. Must be those long legs of his. I was grateful.

"No I don't know who he is, Mac. I didn't really see his face." Not that I wanted to. I told Mac about the flitting movement I'd seen earlier, how I had stepped on the body, and then I told it all over again for the police, who rolled the body over and asked me if I could I.D. the guy. Not anyone I knew, or Mac either, for that matter. White guy, older, balding, small hole in his forehead. Very little blood.

"Likely a .22," Greta Danielson said. "Probably still in there. No casings. Looks like a revolver at close range," she said to Mac. "The man knew the shooter."

She turned her pale green eyes to me. "You still got that gun, Lyle? Mind if I take a look?"

I grimaced and drew the small Taurus .22 from my satchel and handed it to her, grip first, barrel open. At least it hadn't been in my bra.

"New weapon? And this is how you take care of your gun? Like this? That's just shameful!" She opened the tiny automatic and saw for herself it was empty. "Look at this, lint and purse crap all over it. It's just sad." She glared at me.

"It's not loaded, right?" I whined defensively.

"Get a holster, will you? Wear the damn thing if you're going to carry it. You're pathetic!"

Mac turned away, thinking I wouldn't see his laugh, but I saw his shoulders, I knew.

Officer Danielson returned my gun after I showed her that I was licensed and had even taken lessons.

"Las Vegas, yeah, right," she said dismissively. "Tell me, Lyle Hudson, why is it when you come to town you get tangled up in situations like this? Is it your mission in life to create problems for me?" It wasn't a friendly question.

Last time I'd been in Lawrence, Greta Danielson ended up running across Massachusetts Street in a wedding dress, pistol out, thinking she was coming to rescue me from a pair of dog-nappers. Long story, I'm not one of her faves. Greta was a woman cop, a black cop, in a white bread world. Dignity was important to her. I thought we were on the way to becoming friends. Clearly, she felt otherwise.

"OK, you can go. Get inside, warm up, have some hot chocolate or whatever you people do. But stick around. And no more stepping on corpses! We'll be talking again soon. Bye, Mac." If she'd been wearing a hat, she'd have tipped it at him. He had that kind of effect on women.

Mac and I walked around the yellow crime scene tape, past a wad of gawkers, and tried to merge into the line of people single mindedly moving toward barn number two, flashing police lights or no.

"You want to stay?" Mac asked in disbelief.

"No, but I promised the L&L's I'd stop by, and I do not want to come back here again. Ever." I gave him a sharp look. "What's in the bag?"

"Nothing for you," he smiled, taking the small paper bag out of his pocket.

"No?" my eyebrow said skeptically.

"No." Mac's smile widened. "Here, I'll show you." His hands fiddled awkwardly with the small bag for a moment, then he pulled out something that looked like a cookie with antlers.

"What is it?" I asked in horrified fascination.

"It's for Jesse." His Irish setter, who I knew had better sense.

"No," I shook my head. "No self-respecting dog would eat that!"

"Are you kidding? Dogs'll eat anything." He stared at the garish object in his hand and shrugged, stuffing it

back in the paper bag. "It just kind of came over me."
Like a rash, I thought. The Faire did that.

Barn number two was slightly less crowded that
barn number one. No cloying food smells, more room to
move around. I took off my gloves and tried to rub some
warmth into my hands. I scanned the room, trying to out
where my aunts were, but I wasn't really seeing much.

"Is this what people do, Mac? Walk away from
something like that," I gestured behind me to the corn
maze, "and just go shopping? It feels weird."

"We can leave, you know," he said, looking down at
me with concern in his brown eyes.

I shook my head and took a breath, bucking myself
up. "No, we're here. Let's just do it." I set my jaw with
grim determination.

I stopped at a table displaying folded silk scarves,
brilliant colors, finely woven. I was surprised to find
such quality at what was essentially a kitschy crafts fair.
I picked one up and unfolded it, an oblong of deep red
silk. No, "red" wasn't the right word. This color needed
a bigger name, maybe "vermillion." Wow. Mac smiled,
knowing I'd be with the scarves for a while, and
indicated that he'd be up ahead. I nodded OK and
returned to the scarf.

"Silk is just as good as wool, to keep in heat," the
young woman running the table said. "Imported from
Thailand, I bring them in myself. Fifty percent of the
price goes to putting a young man through teaching
school. Look, here's his picture." Her eyes were earnest
and devoted to her cause.

"I'm sold," I told her. "These are lovely. The trick
is making a choice! Give me a minute, OK?"

She smiled beatifically and patted the carefully
folded rows of silk, moving over to talk to people
standing to my right. I chose the vermillion for Uncle

Vern. He'd be totally shocked at something so NOT outdoorsy and unrelated to fishing, but he'd love the color, probably wear the thing to shreds. I found another scarf with an iridescent weave of violet and turquoise that would look great on Loretta. She'd be miffed that I got her and Vern the same thing, but she'd love the scarf for the same reason. The thought made me smile. Sometimes, looking at the two of them, I could almost entertain the thought of marriage. Almost.

And, because I couldn't buy something so lovely for others without a treat for myself, I chose a scarf of pale celadon, wondering briefly if Chas would let me keep it once he laid eyes on it. I sighed.

"Do you have another scarf this color?" I asked the young woman. "I think I'm going to need two." She went to rummage around in some boxes at the back of the booth and I turned aside to pull my wallet from my satchel.

Behind me to my left, a whispered conversation started to heat up, an intense hissing that raised my eyebrows and made me stand very still so I could listen and remain invisible.

"How could you?" was met with condescending denial.

"I know you did, I saw you!" the S in saw was definitely hissing. It was met with indistinct muttering.

"You, you hypocritical, sanctimonious asshole. She was an acolyte! I can't put up with this any more." Darker mutterings. Why couldn't I hear him? Somebody wanted a low profile.

"Let go of me! She may be dead, but this is not over." High-heeled boot sounds ebbed away. I know they were high heels because I snuck a look. Curled red hair, likely dyed, flounced on the shoulders of her fur jacket. I was betting on Nutria. A slim man wearing a leather jacket and a clerical collar watched her leave, smoothing down his hair with one hand, pretending he wasn't looking around to see if they had been overheard.

"Still here?" MacDonald had a cup of coffee in hand, smile crinkles at the corners of his eyes.

"Almost done." I paid for the four scarves and tucked the plastic bag carefully into my satchel. I reached to take a sip of his coffee, maneuvering Mac between motorcycle minister and myself.

"Who's that?" I gestured to the man in the leather jacket and Mac turned his head briefly, a big dog looking at a puppy.

"Him? Edwin Hodge, Episcopal priest." His tone said bad puppy.

"He married?"

"You looking?"

"Yeah, right. I can totally see myself as a clergy wife."

Mac laughed out loud. "Too late. Wife's name is Kirsty or something like that. Redhead, great legs."

"Just my luck," I said, jabbing him with an elbow.

We passed a group of quilters chatting happily at a table of Christmas tree skirts, festive stockings, and a heap of homemade quilts. If quilters have a heaven, this booth was it.

Not too far beyond the quilters was what looked like a scrum of fevered shoppers.

"Oh, no. That's not..." I looked up at Mac.

"Oh, yes, it certainly is," he said, able to peer over the heads from his superior height. "You go ahead, talk to your aunts. I'll meet you over there, by the cuckoo clocks. Just kidding," he replied to my sharp glare. "I'm sure they're really birdhouses."

Mac ambled away taking the empty cup with him, and I studied the knot of buzzing people before me. I didn't want to mess with them, but I did need to figure out how to get past.

"Hold on, there!" Loretta's vice rose above the crowd. "This isn't Target, ya know. There's just the two of us!" The buzzing subsided to an impatient grumble. Someone from the front of the pack peeled away, red of face but smiling. I recognized Deirdre, Luce's yoga teacher, slightly worse for wear.

"It's Lyle, is it?" Luce's girl?" she greeted me. Girl? I was older than she was.

"Luce's niece. Hello. Are my aunts selling Christmas yoga-wear?"

"Ach, no!" she laughed at my lame joke. "Everybody comes to Holiday Faire, girl. It's daft, but it's what we do, isn't it?" Deirdre smiled a pixy smile at me.

"Having fun?"

"Oh, too right!" Deirdre cracked herself up. "Here, have a look at this." She reached around in a white paper bag, the kind my aunts used when they were in the adult chocolate business, a fond memory now that they were into seasonal torment for pets.

"Elf ears!" Deirdre almost doubled over laughing.

"Um, yes, they do look kind of elfish." I cringed at the pointed, wing-like things attached to a bright green headband."

"For my brother's angora rabbit!"

"Really? Won't the ears, the real ones I mean, get in the way?"

"Ach," she waved away such a fool thought. "He won't actually put them on the wee beastie. It's the sheer stupidity of it that gets ye laughing, eh?" Not waiting for an answer, she stowed the elf ears, patted me on the arm, and left, not bothering to remind me about coming to yoga. Deirdre probably knew Luce would take care of that.

While we chatted, the roadblock at the L&L's table had cleared, the crowd thinned down to a few customers.

""Could you take an order for one of these capes, Lenore? Size large?" The request came from a hefty woman in a red sweater.

"Oh, I'm afraid there's not enough time for orders now, dear. But, tell you what. Give me your number and I'll call you tonight if we have one back at the house. I could bring it with me and you'd pick it up tomorrow. How's that?"

"Oh, that'd be lovely! Thank you!" The woman wrote her name and number on a receipt and left. Lenore stuck it in her pocket as I slipped behind the table to give her a hug.

Her twin, Loretta, was scrounging around for something under the table, which turned out to be her Santa hat. She plunked it on her head and sat back and looked up at me.

"You're still here!" Loretta patted her ample lap. "Come give us a kiss!" I pretended to sit and complied, adding the mandatory hug to the kiss.

"You can put some weight down, girl! I'm not feeble, ya know!"

Instead, I stood up and grinned at her. "Everyone knows you can't be trusted, woman." Loretta had a reputation for merciless tickling.

She smiled up at me. "Business is great! Didn't I tell you? Ha! Say, have you heard anything new about that murder?"

"Already?" Was the gossip mill that fast?

"What do you mean, already? That girl was strangled a couple of days ago."

"No, I mean the guy shot in the head."

"What guy shot in the head?" Loretta looked at me as if I was tuned into a different station.

"Outside in the corn maze." I checked my watch. "About an hour ago."

My two aunts and I regarded each other with wide-open Hudson eyes.

11

"Two for two in the dead body department, Lyle! Not very Peace on Earth Good Will Toward Man, is it?" Loretta declared.

"Hey! I didn't kill them! I happened by, after the fact." I raked my hands through my hair, pulling it back from my face. "Truth is, finding that body today upset me. Still does."

Both L&L's became instantly solicitous, making aunt-like clucking noises, insisting that I join them for supper. I said I might do that, surprising the hell out of both of them. Clearly I was not myself.

When MacDonald George joined us, I was discussing Glory's need for a coat with Lenore. I was feeling guilty having to leave her home alone so much.

"I might have some fleece, Lyle, maybe an old pullover I could reconstruct for her," Lenore offered.

"NO, you're too busy as it is."

"Not at all," Lenore began. But to prove my point, a new wave of holiday shoppers approached the table and Mac and I moved off.

"I'm not really in the mood for barn three, Mac. Let's get out of here."

"Glad to. I think there's an aisle over this way."

As we headed out, people ahead of us parted and gave way for a man in a wheelchair. Correction: a gorgeous man in a wheelchair, lethally attractive. The kind of good looking that makes a woman all confused and disoriented. I tried to concentrate n my breathing.

What do such people actually look like? This one was golden brown all over, golden brown hair, golden brown eyes, just all…golden. In a fawn color leather jacket with fringe, hair curling onto his shoulders, which seemed to ripple as he propelled the wheels of his chair. It was one of those customized deals, not clunky like a regular wheelchair. Maybe he's part golden retriever, I thought. One that smells like biscuits.

I half expected Mac to read my mind and tell me to behave myself, but he and Mr. Gorgeous were locked eye-to-eye, reminding me of the way a couple of veteran poker players will stare at each other over a sizeable pot.

"Carl."

"MacDonald."

No one was blinking. I started to hear Clint Eastwood music, which appealed to me more than Christmas carols.

"Here you are, Carl! I totally lost…Oh, hello, Mac. Lyle?"

Andressa Keach joined our happy little group and broke the mood. We all retreated into a round of introductions and holiday chat, and I thought I was home free until I shook Carl's hand and practically fell into the golden brown eyes. Very strong hand. A worker's hand, warm and powerful. It was the hand that saved me from the eyes.

"What are you, a lion tamer? You break horses or something?" I was talking to the hand. Much safer.

"Close to." He had a golden brown laugh, too. "I do some equine therapy west of town."

"When the weather's good enough to get there, " Andressa added. "Which it hasn't been lately. Carl's been pretty much housebound, haven't you, sweetheart." Something in her tone sounded forced.

"You worry too much, Andy. I was fine on my own. No need to rush around looking after me."

Andressa's lips tightened. Evidently *Andy* was not a name she liked.

Carl looked away and then turned his eyes back to me and smiled a golden smile. I stammered something lame about enjoying the Faire and dragged Mac by the arm, trying to get the hell out of there.

Shivering, in Mac's car, I punched him in the arm, twice.

"Ow! Stop that! What did I do?" Mac complained.

"What was that? What just happened? Who is that guy?"

"Yeah, Carl has that effect on women. Always has, probably always will, wheelchair or not." MacDonald clenched his jaw and put the Mustang in gear.

"Oh, yeah? Well, I don't like it! Why doesn't he use some self-control, put a bag over his head, or something. Totally not fair. Like a Svengali or Vulcan mind meld." I had to stop before I worked myself into a rant. Carl Glasser had made me feel like a teenager, and that made me angry. Vulnerability made me angry.

"And what was that with the eyeballs? Some gorgeous man grudge match?"

Mac chuckled at my remark but grew serious, thinking about what he didn't like about Carl Glasser. "Someone was in the car with him when he got himself paralyzed. Someone not his wife. She died."

"Hm," I nodded, thinking about it. "Interesting." Silence from MacDonald George. I knew that he cared for Andressa, seemed to have a genuine regard for her. Odd, though, how Mac grew quiet whenever she came up in conversation. As far as Andressa and Carl were concerned, I was old enough and grown up enough to know that you can never figure out anybody else's relationship. It was hard enough figuring out your own.

"We've got guns," I said brightly. "We could always just shoot him."

"I'd have thought you'd have had enough of that today."

I sighed. Reality sucked. "Yeah, probably right."

The V-8 engine hummed. The car grew warm. We rode back into town in meditative silence.

Mac dropped me at the house, where I met a frantically dancing Glory, happy to see me, needing to get out. I let her out the back door and proceeded to obsess about neglecting my dog. A good topic to keep me from thinking about anything else. I got to feeling so bad that after the skinny white dog trotted up the icy stairs and back inside, I sat down at the kitchen table and took her into my lap. All four paws leeched cold into my legs, making me feel even worse. But Glory was in dog heaven, licking my face, wriggling her bony butt, getting her ears scratched.

"Guilt, huh?" Caitlin padded in, barefoot, and leaned against the stove. I didn't know how she could stand to walk around without at least a pair of socks. Part of "stayin' real", no doubt. Glory leapt down and gave her a Let's Play bow, prompting Caitlin to commence patting and ear scratching. Glory rolled over and showed a non-existent belly. Caitlin joined her on the floor and pitched in there, too.

"Yeah, I get that way, too," Caitlin said. "Winter is tough on Miss B. Can't take her out with me; it's so cold, you know? She's sluggish, not interested in food. I feel rotten."

We nodded, looking down at Glory, thinking about how much Caitlin loves having her boa constrictor wrapped around her shoulders, just feeling the blues.

"I heard you were surrounded by cops out at the Frigging Faire today."

"I was. Found a dead guy out in the corn maze."

"Dude." This time the word meant something like "whoa."

"Seriously." More nodding.

"At first, I thought they were coming for *me*," Caitlin said, chewing on her lower lip.

"You did? Really?"

"Totally." She paused and then filled in the rest of the story. "I was helping at the Animal Rescue table, handing out flyers?" Caitlin is a well-known Animal Rights advocate in Lawrence, very much a take-it-to-the-streets activist. I had a pretty good idea where this was going.

"I was even smiling, right? Going along with all the fake holiday spirit crap, trying to get it into people's heads that we human beings are responsible for animal suffering, right? It is our moral duty to help the helpless animals that are neglected and abandoned!"

I was impressed by Caitlin's passion. This speech was more words from her at one time than I could remember.

"Anyway," she continued, calming herself down, "it was going fine. A couple little kids stopped to check out the piercings. They asked me to stick out my tongue, which I did." She smiled and stuck out her tongue to illustrate, the round metal stud gleaming wetly.

"And then I see over their heads some jerk yelling at his dog, choking him. One of those metal choke collars with those evil prongs?" She made a claw like gesture with one hand. "German Shepherd, beautiful dog but totally whipped, defeated, tail between his legs. I couldn't stand it. I tell the kids to scoot, walk over to the jerk and give him a poke on the arm.

"Dude. What the fuck are you doing to that dog? He brushes off his sleeve, says he's disciplining his dog and it's none of my business, go away. Dim twit.

"For what? For existing? You are abusing that animal, mister. Cut it out.

"Jerk gives the chain a yank, dragging the dog away, and I snap. Give the creep a kick in the back of the knees"—Caitlin wears steel-tipped boots—"and the geezer is down, me stomping on his arm, the dog whining."

There was a light in Caitlin's eyes, remembering the scene. "What happened?" I asked.

"I got the chain off the dog before people stepped in, thinking I attacked the guy. Some professor, turns out. A couple bystanders knew him. Who is he, I ask. Professor at the university, Cassidy or something. Oh yeah? Well, Professor Cassidy ABUSES HIS DOG! I got in the guy's face. Every time I see you, man, I am calling you out! CRUELTY TO ANIMALS! Shame on you!"

Caitlin was up and standing in front of the stove, shouting and shaking her fist.

"So that's why I thought the cops were for me, that he was going to press charges or something. It's criminal he still has that dog. Hey, I made some lentil soup. Want some?" She pointed to a pot on the back burner and turned on the heat.

"You bet," I said. "Cassidy? Could his name have been Cassaday?"

"Medium-skinny dude? Older than you, balding, wrinkly, sour face?"

"Sounds like him." I thought of another such person lying dead in the straw. They couldn't both be him.

We ate the lentil soup and I told Caitlin that if she did get arrested to call me immediately and I'd bail her out.

"Cool," she said. "Oh, wait. I have something to show you."

I washed our bowls in the sink while she pounded out of the kitchen and up the stairs. Glory stood beside me, looking after Caitlin, wagging her stubby tail expectantly. Maybe Caitlin was getting a b-a-l-l.

Caitlin pounded back in, carrying a suspiciously familiar white paper bag. I dried my hands.

"Dig this!" She pulled a small swatch of green velvet from the bag. Was that a fringe?

"You got Brunhilde a cape?"

"No, silly. It's for the rats! Sometimes I like to play with Brunhilde's food!"

*

After a much-needed nap, I sat up and put my feet on the floor, brushed hair from my face. The lump under the blanket that was Glory wagged its tail. I pounced on her and we wrestled a bit, happy growls and muffled yips.

"How can you breathe under there?" I asked the wriggling dog. Glory loved being under things—blankets, hotel towels, a coat someone had forgotten to hang up, preferably black.

It was almost 2:00 p.m. I had to pull myself together and show up at the bridal shop. I hated the place, but what the hell—today was already one weird hallucination. It couldn't get much worse.

I washed my face and slathered on a protective layer of moisturizer as advised by a cosmetic expert friend of Chas in San Francisco. I had a black eye at the time and needed an industrial strength concealer. I was well beyond the anti-aging phase of skin care, she said, and needed to preserve what little elasticity I had left.

"The young can be so cruel, Glory."

I went over to the jewelry box on top of the dresser and took out the ring—nine carat ruby and three diamonds embedded in a wad of gold. "Star Gazer," Ari called it. My Arab admirer, dark eyed and dangerous. His two crazy wives, Mina and Fahdi. Where were they now? Better not ask. To think it might be to summon them. I put on the ring. It would come in handy if I needed to put someone's eye out.

Downstairs, I saw there was a txt message from Chas. YOU SAID YOU'D CALL. Crap. So I did. My call went to his voicemail.

I spoke quickly, "You shouldn't use those adjectives with the word 'beep,' Chas. Keep it simple. Um, no news on the dead guy, no idea who he is. There's also a dead coed down at the morgue, apparently. What else? No, that's all for now. I'm on my way to Hyacinth. Pray for me. Kiss kiss."

Glory looked up at me expectantly. Now that we had spent quality time bonding and napping and wrestling and all, I couldn't possibly abandon her. Again. No, she had complete faith I'd do the right thing. She, Glory, my dog, believed in me.

"OK, you can come." Magic words, maniacal results. Glory did the happy dance and kept running between the closet where I scrounged for something to keep her warm and the kitchen door, in case I forgot where it was.

"It'll have to be blue mohair, girl." I stuck the sweater over her head and tied the sleeves around her slim body, knotting them over her back, thereby transforming Glory into a sumo doggy. It would work. She didn't care, she was going in the car, that's all that mattered.

Snow flurries had set in while I'd napped and the day was a flat gray and white. There was no space in the alley behind the shop, but I lucked out and found a slot around front. The mohair sweater had slipped off, or Glory had slipped out of it, on the ride over, and it had devolved into a nest-like blob. Mohair makes me itch just to look at it. Glory didn't seem to care. I fed the meter and looked across Mass Street to the park and the cupola where Greta had made her grand arrival in wedding dress and pistol.

A man in a Santa hat stood on the sidewalk. I squinted to get a better look through the falling snow. This one was in full Santa regalia, like a 19th Century greeting card. Was that a tree over his shoulder? A little one, maybe. Long white beard, big black belt, shiny boots. He waved at a child leaning out the window of a passing car. His laughter seemed to float to me through the snow. The man turned in my direction and waved. I waved back. I turned slowly toward the shop door but paused and looked back over my shoulder. Santa was gone.

Inside, the bridal shop smelled of cookies—a buttery, vanilla, sugary fragrance. The dress on display in the window had to be Nola's idea of bride as Christmas angel, wings and all. A gold, tinsel halo hovered above the headless mannequin in a way I found disconcerting.

"Hellooo! Welcome! Season's Greetings! Would you like to enter a raffle for a new car?" Nola's cheery voice preceded her as she came from the back of the shop. The place always felt crowded, even with just a few customers moving about. The dresses took up a lot of space with their fluff and frou frou.

"Oh, it's you, Lyle." The cheeriness dropped a notch, for which I was grateful. "Don't you look wonderful! For you, I mean. Lovely coat. Are you moisturizing? I'm so glad." She had Perry the Pomeranian tucked under one arm. Tiny antlers were strapped on to his pointy little head.

"Did you get those at the Faire?" I wriggled my eyebrows at the brown felt and sequin contraption that made the dog look like an insect mutation gone wrong.

"Holiday Faire," Nola corrected me. "Yes, of course, dear. Your aunts are so clever! Who could resist these?" She smoothed Perry's nose, careful not to muss her lipstick. "Why, Lyle, your dog is shivering. Doesn't she have a coat?"

"She's fine, Nola. Brides make her nervous."

"Lyle, come look at my plans for Angel Bride." Nola latched on to my coat sleeve, but I was saved by the jingling of bells on the shop door.

"Hellooo, my dears! Welcome! Does everyone have a ticket for a chance at winning a shiny new car? Right this way! Cookie, anyone?" And she was off.

I found Crista seated at the Queen Anne desk that had been my mother's joy when she owned Hyacinth. She and Nola had developed a strong rapport, and Crista was spending a good deal of her time at the workroom above the shop. At the moment Crista was chatting with a couple of young women who were giggling and nibbling sugar cookies. I'd have to keep track and see if they actually managed to eat one instead of merely reducing it to crumbs with their nibbling.

Crista waved. Her customary Goth attire, more Steampunk, really, all Victorian ornate, was toned down for the season. Forest green velvet, lace collar, green eye shadow, green nails, mauve lipstick, a band of holly leaves in her short, black hair. At least the hair wasn't green.

I winked at her as I passed the desk and took Glory through the French doors into the back room. The shop was more crowded that I'd ever seen it. Way too much estrogen in one place. I hung up my coat and scouted around for Nola's grand plan, which turned out to be a spreadsheet, some sketches, and an assortment of exclamatory statements in red ink, candidates for a banner, no doubt.

I'd barely gotten started when Nola burst through the French doors, free hand fluttering dramatically at her throat.

"Isn't it wonderful? Crista mapped it all out on computer. I know it will be a very, very big night for us!"

"Big Night? Like the movie? Will Stanley Tucci be here?"

"Excuse me?" Nola blinked once to signify she was ignoring me. "I refer to our elegant champagne reception, only for our best customers. It's all right there." She waved a manicured finger at the spreadsheet.

"What do you mean 'best customers?' Wedding dresses are a one shot deal. No repeats, right?"

Nola rolled here eyes at my obvious ignorance. "So not the case, Lyle. Where have you been?" Nola patted her hair coyly. What was that color?

"Nola, are you dyeing your hair? It's the same color as your dog. What is that, peach? Salmonella? Did you dye Perry, too?"

"For your information, Peri and I are 'coordinated.' It's fashionable. Quite the done thing. And no one says 'dyed' anymore, dear. Now, stop being difficult and pay attention, please." She hated me calling the dog Perry, named by her husband for Perry Como. She accented the second syllable, insisting that the name was French, for peridot. Poor dog.

Crista walked in with an empty plate, in search of more cookies.

"They're actually eating them?" I asked.

She grinned at me. "It's the vanilla. They can't help themselves."

Nola practically snatched the plate from Crista's hands. "Make her behave, Crista, dear. Lyle won't listen to me." Nola narrowed her eyes at me and swept off. Crista gave me a quick hug and knelt down to say hello to Glory.

"Fresh cookies?" The aroma was overpowering.

"We microwave them, " Crista explained. "We've got gingerbread men, too."

"Fiendishly clever. Lure them into a sugar trance and make them buy expensive dresses."

"Pretty much!" Crista grinned and stood up.

"Crista Banks, are you moving in on Nola's bridal empire?" I raised an eyebrow.

Crista raised an eyebrow back at me and put one hand on her hip. "No, I'm more of an impresario-slash-designer wizard. Read the plan. We could end up having to expand the shop, Lyle."

"See?" Nola sniffed as she passed with a fresh plate of cookies. "It will be a big night. Very."

Crista's gaze traveled the small workroom, a tiny wrinkle forming on her young brow. "Where's her coat? You aren't taking Glory out naked into the snow, are you?"

I told her about the L&L's pet wear and Glory's humiliation. Crista stroked the dog's head sympathetically and I thought about the hapless Perry.

"That's just wrong," she said. "I have an idea. Glory will come with me. You, Lyle, read the plan. We'll be back. No humiliation, promise!"

Glory followed Crista upstairs to the storage area that also served as Crista's base of operations. I realized I had forgotten to ask her about Blake. We'd have to catch up later.

Forgoing my responsibility to read the plan, I took Crista's seat at the Queen Anne desk and decided to check my email. Two girls hovered near a plate of cookies and played no-I-shouldn't, a girly version of 'chicken,' to see which one would cave first and eat the damn cookie. The caver gets the guilt, and girl number two gets to smirk before generously giving in to keep her friend company in the caloric sinfulness of cookie eating.

Before I could swipe a handful of crumbs to shove up their noses, the girls started to gossip about girl number three, the friend who had lured them into Nola's bridal web.

"You know bout Rozzie, right?" Was she asking the cookie?

"Awww!" a mewing sound of total sympathy. "Soooo sad!"

Girl number one picked up a cookie and nibbled. If you were talking about other people, you weren't actually eating a cookie. Gossip rendered the cookie invisible.

"Totally. And Robin was her BFF, right? They were roommates." At the word 'roommates', girl number two quickly grabbed a cookie of her own. "No way."

"Um hum." Nodding and nibbling.

"Wow." Nibbling and nodding. "Considering the, you know, murder? Rozzie looks great." No cookies for Roz, I thought.

"Well, duh. She couldn't eat a thing when she heard about Robin, you know, being strangled?" Both girls shuddered and finished the cookies in silence, enjoying the frisson of pretending to care.

Girl number two reached for another cookie. Only one left on the plate. She split it with her friend. "I heard she's bulimic."

"Robin? Really?"

"No, Rozzie."

"Nuh-uh. It was Robin. Best friend, hah!" spoken with a sneer. Girl number two licked sugar from her lips. "Took Rozzie's boyfriend, right?"

"Seriously. Total bitch. No wonder she's dead."

"Seriously." Cookies gone, they gazed at the empty plate.

I made tapping noises on the keyboard but need not have bothered. I was so old to them that they probably thought I was deaf, or a piece of furniture.

Girl number one took out a pink cell phone and started to text, with girl number two standing lookout.

"Psst. Here she comes."

Their grieving friend joined the girls, eyes twinkling, all aglow with whatever foolishness Nola had just put into her head. They were all so girly, I couldn't have told you if they were pretty or not. They reminded me of puppies—so young with their lives unwritten. I tried not to hate them for being so empty-headed and consoled myself with the thought that life would take care of them eventually, visiting upon them the usual heartache, disappointments, and inevitable wrinkling that came to us all. Must be the odor of cookies making me cynical.

"OK, ladies!" bright eyes said. "I just got us three tickets to the Angel Bride reception! I want you, my best friends, to be my guests!"

"Yay!" Girls number one and two clapped their hands.

"Oh, wait. Um, we're not getting married, Rozzie," girl number two was trying to do the math. Her friends looked at her blankly.

"That's not the point, Kimmie," said Rozzie patiently.

"Really. That is so not the point," said girl number one, rolling her yes.

"OK! Who wants margaritas?" Rozzie chirped.

"We do!!" the two friends responded. It sounded like a varsity cheer, even had a little jump to it.

Giggling in renewed harmony, the trio trooped out the door and into the snow. I shook my head, wondering about the future of the species.

Nothing in my email. I saved the Vegas promos, out of habit I told myself. I logged off and decided to text Chas. He was the one always hounding me to call; his silence was unnatural. I picked up Nola's reading glasses so I could read the tiny letters on the buttons of my phone. They worked great. I found this worrisome.

"So, what do you think?" Crista's voice made me jump. I turned and peered over Nola's glasses at the happy dog and smiling young woman. I smiled back.

"Crista, you renew my faith in humanity. Well done!"

"It's just a dog coat, Lyle, not like I'm a saint or anything." Like me, Crista had a hard time accepting compliments.

"Moot point," I smiled. She was already three times as worthy as the ditzes who just left the shop. What

Crista had done for Glory raised her to sainthood in my book.

"That color, the material, reminds me of something," I said, vaguely musing. Crista nodded encouragingly. "An airline, maybe?"

"On the nose!" she laughed. "Blake collected a pile of 'complimentary blankets' he calls them. I had some upstairs on the cot and thought one would make neat coat for Miss Glory." The dog stood at Crista's feet and smiled up at her slavishly.

"C'mon, Glory, let's show Lyle. Up!" Crista snapped her fingers and Glory obeyed instantly. The girl and the dog walked in a tight circle, Crista talking as she and Glory danced together.

"I doubled the thickness, trimmed the corners, fiddled around a bit to make sleeves for her front legs, added Velcro to flaps that would wrap around like a belt—see there? And, voila! A snuggly for Miss G! Who's a good girl?" She knelt and patted the dog, ruffling Glory's black ears.

"Crista, thank you." I was touched, and very relieved for Glory's sake. "Can I buy you a drink, a bottle of wine or something?"

"Not necessary, Lyle. She needs to be warm, yes she does," she said to the dog, hugging her.

"Hey, can I have my dog back before she forgets I exist? I'm starting to miss her."

"I don't know, she looks pretty cute in that coat!" Crista stood and tried to brush white dog hair from her velvet dress. I'd have told her it was futile, but she was finding that out for herself.

While we were talking, Nola had placed the CLOSED sign in the window and locked the door to the shop. She joined us, Perry still firmly latched under her arm—did the poor thing even walk—and voiced approval of Glory's new blue coat, even though it would soon be covered in dog hair.

" I'm glad that someone is looking after the dog. Lyle? Are those my glasses?" she held out her hand and kept talking. "Did you hear about that girl? Strangled, they said. Killed during that sleet storm and left by the side of the road. Oh, it's too awful!" Nola hugged Perry close, making him squeak. I decided not to bring up today's new murder victim and wondered idly what had become of Perry's antlers. The dog almost looked like a dog again.

"Did you know her, dear?" she asked Crista, assuming no doubt that all young people must know each other.

"Only by reputation," Crista replied, her face somber. "I don't want to speak ill of the dead."

"Poor creature," Nola barged on. "And she was so popular, they said. It's a shame." Nola tsked a few times and went to the rear of the shop to pack up and go home.

"Was she," I asked Crista, "popular?"

"With guys, I guess, yeah," she replied, thinking about it.

12

"Angel Bride?" I practically gagged. Hater of all things bridely, I found it supremely ironic to be saddled with Hyacinth. If I even thought about selling the shop, my aunts would speak as one. They don't have to use words; they look at me with six unblinking Hudson eyes. My genetic resonance does the rest, and here I'd be again, face with the blood-sucking horror of ...Bridezilla!

Crista and I were sharing a glass of wine in the empty shop. The small fridge held more than cookie dough.

"Angel? Bride? What the hell is that?" I reached down and scratched Glory's ears.

"I know," Crista laughed, "it sounds crazy, but Nola is right, Lyle. They'll love it. I did the research, believe me. Then I did a Pro forma for Hyacinth. With all the bridal consulting that Nola has already done, her marketing the reception via word of mouth, not to mention the designs contributed by yours truly," here Crista took a little bow. "I mean, this reception could take us to the next level, lift our recognition. The spreadsheet shows us definitely expanding."

I was happy for Crista. She was building her own clientele who wanted something slightly different for their wedding dresses. No angel brides for them, I thought. But they'd show up to support Crista. She had a niche, a place in the community. She was happy and it showed.

I closed my eyes, opened them. Gave Crista a wry smile. "I hate brides, Crista, angel or otherwise. Give me a vampire bride and I'd hate her, too. I can't stand the business as it is. I'm not sure I want it to get bigger. When it was smaller, I could just ignore it, but now..." I sighed.

"It's a business, not a disease, Lyle. It won't kill you," she said, drily. "Your problem is you're in town and it's in your face, feels like an irritant. If you were in Vegas and we told you about the plan, you'd say yes and go back to playing cards, no problem.

"Have you been talking to Luce?" I narrowed my eyes at her.

"It's obvious, woman!" Crista laughed. I was getting tired of her laughing at me. "Besides, you do not hate Hyacinth."

"Do too."

"Not so. You stop by all the time. Do you really have to? Do we ask you to? No."

I opened my mouth the shut it, speechless. This was spooky. Crista was channeling Aunt Luce. Maybe Crista had joined the Borg, become one of them.

"I think you're just bored," she said.

"OK, so what do I do?" I really wanted to know.

"You're asking me? You're the grown-up. Lyle. You figure it out." She took a sip of tea. "I feel for you, I really do, " she said. "I get stuck sometimes, too. It totally sucks."

I raised my glass in a toast. "Life sucks."

Artfully changing the topic, Crista asked me about yoga, which led to my story about running into Deirdre at the Faire, which segued into finding the body in the corn maze, at which point the conversation fizzled out.

After being pushed aside all day, the memory came
back hard.

"Wow," Crista said quietly, "that's two.

"Two?"

"Violent deaths," she whispered. I told her about
the girl talk at the bridal shop.

"I wonder if they're connected," she said. "Was it a
young guy?"

I shook my head.

"Huh."

*

A knock at the front door made Crista jump up.
"That must be Blake!" She went to let him in the back
door, turning on a light on her way. There were sounds
of stamping feet, clunks of winter footwear hitting the
wood floor, the scrabble of dog feet as Glory greeted the
young man.

"It's so dark, I wasn't sure you were here," Blake
said, coming into the shop. Glory danced around Blake's
feet.

"Blake Phipps, hello!" I stood up and gave him a
hug. "You look great, kiddo." I grinned and took him in.
He and Crista were together, that much was obvious,
and he looked happy, more relaxed than I remembered,
still fit. Blake's blond dreadlocks just reached his
shoulders. I was glad to see he was growing them in.

"So, are you still traducing?" I asked, going for a
lame joke.

"Traceur," he nodded, "yes. Not much right now,
with all the ice. I do the climbing wall, work out at the
gym. Hey, traduce means, like, con somebody, right?"
Bright kid.

"He's back at school," Crista said, proud of her man.

"Really?" I was pleased. Way back when, Blake was a student of mine at USF. I'd run into him again when I returned to Lawrence after my mother's death. An eternal student, Blake was practically family these days. As was Crista, I thought.

"Yeah, yeah, it's different this time, Lyle!" he said, reacting to my smile. "I'm going to finish it out. And, hey, I got a local gig to make some money over the break!" Blake was referring to the semester that just ended. "Holiday yard work, you know? We don't have a name yet. I'm thinking something like Light Up The Yard, but people might not get it.

"Yard work?" I asked.

"Holiday Deco—set it up, take it down, an inclusive service." Blake read my face and backed up to spell it out for me. "Lights? Inflatable Santas? Illuminated set ups on your lawn or your roof? Or both! People don't want to mess with putting stuff up in cold weather, right?"

"Right." In Kansas, people usually decorated houses in November, in order to beat the frigid weather, not to mention welcome in the shopping season.

"Man, I'm swamped! I had a couple dudes lined up to help, but one went home for Hanukkah. I was out there until way past dark today, out in the snow and everything. It can get, dangerous, too. But when those lights come on, it's awesome!"

"I bet it is," I said, envying Blake's enthusiasm.

"Um, OK. Crista?" Blake looked at her meaningfully.

"Whoa! Totally forgot! I'll be right back!" She raced upstairs to the workroom, to change clothes so they could go out. I was betting that velvet would be replaced by jeans and a sweater.

"We're going down to the Jazz Room, a friend of mine is in town, playing guitar tonight." We talked about music to pass the time until Crista got back. She bounded into the room, ready to go out. Sweater and jeans it was, the former a purple so dark it was almost black. Crista's primary colors. She grabbed Blake's arm and they shared a look.

"Want to come with us?" Blake asked dutifully.

"No, thanks. Go have fun!" I said and shooed them off.

"OK! Well, see you!"

When they were gone I washed glasses, stashed the win in the fridge and locked Hyacinth for the night.

*

Back at the house I threw my keys and satchel on the hall table. The buffalo herd in the painting continued their silent stampede. Glory looked up at me, wagging her little white tail.

"Last out?" I asked her.

The words were no sooner said than she zoomed past me through the kitchen to the back door.

"Get back here! We have to put on your coat!"

The dog pranced back and I put her back in the coat, appreciating how easy it was, how soft and warm, loving Crista for her gift to my dog.

"Gratitude. It's a crazy feeling, Glory. Hey! I think I'll come with you!" I bundled up, and Glory and I headed out the kitchen door and down the steps into the frozen back yard. A light layer of snow had fallen, but I could dimly see the indentations of our previous steps. Snow was still falling steadily. I lifted my head to watch the flakes turn gold in the light from the kitchen window and disappear into the darkness below.

Calling Glory to my side, I opened the alley gate and walked through. I knew every inch of yard and alley, having grown up here. It was very dark, but the light from nearby houses and the reflective quality of the snow was enough to see by once my eyes had adjusted.

I let Glory wander up the alley ahead of me and sniff around for a good place to pee. She dug her nose in the snow, investigating. A few tire tracks stretched up the alley, nothing recent. Most folks were in for the night. Clumps of snow collected on fence posts, dried leaves, and old vines. I paid attention to each step, aware of the icy layer beneath the snow. Silence collected around me. I lost sight of my dog. Hating the thought of inciting an invisible Hallelujah Chorus by calling her name, I tried a pathetic whistle.

"Evening." A man's voice. Large flashlight pointed down considerately instead of blaring into my face. I couldn't see who he was, but the low tone was reassuring.

"This your dog?" Glory stepped into the light and crossed over to my side. "Thought I heard something in the yard and came outside to check it out. Hope I didn't startle you." The man stayed where he was, light still pointed down at the snow.

"Just a bit. I didn't expect to see anybody out here so late. Thought Glory and I'd have the alley to ourselves," I gestured to the dog. "Enjoying last out."

"So I see. I wouldn't spend too long, though. It's a safe area, and the weather might help some, but still," he hesitated. "You never know."

"Point taken," I said. "You a neighbor?"

"Name's Shore, Martin Shore." He reached out a gloved hand and I stepped forward to shake it briefly. "I believe we have previously met." Schnauzer man.

"Giant Schnauzer, right? I'm Lyle Hudson." We shook.

"Yes, I know. Little Miss behaving herself these days?"

"Instead of attacking and trying to maul a dog twice her size? I'm still sorry about that. Really."

"Bygones," he said.

"No, really, really sorry. I'm hoping it was a passing phase."

"Enough said. You head home, and I'll wait here 'til you're in your back yard, see you safely in." Martin Shore was an Iraq vet, still cautious, still in the habit of keeping a lookout. I couldn't for the life of me remember what he looked like. Why was I wondering, anyhow? He'd practically had Glory sent to doggy jail, half way to the big Lights Out.

I waved my thanks and turned back down the alley, Glory running ahead of me to show me the way home.

Even before I reached the gate, I could see the kitchen lights were out. No lights upstairs, either. I was pretty sure no one was home when I left the house. I did not have a good feeling about the lights. My satchel was in the house. No cell, no gun.

"Hey, Shore?" I called back up the alley. "Could you come down here for a minute? Something is wrong." My answer was the flashlight beam bouncing as he jogged to where I was standing.

"What's up?"

"The lights are out."

He nodded, opened the gate and moved the beam of his flashlight back and forth across the snowy yard.

"Those all yours?"

"I think so." The path of prints from gate to house sure looked like they belonged to Glory and me.

"OK. Stay behind me. We'll take it slow." Shore switched into recon mode. I was relieved he was taking my concern seriously.

Glory raced ahead and up the steps and waited for us at the kitchen door. No twitches or alarms from her. I took that as a good sign.

As we reached the bottom of the steps, Shore moved the light over to our right, where a line of prints came around the side of the house. One set of prints, in one direction, toward the stairs in front of us. It had stopped snowing, so each print seemed clearly etched.

"Somebody picks up their feet. Your prints scuff through the snow, kicking it ahead of you. These belong to roommates, maybe?" How did he know I had roommates? Well, Crista lives here more than you do, you dope, I told myself. Why wouldn't he know?

"No one's home," I said.

"Key?"

"Door's not locked. We were doing last out, " I explained. No comment from the man.

He opened the door, and Glory raced into the dark house. Shore tried the switch near the back door. Nothing. He shined the flashlight around the kitchen and stopped on the floor in front of him.

"Looks like melted snow to me. Not from the dog. Where's the fuse box?"

"In the basement, but the circuit breaker is in the pantry, off to the right, beyond the stove."

"Got it. Wait here."

I heard metallic sounds, a couple of sharp clicks, and the lights came back on. I didn't realize I'd been holding my breath. Glory appeared at my feet and I knelt down to remove her coat.

"You can shut the door," Shore said, coming back into the kitchen. "I'll just take a look around. That OK with you?

"Thanks," I said. "Mind if I come with you?"

He thought about it, then nodded his head and turned off the flashlight. Daniel Shore seemed older than I remembered. Maybe it was the stubble on his jaw line giving him a grizzled look. Bags under his eyes, lines of experience drawing down the angles of his face.

The front door was unlocked. I told Shore I had locked it after Crista and Blake left. I locked it again, feeling uneasy.

"Must be the way he left. Wanted you to know someone was here. Assuming it was a he," Shore said.

The rooms all checked out. I told him not to go into Caitlin's room. One look at Brunhilde sleeping in her gigantic cage—I hoped that's where she was—would be a natural deterrent to any intruder. We returned to the kitchen, where Shore declined a cup of tea or coffee. He zipped up his down jacket, flashlight under one arm, shoved his hands in his pockets and looked down at the floor where the snow had puddled.

"No real damage done," he said thoughtfully. "Did you notice anything missing?"

"Nope."

"It might turn out to be so," he said. "Keep an eye out. Looks like somebody's trying to scare you." He gave me a sharp look.

"But why?" I was dumbstruck for a moment. "Oh. Wait. Maybe." I told him about the corn maze, that somebody might have thought I'd seen something.

"Did you? See something."

"I told you, Mr. Shore..."

"Just Shore."

"I wasn't really looking. Just standing there. I caught a movement, maybe a shadow. I thought it was a dog."

"Big dog."

"Apparently."

He turned to go. "Lock your doors. Make it a habit. You need anything, you let me know. Here's my number." Shore wrote on the pad by the defunct wall phone.

"You say you have a gun?"

I nodded.

"Carry it with you."

"Sure. That'll make my aunts happy!" I blurted out.

Shore chuckled. "I'd do it. You never know."

We said good night, with more thanks from me, and Shore stood on the other side of the door, waiting for me to lock it. I listened to his heavy tread going down the wood stairs. Afterwards, a heavy silence set in. I went to work mopping the mess off the kitchen floor.

"What the fuck, Glory." I didn't know if I was mad or scared. "Fuckety fuck fuck fuck."

13

I woke up tired, after a restless night of thinking I was hearing noises. At 2:00 a.m. I settled down after hearing Crista and Blake come in from their night out. Smothered giggles and ssh's going up the stairs, real noises of real people.

It was a bright day, but it looked cold. I stood at the window and watched a squirrel carry an entire sheet of newspaper up a tree to its nest. Definitely colder. I pulled on some jeans, one of Louise's old sweaters, and dragged my scraggly silver hair back into a pony tail, thinking about squirrels, wondering where the paper came from, anything instead of last night's intruder. Looking in the mirror—big mistake—as I brushed my teeth I thought that if a squirrel's nest had gray hair it would look just like me.

Downstairs, I tugged Glory into her coat and let her out the back door. Turning back to face the kitchen, I was surprised it looked the same, no signs of invasion, no angry message scrawled on the refrigerator door, just Martin Shore's number on the pad by the phone as proof that anything had happened.

Calmed by the usual routine—water and kibble for Glory, measuring coffee, making toast—I hummed to myself, let Glory in, and put the blue coat across the back of my chair. Munching happily on cinnamon toast, handing bits of crust to the dog, it suddenly occurred to me that I would have to tell my family, and Mac, and

Crista and Caitlin about last night. Crap. If I didn't, they'd just find out and there'd be hell to pay. Maybe I could sneak out of town, send them all a text message or something.

My fantasies of escape were interrupted by a loud pounding on the back door. Who'd be out there at this hour? It was eight o'clock in the damn morning! The thought paralyzed me. Glory danced and barked at the door, her stubby white tail wagging maniacally. Eight a.m.? What was happening to me? I was a night person, usually out until four, playing poker. Eight? What was happening to my life? The pounding became more insistent, accompanied by foot stomping and hollering.

"Lyle, you in there? Open the damn door!" Pound, pound, pound. Loretta. No way would she be alone.

I unlocked the door and let her in. Glory zoomed out past Loretta's legs, out into the snow without her coat.

"Here, take this." Loretta shoved a cardboard box at me, picked up another at her feet, and pushed me back into the kitchen. "You locked your door? What's wrong with you, you depressed? Got that existential angst nippin' at you again? Keep moving!"

"Where do you want me to go, Loretta? There's a table here, you know! What's in the box?"

"Just keep moving. You'll know when we get there." She pushed me through the kitchen and down the hall.

There was the front parlor. Uh oh. Loretta had me trapped against a wall in a way that I couldn't put my box down, not that it was heavy. That was a clue. It was a very light box. Loretta used the one she carried like a whip and a chair, continuing to corner me. I looked past her fuzzy Santa hat and had my worst suspicions confirmed. Lenore and Luce entered the room; behind them Vern wrestled with a tree.

"Uncle Vern?" I gasped. Usually, when my aunts ganged up on me, fixing to set straight some flaw in my character, Vern was nowhere to be seen, often taking refuge in the garage or out somewhere with his buddies.

Vern set the tree down by the large front window and removed his Santa hat, twisting it in his hands.

"This is a Christmas intervention, niece. We're your family and we're concerned about you, hon. I suggest you comply with the plan." He paused and looked at the three Hudson sisters and then back at me, pinned against the wall by his wife. "Whatever that plan turns out to be." Vern smiled hugely and broke into a laugh. "It appears to be a work in progress!"

My family had strategically placed themselves around the parlor so if I managed to slip by Loretta, I'd have to go through them. The look on their faces told me they'd take me down.

"What are you doing? What's gotten into you all?" I was stalling for time, but I didn't have a prayer. We all knew it.

"Lyle, dear, put the box down." Lenore came over and patted me on the arm and led me over to one of the big, chintz armchairs my mother so loved. I kept a death grip on the box. "We know you've been struggling with certain…issues," she said. "And we surmised that after yesterday's unfortunate corn maze incident, you might need a little emotional support."

"How did you find out about that?"

All four of them rolled their eyes at me. "News media," Luce said, acerbically. No sympathy from her; she was more of a snap-out-of-it kind of person.

"I'm fine, really."

"Really, Lyle? Fine? Really? Look at this house. You've turned it into a cave. Locking the kitchen door?" Luce struggled to get her head around it. No way was I going to tell them about last night. Not even if they applied torture. I looked around at the boxes and the tree. Torture might be about to commence.

Crista and Blake appeared, in slippers and pajamas, and were welcomed enthusiastically by the intervention team.

"What's up?" Crista asked, smiling at their cheerful faces.

"Pulling together a Hudson Christmas!" Loretta declaimed.

"About time!" Blake said. "Want help with the lights? Oh, man!" He shot a look at his watch. "Dude! I am so late! Sorry, gotta go!" He rushed out of the room.

"I do have decorations, guys," I said in a calm voice. "Out by the stairs, remember?"

"That's a start, dear," Lenore said encouragingly, shooting Luce a look that told her to back off.

"Anybody want coffee? Tea?" Crista asked.

"Sticky buns are on the kitchen table," Vern said."

"OK, coffee it is!" Crista headed for the kitchen, Glory at her heels.

"I'll put on some Christmas music," Luce volunteered, taking an iPod from her purse. "I made a mix." She smiled sweetly and left the room.

Vern started messing with the evergreen and asked Loretta to help him get it into the stand. They chatted and joked and laughed in a way that made you laugh with them, even if you don't know what they're talking about.

Lenore opened the box at my feet and started removing wads of ancient newspaper and opening them up. "These belonged to your grandmother. Lovely, aren't they?" Delicate orbs of cranberry glass. Yes, they were lovely.

"We are so happy you are here to have Christmas with us, Carlyle," Lenore whispered.

Dean Martin started singing "Baby It's Cold Outside" and Luce slid back into the room and looked at me brightly. "A touch of Las Vegas, don't you think?"

We all laughed and I found myself having a good time. We waved Blake out the door, and a little later Crista, as well. The tree went up, the old reindeer tree skirt spread beneath it. Swags of evergreen were hauled in from Luce's truck, and I helped Vern tie them to the railings around the porch. The sleigh bells were found and slung around the newel post. Loretta voted for putting them on the front door, but she was outnumbered.

"Now, Elvis, these bells make an unholy noise in the middle of the night. Young people come in late, you know." No one knew why Vern sometimes called Loretta Elvis, he just did. When you asked either one of them, they'd make something up, or catch each other's eye and bust out laughing.

"Well, at least you'd know when someone was coming through your door!" she pointed out.

Point taken. It was almost lunchtime and I had not told them about last night's adventure. I wondered how long I could hold out.

The last ornaments were going on the tree, and Luce and I were stacking boxes, throwing out shreds of newspaper that Loretta wanted to stop and read.

"Come on, let's check it out and see what was going on in 1978! This stuff is like a time machine!"

"Put. That. Down." Luce bossed her, grabbing a fistful of paper with each word.

"It's time to move on, dear," Lenore told her, effectively vetoing Loretta once again.

Loretta was about to protest when the sound of heavy clomping on the porch distracted her. We all turned as Caitlin came in the house and leaned over to take off her Doc Martens. She piled the boots near the door and beamed at us.

"Shoveled the walk, Lyle. Hi, folks! Whoa, bitchin' room! You guys rock. Hey, can I put something on the tree?"

We all nodded various versions of yes, and Caitlin ran up the stairs.

"That girl have a formative experience with a stapler when she was a little girl?" Loretta asked, cracking herself up. "She'd be as cute as the dickens without the hardware."

"Maybe cute isn't her thing," I said.

"Not everyone likes to be called cute, Luce added. "Loretta, I seem to remember one poor soul who tried to call you cute, and…"

Loretta was saved from humiliation when Caitlin hurried back into the room, ornament bunched in her hands. It looked like a jumble of different colors, something undulating, made out of silk.

Lenore drew close to get a better view of the fabric. "Why, it's lovely," she breathed. "What is it, dear?"

We watched, fascinated, as Caitlin uncoiled her ornament, which turned out to be about two feet long, with a bright red ribbon as a tongue. Caitlin held it out reverently.

"This is Rainbow Serpent," she said. "Maker of the world, of dreams and the Dreaming. I made it for Brunhilde." She regarded our nodding, vacant blinking.

"Aboriginals? In Australia?" She proceeded to explain. "The oldest continuous culture for, like, 30,000 years. Rainbow Serpent is the best!"

"Excellent," I said and gestured toward the tree.

"Really? It's kind of big." Caitlin regarded the Christmas tree, searching out a spot amid the mass of traditional objects.

"Really, it'll fit right in." I gave her a nudge.

"Awesome!" We all smiled, watching her, happy as a kid at, well, Christmastime. Caitlin grabbed the step stool and found a place for Rainbow Serpent somewhere near the top of the tree.

"Hey, what's this?" she asked, pointing at the painted cardboard star decorated with macaroni.

"The Star of Davis!" we said in unison.

Amid my aunts' laughter, I explained to Caitlin that I made the star when I was in third grade. The Star of David seemed appropriate at the time, as the baby Jesus had started out in life as a Jew. When I brought it home I announced it was the Star of Davis, and the name stuck.

"That macaroni is older than you are," I told her.

"Awesome," Caitlin nodded her approval. Of anyone I ever knew, Caitlin was the perfect audience. Rainbow Serpent and the Star of Davis would get along quite well.

The crowd of us in the parlor were talking about what went where and who was doing what, and hugging and thanking each other, when there was another knock at the door.

"You sure you don't want the bells up there?" Loretta asked, pointing at the front door.

I grabbed the door as everyone except Caitlin shouted NO and opened it to find officer Danielson standing there. I invited her in and closed the door.

We're voting on Christmas decorations," I told her. Greta nodded to everyone, an officer-of-the-law greeting to the local citizenry, and asked me if I had time for a follow up conversation on the events of yesterday.

"Is Lyle a suspect?" Loretta asked hopefully.

"No, ma'am. Uh, Lyle, if now is not a good time?"

"You could always rescue me from my family, interrogate me downtown?" I suggested.

"Not necessary. This is not an interrogation." Despite her words, I suspected it just might be.

"We were just leaving," Luce said. "We'll catch up with you later." The Hudson clan trooped down the hall and out the back door, leaving Glory bereft as it closed behind them. I went to the back to be sure the door was locked properly, and Greta Danielson followed behind me.

"We can sit in the library," I offered.

"No, the kitchen is fine," she said, placing a small black notebook on the table.

Not so fine for me, I thought. Invisible footprints seemed to glow before my eyes.

Greta accepted the offer of a glass of water. Setting one for each of us on the table, I pulled out a chair and sat across from officer Danielson in her pristine uniform. She patted Glory tentatively, like a person who didn't really like dogs but could put up with them. She seemed relaxed, not tensed up for an inquisition.

"How did Nola ever get you into that wedding dress?" I asked, reflecting on the last time we'd seen each other.

"I told you at the time. She hypnotized me."

There was more than a little truth in the statement. In her own domain, Nola was a force of nature. Greta had been on lookout at the front window of the bridal shop. She hadn't stood a chance. Our laughter was uneasy.

"Yeah. You ever catch me in one of those things," I said, "put a stake in my heart."

"Seriously," she nodded, "I am never going in there again. You couldn't pay me!"

We were joking around, but we sized each other up for the conversation to come. It didn't feel like an inquisition, but it could turn out to be an interview. I let the silence fall and waited for Greta to open it up.

"I am here, Lyle—can I call you Lyle?—to see if you remembered any details you maybe weren't aware of yesterday."

"I'm Lyle, you're Greta, OK? I think we've been through enough together to dispense with the formalities."

"OK, OK," she smiled. "Just trying to be professional."

"Got it. And no, I can't think of a thing I haven't already told the police." I paused, going back to last night, not wanting to tell her about the visitor.

"I mean, I might have caught a glimpse of something, like I mentioned yesterday, nothing concrete, a shape or movement, that's all."

"Hm." Greta watched me avoid her eyes. She would be a demon poker player.

"Why don't you tell me what's on your mind, Lyle."

I shook my head. "It's not the dead guy," I made a grimace, wincing. "Something else. Who was he, anyway?"

Greta gave me a look and answered the question. "Professor up at the university. Name of Addison. English department, tenured, fifty-four years old, lived alone. Few friends. Ring any bells?"

"Never heard of him."

"Hm. And you didn't know Robin Decker, either?"

"Who?"

"College girl found strangled a few days before the professor was killed."

"No, I didn't know her. She was a student?"

"Two university types. There could be a connection," Greta mused.

"You know, I might have heard something about her recently."

"Not unlikely. Girl was a piece of work. Tell me."

I recounted the conversation I overheard between the clergy guy and his unhappy wife, that the girl in question was an acolyte, accusations of hanky panky.

Greta took a few notes. Good looking?"

"Some might think so. Boyish, I guess."

"Pastors," Greta sighed philosophically, "are catnip to women of a certain stripe. For some it's the hero worship, a 'spiritual' thing. For others, the collar is a challenge. They want what they can't have. Add married to that? Irresistible. I've seen it before. And our girl, Robin? If it is her, she probably just wore him down."

"Really?"

"Oh, yeah. Pretty obvious, but hey, a young hottie after you all the time, telling you how hot you are all the time? Yeah, that's hard to take."

"Greta, you are quite the student of human nature. I had no idea."

"And a college professor?" she added, continuing the theme, "same deal, man with a position. Coed groupies. Goes on all the time, take my word."

"Well, she couldn't have shot him, she was already dead."

"And she wasn't in any of his classes. I already checked."

"Wow."

"Yeah, wow." Greta closed her little black notebook with a snap and looked at me, took a sip of water. "So, Lyle, what are you not telling me?"

"It's not about the professor, Greta, or Robin the man-eating coed." My gaze went to the floor and back up to Greta's unwavering eyes. I told her about the intruder, about Shore's assistance. Left out his advice about the gun.

"Hm," she commented, adding Shore's name to the tiny notebook. "He's right that whoever it was might be thinking you saw more than you think you saw. Anything get taken?"

"I don't know. Nothing seems to be missing."

"Might be something small." Greta's face was set, serious. "I'll have a patrol car drive by every now and then, random kind of thing."

"OK, but I'm not reporting it, Greta. Police reports end up in the paper. The aunts read them. I'll catch hell."

"If I were you, I'd tell Mac, though. The man will not be happy to be the last to know. I'm just sayin'." I started to protest, but she held up a hand for me to talk to. "You're not invisible, you know. People see the two of you together. I've got eyes."

"Are you smirking at me?"

"Lyle, Lyle, Lyle, what you don't know."

"What don't I know? What?" I complained, following her to the front door.

"Nice tree," Greta said, stopping to look in at the parlor. "Is that a snake? You got a Christmas snake?" She hooted. "Does it have a sleigh and tiny reindeer?" She snickered and then stopped at the front door.

"I'd be sure this stays locked, Lyle." The she resumed various forms of laughter. "Christmas snake. What next?"

"It's a Rainbow Serpent," I told the door as I locked it. "Cosmic entity, right, Glory?"

Right, the dog agreed. She was pretty cosmic herself.

14

Alone in the house, I was overcome by a need to get out and do something other than shopping. Although I did still need a few presents and time was growing short. I needed fresh air, more exercise. The day didn't look too bad. The sun was out, no looming clouds threatening snow. I walked out onto the front porch to feel the air. Glory stood in the doorway and regarded me with great interest.

What the heck. "Let's go for a walk, Glory."

We put our coats on, and I attached the leash, made sure I had baggies in one pocket, tennis ball in the other. It was a production just getting out the door, I thought as I locked it. I was more used to a warm climate. In San Francisco winter was green, temperate and rainy. Cold Kansas winters I managed to avoid. Christmas, too, for that matter.

Determined to avoid that line of thought, the one that led to what-are-you-doing-with-your-life, I tossed the tennis ball into the front yard. The retractable leash spun out and Glory hunted the ball, pouncing in short, foxlike jumps, burying her snout in the snow. Finding the object of obsession, she pranced back to me and set the ball at my feet. I tossed it high in the air and she leapt to catch it. If a dog can grin with a ball in its mouth, that's what she did. I let her carry the ball up the street.

It was a quiet neighborhood of Victorian houses, shoveled sidewalks, and cars parked neatly along the curb. It all looked so cozy and felt so foreign to me, a walk through the past, a time that felt like it belonged to someone else.

We passed Shore's house, which wore the same traditional decorations as the other houses on the block. I wondered if he was going for invisibility by blending in completely. He was such an odd man, I thought. No odder than you, said a voice in my head. Ha! I bet his wreath has a surveillance camera.

We turned at the top of the hill and walked back to Louise's house, which now looked lived in thanks to Vern and the aunts. From the sidewalk the Christmas tree in the window seemed normal enough, Rainbow Serpent not being visible from the street.

Glory and I exchanged a look. Neither of us wanted to go inside. We decided we were ready for adventure. I dashed inside and grabbed my satchel and swung back out, Glory still in tow. Door locked, we continued down the hill to 9th Street and downtown. Talk about multi-tasking! Glory gets her walk, shopping gets shopped, and I avoid the habitual guilt of driving my car so close to home, not to mention the headache of trying to park on Mass Street. We were headed to The Book Trader which welcomed the occasional four-footed visitor, as long as they didn't mess with the resident cat, Jasper.

As we passed Andressa's jewelry store, I thought about meeting her husband, Carl. What's that got to be like, being married to such a man? Did the charisma wear off? Was she affected by it like the rest of womankind? I reflected on what Greta said about sexual power over others, a game not restricted to coeds.

The Book Trader has three large windows that admit swaths of sunlight into the spacious room that was the store. The place was a paradise for people who loved books. Words on the page felt good in natural light. In addition to shelves on every wall crammed with books, there were stacks of them around the floor, and books arranged on tables invited browsers to pick them up and take a look. There were chairs in every nook for quiet reading, and small wooden step stools helped you reach a book on higher shelves.

The checkout area occupied the center of the shop, a four-sided quadrangle of counters that was always busy with people buying and selling books. I'd brought boxes of Louise's paperbacks here, opting for store credit instead of cash. Joan kept a box of index cards, one per customer, to record credit amounts. No computers for her, thank you. The place felt well lived in, hospitable. It was all about the books. You wouldn't find cappuccino or reading accessories here. And it helped if you had your own shopping bag with you.

Glory and I slipped in quietly. No other dogs in sight. Jasper, dozing among books displayed in a front window, cocked an ear but didn't bother to open his eyes. The shop felt serene as always, despite the number of people browsing shelves and talking in low voices. Glory, in "best girl" mode, stuck right with me as I trawled the books.

What was I looking for? I waited for the books to tell me. A mahogany table held best-sellers, books that had been recently devoured and then sold to Janet. I guess the turn around had to be pretty quick.

There were the usual piles of Christmas books, Hanukkah, and Kwanza books, too. Some were quite old, some shiny and new. No Rainbow Serpents here. Or maybe there were. I scrutinized bookshelf labels. Looking for the mythology section.

In among Edith Hamilton's *The Golden Bough*, and collections of Greek myths, I found *Wise Women of the Dreamtime*, a collection of aboriginal tales, illustrated with woodblock prints. Caitlin didn't go in for possessions, but I could offer her a shelf for books at the house, dedicate a corner of the library, perhaps. I tucked the book under my arm.

On a nearby table, a paperback with the picture of a gray fedora caught my eye, *The Abyss of Human Illusion*, by Gilbert Sorrentino. Cheery title. I sat down in a chair to take a closer look and Glory settled herself at my feet. It called itself a novel but looked like a collection of stories to me, finely crafted little pieces of writing. The style was post-modern irony; some of it amusing, some not so much. Grim little book, really. It soothed my inner angst with pages of brooding prose. I couldn't stop reading.

"Can I pet your dog?" Five simple words, they always caused immediate horror and dread.

"No! She's not friendly!" The sight of Glory licking the child's face gave lie to my words.

"Are you feeding her a cookie?" There were telltale crumbs on Glory's blue coat and on the floor.

"He likes it!" What was it about Glory and kids? I never knew if she wanted to bite them or wander away with them. I remembered a certain child's tea party in Las Vegas. The little girl had gotten the dog to wear a hat.

"She. The dog's a girl. Her name is Glory." I tended to be matter-of-fact with children, no baby talk. They seemed to find that hilarious. Or maybe it was just me they found amusing.

"No, he's not!" the child crowed. "Look at his nose; it's pointy. Girl dogs have pushed in noses." She was merely stating the obvious.

"That would be a Pug or maybe a Pekinese. That's a breed, not a sex," I explained.

The child laughed and pointed at me. "Ooh! You said SEX!"

I rolled my eyes, stood up, and tried to move away, but Glory wanted to stay with her new, sugary friend.

"There you are." I was rescued by mom.

"I'm so sorry," the woman apologized, brushing crumbs from the child's hair. "Are you eating cookies?"

"No! I had one in my pocket. I shared."

"OK, time to go." Mom separated child from dog and left the shop.

"So, what do you think, Glory, boy or girl?" I meant the child, not her. Glory shrugged and started licking crumbs from the carpet.

"Not that it matters, I suppose." For me, all aspects of children were a mystery. One flew through my life every now and then, like a bird outside a window.

I took my books to the counter to pay for my purchases. A man was there ahead of me, fussing over a book. It looked to me like he was making a total ass out of himself.

"*Tale of a Tub*," he said sharply. "By Jonathan Swift. It probably looks like any old book to you," he condescended to the young clerk, "but I believe it is quite rare. I especially asked that the book be held for me!" I bet the creep made children cry just by looking at them.

"I've looked, sir. I did not see the book or a slip with your name. I can ask Joan when she returns."

"Do that," he sneered, "I'll be back."

I stepped aside to let him go by and gave the shop girl a sympathetic look. The man practically tripped over Glory and found himself momentarily blocked by the leash.

"Mind your dog, please," he snapped at me. "This is not a place for pets."

"If I were you, mister," I said, "I'd watch my step." Cowards do not like to be confronted. I found them irresistible. He narrowed his eyes at me and slithered away.

As he reached the door, Andressa entered the bookstore, and the tweedy guy went all unctuous. Andressa's obvious distaste helped me recognize him as the professor we had seen at Reed's the other night, Prof. Cassaday. Dog abuser.

"You got off easy, girl," I said to the dog.

"Cash or credit?" the cashier asked.

"Credit," I smiled at her. She looked for my name in the file of index cards.

"Lyle," Andressa greeted me, "I thought that was you. Hi!"

She seemed on edge. "Hi, Andressa. How are you?"

"Fine, fine," she said nervously as I stuffed the books in my blue satchel.

Andressa chewed her lower lip. "Do you have time for a cup of coffee? We could go to The Mug." She nodded in the direction of the coffee shop a few doors north on Mass Street. Clearly, she was anxious to talk. Curious, I agreed.

Out on the sidewalk, I asked, "Who's minding the store? It is high season and all that."

"Oh, Carl's in the shop today." She cast a quick glance across the street. "It gets him out of the house, which he needs at this time of year." She gave me a look and forged ahead. "It's Carl I want to talk about."

"With me? You're kidding!"

She took my arm and marched us toward The Mug. "You have no idea. You'd be perfect."

The Mug was located right downstairs from Deirdre's yoga studio. I experienced a pang of guilt for not going, and another pang, of dread, that Luce would hunt me down and enforce attendance.

I asked for Earl Grey. Andressa had espresso in a tiny cup accompanied by a curl of lemon peel. We sat at a small tiled table next to the front window and watched the passing scene, slow moving cars trawling for non-existent parking slots, people walking, talking into cell phones. No Santa hats, as far as I could see.

Glory sat beside me, her chin propped on the low windowsill. It was cool enough, sitting so close to the door, so we all kept our coats on.

"I didn't know you had a dog," Andressa said, smiling at saintly Glory.

"She belonged to Louise. You could say I inherited her along with Hyacinth, Louise's bridal shop."

"Ah. She's so pretty, what's her name?"

"Glory. Are we here to talk about my dog?"

"Unusual name for a dog," she avoided my question.

Why was she stalling? The coffee shop was her idea. "Not really," I made a face. "Listen, Andressa…"

Outside the window, people stepped aside to make way for a young man running by. It was Blake. He disappeared from view and then came back, a panicked look on his face. He rapped on the window as if I wasn't looking right at him. Glory stood up and wagged her tail furiously. Blake grabbed the door and rushed inside, unleashing a blast of cold air.

"Lyle! I'm so glad I saw you! Hi," he said briefly to Andressa and turned back to me. "You have to help me out!" He leaned over to pat Glory who was clamoring for his attention.

"What's up? Grab a chair and join us." I prepared to make introductions, relieved at Blake's interruption.

"No time, no time. You have to come right now!"

"Come where?"

"My guy, the guy who helps with my yard gigs? Has the flu! Couldn't get out of bed! I thought he was just late. Whatever," Blake waved the digression away. "I am in such deep Doo! I can't do this alone. Please help me!" Blake was agitated, desperate.

"OK, OK," I tried to calm him. "I'll help if I can. What do you need?"

"You! Now! I do yard decorations, remember? If I don't get this place done today, I am totally screwed."

"Me? Climb on a roof, are you nuts?" Andressa laughed at the expression on my face. "I can't do that! I'm...I'm too old!" Did I really just say that?

"No, really, you'll be fine, Lyle!" He dismissed my objections. "You'll only have to hand me stuff from the truck. No big deal. I need a second pair of hands. But I really need them! Please!"

"What about Glory?"

"We'll drop her off, it's on the way." Blake pulled my arm, getting me out of the chair. It was all I could do to grab the satchel and the leash. Andressa waved sadly as we hustled outside.

*

We dropped Glory off at the house, along with the books, but I didn't have anything in the way of outerwear for extended time outdoors. Blake loaned me insulated overalls, a down jacket, work boots and a ratty watch cap, all pulled from his truck.

"Do these belong to the guy with the flu?" I asked suspiciously.

"Never mind! Just put it on!"

"This stuff stinks, Blake!"

"I'll make it up to you!" Blake did a double take. "Whoa, dude! You look like a dude!"

A deflated Santa balloon was more like it. Or a bum. Sick bum. I glared at Blake and climbed into his truck. Make it up to me? Oh, yes he will. This was on the order of firstborn son, maybe a pound of flesh.

The job turned out to be a few blocks over and up the hill, close to the university. I was surprised anyone would be going over the top with yard decorations in this neighborhood.

"Sweet! We're on time!" Blake crowed. "Let's roll!"

"What do you mean on time? Are you telling me you had time to find someone else? That this isn't the employment emergency you made it out to be?"

Blake bounded up the front walk to tell whoever was home that he was on the job.

"We're cool," Blake said when he came back and started yanking boxes out of the back of the truck. "Here, take this," he shoved a box at me. "And carry it over to that tree."

"Not cool, not cool, Blake!" I refused to take the box and stood there with my fists on my hips, looking puffy and droopy, and totally ridiculous.

"Lyle, you're the best!" Blake grinned a happy grin. "I completely lost it there, I know. I panicked, was totally freaked that I'd be late, lose the job, but you were there, and here we are! Isn't that great? You saved me!"

"Yeah, I'm a goddam angel," I muttered and stooped to pick up the heavy box.

"What?"

"Nothing. That tree?"

"Yeah!"

I carried the box over and set it down, seeing the color label for the first time.

"Pink?" I looked from the box to the tree. "A pink tree?"

Blake joined me with a second box. It was a tall tree. "The lady wants pink lights, she gets pink lights. OK with me."

"Maybe it's a Mary Kay house," I said.

"What?"

"Never mind." It would take to long to explain.

Blake and Company had already completed the majority of decoration. There was an angelic choir lined up along the rooftop, apparently singing to the chimney. A Santa in a sleigh of bulbs sat further down on the roof. The angels would blink on and off from left to right, Blake informed me. The Santa would glow steadily, except for the tiny running lights around the huge sack of presents.

"There are only four reindeer," I said.

"Yeah. Not enough room for eight."

"Couldn't you have smaller reindeer? That way they'd fit."

"Tried that," Blake explained patiently. "It looked like Santa was being pulled by a dog team wearing antlers," he laughed.

"What are those over there?" I pointed to a trio half way between Santa and the angelic choir, in the middle of the roof.

"Chipmunks."

"Chipmunks?"

"You know, Alvin, Theodore? Chipmunks."

"That your idea?"

"No way. Every decorative element is entirely determined by the customer. Custom design." Blake sounded like a brochure.

"Well, that's a relief." I didn't have to worry about the boy's taste.

Blake deftly braided strings of light up the trunk of the tree into the branches. I'd have thought it would go from the top down, but apparently not. That would take too long. This way, each string shoots out, like a fountain. Whatever.

Three smaller trees had their trunks wrapped in lights, also pink. We hung LED snowflakes in the branches. All the movement to and from the truck, up and down the trees, kept me warm. Working with Blake turned out to be a lot of fun. We chatted about his return to college, his major—communications—and how cool Crista was.

"Almost done," he told me when we stopped for a break, drinking water from Nalgene bottles.

"There's more?" I examined the yard. It had become a veritable grove of pink trees and snowflakes. Well, they'd be pink when the lights were turned on, Blake assured me. Candy cane stripes of lights up the pillars of the porch, nets of lights covering the shrubs below. No room for anything on the roof. "Where will you put it?"

Blake pulled a couple of stakes out of the truck and pounded them into the ground on each side of the walk. He then attached taller stakes to them, with triangular supports to keep them upright. Blake moved quickly. It was like watching a stop action movie.

I helped him attach a frame of lights of each upright and then run an electrical cord to connect the luminaria that bordered the sidewalk to the electrical control on the porch.

"Guardian reindeer?" I guessed. The frames of lights reached over our heads and I couldn't tell what they were.

"Pretty close! You'll see when the lights are turned on," Blake said, brushing his hands together with a sense of accomplishment.

I helped Blake stow tools and empty boxes in the truck, and he went up the stairs to knock on the door. I waited down in the yard. The daylight was fading rapidly into a violet-hued winter twilight, the air suddenly colder.

"Would you two boys like some hot chocolate?" The woman asked.

"No thanks, ma'am. Want to turn on the lights and take a look?"

"Oh, my, yes! Let me grab a sweater and I'll be right out!"

We retreated to the truck and turned to face the house. In a matter of seconds, the roof display and the yard blazed into light and the woman hurried down the walk to join us.

"Oh! Isn't it glorious!" she sighed. She walked up and down the sidewalk a couple of times in a state of rapture, oohing and ahhing, and bathed in pink.

"Reindeer." I pointed to the figures bobbing back and forth, bringing their antlers together overhead.

"Not just any reindeer!" the woman said, passing between them. "They're prancing, just like I asked! Oh, Blake, you're a genius! Here's your check." She handed him an envelope and then gave me one, too.

"And here's a tip for you, sir!" She smiled at me, full of Christmas spirit.

"Thanks!" Blake said for both of us. "That's very generous, isn't it, Grandpa Lyle?"

I nodded, tipping an invisible hat to her. The woman giggled and skipped up the pink, glowing path to her house.

15

"When were you going to tell me?" Mac shouted above the noise.

"I'm telling you now!" I shouted back.

We were lying on the floor of the front parlor, keeping our heads down among the debris and broken glass. I don't know how many shots were fired, a small spate that shattered the window and tore into the Christmas tree. In the sudden silence, I thought I'd pop my head up and take a look, but Mac pushed me back to the floor.

"Stay down!" He hooked me with one arm and flattened me.

A few more shots were fired into the room, followed by louder gunfire outside and the squeal of tires as a car pulled away. We lay there listening to the sound of our breathing. A heavy tread came up the porch steps and crunched over to the ruined window.

"You can get up now. Want me to use the door?"

I looked up and saw Shore holstering his weapon, snapping the cover securely. "It's locked," I said.

"Hm." Shore crunched out of view and let himself in through the door. "Guess not."

Mac and I had just come in, having left the Mustang parked at the front curb. I was showing him the tree and talking about yesterday's Hudson invasion when bullets spat through the window and we dived for the floor.

I got to my hands and knees and looked up at Shore standing in the doorway. Mac helped me the rest of the way up. My hands were scratched from scrabbling around in broken glass. My sweater felt sticky.

"Your cheek is bleeding. Must be when I pushed you down," Mac said.

I put my hand to my face and my fingers came away slick and red. The cut was bleeding freely, drizzling down neck.

"Sit down," Shore said, "I'll get some tape." He turned toward me and leaned close to my face, like someone speaking to a child. "Lyle, It's just a scratch, OK? You got some tape?"

"Kitchen."

He walked away and MacDonald sat me down on the stairs in the hall. The chairs in the parlor were covered in plaster dust and splintered ornaments.

Shore returned with a wad of paper towels and a roll of duct tape. I held the towels to my face but Mac said to let him do that; I was just making a mess. Shore ripped off a swatch of tape with his teeth and patted it on where Mac was holding the cut together.

"Neat trick," Mac said.

"Field dressing 101," Shore told him. "I heard shots and came out to take a look, some runty guy shooting across the roof of his car, wearing a ski mask, for cripe's sake. Even an idiot knows you can't see to shoot in those things. It's amazing he even hit the window. I advanced and put a couple rounds into the car to give him something to think about. Volvo, I think. Car was the better target. Hard to hit anyone when you're moving, anyway."

"Mac nodded. "Get a plate number?"

"Kansas. RVW something. Couldn't see the number. It looked like he smeared mud on it. Find a Volvo with .38 slugs in it and you've got your shooter."

"Unless it's stolen," Mac said.

"Always a possibility. Where's your gun?" Shore asked me.

I made fish mouths at him while Mac looked back and forth between us.

"Gun? You told her to carry a gun? Wait. You," he turned back to me, "told him about the home invasion before you told me? Am I the last to know, Lyle?" His voice dropped down into the slow, quiet tone that hints at future explosions.

"He was here when it happened. I didn't have to tell him."

"A firearm seemed advisable considering the circumstances," Shore commented, still kneeling and scrutinizing the duct tape. "Still is, you ask me."

"Water?" I was feeling shaky and put my head between my knees.

Shore stood up, and as he did so an unholy bark fest erupted in the parlor. Glory and Shore's Giant Schnauzer were exchanging insults and threats. Shore gave one of those ear-piercing whistles and the dogs went down, flat on the floor. Shore went over and put a hand on each dog's neck to keep them there.

We heard the wail of approaching sirens. No need to call this one in, the neighbors had doubtless already done so.

"Shit," Martin Shore hissed. "I have to keep a low profile." He cocked an eyebrow at Mac.

"Got it," Mac said. He could ask why later.

"I'll take these two up to my place for a little behavior modification, that OK with you, Lyle? We'll probably not need to call animal control again." He grinned at me.

I gave him a wry smile in acknowledgement of our initial neighborly encounter. "She won't get hurt, will she?"

"I never bite dogs," he said. "Don't worry. Come get her when you're done."

Car doors slammed and Shore nodded to Mac, leading the dogs past us to the kitchen and out the back.

Mac stepped out onto the porch to indicate that the excitement was over and folks could holster their weapons. Everyone wanted a closer look, so all six officers trooped up the steps to greet Mac. Among them were Mac's friend Drew and Drew's young partner Matt, whom we had encountered when the first body was found. The thought crossed my mind that I should be grateful that I was not body number three.

The police were respectful of the scene and satisfied their curiosity by looking through the broken window. Shreds of gratitude evaporated when I saw Greta Danielson's angry face glaring down at me.

"The hell is this?" she said marching right up to me where I sat on the inside steps, duct tape on my face, dried blood on my neck. "I warned you, did I not, told you to be careful? Oh, hello, Mac."

"Greta?" Mac stared at me. "Greta knew? When? Why didn't you tell me someone was after you?"

Greta turned toward him. "I was following up on the corn maze incident, Mac. That information is confidential, as you know." She gave him a look and then turned back to me, hand on her hip. "I told you to tell him, didn't I." It was a smug I-told-you-so.

I was shivering violently, probably blue in the lips, which they finally noticed.

"Right." Greta raised her voice at the gaggle of uniforms on the porch. "Everybody out! You and you," she pointed at two of them, "I want you door to door. Anybody who saw anything or imagined they saw anything, I want details."

"Drew, you take Matt and cruise downtown looking for a, what? What kind of car did you say?" she asked Mac.

"Green Volvo, older model," he called over his shoulder as I sagged against him. "Look for bullet holes, shouldn't be hard to miss."

"You carrying?" Greta asked, eyes narrowed.

"No, I am not. About to start though," he murmured into my ear.

"So, what you are saying is this person stops shooting at you and turns his gun on the car? Tricking out his Volvo with bullet holes?"

"Long story," MacDonald said as he picked me up and carried my sorry ass to the kitchen, where he shut the door against the cold air blasting through the house and went to find me a blanket.

While I was coming around, Greta finished giving orders, posting a cop in the yard to keep gawkers away and to let her know when the scene photographer arrived. She entered the kitchen complaining about the cold, then settled in to take my story, with ancillary comments from Mac. It didn't take very long.

"Not very observant, either of you," Greta said caustically. "And how did the car get itself shot up? Anything to do with your helpful neighbor Mr. Shore? Who is that guy, anyway? Think he's Clint Eastwood, showing up with a flashlight and a gun? I'm going to have to talk to that man, find out what the hell is up with him. His uncles are driving me nuts."

While she was grumbling at us, officer Danielson pulled out her cell phone, checked her address book and punched in a number.

"It is too damn cold in here. Can't leave that window exposed. Anybody could get in." She growled to disguise the kindness.

Greta called a glazier she knew and asked him to come over and help a nice older woman out. When she said *older*, she smiled evilly at me. How old was the person at the other end of the phone, seventeen?

"Fifty is not older, Greta," I complained.

"Oh, shut up. I'm just messing with you. And you're welcome, glad to help."

Mac laughed, shaking his head at us. The kitchen door opened and a young cop stuck his head in, nodded to Mac and said, "Um, ma'am? There's a person outside who says she lives here. Street person type, I wasn't sure…"

"That's probably Caitlin," I said, standing up and bunching the blanket against the fierce draft. Yes, she does live here, officer."

"That kid that's all pierced and everything? You got a roommate now?" Greta asked.

"Please, just let her in."

We all trooped back to the front door. Caitlin was standing inside gazing at the mess in the parlor—the window, the toppled tree—her face pale and worried.

"Lyle!" Caitlin ran down the hall and grabbed me and held me tight. "You're all right! You are, aren't you? OK. The uniform wouldn't tell me anything."

I hugged Caitlin back. "I'm fine." I started to shiver again.

"Man, this is cold!" she said, anxiously. "Way too cold for Brunhilde, she'll get sick!"

I explained about Greta's help in getting the window fixed ASAP, and Caitlin stepped over to her and shook her hand, thanking the policewoman with all the passion of a girl who really loves her boa.

Greta smiled a modest-officer-of-the-law smile and asked about Brunhilde. "Is that your cat?"

I explained about the boa constrictor and Greta calmly slowed down the shaking of hands.

"Oh, I see," she said politely.

Caitlin ran up the stairs to check the temperature in her room.

"Well played, Greta," I told her.

"Excuse me? You think I'd get all fussed about some boa constrictor?" She rolled her eyes, cracking Mac up.

"No, I mean Caitlin shook your hand, a cop's hand. Man, I wish I had a camera. That was right up there with World Peace!"

"Should I smack you? Bring you back to your senses? What are you talking about?"

"Seriously. World Peace. You should be proud."

En route to her patrol car, Greta shooed away a few curious neighbors. She sent the young cop back to his car, perhaps figuring that the excitement was over for now. I'd be admonished to be vigilant, and MacDonald agreed I certainly would. His comment rankled.

"Are you talking for me, now?" I was gearing up for a spat.

"Am I feeling protective, Lyle? Yes. It's something that happens when I lie on the floor with a woman, getting shot at."

"OK, well, cut it out," I grumped, trying to pull strands of hair from my face where they were caught on the edges of the duct tape bandage.

"Let's get that cut looked at."

"Later. I want my dog back."

"Make the call now. You can actually go later," he said patiently. He kissed my lips gently, the moustache tickling in a very nice way. "Do you even have a doctor? Never mind. We'll call my guy."

"I've got a vet," I said, "a good one, too."

"Don't tempt me," Mac said. "Get your coat and I'll make the call."

I told Caitlin we'd be right back. Mac and I went up the alley to Shore's house. It was the same style as all the other Victorians on the block, with the same back steps, only his looked newer and had a small deck. Inside, the kitchen looked new, as well, all stainless steel and granite countertops.

"Wow," I said, "what did you do, take out a wall?"

"Larger windows. They make the room look larger. I like to see what's going on outside," Shore said with a slight smile.

"So, where are the dogs? I don't see any signs of canine mayhem."

Shore whistled and Glory and the Schnauzer trotted into the kitchen and dropped into an immediate sit, waiting for further instructions. Glory grinned at me but stayed where she was.

"Did you drug my dog?"

Shore made some kind of release gesture and Glory came over to greet me and Mac, her small tail wagging happily.

"Nah. She's a good pup, very responsive," Shore said. "All these two needed was a little supervised get acquainted time, a firm hand, and clear expectations." He patted his chest, inviting the Schnauzer to jump up, which she did.

"What's her name?" Mac asked.

"Margot." Pretty normal in the realm of dog names, I suppose. It could be worse.

We were half way out the door when Shore asked about my cut. "Want me to sew that up for you?"

I looked at Mac who looked back. "Your face," he shrugged.

"Why not." I accepted the offer. I hated doctors' offices and occasionally had a hard time at the vet's.

Shore set up his kit on the kitchen table, scrubbed his hands, and set to work with neat, efficient movements. The tape coming off hurt like hell, making my eyes water. I held a gauze pad where directed and watched him take a syringe and fill it.

"What the hell is that?"

"Local anesthetic for the stitches."

"Crap! Where'd you get all this stuff?"

"Sit still, please. It's like I told you, field training." He waited for me to stop squirming. "I like to be prepared."

He put in three very tiny stitches and covered them with a light, surgical tape. Handed me a cold pack for the swelling.

"Thanks, Shore."

"No problem. Take some acetaminophen when you get home. Don't move around too much."

"Will do."

We collected Glory and walked back down the alley.

"Interesting man," Mac said thoughtfully.

Back at the house, we followed sounds of hammering to the front parlor where Caitlin was watching a large piece of plywood being put into place. She told me she'd tried my cell but guessed I didn't have it with me.

The glazier told me the glass would have to wait until the next day. But the plywood would help with the cold. I thanked the man and made sure to lock the door when he left.

"I don't know if I'm up for this," I sighed, surveying the debris in the room.

"It can wait," Mac said.

'Totally!" Caitlin agreed. "And maybe we can tack up a blanket in the entrance? You know, to cut down on the drafts?"

"Good thinking, Caitlin," Mac said, making the girl blush. His eyes did that crinkly thing when he smiled. The man was irresistible.

I told Mac where to find the toolbox, and Caitlin went upstairs to find a blanket. I went into the library, Glory at my heels. We settled into the leather couch and I held the cold pack to my cheek and closed my eyes.

When I opened them again some time later, there was a fire going in the fireplace. Outside, daylight deepened into dusk. I heard voices in the kitchen, the back door opened and closed, the dog tapped along the hallway. Glory entered the room, dressed in her blue coat.

"You're awake," Mac said, following the dog into the room. "Can I get you anything before I go?" Mac had a dog to look after, too.

"No, I'm good." I stood up and went over to the tall man. "Where's your hat?"

"I left it in the car, remember?" We were standing very close.

"Guess it slipped my mind."

"Busy day," he smiled, and kissed me. It was a really nice kiss.

MacDonald George left and I went upstairs to my room, pulling the sweater with its dried blood over my head and dropping it on the floor.

"Gross!" I accused the ruined sweater.

After a shower, where I had moderate success keeping the stitches away from water, I put on a fresh pair of jeans and one of the hoodies Luce had loaned me from her collection. I took a couple acetaminophens. Luce. Crap. What was I going to tell them all?

Back downstairs, I got a glass and ice from the bar and went to the library and poured myself a scotch. My life felt like a sore tooth. The bullets had created a surface level of excitement, the thrill of staying alive, but at a deeper level I felt like a stranger to myself. I was still brooding when Caitlin joined me.

"Look! He's intact!" She held out the Rainbow Serpent, which looked none the worse for wear.

"Excellent. Set him on the mantel for now. We'll put him back in the tree when we put the room back to rights.

"Did you go to the doctor?" Caitlin asked, looking at my cheek.

"No, Shore did this."

"He sewed you up? That is so cool!" She scooted closer to get a better look. "It's pretty small, but I bet it leaves a scar. Bangin! You're so lucky!"

A scar? What the hell, it was better than being shot dead.

16

After the attack I felt pretty wired. Any idiot could see that the intruder and the shooter were the same person. Did I feel safe? No. But I wasn't about to go into hiding, stay with one of the aunts, or leave town. Truth be told, I felt a familiar rush of stubbornness and determination, a lot like the start of a poker tournament. Someone was out to get me? Well then, maybe I'd find out who and get them back.

I needed a map of what was going on, and then a plan of action to fit the map. I dug out the deck of "thinking" cards that I used to analyze problematic situations. The cards were so well used the paper was as soft and pliable as leather. They no longer snapped and would not stand up to a dealer's shuffle. I fanned them out and looked for faces and connections.

I centered the queen of diamonds on the table. That would be me. No hearts involved here, I felt tough and pointy. I was being attacked by the king of spades. I set the king to the left of the queen. OK, why the attack?

The ten of spades would stand for the corn maze. The highest non-face card, the ten looks complex if you stare at it long enough. I placed it underneath the queen, with the ace of clubs underneath the ten, on its side lying down. The dead professor.

What I had looked like a simple triangle. I might have seen the king of spades, so he wanted to eliminate me. That seemed rather extreme. He might have had a good reason for killing Professor Addison, maybe could get off on some kind of plea. If he succeeded in killing me, he'd never get off. Much deeper shit, why go there? I studied the cards.

Who would kill a professor? An angry spouse? A jilted lover? Disgruntled student? A colleague gone postal over arcane departmental politics? It could happen. In Kansas people were generally hospitable and polite, but infighting among the tenured, the old guard and the new, could be vicious.

How did I know? You get a Ph.D. in English Lit. you see things. You see even more as an adjunct working on the front lines. It was a world I gladly left behind for poker. It could get ugly. I knew. It's a wonder they didn't kill each other more often.

I picked up the jack of hearts. Are you a coed? Who killed you, I wondered. Gossip pointed to boyfriends and married men. What might she have to do with the dead professor? Would someone shoot me because of you? I placed the jack across from the queen of diamonds, between the two black kings, one alive, one dead. Maybe this situation wasn't about professors at all, or only incidentally. Maybe it was something I overheard. Another game entirely.

I stared at an ace high straight. A full boat would beat it.

My meditations were interrupted by the cell phone, which told me it was Luce and I better answer, or else. I stood up, took a deep breath and smiled. An insurance salesman I met at a poker table in Tahoe told me you always sound more confident on the phone when you smile.

Luce didn't mince words and got right on me about yoga. I told her I had a cut that needed to heal before I could do any downward facing dogs.

"Cut how?" she asked. Damn. I needed a good lie, fast. Keep it simple, I told myself.

"I dropped a glass in the kitchen sink. It slipped out of my hand and, BAM! It shattered on impact. A piece flew up and cut my cheek." Totally believable.

"So, what is that piece of wood doing on the window?"

"What wood? Where are you?" She must be out front. Curses.

"I'm in front of the house. I was just driving by, wondering if you were home." Yeah, looking to Shanghai me and haul me off to yoga.

"If that door is locked, you better unlock it and let me in. What on earth happened?"

I met Luce at the door and watched her as she surveyed the damage. Glory was a minor distraction but didn't make a dent in Luce's concentration. It didn't look too bad, I thought. I'd taken down the blanket, and Caitlin and I had swept, cleaned, and dusted, returning the parlor to order. The tree was back in place, albeit with fewer ornaments and minus the Star of Davis. The bullet holes in the wallpaper were almost unnoticeable.

"The glass people will be here any time," I told her, looking at my watch.

Luce remained silent. Not a good sign. "And what is that," she asked.

"This?"

"Yes, that."

I stared at the gun in my hand. Taurus PLY22 automatic pistol. My gun. "Um, someone suggested I have it on me, after, you know." I gestured to the parlor.

"No, I don't know, Carlyle. Perhaps you should tell me."

I rushed through the narrative, talking more quickly the longer she remained silent. Luce's eyes never left my face. They saw the cut and the lie that went with it.

"So," I got back to the gun, now stuck in my waistband, making a mental note to get a proper holster. "It's smaller than mom's gun, right, the one she kept at Hyacinth?"

Oh, yes it was. That gun was a sore point with Luce from the time I found it at the shop after Louise's death. Louise, my mother and Luce's sister, had the gun at the shop long ago when the murderous Ann Hadley had threatened to harm her young daughter. Luce never knew, at least not until Ann shot me when I went snooping around into Louise's past. I still carried the scar on my left arm.

"Is it loaded?" Luce's voice was carefully neutral.

"The safety is on, I'm good."

Luce took out her Blackberry and tapped away. No iPhone for her. The Blackberry suited the way she was wired, she said. Was she texting?

"What are you doing?" It was more an accusation than a question.

"I am," tap tap tap, "telling Lenore and Loretta what happened to the window and," she looked over her glasses at me, "that you, and Glory of course, will be staying with me."

"No, Luce." I moved the gun around to the back of my jeans, the way you see it done in movies. Still uncomfortable. I took the gun out and stuck it in my coat pocket, in the hall. "I won't."

"Yes, you will. Listen to reason, please."

"No! Do you really think that whoever shot at me—I didn't mention the preceding nocturnal intrusion—

won't think to look for me at your house, or the L&L's? It is a small town. If they know me, they know you."

We locked eyes in traditional Hudson manner, and I held her gaze while Luce thought it through.

"I appreciate the concern, Luce; I know you are upset and worried. But I can't see us all hunkered down with a pile of firearms. Greta Danielson would throw us all in jail." I tried to make her smile, but no dice.

"You can't stay here," she gestured to the boarded up window, her hand including the whole room.

"Yes, Luce, I can."

A knock on the door interrupted our tug-o-war. The glass folks arrived and proceeded to go about the noisy business of repairing the front window. I grabbed my coat and walked Luce out to her yellow Chevy truck, leaving Glory inside happily sniffing the workers. I gave Luce a hug and told her everything would be OK.

"What will you do?" She was unhappy and didn't want to leave me alone, workmen or no.

"Well, I've been thinking that I might just scout around, ask a few questions. You know, take a more pro-active stance." *Pro-active stance* being a phrase that exuded confidence and can-do spirit.

"Snooping around, you mean." Luce cocked an eyebrow at me.

"Exactly! Maybe I'll go up to the university and see if anyone's around to talk to, plant bees in bonnets, et cetera. I'm thinking of following up on some town gossip I overheard." I paused, mulling it over. "Does Loretta go to the Episcopal church in town, Luce?"

"Yes, ever since Father Bob retired. She seems to like the new priest, Edwin something. Says he has sizzle."

"Anyway," I said, moving on, "at least I'd be a moving target, not hiding out in a dark hole."

"You're pretty good in that department, if I recall," Luce quipped and climbed into the vintage truck to start the engine. "Try not to be any kind of target, please. Figure out some kind of camouflage." She put the truck in gear. "Call me. I need to know you're in one piece!"

"Will do," I said, waving her away.

I stepped back onto the sidewalk to find Shore and Margot standing there. I told myself not to be paranoid.

"I love that truck," Shore said.

"Yeah, it's great. How are you?" I turned to face him and held out my hand for Margot to sniff.

"Can't complain. Did I hear you talking about being a target?" It was a rhetorical question. "Got your gun on you?"

I turned aside discreetly to pull the gun out of my bra and held it barrel down and slightly to the side, so he could see I had minimal training in gun etiquette.

Shore shook his head. "I suppose, if you were standing right next to someone and poked them in the eye with that little thing before you pulled the trigger, you might do some damage. Put it away."

"Hey, don't insult the gun! It's the right size. Besides," I continued, "I don't usually need a gun when I play poker. Casinos have security cameras and bouncers for that kind of thing."

Shore surveyed the street, just a casual scan, and then turned back to me. "The point of having a gun, Lyle, is to stop somebody who means you harm. Punch a hole in them. For that, you need the largest caliber you can carry. And you have to draw it quickly, without making people laugh." He wasn't exactly condescending, but I felt like he was telling me my ABC's. I bristled at the lecture, not in the mood.

"That man in the corn maze had a tiny little hole in his head. Small caliber seemed to work just fine," I said.

"He was shot up close, then," Shore nodded, "probably someone he knew. Your example does not disprove my point."

"My .22 feels heavy enough to me," I said. It really did. People in the movies look like they are waving toys around.

"You don't look like a weakling," Shore squinted mean Clint Eastwood eyes at me. "Sorry, no offense. Just trying to make a point." He rubbed his unshaved jaw, looking for a polite way to hit me upside my head. "Why don't we visit a shooting range?"

"I've been to multiple ranges, Shore. How do you think I learned to use the gun?"

"I think you would benefit from trying out a couple of auto-loads, see how they compare to that little automatic of yours. Think about it." He swiveled his head and surveyed the street again, took in the work going on with my front window, too.

I had to admit it sounded like a good idea, convincing a middle-aged woman to carry a bigger gun. The plan held a certain charm. Maybe not an idea that would make the aunts, Mac, or Greta very happy, but hey. I told Shore it was a date. I needed a day or two to get some business done, I told him, but we could meet up at the end of the week.

Inside, I was met with a burst of laughter from the parlor. As I hung up my coat it happened again. No one was talking or telling a joke; there'd just be a moment of silence followed by laughter. I poked my head into the room.

On the floor by the newly installed window, a dark haired young woman with a ponytail and white overalls sat holding one of those snack packets you pick up in convenience stores. The other worker, slightly older, stood beside her. Same overalls. Across the room in the far corner by the fireplace, Glory sat up attentively, a dark blue bandana wrapped around her head. A blindfold?

"No way she can do it again," the man said.

"Oh yeah? Five bucks," the girl said. She popped a snack bit into her mouth, crunching loudly so Glory could hear and held her hand over her head, waiting for the money.

"El, you don't have five bucks. What if you lose?"

"I won't lose. This dog and me, we got a connection, don't we, chica?"

Glory stood up and wagged her tail, starting to move toward the young woman.

"No, no! Sienta te! Sit! Good dog." She made calming sounds and Glory sat. "OK, ready? One, two, three!" At three, she tossed something orange into the air and Glory sat up tall and caught it and munched it down.

"See, what did I tell you?" The young woman stood up to collect her money.

"Food is always a sure bet with Glory," I said, entering the room.

The two workers turned to me with guilty faces, ready to apologize and disappear from the face of the earth.

"No worries," I said, leaning down to remove the blindfold. Glory hopped up, placed her front paws on my knees to give me a kiss. I sniffed her dog breath.

"What is that, Cheez-its?"

"That one was. It's a mix, got pretzels and stuff, too. Elena Mendoza," she introduced herself. "This is my brother, Mike. We were just…"

"Cleaning up, I can tell." I walked to the window. "Looks good. Mendoza? Do you live near Luce?"

"Lady with the Chevy truck?" Mike's eyes lighted up. "Oh, man!"

My guess was correct; they were Luce's next door neighbors. We chatted for a bit, and Elena gestured to the new window.

"Paper said somebody shot this out. In this neighborhood? I don't buy it." She laughed and shook a finger at me. "What did you do, make eyes at someone's husband?" The thought cracked them both up.

"Hey, it can happen!" I defended myself. "I'm not dead yet!"

Elena nodded, considering me head to toe. "No, you look good. Maybe it was a younger dude with a jealous wife, oh yeah!" That started them yukking it up all over again.

I showed them out and locked the door, the blue bandana still in my hand. I folded it slowly, wondering if it was worth the effort to give it back or if that would just embarrass Elena more. What I was not going to do was put it on my dog.

"No antlers, no bandanas, Glory. It's a rule." She ignored the comment, carefully licking invisible crumbs from the floor.

A shadow appeared at the window, followed by a tap on the glass. It was MacDonald George.

"Wait, don't tell me," I said, letting him in, Glory bouncing around his legs, "you were just passing through and thought you'd stop by."

Mac removed his jacket, stuffed his gloves in the pockets and looked for a place to put his hat. I took the Stetson from him and placed it on the table in the hall, beneath Louise's serigraph of buffalo on a mesa.

"Not passing through, Lyle." He looked straight into my eyes, deepening the crease that ran diagonal to his mouth, controlling the smile. "I came exactly and specifically to see you."

"Well, that's a relief," I said drily, dragging my eyes away from his. "I was beginning to think I had my own neighborhood watch, a patrol with shifts and everything. A visitor is a refreshing change."

We sat in the library and I told him about Luce and Shore, explaining the neighborhood watch reference.

"A bigger gun?" Mac was incredulous. "Is the man insane? I'm not sure you should even be carrying that .22. Where is it, by the way?"

"In my bra." Rushing past his exploding eyeballs, I continued. "And why shouldn't I have a bigger gun? Because I'm a woman? Greta has a gun." My argument sounded lame but it was all I had.

"Greta," Mac said patiently, "is in law enforcement. You are not."

"So, what is it—I'm flighty? Irrational? I think I'm in danger, Mac." I glared at him where he sat on the couch with my damn dog in his lap.

"I've been shot at, right? Why shouldn't I carry a gun?" Oops, wrong turn.

"Can you hear yourself? Lyle, be reasonable." Was he trying to make me mad? I stared at him.

"OK, reasons you should not carry a gun, any gun. Number one: you beat a kid up in a parking lot. What if you had had a gun then?"

"He stole my satchel! He started it, remember?"

"Not my point. Number two: that guy in the Kinko's you took down. It would not have gone well if you'd had a gun, Lyle. I know that and so do you."

"Oh, yeah? Well, what about Ann Headley? I had a gun there!" Bad choice. Had the gun but couldn't get to it. It was Mac's shotgun that got me out of trouble there.

"Exactly. The gun did not help. In your tits, a gun is like a grenade. You go off, it could too. Not a safe situation for me, even if it is only a .22." He took a breath. "Let's not get off track here. I am not blaming you. Police. It's police who have guns. To protect people. That's their job. Police will solve this problem, Lyle. Really, you don't need a gun, OK?" Mac slid out from under the dog and stood up.

"No. Not OK. We totally disagree here, Mac." I looked up at him. Disagreement worked for me. I was not going to stand there and be lectured. "I'm going to the shooting range with Shore."

"I'm sure he is an able instructor. I have no problem with a lesson in a controlled environment. It's going around town or wherever looking for trouble with a loaded firearm that concerns me." He put his hands on my shoulders.

"You're not jealous?"

"Of Martin Shore? Should I be?" His eyes were laughing.

"No, not really." I tried not to sound disappointed. "What if it were Carl Glasser?"

Mac took a step back. "Oh, yeah. Big problem."

"Really?" Now I was trying not to sound too pleased.

"Absolutely."

I beamed and gave the tall man a big hug. Oddly, Carl Glasser's charismatic beauty creeped me out. But he had served his purpose.

17

As with most mid-western towns that built spacious campuses in the nineteenth century, full of idealism, civic pride, and an abiding belief in public education, Lawrence felt that in every way the University of Kansas was its crown jewel. KU was valued as a center of culture as well as learning, with the Spencer Art Museum, Lied Center, and—the pride of all Kansas Republicans—the Bob Dole Institute. Nor must we neglect to mention the success and glamour of the Jayhawks, the pre-eminent basketball team; basketball itself being the invention of James Naismith, whose resting place in Memorial Park Cemetery has granite benches for those who wish to meditate on the wonder that is basketball. Rock Chalk, Jayhawk!

KU's eminence in town life is symbolized by the visibility of Fraser Hall atop Mt. Oread, twin flagpoles gloriously waving the U.S. and Kansas flags high above the river valley and rich farmland below. Driving along I-70, coming home from riverboat casinos, I could always count on looking up and seeing those flags smirking at me. When I was flush I'd smirk back.

As with all smugly superior universities surrounded by towns full of working folk, there was a sharp divide in Lawrence between Town and Gown. University people would disagree, of course. They see themselves as egalitarian, part of the larger community, with lots of friends "out there," even farmers.

But if you are "out there," not "of the university," you can't get in. It is less a club than a walled city, complete with gates, ID badges, clipboards, and other appropriate screening devices. Students are the only citizens with dual passports, but their primary allegiance is to KU. Any hapless soul not wearing red and blue on game day, someone wearing the heinous purple of archrival K State, for example, risks life and limb should they be seen walking the brick sidewalks of Massachusetts Street in Lawrence's historic downtown.

To accomplish anything in my information gathering, or snooping around, as Luce put it, I'd need a cover, some way to convince the inhabitants of OZ that I was already "in", a Jayhawk just like them.

I'd have to move fast. As Blake informed me, finals were over. Students had fled town, but professors, adjuncts, and administrative staff would still be around, furiously grading exams, reading term papers, ready to flee town themselves.

After a day on the computer updating my academic resume, researching English department faculty online, and zipping down to Kinko's for copies, I was ready to go, no disguise needed. I would, however, leave the ruby ring and diamond earrings at home.

My genius plan was to apply for an adjunct teaching position. I didn't want the job, but applying in person would give me the opportunity to chat up English Department denizens. There was a significant hole in my resume in terms of how long ago I'd taught at USF, but it didn't matter what I said to explain it. Kansans were eagerly receptive to the sacred words of the prodigal: "I wanted to come home," a version of the apocryphal Dorothy Gale. They'd get all teary-eyed and do anything for you.

I wasn't sure what my story would be, but I knew that once I opened my mouth, I'd believe in it completely. I generally look at lying as a form of creative self-expression. Lying has served me well over the years, at the poker table and away from it. Lying keeps things friendly. I don't have to tell people off; it provides a credible narrative and gives us something to talk about. At the poker table, you might even think I'm sweet and throw more money on the table. That's kind of what I was hoping for here.

Sincerity is the key, I reminded myself as I pretended to rummage through my blue leather satchel for a non-existent key to Wescoe Hall, the building I wanted to enter. Silver hair held back by colorful reading glasses, manila folder under my arm, exasperated scrounging in the bag—I certainly looked academic. Safe enough for a young Samaritan to escort me into said building.

"Let me get that for you," said the helpful voice. The door was unlocked, smiles were exchanged, and the young Samaritan walked on down the hall.

The building was quiet. As I studied the location index on the wall, I wondered about the odds of my getting to talk to anyone. Was I too late?

The administrative assistant's desk in the main office was cluttered with the usual English department debris. In and Out boxes lay at lopsided angles, spilling paper. A decorative Christmas tree the size of a large rat sat on top of a filing cabinet that looked like it had suffered a minor explosion, drawers open, files akimbo. If the administrative assistant was that mad, I didn't really want to meet her. The computer was on, screen savers of tropical islands fading in and out. The phone was ringing, not a soul in sight.

I walked around the counter to a bank of mailboxes and scanned names, determining by the contents or lack thereof who was likely to be in the office today. Empty box meant someone could be holed up in his or her office, teeth gritted, pen slashing through paper. The unanswered phone told me that anybody who was here did not want to be bothered. Didn't they have an answering machine?

Breathing in the overheated air of hiring freezes, tenure disputes, and exploited/underpaid TA's, I thanked the gods of poker for rescuing me from a pit of despair such as this.

I winced at the thought. What was I doing here? Why wasn't I out at some nice, dark casino, playing cards, making money, lying my head off and staying up all night, soothed by the music of slot machines? The sad truth is that I didn't want to be there, either. I was in the middle of a road in a dark wood. Beasts loomed, and Virgil was yet to appear. I felt heartsick, like Dante at the beginning of his quest.

I gave myself a mental shake. It must be the narcotic effect of the English department ambiance. Time to snap out of it.

Exiting the office and its end-of-semester chaos, I turned right and entered a barren hallway, looking for open doors, someone to bump into. No luck.

At the end of the hall, I could turn left into another hallway or go back the way I came. I opted for a return to the infernal office. Perhaps the absent administrative staff might have returned. Or maybe I'd find a boatman waiting to take me to hell. I started to sweat inside my heavy coat.

As I retraced my steps, a door on my left opened and a young kid, clearly an undergraduate, stepped into the hall right in front of me, greasy hair hanging in his face. He held his pants up with one hand and expertly popped ear buds in with his other hand, a tricky maneuver given the bulky KU jacket and backpack. He shuffled down the hall, not even seeing me. I caught the door before it closed and popped my head in the office.

A severe, dark-haired woman sat at a desk below one of those sets of mounted bookshelves, a plaster bust gazing off into the far corner of the small room. Her chin was in her hand and she leaned in as she scanned the monitor in front of her. Narrow tortoise shell reading glasses reflected light from the screen, giving the impression of opaque lenses. I examined the room briefly; it was a spartan place, no comfy rugs, no family photos or cute tchotchkes. Not a plant person either.

"Excuse me?" I began tentatively, leaning in past the doorframe, not quite stepping over the threshold.

"Yes?" The woman sat up abruptly and leveled a baleful look over the top of her glasses. I've used that technique often, still do. But as a recipient of the Hudson version of the sharp-eyed look, I wasn't fazed.

"Can I help you?" She had a flat, nasal, East Coast voice. What she really wanted to do was close the door and lock it.

I responded with a tight little smile. "Sorry to bother you," I said, indicating that I wasn't sorry at all. "I'm looking for Ron Addison." Ron, not doctor, not professor. Ron told her we were peers if not friends. "Could you tell me where his office is?"

As I spoke the dead professor's name, I checked my watch, indicating that I had places to be. I then met her eyes with the blandest Hudson gaze I could muster, as if I had no idea that Addison was dead and not likely to be in his office today.

The woman took her glasses off and set them on her desk, next to the computer keyboard. She stood up slowly, two vertical lines creasing the space between dark eyebrows, a very small, very thin, tightly wrapped woman dressed in black. No Santa hat for her, thank you very much.

"I think you'd better come in," she decided, measuring the situation and the obvious degree of my ignorance. "Close the door, take a seat." She gestured to the chair by her desk.

I sat, after extending my hand mid-western style and introducing myself with a smile. "Carlyle Hudson. Call me Lyle."

She looked at the hand for a moment, emanating disdain for all things Kansan, and took it reluctantly, giving it the smallest of shakes and withdrawing her hand quickly. No smile.

"Domenica Mancuso." The introduction was followed by a heavy moment of silence and a look of distaste for what she was about to tell me. She sat down and folded her hands in her lap, back straight.

"There is no nice way to put this, so I'll just tell you. Ron Addison is dead." She picked up the reading glasses and put them back on, creating the first line of defense in case I got, God help us, emotional.

"What?" I whispered the word. "You're not serious." I studied her face as if looking for some misguided joke.

"Oh yeah, he's dead," she said with a straightforward practicality, her shoulders relaxing since it didn't look like I was going to get hysterical on her. "Murdered," she added helpfully.

"Ron murdered? Ron? Who would kill him?" My mind appeared to boggle.

"Oh, I know," she said, drawing out the O sound that had probably grown up in one of the five boroughs, or possibly New Jersey. "It's crazy, like someone would shoot a sofa or a potted plant, right?"

"I beg your pardon?"

"No disrespect, Ms. Hudson. If you were friends, I mean." She shook her head. "But the man was such a...a..."

I waited for her to find the right word, unable to supply one of my own to help her out. I stayed with her and tried not to look clueless.

"I don't know, a puppy dog, or maybe somebody's goofy uncle. He was soft-spoken, right? Very friendly." She said the word the way a dentist might say gingivitis. "Always smiling, shaking hands, even with students. Who would shoot that?" She removed her glasses and regarded me.

"Pardon me for saying so," she said, "but I can't see you as Ron's friend. You look like a serious person, you know what I mean?"

"Thank you. I think. No, not exactly friends. We met at a conference on semiotics, got talking about what a crock it is. He was entertaining."

"Interesting," Domenica Mancuso nodded. "Total bull. I bet our boy was giving you what you wanted to hear. He could be sly that way. He's very much a post-modernist. Was, I mean."

"Really?"

"Oh, yes. Cynical bastards, all of them."

I laughed outright, cackled, despite my best effort at self-control. Professor Mancuso was turning out to be a piece of work.

"He was a bit of a gossip," I conceded, looking to prime the pump. "He went off on this guy in his department, Cassidy? Very funny guy, Ron." I went sad for a moment, remembering he was dead. As if I hadn't almost stepped on him in a corn maze.

"Oh my God!" Domenica threw her hands in the air. "They were like the Three Stooges rolled into two. Punch and Judy, whatever. They'd start in at faculty meetings and I'd stand up and walk out. Who has time for such nonsense!"

"So, did you shoot him?" I asked, nonchalant.

She blinked, once. "Ha! What a kidder you are. NO, I'd shoot the other one, Cassaday. That's his name." She spelled it for me. "Pompous ass," she continued, warming to her subject. "Thinks he's God's gift." She shifted gears on me. "So why did you want to see Ron Addison, not being friends, I mean."

"Oh," I grabbed the manila folder and waved it at her. "I told him I was moving back to Lawrence and might be interested in an adjunct position, you know, keeping my hand in? He told me to look him up, he'd see what he could do."

"I'll bet he did." She took the folder. "Look at you. Old Ron was probably falling all over himself." She started to read. "USF? You left San Francisco to come here?" Her eyebrows rose like wings.

"I grew up here, Domenica, it's my home." The magic words had no effect whatsoever. If anything, I must be a nutcase.

"You want my advice? Go back to San Francisco."

"I get that a lot." I remembered other time when people told me to go back to SF. I didn't think I needed to mention them.

"You've done this before, yes? You know that adjunct pay is shit, right? You could make more at just about anything."

"True," I nodded, "but the university atmosphere…"

"Oh, please, spare me." Domenica cut me off. "College classrooms." She rolled her eyes. "To these kids, plagiarism is a way of life. Open access, who needs attribution? Information is free on the Internet, they say, which means it is free to them, like the air they breathe. Why the big fuss? Lyle, you want to fight that fight?"

Absolutely not. But I kept my mouth shut and looked at her hopefully.

She sighed at my blatant idiocy. "I'll give your resume to Roberta, our department chair, Lyle. But if you're wise, you'll stay far away."

I thanked her for her time and wished her well with the exams and term papers.

"Don't remind me!" she complained. "And about Ron, it's a terrible thing."

"Yes it is."

18

Outside Wescoe Hall, I pulled out my car keys and moved them to my coat pocket. My cell still had plenty of juice—always a surprise—but no messages. I wondered about Chas, whether I should leave an annoying voicemail or just call and hang up, letting the record of my number do the talking. I missed him.

Walking to the Benz, I buttoned the coat and pulled on my gloves. The sunny sky had turned gray and a sharp breeze threatened to turn into an icy wind. There was nothing to stop its journey from the Rockies; the wind grew teeth along the way that would send needles of cold up your sleeves and riming the inside of your nose with frost. It was the kind of wind that scraped snow off the land and plastered it against houses and trees, and it was heading this way.

Three crows took off from branches overhead, cawing and complaining. I lifted my head to watch them and caught a dark flutter out of the corner of my eye. Stopping in my tracks, I whipped around to look the way I had come. Nothing moved; I was alone on the sidewalk. Opening my coat, I reached up under my sweater, unsnapped the holster and removed the gun, holding it straight down, safety still on. I walked slowly along the line of cars parked in the street, stopping to listen every few steps, peering over hoods and around fenders. Nothing.

I stood still a full two minutes, listening and surveying the area, eyes tearing every time I faced into the wind. I took a slow breath and released it, feeling my head pound in my chest.

Reversing course, I picked up my pace and replaced the gun in the bra holster. Cold and not exactly comfortable but no frantic scrabbling around in the bottom of the satchel. I snapped the nylon flap into place and re-buttoned my coat. I beeped the car open and took a last look around. It didn't feel like anyone was aiming at me, but what did I know?

Next stop was the Lambda Chi sorority house, which, I had discovered in my research, had been the residence of Robin Breck before she was strangled and thrown in a ditch. I'd made an appointment with the housemother, Irene Worth. "Like the perfume!" she giggled when we were on the phone. I tried not to judge her for giggling. Surrounded by so much estrogen, she was likely a victim of circumstances.

Here too, my story was a job search. No resume this time. I assumed that such positions were obtained through personal connections. Turns out I was wrong, but I didn't want the job anyway, just the opportunity to ask a few questions.

Lambda Chi house, a large white antebellum birthday cake of a building, sat in the middle of a row of other prestigious Greek houses on Tennessee Avenue. A vision of white on white, the house had a sweeping lawn under the snow and a curving drive around the house to a tidy parking lot with numbered spaces. There were five cars in the lot, most of the girls having already left town. Irene told me not to worry about getting ticketed, but I decided to play by the rules and took one of the designated guest spots. Guest was lettered in a gothic gold print on a discreet black sign.

I sat in the car after turning off the engine, telling myself that the nausea and lightheadedness was the effect of skipping breakfast and lunch. Maybe I was dehydrated. I felt clammy and my teeth itched.

A sorority house was on a par with the bridal shop. I was a yellow lab walking into poodle land. I expected the worst.

I rang the bell labeled "Housemother," also in gold letters, on white this time. A musical chime rang far back in the house. Did sororities have theme songs? The tune sounded like the opening bars of "Younger than Spring Time."

The door was eventually opened by a woman with apricot hair who was turned around and calling over her shoulder.

"No, I've got it! Thank you, Shelby dear!"

Irene Worth turned back to the open door and smiled down at me where I stood on the stoop. One had to step *up* to pass the threshold. Highly symbolic, no doubt. I was mesmerized by the twin reindeer on the front of her red sweater, tiny green silk bows and small jingling bells in their antlers. Were the reindeer wearing lipstick? My trance gave the woman a chance to look me over from head to toe.

"Well, I'll be! Carlyle Hudson, I remember when you were just a little girl! What a surprise!" Irene Worth looked over my shoulder. "How odd. I was expecting a...a..." she drew a tiny card from a reindeer pocket. "A Carol Tremblay, Lambda Chi 1980?"

I gave her a sheepish grin. "That would be me, Mrs. Worth."

"What on earth?" She laughed a jolly kind of laugh. "Come inside and tell me all about it!"

I took the huge step up into the sorority house and thought feverishly about how to handle the unexpected situation of being recognized. Whatever I told Irene Worth would be sure to enter the gossip mill of whatever circles she swam in. Her resemblance to Nola could not be coincidental. I took it as a warning.

She led me to an apartment off to the right of the entrance hall. We passed two gigantic pots of poinsettias, pink of course, and group photos of young women dressed in white, sisterhoods of ages past.

The housemother's apartment was a study in chintz. And lace. And ruffles. But it was light and airy, pearly daylight sifting through filmy curtains on the tall windows. The sitting room, with two ladylike wingback chairs and a small tea table set before a small fireplace had one of those metal contraptions on the mantel, an angel/candle ornament. You lighted the candle and the flame made the angel go around, strumming its harp or blowing its trumpet, as the case may be. There were no other ornaments, the room was just too small.

Irene took my coat and gestured to the chairs. I was to sit down and she would bring us a nice pot of tea. I was grateful for the offer.

If the apartment was anything to go by, our Irene ran a tight ship. Every item was polished, dusted, and symmetrically aligned, indicating a world of order that was probably reassuring to young girls far away from home.

As she set the silver tea service on the table, I asked if by any chance she was related to Nola. Irene was much younger than Nola, maybe ten years older than me, but the resemblance was uncanny.

"Oh, no. But I do know who you mean. I visit Hyacinth every now and then with the girls. She has a lovely sense of style. I'm flattered, Carlyle."

"Please, call me Lyle. Carlyle makes me feel I'm in some kind of trouble."

"Speaking of resemblances, you are the image of your mother! Louise and her sisters were quite the beauties. And that Loretta, what a tomboy!" She laughed, remembering.

"So, what brings you here, Lyle? Surely you don't want to get into the business of being a sorority housemother. The girl I remember broke rules instead of observing them. Am I right?" She handed me a plate of finger sandwiches and a small linen napkin embroidered with holly leaves.

I ate one immediately. Egg salad on crustless slivers of white bread, delicious. The second one was traditional watercress.

"Did you make these? They're delicious. " I stuffed another egg salad finger into my mouth.

"Every day," she said, pouring tea into delicate teacups. "I store batches of them in plastic containers to keep them fresh. The girls have come to expect them when they come in for a chat. These are my contribution to Lambda tradition," she added proudly. "Sugar?"

"One, please. And a splash of milk?" I could totally see girls who had grown up with tea sets and Barbies loving a chat with Mrs. Worth.

"Louise took her tea with lemon," Irene observed, placing a small cube of sugar in her cup with small silver tongs.

"Yes, she did. I'm sorry, Mrs. Worth, but I don't remember you."

"Please call me Irene. Worth is my married name. Peter and I divorced some time ago, but I kept the name. Not so many young women do that nowadays. When you were growing up my name was Dalhoudie."

"Ah." Nothing. I'd have to lie. "So you all had that Scots-Irish thing going, I'll bet. Now I think of it, you always used to give me candy." Safe bet; everyone gave kids candy.

"Mary Janes, yes! You do remember, how sweet!" I swear her eyes teared up. What horrible person would lie to such a sweet woman?

"Do they even make those anymore?" I asked. "That combination of molasses and peanut butter, it was addictive. I try to explain it to younger people sometimes, but they look at me like I'm nuts." OK, maybe that was going a bit too far.

"The past can never really be explained, can it?" she said, achieving a philosophical insight I would not have expected based on the apricot hair and reindeer. "It can only be shared with people who were there."

I sipped my tea, feeling a tad nostalgic myself. Like a mid-western version of a Chinese empress, Irene Worth nee Dalhoudie waited for me to answer her question. I devoured two more finger sandwiches and the woman didn't bat an eye. My mother's scolding voice in my head told me that taking more than one sandwich was not ladylike. I patted my lips with the napkin and started eyeing the shortbread cookies, buttery squares of caloric delight. The voice in my head held its breath.

Resisting the temptation to eat the cookies, I set my cup and saucer on the table and placed my hands in my lap, stopping just short of crossing my ankles.

"The truth is, Irene, I have been thinking of this type of position." Just like I've always wanted to know what it felt like to swallow my tongue.

"Don't tell my aunts," I continued, "but I've been feeling at loose ends lately, kind of rudderless, you know?" Maybe that part was true? No time for truth, back to the lie.

"So, I'm looking into it as an option, provide a little tough love and guidance. I did teach at USF for a time. I know the kind of stresses undergraduates face." Also true. Huh.

"But this," Irene's manicured hand indicated the whole building around us, "is more about tradition and ritual, Lyle. And you were never a Lambda Sister, were you?"

"No, that's true. But it's not essential, is it? I mean, it's not like you have to be a birthright Quaker to join."

"Oh, I'm afraid it is. To be one of us is to know us and understand us better. That's what a housemother does, it's who she is." Irene spoke the words kindly, and I really had to struggle not to roll my eyes.

I thanked her for speaking so directly. She patted my wrist and reassured me that life would work out and I would be just fine. God, she was good!

"Stick with what you know, Lyle." I wondered if she knew about the poker. Was she psychic? "Who knows, maybe you could find an adjunct position here."

"I'll give it some thought."

"Of course, the pay is…" she gave a ladylike sniff and shook her head.

"Hey, that reminds me!" I sat forward, signaling an inclination to gossip. "Weren't a couple of people at KU murdered recently? I just got back into town, and that's all that people are talking about."

Irene set her cup down and leaned forward herself. "Yes," she breathed conspiratorially. "Not just that professor, Lyle, but one of our own dear girls! Quite shocking. Our House was in complete disarray. Some parents came and whisked their girls away. Oh, it has been so upsetting!"

I stared, apparently agog at the drama.

"Yes, yes, it's true. Robin was one of ours, Lambda to her toes." Irene sighed. "Such a sweet, helpful girl. Very active at church. Loved Father Edwin at St. Alban's, couldn't do enough for him. She was going to be an angel in the Pageant. The children adored her. Such a shame." Now Irene really was crying, wiping silent tears from her cheeks.

"I'm so sorry, Irene. I had no idea. It must have been awful for you." I patted her hand. "Will you be OK? You know, here by yourself?"

"Oh, it's perfectly safe. I'll be fine." Irene gave herself a shake and produced a thin smile. "It's sweet of you to ask, Lyle. My, you are so like Louise."

No I was not. My mother was genuine and caring, always. Irene meant well, but I felt a twinge.

"A Lambda Chi girl... I didn't know," I said, returning to the subject at hand. "I can tell you really liked her."

"She was a love," Irene said. "Oh, there was the usual girl stuff—boys." She raised her eyebrows in a grown up version of Duh. "But pretty girls like Robin are often the target of petty jealousies and resentment. She felt it deeply. I can't tell you how many times she sat right here, where you are sitting now, Lyle, and she would just cry. Girls can be so cruel."

I nodded in sympathy with dear, sensitive Robin. When I was her age, I didn't have much to do with other girls, was pretty much a loner even then.

I followed up with soothing noises, encouraging Irene to calm down. I stood up, saying I had to get going, and Irene went to retrieve my coat. Behind me there was a brief tattoo of knocks and the door flew open, admitting a Lambda in a Santa hat and a high state of excitement.

"Reenie! Reenie! Mom's taking me to The Angel Bride Reception! Do you want to come with us?" The girl's eyes were squeezed tight shut—paroxysms of delight, no doubt—so she walked right into me before she realized I was there and that I was not Irene.

She gasped, Oh! Excuse me, ma'am!"

I hate being mammed. I wanted to bite her. But before I could, Irene Worth came to her rescue.

"What? LuAnn, is that you?" Irene handed me the coat and turned her full attention to her baby chick.

"Reenie! You have to come! Angel Bride, remember? OMG, I am SO excited! You have to come with us!"

"I would love to, dear. But I hear that tickets were sold out. I'm sure your mother obtained hers weeks ago. You two go and have simply a wonderful time. You can tell me about it after, all right?"

"Aw, Reenie!" LuAnn hugged her housemother tearfully. "I wanted to go with you." There were sniffs and pouting. The urge to bite returned.

"There, there," Irene murmured, hugging the girl back.

I cleared my throat. I do that when I'm about to say something I will regret.

"Um, I can get you a ticket, Irene."

"You can?" two voices said simultaneously.

"I own the shop, Hyacinth? I inherited it from my mother. It's not my thing, really, brides." I nattered on, apologizing where no apology was necessary. "But it's mine, and…" I stuttered to a stop. "Well, it would be my pleasure if you would be my guest, Irene."

LuAnn squealed, jumping up and down, and Irene clasped her hands and held them up to her chin, like someone was throwing a bouquet at her.

"Carlyle Hudson, you are the dearest creature!" She was about to throw her arms around me in a full-on housemother hug, when yet another Lambda Sister threw herself in the open door.

"Reenie, Reenie! Oh, thank God. Here you are! Something awful has happened. You have to come!" Sister number two started to cry, causing LuAnn's lips to tremble.

"What...what is it?" LuAnn asked fearfully.

Sister number two moved in fast, seeking Irene's maternal hug like a heat-seeking missile.

"Someone broke into Robin's room! It's awful! You have to come!"

I left Irene to calm the distraught girls while I called 911, wondering if I should have it on speed dial. After determining that there was no immediate threat, the operator advised me to stay away from the scene and wait for police to arrive.

I told Irene and the girls the police were on the way, that they should stay where they were and eat a cookie or something, I'd be right back.

Upstairs on the second floor all was quiet. I didn't have to look too far, the second door on the right was open, gray light from the window leeching out into the carpeted hall. I trotted over to the door and peered in, knowing I had two minutes at best.

The girl's clothing and possessions had evidently been boxed up, ready to be claimed by family or shipped home. But the boxes had been cut open, contents piled around the room. The piles intrigued me. They indicated a neat, orderly mind. Not rage. Not girlish abandon. It wasn't malicious, rather that somebody was looking for something specific. I wondered if they'd found what they were looking for.

At the sound of sirens coming up the drive, I sprinted back downstairs to Irene's apartment. "Younger than Spring Time" chimed, and Irene excused herself to go answer the door. I smiled at the two girls and stuck my hands in my pockets.

"You really own Hyacinth?" LuAnn asked me.

"She does?" The second girl asked, jumping up to join LuAnn and gaze upon the wonder I represented.

"She does!" LuAnn whispered loudly. "Steph, she invited Reenie to Angel Bride as her special guest!"

The door opened and Irene Worth entered, followed by Greta Danielson, who stopped dead at the sight of me.

"You breaking into sorority houses, Lyle? These girls catch you red handed?"

Irene was shocked at Officer Danielson's tone. "Why, no, officer. She is here as my guest."

"Right," Greta held a hand up. "Everybody sit tight until I get back. No leaving!" she pointed a finger at me. "The room is on the second floor?" She checked with Irene. Receiving a nod, Greta left the apartment, closing the door quietly behind her.

The four of us stood still, listening to the sounds of official voices and heavy treads going up the stairs.

"This is how it works," I informed the three women. "They'll come down pretty soon. There are no bodies or anything, and we'll all be taken aside for separate, probably brief, interviews. Piece of cake."

LuAnn and Stephanie huddled close to Irene; they looked very young and scared. Irene put an arm around the shoulders of each girl.

"Don't worry," I said. "You didn't do anything. The police are merely looking for information and trying to figure out what happened, OK? Nice people, really. I'm sure your interviews will be pleasant. So," I said, turning to Stephanie. "I'm curious. That room is close to the stairs. You must have passed it lots of times. You didn't notice anything?"

"No," the girl shook her head. "It wasn't all the way open, just a crack."

"What made you notice it today?" I asked, sounding way too much like Greta.

Stephanie held up her iPod. "It was on shuffle and I didn't want to listen to the song that was on, so I stopped to change it. The crack of light caught my eye and I looked in. Wouldn't you?" She turned to LuAnn for support. LuAnn nodded sympathetically, one sister there for the other.

A polite knock on the door ended our conversation. After determining that Stephanie had discovered the break-in, Greta sent the girl off with an officer to take her statement. She recommended that Irene and LuAnn stay where they were for a few minutes, and then she took me by the arm and escorted me out the door.

We walked to the back of the sorority house, where Greta found a room with a flat screen TV, couches and comfortable chairs grouped around it. She did not invite me to sit down.

"What do I have to do, lock you up?"

"On what grounds? I am merely a visitor here, Greta. Irene Worth was a friend of my mother's." It was ironic how handy the truth could be sometimes.

"That room upstairs," Greta raised a finger, "belonged to Robin Breck, murder victim, as you probably know. And coincidentally here you are, where her room has been broken into." She held up a second finger, soon followed by a third. Then there's that shooting at your place, oh, and the intruder, right? And, lest we forget, " finger number four joined the others. "There's Professor Addison, found dead by you in the corn maze." She glared at me. "Do not insult my intelligence by telling me this is *all* coincidence, Lyle. I will shoot you myself."

"OK, OK, not coincidence, I get it." I held up my hands, making peace." But you have to admire the symmetry of it all."

"Bullshit. Symmetry, my ass. You are snooping into things, poking your nose in…"

"Hey. Hey!" I stomped my foot at her, working up to getting mad. "You can't blame this crime spree on me, if that's what it is. I didn't strangle that girl or shoot the guy. I was shot at, remember? Let's just calm down."

"No, Lyle, the word is *suspicious*. The situation stinks. I have to ask myself questions about you, about your motives and intentions. You are making a bad situation worse. You're butting in and it could get you killed. Right?" She raised an eyebrow at me, the angry one.

"Right." Point taken.

"How's the face?" Greta tilted her chin, indicating the cut on my cheek.

"Fine. It itches, but it's fine." I touched my cheek briefly.

"Come on, I'll walk you to your car."

"Wait, I have to say goodbye to Irene," I protested.

"I'll tell her for you. I want you out of the way."

"Fine. I'll walk myself to my own damn car."

"Fine. And, Lyle?"

I looked at her stonily.

"No number five, OK?" She held out five fingers. "Do not make me add the thumb." She waved the thumb at me and we shared a weak smile.

I escorted myself from the premises.

19

Greta had let me off easy and I wondered why. She was a woman of sharp contrasts, and I had a hard time reading her. She vacillated between suspicion and concern. Not too long ago, she was convinced I was part of a money-laundering scheme involving shady real estate transactions and my Arab admirer and his lovely gifts.

Gifts led me to Christmas presents. Would I never be done? Was there a gauntlet to walk if you left anybody out? I sighed in frustration. Families! It was a problem I didn't have when I was on the road, going from tournament to tournament, playing poker. When I was really flush, I'd ask a concierge to shop for me, scribbling out a few guidelines on a piece of hotel stationery and handing her a credit card. Easy peasy.

I parked the Benz by a fire hydrant and ran into the Zen teashop on 9th Street and grabbed a Chinese tea set on a lacquer tray and some bubble tea, all for Crista. I was in and out in twenty minutes, no ticket waiting for me on the windshield. Lyle Hudson, law-breaker. I started to feel like my old self again.

What Lyle's old self needed, I thought, turning the car in the direction of home in the fading light, was time to write out my notes on my interviews with Domenica Mancuso and Irene Worth. I could lay out the deck of cards again and see what connections might have turned up in my intuition. Alone time sounded good.

Walking in through the alley gate, coming in from the garage, I saw lights on in the kitchen. Was Crista home from work early? I made a mental adjustment: maybe not alone. But Crista was a quiet person; she'd leave me to my own devices.

Reaching the top step, I heard the clatter of pots and a roaring laugh that could only belong to one person. Dreams of solitude evaporated. I pushed open the kitchen door and heaved myself and packages inside.

"What's this, another invasion?" I asked as Loretta greeted me.

Lenore stood at the counter by the sink, chopping vegetables. Loretta was at the stove, Santa hat slipping back on her head, generating noise with pots. A couple of skinned carcasses lay on the kitchen table, a shining cleaver waiting beside them. Lenore dried her hands on a dishtowel and made a move to greet me.

"Are those what I think they are?" I asked, hugging Lenore.

Loretta slammed down the pots, pushed past her sister and picked up the cleaver. She held a finger to her lips.

"Ssssh! We're hunting Wabbits!" It wasn't the oldest joke in the world but it was a classic and never failed to make us laugh.

Lenore grabbed the Santa hat and righted it on Loretta's head. "Put that down before you hurt someone."

Lenore rescued the cleaver and returned it to the table. I was engulfed in hugs and pats. Glory came out from under the table and danced around us.

"Stop, stop!" I pleaded. "Let me put this stuff down! What are you doing here? How did you get in?" I was a fanatic about locking up these days.

The two women stepped back and communed, eyeball to eyeball. Lenore raised a finger, indicating she'd take this one.

"We grew up in this house, Lyle, dear. There are many ways to get in." She paused. "However, this time we chose to use a key."

"Whose key? Wait. Luce told you about the window, didn't she. That's why you're here."

"No, Luce kept that confidence, as she will tell you," she said, pushing me and the packages through and out of the kitchen.

"Luce is here, too?"

"Not at the moment, dear. She's out with Vern at the grocery store. You have the oddest things in your refrigerator," Lenore said.

"Your officer friend, Greta gave us a call this afternoon," Loretta volunteered. "Said you kept showing up at the wrong time and place, like a bad penny. She suggested we keep an eye on you. So, here we are!" Loretta beamed.

"She did not," I said, horrified.

"Oh yes she did!" they replied simultaneously.

I had not gotten off easy after all. Damn Greta Danielson. I wondered if she broke some law by siccing my family on me.

The L&L's shooed me from the kitchen to put my things away and Loretta took up the task of dismembering the rabbits with her cleaver. I loved rabbit, especially when Lenore was cooking.

"Hey!" I called down the hall, taking my coat back off the hook, "I'll go get the wine!"

"No you won't, Lyle," Lenore answered cheerily. "Vern and Luce are taking care of that." Drat.

"Get yourself a drink!" Loretta yelled, appealing to my vice, "and come join us!" I was thinking Johnnie

Walker, very little ice. A nap would have been nice, but that wasn't going to happen.

Glass in hand, a healthy dose of J Walker in my system, I sat at the kitchen table and nibbled at the heel of a baguette Lenore was tearing up for her cassoulet. I was mulling over a respectful way to broach my opposition to the family butting in, when Lenore beat me to the punch.

"It's not right to keep us in the dark, Lyle, especially when…"

Lenore's lecture was interrupted by a knock at the front door and Glory skittering down the hall in full cry. I took a healthy swig of scotch and followed her.

"I saw the lights," Andressa explained in a shaky voice. "I would have called," she wave her cell phone at me, "but I didn't know what to say…" her words dwindled into silence.

I took her coat and invited her back to the library. "I've got white wine and scotch, take your pick. Red wine should be arriving shortly." Andressa opted for wine and followed me to the kitchen where she greeted the L&L's.

Lenore was braising floured chunks of rabbit and onions in two frying pans.

"That smells wonderful," Andressa said, receiving a radiant smile from Lenore.

"That's a lot of meat, isn't it?" I asked, plunking a few cubes of ice in my empty glass. "You planning to feed an army?"

"You never know!" Loretta winked at us.

I ignored the sinking feeling and headed back to the library, handing Andressa her glass of wine. She broke down before she took two steps out of the kitchen

"He left me! Carl's gone and I don't know where he is!" Andressa's chin quivered.

"At Christmas?" Loretta boomed. "Son of a bitch!"

"Stay right there. Do not cry," I ordered the miserable woman. I grabbed the bottle of wine from the fridge. "Got it," I told my aunts. "She'll be fine."

I dragged Andressa to the library and set the bottle down where she could reach it.

"How long has he been gone? Is that what you wanted to talk about at the coffee shop?"

"Yes," she nodded. "I mean, no, he left later. Two days. Yesterday?" Tears started leaking quietly down her face. "He." She had to stop and take a drink. "He said he was worried. The police stopped by the house and asked him questions about that girl."

"What girl? Do you mean Robin Breck?"

"He said, he said, he thought he was a suspect."

"Why?" Andressa just looked at me. "Oh." I made a sympathetic face, more like a wince. All that golden brown yumminess. Poor Andressa.

"Carl admitted he'd had a fling with her, as he called it. But it had been over for a while, that he'd dumped her. She had said some nasty things and stormed out. He said he wasn't going to stick around and get blamed. I don't know where he is, Lyle. I don't know what to do!"

Like I would? She was better off without him, but I couldn't say that. Andressa had moved from weeping to loud, wrenching sobs.

"Hey?" I called to the kitchen. "Luce? Is Luce back yet? I need help here." The best I could do was find a box of tissues for her.

Luce entered the library through the small bar area connected to the kitchen. "Yes?" She pulled off her gloves and coat and threw them on the arm of a chair. "What's up?" Thank God, the cavalry had arrived.

Luce took Andressa to the front parlor where they could have some privacy. I was instructed to tell Lenore that Andressa would be staying for dinner.

Vern sat across the table from Loretta while she made a vinaigrette for the salad. He raised his beer in greeting. I slipped behind Lenore, trying to reach around her and pinch a bit from the mixture she was pouring into baking dishes. I got my hand smacked but the tidbit made it into my mouth.

"Lyle, stop that. It's not cooked yet!"

'That piece was, Lenore. Is that rosemary?"

"You know it is. Now, go on."

"So," I said, licking my fingers, "anybody know Irene Worth?"

Vern started laughing, trying not to pass Christmas ale trough his nose. Behind me, Lenore giggled and had to put down the baking dish before she pilled it. Loretta's face turned bright red.

"Well, let me think, Lyle," she said. "The name does ring a bell." Her understatement brought hoots from the other two. "Perhaps you better ask Luce." Howls of laughter.

"Luce is busy, talk!" I pulled up a chair and sat at the kitchen table waiting for the laughter to subside.

Lenore put the second casserole in the oven and covered her smile with the dishtowel, avoiding eye contact with her sister and brother-in-law. "I think I need a glass of wine," she said.

"Hell, yes!" Loretta agreed. "Open a bottle of that red, will you, Vern?"

The man was wedged in at the table and couldn't move. He directed me to the case of wine he had just put in the pantry.

"Case? You bought a case of wine?"

"'Tis the season! Just shut up and make yourself useful," Loretta said.

I opened the wine, poured glasses for the L&L's, got Vern another beer, and not wanting more to drink at the moment, asked Lenore what I could do to help with dinner while they told their story. I was directed to chop peppers, shred some lettuce, and get a salad started.

"Irene Worth, lord, lord," said Vern, raising his eyes to the ceiling.

"She was Irene Dalhoudie," Lenore clarified.

"Why when that girl was fourteen she looked like she was twenty-four," Vern said nostalgically. "A young man could get arrested just looking at her."

"She was something else," Loretta said. "I had to admire her flair. And you, sir," she said to her husband, "are a man of wisdom with a strong survival instinct. You might not have made it to thirty if things had gone differently." Loretta's eyes sparkled mischievously.

"It was always you, Elvis," Vern said, "Only you."

Loretta shook her head, thinking back. "That girl, when she was eighteen, was dating three different fellows. None of them," she emphasized none, "knew about the others." She started to laugh again and had to put down her glass to keep from spilling the wine.

"I don't think those boys ever found out," Lenore added. "Oh, my, she was a vixen."

"Vixen! Oh yeah, that's the word!" Loretta boomed, reducing them to cackles all over again.

"Wait, wait," I crunched a piece of green pepper. "This is Irene Worth, like the perfume, right?"

They nodded.

"The same Irene Worth who is housemother over at Lambda Chi?"

"She's what?" Lenore's giggles set us all off.

I stared into the leafy greenness of the completed salad, crunching another piece of pepper. "Um, Lenore, where are we going to eat? We can't all fit in the kitchen."

"Why, in the dining room, of course." She looked at me for a moment and crossed her arms. "You really don't get home much do you?" It wasn't a question.

"Front of the house, you idiot!" Loretta said. That would be the other room with all the lights on. You'll recognize it when you get there. There's a table with plates on it!"

I looked at them blankly. "But. That room has been closed up for years. Louise never used it."

"How would you know, Lyle, you weren't here much then, either." Lightening her tone, Loretta added, "We're using it now, go take a look! And here, take the salad dressing with you."

Glory walked ahead of me, checking over her shoulder to see if I was following. Sure enough, there it was, right across the hall from the parlor where Luce and Andressa talked quietly. How could I have forgotten an entire room?

The dining room was Wedgewood blue, with white trim and wainscoting. It had its own fireplace, with a mirror above the mantel. An antique mahogany sideboard by the door was loaded with bowls, trays, and serving utensils my aunts had decided would be needed for dinner, along with two apple pies cooling on trivets. How long had the L&L's been here, anyway?

The table was dressed in white linen, two candlesticks the only decoration. Pride of place would go to the food. The table was set for ten people. I counted people in my head. All the usual suspects added up to eight. Add Andressa and there were nine.

Ten? Glory wasn't interested in counting and disappeared under the table.

I set the salad on the sideboard and walked around the table, taking the room in, the botanical prints, light gleaming off silverware that had belonged to my grandmother. The room had a large picture window that was twin to the one in the parlor, and light spilled out onto the porch. A passerby might look in and see a dinner scene from a play of a Henry James novel.

The room spoke to me of another world, of childhood and dinners past. How could I have forgotten?

"Carlyle," I recalled a conversation on the subject with my mother. "Why do you keep pretending to be an orphan? We're your family. You belong here."

I sighed. No-place-like-home never worked for me. The idea was suffocating, squashed me flat. This room had home written all over it. Yet here I was, drinking it in.

I left the dining room, the dog beside me, and headed back to the kitchen, where I could hear the L&L's laughing and talking about Irene, their memories freed by my absence. I took a quick detour into the library to pick up my empty glass. I wasn't a neat freak, but finding glasses left lying around bothered me.

Caitlin was sitting on the leather ottoman that she had moved closer to the fireplace, her jacket still on. She was looking at the low flames with a content expression.

"Hello, Caitlin. When did you come in?"

The dog greeted her and she scratched Glory's ears before turning the dog around and sending her from the room with a gentle pat on the butt. That was unusual, but Glory was used to doing anything Caitlin asked her to, and she trotted out in the direction of the kitchen.

"I just came in. You were all in the kitchen telling stories of the old days." She didn't mean to make me feel old; Caitlin just had this gift.

"What's up?"

Caitlin smiled up at me then untucked her winter scarf from her jacket. She reached in and carefully drew out a small, bedraggled creature with pointy ears. Not a rat, I was relieved to see.

"Is that a cat?" It looked half dead.

"I found it on 9th Street. It was just lying on the sidewalk." Caitlin spoke softly, all her attention on the inert swatch of fur in her hands.

"Is it dead?" I asked hopefully.

"I thought so at first. But I picked it up and held it to my ear. It was still breathing." She repeated the gesture. "Still is."

I resisted the urge to drag Caitlin upstairs and make her wash her hands. The thought of how filthy that cat was made me feel slightly nauseated.

"What's your plan?" I asked. "Going to feed it to Brunhilde?"

"Not funny, Lyle." Caitlin stood and held the thing close. "You can be a jerk sometimes, you know?" She shot me an angry look and headed out of the room.

"Caitlin, hey." I touched her arm and she turned around, not meeting my eyes. "Sorry, OK? Let me go get Vern. He has a lot of experience with strays and barn cats. Maybe he can give you some pointers on how to keep it alive."

She nodded and carried the filthy, pathetic creature slowly upstairs. I went to the kitchen and recruited Vern, who picked up a dishtowel and a few other items from under the sink to take with him on his errand of mercy.

At the bottom of the staircase, he turned and looked at me. "She still got that big old snake up there?"

"It's in a cage, Vern. Pretty sure, anyway."

He shook his head and started up.

I stood in the hall, feeling like a creep for my snake food comment. Where was Glory?

"I want my dog back!" I yelled.

"Come and get her," Loretta yelled back. "Nobody's keeping her from you!"

Glory, like most dogs, was an opportunist. The warm kitchen was filled with wonderful smells and tasty crumbs, possibly a bit of rabbit.

I sulked into the kitchen where Loretta accused me of being neurotic about my dog. I got down on my hands and knees to drag Glory out from under the table. At Loretta's words, I turned and grabbed her ankles, pulling her off the chair onto the floor with me. We shrieked and wrestled, while Glory tried to lick our faces. She liked a good tussle, too.

Lenore grabbed a wooden spoon and smacked our legs, commanding us to get up off the floor and act our age.

"The hell we will!" Loretta roared, snatching the spoon and attempting to pull Lenore down with us.

The uproar brought Luce and Andressa in from the front parlor, just in time to see Lenore haul off and smack her sister on the Santa hat with the spoon. The look of horrified delight on her face had us all rolling with laughter. I was just managing to get to my knees and crawl out, when the kitchen door opened and Crista and Blake bustled in, bringing a wave of frozen air with them.

"Welcome to the WWW!" Loretta said from where she sat on the floor. "Whatcha got, kids?"

Crista held up two bottles of champagne and Blake held up a third, along with a crinkly cellophane bag in his free hand.

"Champagne and mistletoe," Blake grinned.

Loretta got up and chased Blake from the kitchen, making frightening smoochy noises. Champagne was stowed in the fridge, and Luce and Andressa moved into the kitchen as Crista and I moved out, into the library, where she piled coats on top of Luce's in one of the leather chairs.

"Wow, full house!" she said.

"More upstairs." I told her about Caitlin's rescue kitty and Vern's helping hands, leaving out my snarky comment about snake food. I pushed the ottoman back over to the couch, where it served as a coffee table. My glass had yet to make it into the kitchen. I picked it up and tossed it back and forth between my hands.

"Crista, I need a ticket. To Angel Bride."

She took the glass from me and regarded me silently, wondering how much I'd had to drink, perhaps.

"For a friend," I explained. "I invited someone to be my guest."

"Really? You're going to come? Seriously?"

I nodded, made an equivocating shrug, uncomfortable with the situation.

"Cool! Nola will be pleased, Lyle."

I sighed, thinking that maybe I did need another drink.

"I'll add the name to our VIP list. Who is it?" She handed me the glass and took a cell phone from her purse.

"Irene Worth," I said quickly. "What is that, an iPhone?" I hoped to distract her from the name, but she didn't recognize it.

"Worth? Like in value, self-worth?" She was too young to know about the perfume. "Yeah, this thing is great, and the apps are so cool! It's like carrying a tiny computer with me. There, she's in."

"Thanks, Crista."

There was a knock at the front door. "I'll get it," I said. "Could you take this to the kitchen, please?" Crista took the glass and went to join the mayhem in the kitchen.

MacDonald George stood there, a gift bag cradled in one arm, his Irish Setter, Jesse, standing obediently beside him. I just stood there looking up at him, not feeling the cold air gusting in around the tall man and the red dog.

"Lyle, close that door!" Loretta bellowed from the kitchen.

I stepped aside to let them in. "Um," I began.

"We were invited," Mac said, "ask Luce." He leaned down to whisper in my ear. "Hello to you, too." Mac took his hat off and kissed me.

20

The dogs let us know it was time to get out of bed. Not that Mac and I had slept in, but they knew we were more than awake, and they needed to go out. I jumped out of bed before Mac could grab me and took the dogs downstairs and let them out back. It was a cold, snowy morning, so it was a quick out. Last night's dinner played in my head, flirting with Mac across the table, the affection my family has for him, the easy decision to invite him to stay. What was wrong with me that I was suspicious of such a good time?

Back upstairs, I jumped back under the covers and tormented the man with my frozen toes. "No coffee for you, mister. Talk!" We tussled and ended up with our arms around each other. "No fair, Mac. You brushed your teeth while I was downstairs!"

Mac nuzzled my neck with a minty moustache.

"Cut that out!" I complained. Nuzzling continued and my toes warmed up real fast. "You have talked to my aunts, haven't you? They're on your side, you're all conspiring against me, it's clear."

Mac pushed my hair off my face and moved the nuzzling up to an ear, where he whispered, "You were warned, Lyle, remember? You are a woman pursued."

"Well, maybe I'll pursue you right back!" More tussling ensued.

"To what end?" Mac took a strand of my silver hair and tugged. "You think that hot sex will chase me away?"

"I don't want you away, not really, " I sighed, looking into his eyes.

"What do you want, Lyle?"

"You know, I think I figured that part out!" I sat up and smacked the comforter. "I want you—us—to be together but not nailed down!"

"Nailed down?"

"As in married. I want us not to be married." It made sense to me, yet didn't sound too cool when I said it. But it was out and I was going with it.

"So, you're asking me *not* to marry you."

"Exactly."

His smile flickered and then went and hid somewhere while he thought about it. "What would we have, then? What would I have with you?" he asked.

"What do you want?"

"I want more."

"Married more?"

"Not necessarily. But present in my life, Lyle. With me... with, with, with."

"Like partners?"

"Yep."

"Living together?"

"Yep."

"Oh, man! I suck at living together! What would I do here?" I threw a pillow on the floor.

Mac laughed. "Do what you do best, play poker. Who said you had to give that up?"

"Cards," I shook my head. "I don't know...anymore."

"Oh, stop."

"Stop what? I'm conflicted!"

"Are not. You're hungry, you need food."

Food meant jeans and a t-shirt for Mac and a ratty bathrobe for me, dogs and feet down the stairs into the kitchen in search of coffee, toast, leftovers, and kibble for Glory and Jesse.

The kitchen was immaculate. Hudson women are a well-oiled machine after a big dinner like last night's. They all know where everything belongs in each Hudson household. Items magically returned to their proper places, where they have lived for generations.

I grabbed plates and cutlery and rummaged around in the fridge, talking over my shoulder. "No, really, I'm conflicted."

"Are not." Mac pulled me out of the fridge and sat me at the table. "You're mostly feeling insecure. It happens when you lose. You take it personally."

"What are you, a poker psychologist?" My stomach growled.

"Bagel. Eat. Coffee." Mac put a steaming mug on the table and pushed the milk over where I could reach it. I was pretty sure I was the only person in the whole of Kansas who did not take coffee black.

"Luce explained it, and the L&L's agreed," Mac said.

"You talked to my aunts about me."

"Damn right. I'm in pursuit, remember?"

"I was warned. Got it." I ate my bagel and cream cheese in silence, looking down at Glory for support. The dog wrinkled her brow at me. She had nothing.

"What else did they say? Good coffee, by the way."

"Thank you. They said that you have *oscillations* I think Lenore called them, highs and lows. Like light from a distant star or something, was how Loretta put it. Their language confused me a bit but I got the point." Mac held up a hand to keep me from interrupting. "You

want to hear this or not? Nod yes and I'll continue." I
nodded and invited Glory up into my lap. She's a bony
little dog and gets cold. I was *not* feeling insecure.

"Luce explained that you get so used to winning
that losing at cards always comes as a shock; you get
pouty and take it personally. Generally, that's when you
come home—yes, Lawrence and this house are home—
and start stirring up trouble to distract yourself." What
none of them knew was that I had been winning,
consistently. Their picture was incomplete.

"I do not pout." Glory licked my face. "Or stir up
trouble, that's a lie! And no counting examples on your
fingers. Greta does that and it drives me crazy."

"Lawrence is a quiet town, Lyle. You show up and
peaceful folks turn violent, local youth go on crime
sprees, you get shot at, bodies appear."

"Not fair," I said defensively. "Those bodies were
already there. I didn't kill anybody, you know." I smiled
sweetly, avoiding the temptation to pout.

"Lyle, where are you going?"

"Wait, I have to check something."

MacDonald followed me down the hall to the front
of the house and into the dining room, where daylight
illuminated Wedgewood blue walls making the glow.

"It's still here."

"What is?"

"This room. I totally blocked it out, like it was
bricked up or something. I did not even see this room
until last night. How can you miss an entire room?"

Mac looked down at me skeptically. "Nice try, Lyle.
Do not change the subject."

I was about to protest, probably get all pouty, when
a scuffling noise drew our attention to the dining table.
Something was going on beneath it.

"Better not be a rat," I said.

"Excuse me?" Mac probably thought I was changing the subject again.

"Long story."

We leaned over and peered under the table. Glory was opening and closing her mouth, weaving and bobbing her head to keep from getting swatted by cat paws. The little cat was sitting up on its haunches, boxing at her. Caitlin's stray, no doubt. I knelt down and tried to tell who needed rescuing from whom. The cat turned and raised a paw at me.

"Wait till you meet Tetley, cat. He'll mop the floor with you." Tetley belonged to Luce and had once been the occasion of my encounter with a psychotic veterinarian.

On the other side of the table, MacDonald's legs remained stationary. Jesse was standing beside the legs swishing a feathery Irish Setter tail. The smiling dog and the motionless legs seemed faintly amused.

Glory sneezed, making the small cat puff up like it had been electrocuted. It hissed and swatted with increasing fury. I could throw my bathrobe over the cat, but then I'd be naked. What the hell. Teach those legs a lesson.

I squirmed out of the robe and held it in front of me like a matador's cape. Before I could toss it at the angry cat, Caitlin slid under the table next to me. She bagged the cat in a bath towel in one swift move and hugged the writhing beast to her chest.

"That thing wouldn't work, Lyle. His claws would go right through chenille. You'd have got hurt. Thanks for trying, though. Sorry about the cat. Glory OK?"

"She's fine, didn't even try to hurt your cat." I tried to untangle the robe and bumped my head on the table.

"Cool," Caitlin said. "That'll be easier if you stand up."

So I did, in all my (I can't help myself) glory. A couple of interesting things happened next. Mac stumbled back and bumped the sideboard, making the china rattle, Shore walked by outside with his dog, Margot. He looked in and I waved one of those Queen of England waves, hand about even with shoulder. Shore held up his watch and pointed to it. Cripes, I'd forgotten the shooting lesson. I held up my naked wrist and pointed. No watch. He checked his watch again, checked the sky, and held up ten fingers followed by two. Noon, got it. I gave Shore a thumbs-up. Message received. He and Margot continued on their way.

I put my robe on and belted it. Caitlin took her squirming cat upstairs, and Glory presented me with a yellow tennis ball.

Picking up the ball, I said, "Well, that was fun."

Mac shook his head and gave a wry smile. "You make my point."

I shook an index finger in front of him slowly from left to right. "Oh, no you don't, MacDonald George. I don't make animals crazy, they do that by themselves."

"And what are you doing at noon with Martin Shore?

"Shooting range."

"Naked?"

"What's wrong with you?" I rolled the ball down the hall into the kitchen and watched Glory chase it.

21

The shooting range was west of town; let's just say well outside of developed housing, where even farmland meets what can only be called the outback. It was a private club, Shore informed me, for serious people who took their guns seriously. He made no mention of seeing me in the window the day before. Did Shore think I was too old to mention it? Was he gay?

Shore turned in at an unmarked road and stopped before a chain link fence that bore a small black No Trespassing sign. The gate was closed with a chain and padlock that had to be unlocked and then reclosed once the car entered the gate. Shore's vehicle, a Toyota FJ Cruiser, had no trouble with the rutted, gravel road. New slush joined the drier remnants on the side panels.

We followed a trail past a low wooden building and an open area that Shore explained was used for competitions, to a series of narrow practice ranges that looked like banked pits, walls of dirt ten feet tall around three sides of each area. He pulled into one and cut the ignition. Shore was in a non-verbal mode of communication possibly brought on by the presence of side arms and ammunition. That was my best guess for the grunts and gestures that indicated I should get out of the vehicle and make myself useful.

He pulled out two canvas gun bags from the back of the SUV, hitching the smaller one over a shoulder, then nodded to a cardboard form and pointed me to the metal stand near the far wall of dirt. Apparently my job was to set up the target. It was a lot like standing sheet music in a music stand, the kind of task that makes idiots feel competent.

Shore set the gun bags on a picnic table under a freestanding awning and returned from the Toyota with two sets of ear protection and boxes of cartridges, copper tips. "Do not scrimp on the bullets," he explained, "quality ammo is good for your gun."

Before he let me handle any of his guns, Shore reviewed gun-handling etiquette with me and told me I'd better be religious about the rules, especially the basic assumption that all guns are *always* loaded; the more often you check the safer you are, period.

I shivered in the cold and reminded him that I had taken lessons in Las Vegas, knew the basics, and could we please get on with it.

Shore squinted at me. "Bullshit. Don't be stupid, Lyle. This is outdoor training, right? Not some Las Vegas indoor party range. And another thing, why are you dressed like that?"

Clothes? He'd seen me naked and was asking me about clothes? What's so wrong with me? Am I not attractive? I was starting to get mad.

"Hey, people in Vegas are serious about their guns too, you know!" It seemed like a safe bet. "And these are the clothes I wear and probably would be wearing if—no, when—I have to use a gun. No one's going to give me a time out to go home and put on warmer clothes, OK?"

"Point taken." His mouth twitched. "Let's move on. First rule of a gunfight is?"

"Have a gun."

"Exactly right. You carry the highest caliber you can handle. Point is you want to stop them, punch a hole. Will you please put that on the table?"

I was fiddling with my gun, watching the way the light reflected off the barrel. Shore held out a hand and I opened the magazine and handed the revolver over to him open.

"Good girl. Now pay attention."

"Not a girl, Shore. You wouldn't call me that if you didn't have all the guns."

He gave me a look and pulled four guns out of the small, canvas bag, laying them out on the picnic table as he made introductions

"This is Mr. John Browning's Model 1911, his most popular and a personal favorite of mine." He admired the gun for a moment as he held it in his hand. "Outstanding. See how slim it is? Very easy to handle, takes .45ACP cartridge, which makes it a powerful gun." It looked like a pretty big gun to me, and I told him so.

"As you will discover once we get started, how well you use a gun is a matter of stance not muscle, Lyle. Moving on."

Next up was a Walther PPK/S. "Elegant little thing," Shore said. "Ian Fleming gave James Bond one of these, and it's been popular ever since. Has a double action and single action trigger right here." I gave Shore a blank look. "Hm. Maybe not."

The third gun looked really lethal. Or maybe it was seeing them in a group, they all looked lethal.

"Sig Sauer P226 takes 9mm cartridges. This is the elite model, Lyle. It could work well for you. It has an ergonomic beavertail grip that fits snug into the hand." Shore smiled. "Very pretty, see this custom wood? The Sig has really fast trigger return, about 60% faster than most, which gives you surgical control for high speed shooting."

Shore took the last gun from the bag and held it out to me after checking to see it was empty. "Those are all autoloaders. I thought you might like to try this revolver, seeing how partial you are to that baby .22 you carry." Shore's attempt at sidearm humor.

"This is a Smith & Wesson model 642CT Revolver, basically a .38 special. It's an *air weight* version, easy to carry in a purse or whatever that thing is. Like yours, it has a snub nose 2" barrel. The trigger is shrouded, concealed, so it won't catch on clothing or anything if you have to access the gun in a hurry. CT stands for Crimson Trace. Here, close the magazine and point the gun at me, go ahead."

It felt a lot heavier than my brassiere-special. I gave the cylinder a twirl before snapping the gun closed and pointed it at Shore. A tiny red dot appeared on his jacket. "Whoa, very cool!" I said, moving the dot around here and there, a big grin on my face.

"Cut that out." Shore took the revolver back. The laser module is in the grip, see? It gives you a psychological advantage with the bad guy."

I was definitely interested in getting my hands on that revolver.

" Only downside is that the sights suck, are practically useless. The CT is more of a belly gun."

"Belly gun?"

"You are standing seven yards or less from your target, in most encounters. You pull the gun and use it without stopping to set up the perfect stance. The gun is reliable and accurate. The laser points the gun."

We worked with the semi-automatics first, so I could adjust to the recoil, Shore explained. More firepower meant more knowledge on my part and developing skills to use side arms that are harder to handle than my .22. He was a good teacher, and Shore's calm focus on the target, the stance, the details of each gun helped me get past self-consciousness about how awkward I was. After getting pushed around by recoil for a while, my grip began to feel more secure and I had an easier time controlling my breathing. It was hard work.

Signaling for a break, I opened the cylinder of the Crimson Trace and caught the shells in my hand. We had picked up spent cartridges as we went from model to model, so the ground at our feet was clean. Shore handed me a bottle of water and gave me a nod of approval. We wore the headsets around our necks and studied the target.

There was a sound of gunfire from the next bunker over, not very loud, a percussive sound punctuated by silence. I felt secure behind the solidity of the mounded walls.

"You're doing a better job holding the revolver steady, Lyle, not jumping the laser around so much."

"Thanks." I rubbed my shoulders, ready to call it a day.

"Remember to be aware of your background when you shoot. I know you're focused on the target, but you need to know what's down range. It helps if you know how far your bullet will go, as well. They're marked for range, you'll figure it out."

Shore refilled the cylinder, handed me the .38 special, and stepped well back behind me.

"Visually explore the situation!" I yelled.

"Damn right!"

We put our headsets back on and I addressed the target.

On the ride back to town, I saw his point about a bigger gun, but I wasn't sure if I was ready for any of the guns I had tried today. He agreed.

"You're still pretty skittish, need more confidence is all. Practice will take care of that. I'll bring you out any time, just let me know."

Hanging out with Shore, shooting all those guns, had improved my mood. I decided Martin Shore was taking higher ground, being a gentleman about seeing me naked. Maybe those uncles of his pushed it from his mind. A good story, I was sticking with it.

22

According to Nola, Angel Bride was not going to be like ordinary wedding fairs with their displays of cakes, limo services, tuxedoes, and gift ideas. It was all about the dress. From her description, it also seemed as if it was going to be a kind of girls-only prom, or rush day at a sorority, which made sense since most of the women who would be attending had known each other since high school. Nola had planned well, marketing the exclusivity, the excitement, the aren't-we-special-ness of it all.

She managed to convince a real estate developer that he could capitalize on the event as a way to promote his houses. So Angel Bride would take place in a model home with a two-story atrium. The house was huge, large enough to accommodate a political fundraiser, complete with marching band. Fortunately, Nola opted for a pair of harpists. They didn't have to wear wings, but white was mandatory.

I showed up early hoping to score a parking space near the house, but with caterer's vans, other assorted vehicles, and valet squad already in place, I didn't have a chance. I checked my watch: 10:01 a.m. Angel Bride started at 11:00. What to do? I considered parking at the house under construction next door, but that looked like a cross-country hike in the snow. On-the-street parking wasn't any nearer. Yielding to the inevitable, I handed the valet kid the key to the Mercedes and a ten.

"I'm leaving early. There's another one of these for showing up quickly."

"Yes, ma'am!" He accepted the bribe cheerfully and drove the car away at a reasonable speed. I wondered briefly where all the cars would go and whether valet staff needed marathon training, but I let the thought go and entered the architectural vision before me.

The day's raffle prize, a red Camaro convertible, was parked near the fountain at the center of the circular drive, an electronic prancing reindeer in front of it, a pile of decorative "presents" tumbled in the back seat and spilling over onto the trunk of the car. It would make some little girl very happy.

Inside, I passed a sitting room that had been transformed into a coat check area. Across the foyer, Crista was checking an array of laptops in what looked like a private office carpeted in dark green. The drapes were closed and the lights dimmed so she could better see the information on the screens. It looked like she was talking to herself. When she caught sight of me, Crista tapped the Bluetooth in her ear and came out of the office to join me.

"Lyle, you're here! Awesome!" she laughed, knowing how I hated bridal shows and the disasters that attended my appearance at same. "Nola will be delighted!" Somehow I doubted it.

"Let me show you around. Here, leave your coat in the office, in case you need to make a quick exit." Just the thought of leaving made me feel better about being at Angel Bride.

Crista's concession to seasonal attire was a shimmering emerald garment trimmed with black lace and jet beading. On anyone else, it would look absurd, like a cucumber gone over to the dark side. She pinned a stray lock of black hair behind her ear so the Bluetooth could fit more securely. Crista checked her smartphone, stuck it in an invisible pocket, and we were on our way.

At the entrance to the atrium we paused to admire what Nola had wrought. The harpists were tuning their instruments directly beside us. Behind them and to the right, the catering crew were setting up in an open kitchen area—young people in black pants, white shirts, string ties, and Santa hats.

"Santa hats?" I asked.

Crista rolled her eyes. "Nola wanted halos and wings, but I persuaded her that they would get in the way, get feathers all over and up people's noses. The hats are a compromise."

Before I could think of a clever comment, Crista started describing the battle plan. "We're serving mimosas and canapés, pretty basic; we don't want food to distract attention, you know? It's what I call a clean focus: first the car raffle, then the dress." She checked to see if I was listening.

"Lean focus, got it." My gaze drifted to the bank of two-story windows at the far end of the atrium.

Crista stepped between my line of vision and the dress and turned my attention to a large room adjoining the atrium, intended as a formal dining space, perhaps. There were two long tables, side by side.

"This is the info room," Crista told me, "part of our agreement with Mr. Hampden. He gets to display brochures, photos of houses, etc. 'Makes sense,' he says. 'You get married, you need a place to live!' I try not to think about him." Crista grimaced.

"Sounds like a charming guy."

"Yeah, right. This table," she changed subject, "is ours. One laptop for appointments at Hyacinth, a second one for our wedding dress catalogue, and," Crista went over to a basket filled with white lace, "these!" She grinned an evil grin, advancing on me.

"No, I won't. You can't make me!"

"Now, Lyle, you do represent Hyacinth, you know."

"How come you're not wearing one?"

"No room." She pointed to her wrist, where the sleeve of her green dress came to a narrow point over the back of her hand. "Besides, it would clash with the black."

"Luce would call that a feeble excuse."

"Luce will be here shortly. She's helping me with the computers in the office. You can complain when she gets here."

I allowed her to tie the lace wristband with its tiny gold angel charm, promising myself to dispose of it as soon as Crista's back was turned. Childish? So what.

"These little angels are the perfect keepsakes. The girls will love them, moms, too. I hope we have enough." Crista wrinkled her brow.

"If you run out, they'll be even more valuable. Maybe I could sell mine!"

"Don't be silly. OK, now you can look." Crista turned me around so I faced the two-story windows, where Angel Bride itself, that white explosion of a wedding gown, stood on a dais, an enormous pair of wings invisibly attached to the window behind it.

Freed from the display window at Hyacinth, the dress seemed even larger than I remembered, an operatic gown. You'd probably have to move pews to get it down the aisle.

Below the dress, Nola O'Neal stood at a podium, talking to a man and woman dressed in black.

"He's the auctioneer," Crista explained, "and she's the photographer. Nola says hi, by the way." Crista tapped her earpiece.

"My god, Crista! Look at all this…" I waved my arms around like a drowning woman, which Nola construed as a bid to catch her attention. She gave me a busy little wave, spoke into her headset, and went back to her discussion, all in the time it took me to finish my sentence."…expense! How can you and Nola hope to make any money?"

Crista smiled serenely at my concern. "Oh, we'll do fine, you'll see, Lyle. See, the way the Angel Bride dress is set up? For a small fee, the photographer will take your photo as The Angel Bride."

"I don't get it."

"It's like those George and Martha Washington cutout. Stick your head here and take a photo."

"Really? People pay for that?"

"Absolutely. And," Crista pointed to a flat screen mounted on a wall to the left of the dais, "we create a slide show of all the Angel Brides! They'll all want to be seen in the dress! It's brilliant!" She clapped her hands in excitement.

"We've lost you, Crista," I said solemnly, "you are now officially a minion of the Dark Side, part of the Borg. I could weep."

"Oh shut up," she replied. "You just need food. Have a canapé. We're also using the slide show for messages from family and friends."

"Messages?" Would the horror never end?

"Come back to the office and I'll show you. I already have a few samples cued up."

The laptop showed a smaller version of the image on the screen in the atrium, currently the jowly smile of Mr. Hampden. Crista tapped a key and the face dissolved into a cheery message, white script on a blue background: *You'll always be my little angel! - Love, Dad.*

"Eeew!" I complained.

"Yes, Lyle, people *will* pay for that." Crista tapped again and a new message appeared, this one was a black font on a background of red: *Bang! You're dead, Lyle Hudson.*

Crista killed the screen immediately and stared at me.

"Maybe I need a bigger gun," I muttered.

"What?" Crista's attention was focused on the computer.

"Here," I pulled a flash drive from the satchel. "Put the slide show on this before you delete the message." She nodded, plugging the drive into a USB port.

Nola appeared at the open door of the office. "What was that last message, Crista? Was that a black font? I didn't catch what it said, dear, but we agreed that all messages would be white, yes?"

"I'm fixing that now, Nola."

"Thank you, dear. Oh, hello, Lyle. I see you're one of us now!" She dangled the angel on the lace wristband girlishly and went back to work. I wanted to shoot myself. The message on the screen told me I wasn't the only one.

"Crista, who could get in here? Who had access to the slide show?"

"Pretty much anyone, sorry Lyle. Once we start the show, it'll just be me and Luce, but right now the room is open." She handed me the flash drive and we stepped out into the foyer where Crista gazed around. "I don't see anyone who doesn't belong here."

A humming noise was growing louder outside the front door. Crista stepped back into the office area, talking quietly into her headset. Harpists started playing, the door opened, and I looked for a nice wall to hug up against.

23

For an onslaught it was disappointing. No pushing, no pandemonium, nada. I opted to keep my place by the wall and fiddled with my cell phone as the stream of well-behaved women glided by in their perfumed air of entitlement. A cell phone confers instant invisibility; people avert their eyes. I wonder why that is, whether it's respect for privacy, maybe an assumption that they know what you're doing, or perhaps it's relief that what's in your hand is a phone and not a gun.

Conversations rose and fell around me, occasional lulls filled with harp music. Girls lined up for photos with the Angel Bride dress, wings, pom poms, and all. Soon, slides began to appear on the Jumbotron, along with affectionate messages of hopes for the future. It made me want to smack somebody.

I kept an eye on the messages. Who was threatening me? How did they know I'd even be here? Maybe it was a prank of opportunity. Whoever it was had to be on site to have access to Crista's computer. Maybe I should write a message of my own. I glanced into the office where Crista and Luce were hard at work. Not a chance. Truth be told, I wouldn't want to make Nola O'Neal unhappy, she was scary enough as it was. What kind of evil genius comes up with an idea like Angel Bride? I shuddered.

Catching sight of Irene Worth at the coat check with two beaming Lambda Chi's, I put the phone away and went to greet her.

Rosy-cheeked and eyes shining, Irene was the picture of happiness. I caught a glimpse of the young girl she must have been when the L&L's and Vern knew her as Irene Dalhoudie.

We air-kissed, the customary greeting at events such as this, and Irene smiled beatifically.

"Oh, Lyle, this is so wonderful! Thank you so much for inviting me!"

Before I could reply the sorority sisters squealed and grabbed their Reenie and whisked her away. I felt oddly bereft.

Angel Bride was now in full swing. Nola's well-timed announcements sculpted the excitement in the room, reminding women about the car raffle, the info tables, Hyacinth appointment books, and the time left for posting messages and having photos taken with the dress, dress, dress.

The place was full but not overcrowded. I spotted familiar faces in the crowd, people I'd seen at the coffee shop or at Hyacinth. I recognized the minister's wife with what looked like a bunch of girls from a youth group. Andressa waved at me across the atrium, and I waved back, wondering about her computer skills.

For the car raffle, a little girl in full angel regalia hopped over to the podium and presented Nola with a box wrapped to look like a present. Nola removed the lid and invited the 'little angel' to reach in and grab a ticket. The queasy feeling I experienced reminded me of eating too much maple sugar candy as a child.

The room hushed and Nola read the number of the winning ticket. After a pause, a stout woman in a Santa hat waved her ticket over her head and made her way forward. Two teenage girls followed her, whooping and cheering, "Go, Mom!" It looked like borrowing mom's car was soon going to be a lot more fun.

I ducked out when the Angel Bride auction began, knowing there would be a mass exodus once the victor claimed her gown. Tears would be shed, but there were photos to post online, stories to tell, and wedding dreams for the future.

The valet guy sprinted off to retrieve the Benz and I enjoyed the silence of the empty driveway. A flurry of movement caught my eye and I turned toward the red convertible.

A disheveled man in a grimy Santa hat sat up in the back seat and began stuffing presents into a black trash bag. I *visually explored* the situation, fumbled with the buttons on my blouse, and drew the .22 from the bra holster. I held it straight down, as trained.

"Hey, Santa the presents are fake. Empty boxes, get it?" Just trying to be helpful.

A couple of boxes went flying and Santa pulled a rather large gun on me. "Oh yeah? Then why are they wrapped?" He waved the gun around erratically.

"It's a display, like lawn ornaments."

"This is a car, not an ornament, lady."

"Are you stoned?" Nobody could be that stupid. "Hey, what is that, a .45?"

"I don't know. It's heavy, OK? A real gun!"

He pointed the gun at me and I shot him. In the arm, apparently. I was relieved. He dropped the gun and fell back in the car, grabbing his arm and yowling.

"OW! That hurts! What did you shoot me for? It wasn't loaded! Ow! Ow!"

I kept my gun on him and went over and picked up what turned out to be a M1911 .45 automatic pistol. I wouldn't have known what it was if I hadn't seen one the other day. I stowed the .22 and buttoned the blouse and checked Santa's magazine. Full clip. The idiot could have hurt someone.

The valet kid came back as I was calling the police. I handed him the ten I promised him and asked him to move the Mercedes off to the side. I wouldn't be leaving just yet.

"Um, ma'am?" He handed the bill back to me and pointed to the Benz, where angry key scratches ran along the driver's side of the car. "I can't take your money."

"Are the tires OK? No dead animals? We're fine." I gave the kid the ten. "Keep an eye on Santa for me?" I knew I had some serious 'splainin to do. I also planned to get a bigger gun.

I didn't hear the door to the show house open and close behind me, but I did hear high heels click down granite steps and crunch across the gravel drive. Dressed in a heather green blazer, white t-neck sweater, and gray wool slacks, Greta Danielson looked great. She did not, however, look happy.

"Hey, Greta, you look…"

"*Supposed* to be off duty. What is going on here?"

"What are you doing here?" Not a cop car in sight. I put the phone back in the satchel.

"Don't look so surprised. Black people have weddings, too. I'm here with Danielle, my brother's girl."

As she spoke, Greta took in the scene—sprawled packages, valet kid doing his best to calm the unhappy man in the back seat of the Camaro. He didn't seem to be bleeding very much at all.

"You *shot* him?" Her eyes blazed at me like pale green flames.

"Self-defense! He pointed this at me." I waved the
.45 by its barrel. "I shot first, is all. Barely winged him.
His gun is way bigger than mine. I could be dead,
Greta!" I looked at the full clip of bullets I held in my
other hand. Crazy. "And he keyed my $175,000
Mercedes!"

Greta wasn't buying it. "Give those to me." She
snatched the gun and cartridges from my hands. "There
are so many prints on this now, we'll be lucky to find
one that belongs to your friend here." With no evidence
bag, she stuck the gun and the clip in her blazer
pockets.

"You stay right there. I'm calling an ambulance."

As Greta stepped away from me, the wounded man
called out, "Hey! Where's my gun? Give me my gun
back or I'll sue your ass!"

That was helpful of him, I thought. Probably
wouldn't be much suing going on, maybe a plea bargain.
He was not one of heaven's brighter angels.

After the EMT's patched him up, Santa was taken
away in a squad car. Greta escorted me to the Mercedes,
scolding and warning me all the way. I had ruined her
day off, she was going to have to go back into that ugly-
assed house full of crazy people, find her niece, and pray
the girl had not been brainwashed. She, Greta, was well
aware of Nola's powers when it came to wedding gowns.

"Danielle is only seventeen, no way we are gonna
let her start planning any damn wedding." She paused
and gave me a look. "So, you making friends here,
Lyle?"

We had reached the car with its scratched paint. I
told Greta about the power point threat. The vandalism
she could see for herself. I was pretty sure the two were
related, same day, same place.

"Could be," Greta said. "How many people can you make angry enough to shoot at you and do stuff like this? I mean, do you have a goal, a certain number in mind? You are a menace, Lyle. We need a place for people like you, like a police hostel, where we could put you and keep you when we can't charge you with anything other than being a major pain in the ass."

She touched one of the gouges on the left front quarter panel. "Looks expensive. Might be it will slow you down and keep you from snooping around."

"Greta, I did not want to be here today. Angel Bride and me, really? I was not snooping!"

"Well, looks like somebody thinks you're up to something. Go home. Watch your back."

"Thanks, I will. Good luck with your niece."

She rolled her eyes and walked back up the steps to the show house, the gold heels on her black stilettos catching the light. One stylish woman, our Greta.

24

The levee was deserted, a perfect place for solitary brooding. During the warmer months, the path along its length was full of joggers, dog walkers, strollers, and kids on bikes. Trampled snow indicated foot traffic, but I had the levee to myself. Bundled in black coat and wool beret, I turned my back to the wind and watched the Kansas River below me, ice-crusted along both banks, muddy and slow moving. I remembered seeing foxes out here, and deer in the woods to the east. Just a few blocks from downtown Lawrence, the place was a haven of quiet, a welcome contrast to Angel Bride.

I had just shot a person for the first time in my life. I felt queasy, guilty, and ill at ease, regardless of what I told Greta. I wondered what made me so quick to shoot that man. A gust of wind blew along the rocks, making me shiver.

I was pretty sure that idiot Santa was unrelated to the bang-you're-dead slide, but was the slide connected to the corn maze? If so, it seemed harmless by comparison with blowing out a window and shooting at me. Maybe I wasn't a trigger-happy maniac, maybe I was merely paranoid.

The levee wasn't much fun without Glory. I scanned the bare trees along the river, hoping to catch sight of an eagle. The gray sky and gray trees felt ominous. The afternoon was emptying out and growing dark. It felt like snow was on the way.

Back at the car, I surveyed the scratches, which appeared only on the driver's side, aimed at the driver more than the car. A Mercedes CL600 is a thing of beauty. The car was starting to feel like bad luck, though. Gamblers tend to be superstitious people, and although I was not playing cards at the moment I was susceptible. At one time I was convinced that the Infiniti I'd won in a poker game was the only car for me. It had ended up in a chop shop.

At home, I put the Benz in the garage. Hiding scars, Lyle? Nah—more like not inviting trouble. Trouble had a number of different faces. Mac would have a fit and so would Shore. One would want to lock me up; the other would make me get an Uzi. Neither prospect appealed.

Glory danced around me as I entered the kitchen. After a brief foray outside for biological relief, she was back at it, wagging her entire rear end in delight. I rewarded her with a dried chicken strip and walked through the house to hang my coat in the hall. It was so quiet that I could hear Glory crunching her treat at the other end of the house. The place felt empty.

In my mind, it was *the* house, not Louise's house. There was more me here now. The library was still my favorite room, with its leather couch and chairs, Native American rugs, bookshelves and fireplace.

"Anything going on, Glory?" The dog ran to the stairs and pointed upstairs. When I gave her the OK, she ran ahead of me, making a rumbling noise on the carpeting, as if she had twenty-six legs.

I had to call her away from Caitlin's door, where the dog tried to inhale whatever was on the other side. A small, dark paw whipped out at her, Caitlin's stray, no doubt.

I shut my door to keep Glory with me and sat on the bed and pulled out my cell. Where the hell was Chas? I hadn't heard from him in forever. No messages. *I shot Santa. Who's a bad girl?* If that text didn't get him, he'd have to be abducted by aliens. I plugged the phone into the charger and stuck the *.22* in the back of my pants, for a change. I might have to shoot a rat. The thought made me smile.

The spacious, bright room had been Louise's, but a coat of pale yellow paint, the addition of a sitting area and chairs declared new occupancy. I was not ready to call the room mine yet, but I was comfortable in the space and only heard my mother's voice on rare occasions.

Glory dived under the bed, leaving her hind legs peeking out. Figuring I wasn't going to go off and leave any time soon, she took the opportunity for a quick nap. A contented groan from under the bed confirmed my conclusion.

I pulled presents out from various drawers and shelves in the closet and set them on the bed to be wrapped. Scissors and tape came out of the desk. No wrapping paper. Crap. No ribbons, bows, or tags. I groaned, making the dog's legs twitch. I was in no mood to go out and be around people of any sort. I raked my hands through my hair, cursing and mumbling, trying to think.

Lenore answered on the first ring, which told me that Loretta was not around. Loretta prided herself on beating her twin to the phone. She'd come running in from another room and Lenore would stand back and let her pass, like getting out of the way of a freight train.

"No, it's just me today," Lenore said. "I'm finishing up orders for festive wear, last minute jingle bells, if you know what I mean," she laughed. "I have no idea where Loretta and Vern are. They're plotting something, I can feel it. Why, I can't remember the last time those two spent so much time together. They're acting like a couple of old married people!"

We pondered the mystery. It was usually the L&L's who were out and about together and Vern the one left answering the phone. I was sure we would find out what was up, eventually.

"I remember you always had a truckload of wrapping paper, Lenore. Could I borrow some?"

"Borrow? Like I'll get it back?" she teased.

"Well, in one case, yes. On your present. So pick the paper you like best!"

"That way I'll know what to look for under the tree!"

I offered to drive over but Lenore insisted on bringing the Christmas wrap to me, saying that she needed to get away from pet wear for a while.

Lenore arrived with shopping bags full of bows and ribbon, rolls of giftwrap in her arms. I helped her in and she dropped everything on the floor and gave me a vigorous hug. No air kissing for Hudsons. Lenore took a minute to greet Glory, commenting on how much Louise had loved the dog.

"I know you don't like to hear how much you remind people of your mother, Lyle, but sometimes it's quite startling—this," she gestured to the last minute supplies, "and your love for this sweet creature." She took me by both arms to forestall a protest. "Try not to take it personally, dear, it's merely an observation."

Standing eye-to-eye like that, I was struck by Lenore's individuality, her difference from her twin. Details of size and fluffy white hair—they both favored bouncy ponytails—facial features, and gray-green Hudson eyes were indeed identical, but where Loretta was boisterous, Lenore was gentle and reserved. Unless her passion for justice was aroused. She practically turned into a vigilante. I suspected that Lenore had as much a likeness to her sister Louise as I did.

We made mugs of tea and Lenore suggested we take them to the front parlor. She gave the sleigh bells on the newel post a shake, startling Glory with the loud noise. We sat in the large chintz chairs and Lenore admired the reconstituted tree as I dug into the bags of ribbons and bows.

"Why, the room is none the worse for wear, is it?" Lenore observed.

"Other than the bullet holes, you mean?" I rummaged around. "What paper do you want on your present?"

"Which do you think?" She wasn't going to make it easy for me. I smelled a test.

"I'm thinking this dark green with holly berries."

"Exactly right." Lenore sipped her tea, smiling into the mug.

"You are so bad," I scolded her. "If I said the one with silver Noels, you'd have said that was the right one!"

"Yes, dear, I would."

"You may be quiet, aunt, but you are just as sneaky as the rest of them."

"Thank you, Lyle."

"Why would you do that, say yes to whatever I chose?"

"You're an intelligent woman, Lyle, most times, anyway. You'll figure it out."

Glory trotted into the room, looking for a warm lap for her bony little self. She really was a tad too large to fit comfortably, but the chair was large, so Lenore invited the dog up and watched as Glory arranged herself in the smallest curl a happy dog could manage.

Lenore used the distraction to introduce a typical change of topic.

"So," she said brightly, "How was Angel Bride? Nola and Crista worked so hard. I do hope they will be pleased."

I told her most of it, omitting the threat. Lenore laughed at my cynical descriptions of angelic brideliness. She applauded the middle-aged woman who won the red Camaro convertible.

'Who won the dress?" she asked.

"I didn't stick around for the dress auction, Lenore. I went outside and shot Santa instead. I'm pretty sure Greta Danielson is mad at me."

"You took a gun to a bridal reception, Lyle?" Like she must have misheard me. "And then you used it?" She petted Glory's head but kept her eyes on mine, possibly examining me for signs of early onset dementia.

"It wasn't like it was a wedding," I explained, "And Santa had a great big gun, huge compared to mine." I held my hands out, as if I was measuring a good size fish. "It was self-defense, Greta agreed." Greta was pissed off about it, but I chose not to mention that detail.

"Hm. And are you wearing it now because you think I might draw on you, too?" she asked sweetly.

I touched the gun in my waistband, as if surprised to find it there. "I couldn't decide where to put it," I grumbled.

"Oh, Lyle!" Lenore laughed, "That has to sound lame, even to you!"

I stashed the .22 under the chintz-covered chair, but Lenore gave me one of her calm, cool stares and waited me out. Trying not to sulk, I stomped into the hall and stowed it in my blue satchel.

"Minimally better than on your person, I suppose. But that is a place an adult would keep it," she said a bit tartly.

Reassured by my minimal display of adult behavior, Lenore informed me that she had to get back to work on the pet wear. She shooed Glory off her lap with gentle apologies.

Seeing Lenore on her way with a hug and warm thanks for the Christmas wrappings, I closed and locked the door, retrieved the gun from the satchel and took it and a load of stuff upstairs. As was her custom, Glory stopped by Caitlin's door and inhaled. It must be a dog's version of a candy store window, I thought.

Sitting amid the clutter of wrapped, half-wrapped, and unwrapped presents strewn across the bed, I realized that wrapping presents was a distraction. I wasn't doing anything productive, except maybe keeping Glory company while she napped underneath the bed. I stared out the window at the snow, which looked pretty half-hearted itself.

The sudden marimba tone from the cell confused me for a moment, and I had to dive into the mess of tissue paper, wrapping, and bows to find it. I answered without checking caller ID.

"Chas! Oh, Crista. Hi, how did it go?"

"Could you come back to the show house, Lyle? There's someone you need to talk to." Her voice sounded tense.

"Crista," I started to protest but she interrupted me.

"It's important. About that ... message."

No more argument from me. "I'm on my way."

I threw the phone and the gun in the satchel, threw Glory in the car, and hotfooted it back to bride-to-be land.

With the reindeer and the red convertible gone, I almost missed it. Empty house, no valet. Inside, the huge house was almost deserted, the atrium a vaulting dim space where you could watch the snow fall two stories to the ground. Glory stood still beside me, not interested in sniffing around. No cool smells here.

We turned into the office area to find Crista snapping laptop covers closed and piling power cables into a large cardboard box. I knocked on the doorframe.

"Hi, where's Nola? Are you the only one here?"

"Hi." Crista stepped around the box and came over to greet the dog. "She's at Hyacinth with the appointment books, in absolute Angel heaven. Come in and shut the door." Was it my imagination or did Crista sound a lot like my aunts? Clearly, she'd been spending too much time with Luce.

I followed instructions and turned to find a red-eyed, tearful young woman dressed in black and white catering garb. She sat on a folding chair against the wall, wringing a damp tissue in her hands.

"This is Nicole, she has something to tell you," Crista said in a stern tone.

The girl looked up at me, lower lip trembling. "Did you really shoot Santa? You're not going to shoot me, are you?"

"Santa pulled a gun on me, Nicole, and he tried to steal presents." I sat down on the edge of a table and tried to look harmless. Old poker trick. Throw in a cute white dog and it works even better. "Now, whatever you tell me, I won't shoot you. Promise."

"Well…" she looked at Crista and hesitated.

"I asked around," Crista said, "and a few people had seen Nicole, here, at the computers, messing around while I was out of the room."

"It was a joke, OK! He gave me fifty bucks to insert a slide in the loop, said it would make you laugh," Nicole said.

"He who?" I asked.

"Your age? Maybe he was older? I don't know. He was so friendly, like somebody's uncle, maybe. I thought this Lyle person was one of the brides-to-be, like, young." She shrugged.

"Details, please, Nicole. What did he look like?" The girl stared at me blankly. Clearly, all old people looked alike. It took a fair bit of prodding to get her to remember anything specific. She said he was average height, not heavy, and he wore a Santa hat, so she couldn't tell if he had hair or was bald. He looked neat and clean, she said, like clothes were important, and he wore one of those school rings on his right hand. OK, that was interesting.

"Crista, who knew about the slide show?"

"It was common knowledge. We all thought it was a cool idea and we talked about it a lot. News would've got around quickly, Lyle. It was a major selling point for the reception: 'Be an Angel Bride!' that kind of thing."

"OK. We'll think about who might have told who. Look, Nicole," I turned back to the unhappy caterer. "We're not—I'm not—mad at you, OK? The gun stays in the purse." I smiled thinly. "Just, don't be so trusting when people tell you to do things you're not sure of, especially when you don't know them. Make good choices." Crap. I sounded like my mom.

After a sadder but wiser Nicole departed, I helped Crista finish packing computer gear. The jowly real estate agent showed up to turn out lights and lock up, and we toted boxes to Crista's VW bug and loaded it up. I put Glory in the Benz and started the engine so the dog would have a warm seat.

Crista quickly brushed snow from her windshield and jumped into the car. She rolled down the window and yawned.

"Thanks for finding Nicole, Crista. I have a pretty good idea who the prankster is."

She held up a hand and stifled another yawn. "Don't want to know. Just be careful and watch out for Nola. She is relieved that the shooting didn't interrupt Angel Bride, but it 'tarnished the beauty of the day' she said."

"Valet guy talked, did he?"

"Most likely. I'd watch out for Greta Danielson, too. She and Nola had their heads together after the show. It was a toss up which one would melt down first." Crista gave a tired smile.

"My money's on Nola," I said, "but I bet it was a close call."

I stepped back from the tiny car and watched as Crista drove off in the falling snow, her taillights winking down the hill and into the night.

25

"Forgot your coat, didn't I," I said to Glory as we drove away from real estate heaven. "That doesn't mean we have to go right home, right?" Glory liked it when I talked to her. She'd sit right up and look at me, cocking her head, waiting avidly for the words *ball* or *treat.* "Home is boring," I told her. "Let's go downtown and see what's happening." The dog yawned and looked out the windshield. I took that as a yes. It was dark, but the night was early, and the car had warm seats. If it was snowing, so what? The Mercedes laughed at snow.

The twinkling light along Mass Street illuminated the falling snow, making halos of light in the darkness. People were picking their way along the sidewalk, ducking into coffee shops and bars, brushing snow off windshields, keeping their heads down. Parking spaces were opening up in each block, which was unusual, even with the snow. I was tempted to pull over and park just because I could.

We stopped to let a car back out of a spot ahead of us, when a nondescript door opened and closed on the right. A drift of music, possibly jazz, hung in the air before it was muffled by the closed door. This was not a place I knew, and there was no sign to tell me what it was. A neon sign in an upstairs window declared Live Music.

"We're curious, aren't we, Glory?"

I pulled into the spot vacated by the departing car and sat there looking hard at the dog. Melting snow drizzled down the windshield in streams of neon red.

"OK, we'll give it a try. It's not like we haven't been kicked out of bars before, right, girl?" Glory wagged her tail, indicating that it was no big deal. She was game.

Upstairs, the club was dimly lit and practically empty. The sound system was playing Melody Gardot, "Worrisome Heart," a favorite of mine. A man with no baggage who loves you as you are? That's my kind of song.

Glory and I waked over to the bar, and I waited for the bartender to walk over before I took a seat. A young (well everyone looks young to me these days) blonde with worldly eyes, a velvet choker around her neck and tats up both arms, she put all her curiosity into one word.

"Yeah?"

"I'm stopping in for a drink on my way home, and didn't want to leave Glory here alone in the car. Is it OK?"

She walked around the bar and looked down at the dog, who looked up hopefully.

"She bite?"

"No, but I do. A scotch might calm me down." I grinned at her.

"What kind of scotch?" she dead-panned back.

"Johnnie Walker Black, rocks." She walked back around and set a glass in front of me, covering the ice with a generous pour. "That looks like a double," I said.

"Well," she gave me a lazy smile. "You are drinking for two." She glanced at Glory.

"Good one," I acknowledged.

Glory sat peacefully by my bar stool, I sipped the scotch and looked around. The place was small and spare, clearly emphasizing space for music, small though it may be, no menu to speak of. They had to serve food to keep a liquor license, but you wouldn't go there for the best burger in town.

"This was a jazz club, right?" I was guessing, just making friendly conversation with the nice bar tender.

"Still is," she said. "New owner. He's bringing in folk music, too, that way old music? I wasn't sure about it at first, but the bands are good, small combos, you know?" I nodded as if I had a clue. "We have a poetry slam, too." No cynical mocking there, she was thinking about it. "What do you think about that?" she asked.

"I prefer traditional poetry readings, myself. Slams are competitive, maybe more spontaneous, and I can see how people would like that, but I think poetry should convey a deeper experience, you know what I mean?"

"Yeah, I do." She poured herself a shot and took a delicate sip. "It's intense. Poetry. Take Baudelaire, the *Fleurs du Mal*? It's like he wrote that stuff in blood." Heady thinking for a young person.

"Exactly. I used to feel that way about Blake, *The Proverbs of Hell*? 'The road of excess leads to the palace of wisdom,' catnip, isn't it?"

" 'The nakedness of woman is the work of God'," the bartender quoted.

"I don't remember that one."

She laughed and headed off to talk to a guy with a bass fiddle shaking snow out of his hair.

My eyes adjusted to the dim light, and I noted the slight buzz of scotch on an empty stomach. Curiosity satisfied, I would finish my drink and take Glory home. Behind me, a jumble of tables was grouped around a small space where a couple of young men unpacked instruments and greeted the kid with the bass. There was no backstage area to speak of, the scene was intimate and friendly. I thought of bringing Mac here sometime.

"Excuse me," a voice right beside me was trying to get the bartender's attention. I looked over and past him. He had a whole array of barstools to choose from. I didn't appreciate somebody moving into my space.

The man unwrapped his scarf, rubbed his hands together and sighed loudly as he realized the bar tender was ignoring him.

"Pardon me," he said, leaning toward me, "but don't I know you?" He was not an original thinker.

"You must think so, or you wouldn't be sitting in my lap this way," I said to my scotch glass, refusing to make eye contact.

"So sorry." He scooted his stool back a whole half inch. "It's so dark in here. I didn't mean to…"

I cut him off. "No."

"Beg pardon?"

"No, you don't know me. I'm leaving now. You stay here." I picked up my drink and satchel and took a step down the bar. The man reached out a hand and touched my elbow. He smiled blandly at my hostile stare, completely missing Glory's preliminary growl.

"I'm sure we've met. You're that friend of Andressa Keach's, yes? Linda something?"

I leaned down briefly to calm Glory. "Lyle." I hated it when people called me Linda. The man was a creep.

"Ah, yes. Lyle Hudson. Richard Cassaday. How do you do." He held out his hand and smiled. Some people should avoid smiling. He was one of them. I declined the hand. I recalled Andressa's aversion, his pompous superiority in the bookstore, Caitlin's description of dog abuse. Yeah, he was a charmer.

One of the musicians was picking out a melody on a mandolin, talking with his friends as he played. They laughed and encouraged him to 'play something real, man'.

Cassaday stood and tried what he thought was an ingratiating smile. "Please, do join me for a drink?"

"Why, what do you want?"

"Well..." he lowered his voice even though it was just the two of us at the bar. "It's Andressa, you see. I'm worried about her."

Women are suckers for friendship issues, as Cassaday assumed. I was not taking the bait. I swallowed the rest of my drink and the ice rattled as I slammed the glass on the bar.

"Andressa's a big girl. She's fine. I'll tell her you were asking after her." Yeah, that'd give her the creeps.

Taking Glory's leash, I brushed by the man and headed for the door. I took a couple of steps and stopped, turning to face him.

"Wait," I said in a voice loud enough to be heard across the small room. "You're Cassaday the professor, right? You worked with that guy Addison. He was murdered, wasn't he? I heard you two didn't get along. Want to talk about that, Dick? Or would you rather talk about a death threat masquerading as a prank? Didn't think so."

I turned my back on his astonished face and left, hoping I wouldn't trip over a chair and mar my dramatic exit.

Glory and I hurried through the snow to the car. What was he doing in that club in the first place? It didn't seem his style. Had he seen me go in with the dog? Was I being followed? If so, it was a cheeky move to talk to me. Arrogant bastard. And I was a total idiot, having just told him what I knew.

Greta Danielson's voice scolded me all the way home. The snow in the back yard was up to Glory's shoulders, and she was not happy, even in her warm coat. I shoveled a path for her from the steps to the shrubs by the garage, where there was a tiny dry space for her to use. This was prime opossum territory, but the dog just needed to get out, do her business and get back. Practical Glory.

I piled our wet things by the kitchen door and locked it. The snow was still falling hard. I watched the flakes passing through the light shed by the kitchen window and picked at the plate of scrambled eggs and toast I'd made myself for supper. I twirled the .22 on the table. I looked at my cell phone.

Glory settled herself at my feet under the table and sighed her full tummy sigh. Occasional flecks of snow made minute taps against the window, caught in sudden drafts. Twirled the gun. Stared at the cell phone.

"Speak."

"The Crimson Trace and a box of cartridges?"

"Can do. When?"

"Tomorrow. How much?"

"It's got a customized grip. Eight hundred. A good price."

"No problem."

"Everything OK?"

"Yeah. The Taurus here will get me through the night."

"You get to keep it, you know," Shore chuckled.

"I guess."

"Buck up, Lyle. See you tomorrow. Oh nine hundred?"

"Fine. We'll have coffee."

"Outstanding. Keep your shirt on." He hung up.

"Keep my what? Oh. Ha, ha." Guess he did notice.

It had been a long day, a long couple of days, and I was feeling burnt out. I took the phone, the gun, and the dog and retreated to the bedroom. In PJ bottoms, and t-shirt, hairbrush in hand, I came out of the bathroom expecting to find Glory asleep on the bed. No dented pillow, no dog under the bed either.

The bedroom door was open, the hall was dark. I took the .22 out of its holster and headed for the door just as Caitlin and Glory showed up.

"Am I in trouble?" Caitlin asked, nodding at the snub-nosed revolver in my hand.

"This? I thought I might go on a rat hunt. They're nocturnal creatures."

"No need. Miss B. is on track with her food these days. Here, this came for you." Caitlin handed me a small parcel, which freed up her hand to scratch the ears of the small cat she carried.

"Thanks, Caitlin. Was Glory bothering you?"

"Nah, she likes to stop by and sniff under the door. Cat here threw a fit tonight, so I thought I'd walk her back."

"Cat? The cat's name is Cat? That doesn't sound like you, Caitlin."

"Well," Caitlin came over so I could take a closer look at the creature. "I thought of calling him Spit." The cat spat at me to demonstrate. "But running around calling, 'Spit! Spit!' when I can't find him?" Caitlin snorted.

"Yeah, I know. People always respond when I'm looking for Glory."

"Hallelujah!" Caitlin said.

"Exactly. Spit suits him, though. Any other candidates?"

"I like Hecuba, Heck for short, you know, the witch? But Cat's a boy." She turned the cat over in her arms and rubbed its belly. Extremely loud purring ensued. B-52? Wood chipper? I kept my thoughts to myself.

"I'll just have to keep thinking," Caitlin said.

"Sounds like a plan. Good night, Caitlin."

"Night, Lyle. C'mon, Cat."

They left, I closed the door, and looked for Glory, whose hind legs peeked out from under the bed. I invited her up, but Glory grumped at me, preferring not to be disturbed. The box addressed to me was about the size of a box of checks, slightly longer. Inside, I found a velvet case and a gift card.

"Oh, Glory," I said to the dog, "I don't have a good feeling about this." I lifted out the gift case and opened it slowly. Inside, nestled on white satin, lay a strand of pearls.

"Shit."

I closed the case and opened the card. *Come to the Prom with me? ~ Chas.*

"Shit, shit, shit."

Come to the Prom was a request that could not be refused. The pearls were overkill. I texted Chas: *When is the Prom, Chas? Where are you?* Then I rummaged around in the medicine cabinet until I found a sleep aid that wasn't past its expiration date. I got back into bed, shut the .22 in the bedside table, and turned off the light. I flounced and flopped under the comforter, cursing.

"Prom. Shit! Just shoot me!"

Glory grumped in response.

I had to leave. Now.

26

"You're where?"

"Vegas. It's Chas. I have to find him, Mac."

"Now? You have to find him *now*?"

"I have to find him yesterday. It's the Prom. He's in trouble."

Mac sighed. "What Prom? Lyle, you're not making sense."

"I am, I just don't have time to explain it."

Silence. He was waiting for the explanation.

"Look, Mac, I'm calling you first." Maybe even only, I thought. So many explanations. It'd take forever to go through it with everyone. "Because I don't want to mess up what we have, don't want you to hear it from someone else."

"Hear what? What do we have, Lyle?" The man sounded exasperated. "And you just leave, just dump everybody. Where is Glory in all of this? You left your dog, too, didn't you?" OK, Mac was beyond exasperated and into full blown mad, working toward righteous indignation. I didn't know he could go there. Maybe he was human, after all. Unfortunately, I had no time for human, not time to talk him down.

"I understand that you are upset with me. I get it and I'm sorry, but I don't have time to explain. Glory's fine. Caitlin's looking after her. I've got to go, bye."

"Whatever." He hung up before I did.

That, I told myself, is why I avoid relationships. They're messy. Feelings get hurt, blame gets flung around like crap in a monkey house. I hated that, hated the demand for explanations. What's the point?

I do not ask people to explain themselves. Explain what—motives, intentions? Like they even know. People lie, and they lie to themselves. It's one of the reasons I like poker. People lie, but the cards are the cards. Truth will be revealed.

I looked out the hotel window and fingered the pearls at my neck. It was morning on the Strip, a cool, bright day. Few taxis at this hour, few pedestrians. Casino workers were already on their shifts, and the tourists were looking for breakfast, waiting for shops to open. Any serious gamblers, I knew, were either finishing marathon all-nighters, or sleeping till noon, sealed in behind lightproof drapery.

Still no reply to my text. Damn you, Chas. You don't invoke the Prom and disappear. I was pretty sure he was here in Las Vegas, the pearls were mailed from here. But which shop? The box was cryptic. I'd have to visit jewelry stores up and down the Strip.

Restless and itching to get moving, I shrugged into the black coat and knotted the pale green silk scarf I'd bought at the Holiday Faire around my throat. The iridescent color highlighted the contrast between my silver hair and the black coat. With the string of pearls, ruby ring and sunglasses, any jewelry store would be glad to see me walk in the door.

The Faire reminded me of the corn maze and the dead Ron Addison. Maybe it was a good thing to be out of town right now, I thought, put the whole thing on the back burner and deal with it later. Maybe by the time I got back to Lawrence, the police would have the case closed. Greta Danielson would be delighted to have me out of the way.

I threw the blue satchel over my shoulder and headed for the door. Damn. I caught sight of myself in a mirror. The bag would have to stay here. It called my whole outfit into question, like seeing a poodle in hiking boots—just wrong.

Dumping the contents of the satchel out on the bed, I groped for pockets and tried to figure out how not to look too lumpy. I could pick up an appropriate purse in one of the Bellagio shops downstairs. The cell was no problem, ditto comb and lipstick. The Taurus .22 was locked safely in a dresser back in Lawrence. The .38 special Shore sold me came with its own holster. Now on my hip, it made a bit of a lump, but not too bad. I stuck the wallet in my right pocket and squeezed the jewelry case in with it. OK, I looked like a rich lady with hips, no big deal.

There was no problem with the gun and airport security. I just completed the paperwork and put it in my checked luggage. I was not a danger to myself or other passengers. As for carrying a gun in Las Vegas, I was home free. I had a local permit for the .22, and as far as the state of Nevada is concerned, a pistol is a pistol. The only thing I had to remember was not to bring a firearm into a casino. But if I wasn't going to risk public exposure carrying it in my bra, I had to have a bigger purse.

Argh! It took me forever to get out of the room and find a shop that had a black purse I could bear to carry. Beaded clutches, palm-sized bags on strings, gold, silver and bronze leather bags made my teeth itch. I settled on a black suede handbag with an articulated bone handle that fit a bit snugly worn over the shoulder, but it would work.

I charged the purse to my room, signed the receipt, and emptied the stuff in my pockets into the handbag. The sales clerk gasped when she caught sight of the gun on my hip.

"I just paid for the bag, right? This is not a stick up."

She nodded tentatively and took a step back.

"But, hey," I added, all friendly, "somebody bothers you, you let me know. My name and room number are right there," I pointed to her copy of the receipt. "You have a good day." I snapped the purse shut and left the shop.

On my way to the street, I passed through the Bellagio's botanical gardens, which were decorated in full seasonal regalia. There were flying reindeer made of whole pecans, a polar bear family made of white carnations, and a 42 ft. fir tree covered in thousands of lights. I toyed with the idea of taking a photo with my phone and sending it to Blake. Maybe later.

Outside, the day was warming up, but not much. I turned left and headed for Caesar's palace and the Forum shops. As I walked, I brooded on Chas and remembered a cold night in San Francisco when the idea of *The Prom* invitation first came up. We were at Chas's place, cuddled under a throw on the couch, watching a DVD of *Carrie*. I hated horror movies, but it was his house, his choice. When we were next door at my apartment, I got to choose—French films, westerns, anything with Clive Owens. Basically, we had one rule: no Nazis.

A cold night in San Francisco meant it was July or August. We were watching *Carrie* and talking about the cruel irony of special dates, which were doomed to go horribly wrong. We drank white wine and shared stories.

"Time to put out? He actually said that?" Chas was aghast. "In a cemetery? Oh, you poor dear!"

"Asshole. He must've asked me out on a dare. I still can't figure it out," I said.

"Well, cara mia, why did you go out with him? And what happened next?" Chas put *Carrie* on mute, the screaming was getting louder.

"Chas, *you'd* have gone out with him, the kid was smoking hot. Can't remember his name, though." I sighed and flicked the rim of the crystal glass with a fingernail, making it ring. Chas loved crystal. I bought my glasses at Target.

"And?" he prompted.

"I pushed his face out of my face, twisted his nose, and got out of the car. He'd never been treated that way, I could tell. He was shocked!" I laughed. "Tried to get me back in the car, said he'd drive me home. I told him to fuck off. Never saw or heard from him again."

"How did you get home?"

"A long walk. It wasn't too bad. It was Lawrence, Kansas, after all. I knew every inch of it and felt pretty safe."

We returned our gaze to the increasingly gory movie and its vision of blood vengeance.

"I'll never ask you to the prom, Chas, promise."

"Oh, but I'd want you to, sweetie. I'd ask you, too."

I laughed. "What?"

"Well, if the shit hits the fan, and the walls are dripping blood," he nodded to the screen, "I'd want to be rescued, wouldn't you?"

So, *Prom* it was—an invocation for special emergencies.

"Panic attacks don't count," Chas stipulated.

"Weight gain? Wrinkles? Bad dates?"

"Them either," Chas said, turning off the DVD at the credits.

"Well, OK." We shook on it.

I'd use the Prom invitation only once and sent Chas a corsage with the message: *In Reno. On a bender. Suicidal, want to help? Come to the Prom with me.* It was ugly. Chas chided me for the double-entendre of the *want to help* part, but I didn't care. It felt like a toss up at the time. And I had told him where to find me.

In one of the Forum shops, I found a salesperson who knew his pearls. Like the other jewelers, he told me what I already knew, that the box did not originate with the necklace. It revealed nothing about where the pearls had come from.

"You're sure they're from Las Vegas?" he asked, examining the pearls through a loupe, holding them gently in cotton-gloved hands.

"Pretty sure. 90%? 95?"

"OK." He paused. "I can think of only two places that would have pearls of this quality." He wrote the names of people to ask at the Grand Canal Shoppes at the Venetian and at Wynn Esplanade. Insisting on helping me into the necklace, he complimented me for not wearing perfume.

"Horrible for pearls. But some people just do not listen."

I thanked him and exited the shop to find *The Fall of Atlantis* going strong—thundering noise, flashing lights, moving statues of gods at war. I made my way past immobilized tourists and headed for the door as quickly as I could. The noise was deafening.

A jostling at my elbow told me someone was trying to get into the fine new handbag on my left elbow. I went down on my left knee, pulling the woman—it turned out to be a woman—off balance and onto the floor. I swiveled on the knee and came around with my right hand and grabbed a hank of well-sprayed hair.

"Bad idea," I said, yanking my purse away.

"Stop! Stop!" she panted. "You're ruining my hair!"

"You OK?" asked a young man in fake Roman armor. "Yeah, you're OK. We don't see that much." He pointed his sword at the squirming woman and told her not to move.

"Women pickpockets?" I suggested, catching my breath and getting back to my feet.

"Take downs. That some kind of Kung Fu?"

"Aikido. Once upon a time. I'm going now, OK? She's all yours."

"OK," said the helpful Roman soldier. "Don't take that into the casino." He gestured to my hip.

"Wouldn't dream of it."

27

The jewelry stores at the Venetian were a wash. No one knew my sales friend's friends, and the story of the pearls didn't interest them; they were all about selling bling. Big bling. The canals confused my sense of direction and seemed small and crowded, like somebody put gondolas in a swimming pool. I escaped back onto the Strip as quickly as I could and headed over to the Paris and a much-needed coffee at a Boulevard café. It was more my kind of kitsch than the canals. There were cobblestone streets, nineteenth century lampposts, and Edith Piaf on the sound system. Behind Piaf, you could hear the incessant gibberish of the slots luring people in with the promise of something for nothing. The lighting was dim, and eternal Paris evening, the eternal present of the casino.

I ordered coffee and a croissant and yawned. I was slipping back into old habits without realizing it. The coffee arrived and I inhaled the croissant like a frog with a butterfly. Not very French of me. The French linger over their food, savoring instead of ingesting it. I shrugged and examined my nails, which were too long. I liked short, businesslike nails at the card table, no distractions. I needed a manicure. I checked the cell for the millionth time, wondering what kind of trouble kept Chas from contacting me.

"I'll be damned if he didn't nail it to the day and minute!"

I looked up to see a short, swarthy man pulling out a chair and seating himself at my table.

"Have a seat."

"Thanks, I will." He had a stocky build, round cheeks, but the smile reminded me of Caitlin's rats.

"Snake food."

"Pardon me?" The small man put both hands on the table. The smile disappeared.

"Did I say that out loud? I apologize. Early onset dementia, or maybe Tourette's."

"You saying I look like snake food?" His beady little eyes got even smaller. One hand moved under the table.

"A gun? Ooh, I'm scared," I sneered at him, comforted by the weight of the .38 special. "So—what— we have a shoot out right here on the streets of Paris? Or would you like to talk about Chas? I hope you're feeding him properly. Chas gets bitchy when he's not fed."

The man gave a raspy, dry laugh and put his hands back on the table, hunching forward.

"Feisty too, just like he said." More rasping.

I put my hands on the table, hunching forward to mirror his pose.

"He? Are you referring to my friend, Charles? Where is he?"

"Sure, why not. Nice ring, by the way."

"Yes, it is." I drank the last of my coffee and stood up. A couple of men in black coats at a table across the boulevard stood up also.

"Sit down, sit down. We ain't finished yet."

"Ain't? Watch a lot of mafia movies, do we? Where's Chas?"

"I'm asking you nicely. Sit down."

I sat, crossing my arms and staring at the man. Across the way the two men also sat, slowly.

"So, here's the deal," my visitor said. "Our mutual friend is into me big time. I can't front him any more money, see, 'cause the idiot pisses it away. Now, I have a reputation to uphold. So, I talk to him about giving up a—oh, let's say—hand. But the kid gets the idea to call in his ringer—that'd be you—to win back the cash for him and cover the vig. My question for you, Ms. Hudson, is—are you in?"

"Call me Lyle. Chas couldn't just call? Why all the smoke and mirrors, the mysterious pearls?"

"They look good on you, Lyle. You should keep them, they could bring you luck." He gave me a brief, ratty smile. "We wanted to be sure you understood the gravity of our friend's situation."

"Mentioning the Prom was enough to make me see that, Mr...."

"Call me Max. Not willing to take Chas at his word, I wanted to see: A) How important he really is to you, B) If you were smart enough to figure it out and hence smart enough to win, and C) To assess your determination, which is impressive. My conclusion is that this could work!"

"So, I'm here to play cards for you?"

"For Chas, sweet pea, for Chas. You win and the kiddo gets to keep his hand. Shake?"

"And if I lose?"

"Now, come on, you don't want to go there. Let's stay positive."

"Play what? When? I haven't touched a deck of cards in a while, you know. I need practice, and I need to see Chas."

"Here, I'll get him on the phone." The little man started patting around his pockets, looking for his cell.

"See. Chas." I pointed two fingers at my eyes and back to him. "Eyes. On."

"OK, OK. Relax. Jeeze." Max signaled Thug One and Thug Two and we walked out to the Strip where a limo was waiting.

"No Hummer?" I asked.

"Old School. You need to remember that." His voice was dead serious.

Chas was housed in a condo near Lake Las Vegas, well away from the casinos. It seemed comfortable enough, but Chas must've been bored out of his mind.

"You all roomies together?" I asked Max.

"Nah. I need to be where the action is, keep an eye on my investments. Our boy is here to keep him out of trouble."

"So, who keeps an eye on Chas?"

"Who do you think?"

"No locks, no minders?"

"Ha! Where's he gonna go?"

I could think of several places, mostly out of the country.

"He's likely to remain intact if he behaves himself," Max observed. Point taken.

Max told his guys to stay with the car and we went in.

"Lyle, you came! Oh, thank you. I'm so sorry," Chas rushed the words, holding on to me.

I hugged him back, relieved and grateful to see he was OK.

"No apologies."

Edgy and thinner than I remembered, Chas was still Chas—blond, green-eyed elegance. He avoided my eyes.

"Chas, look at me. We'll get through this, OK?"

"Yeah, yeah, yeah. Very nice," Max interrupted. "Let's get on with it. You," he said to Chas, "owe me 70K"

"What? It was 50!" Chas protested.

"Time marches on. 70K."

"You," he said to me, "have two days, then I start taking fingers."

"Oh, please. Cut the crap, Max. I can't do it in two days. You want to set me up to lose, or do you want the money? Your choice."

"OK, wiseass, what do you want?"

"Four, maybe five days. I need practice."

"No can do, Lyle. Reputation, remember?"

"Old School, got it. It has to be four days, Max. I need to move around, so the casinos won't mark me. They are not charitable institutions, you know." Casinos don't really make money from poker, they charge for time and space. I was betting Max didn't know that. The real moneymakers are the slots.

"You got three days. The best I can do. Time's up." He checked his Rolex. "Let's go."

"Answer the damn phone," I said to Chas.

"Love you, too."

We hugged. I left with Max.

28

Max dropped me off at the Bellagio, saying he'd be in touch.

"You can follow me around, whatever, Max, just don't let me see you—or any of your minions."

"What's a minion?"

"Never mind. You catch my eye, you make me anxious. That's a distraction. You interfere with my play. You get in my way, all bets are off."

"Oh, yeah?" He started to bluster, but I cut him off.

"Don't threaten me with Chas, Max. In fact, do not threaten me, period. I've agreed to play, that's the deal. You put a kink in my concentration, that's on you. Clear?"

He gave a rodent-like chuckle. "One tough lady."

"I can be. If I were you I'd want me to stay that way." We parted with mutual growls.

Back in my room, I played some online practice rounds of Texas no limit hold 'em. Virtual poker doesn't really work for me, even when I'm winning. It's more math and less psychology. Even so, it helped me reconnect with a few basic truths about poker. With Texas hold 'em, position (where you sit in relation to the dealer) is huge. To the dealer's left, out of position, like most players, I did better playing tight and slow. Seated to the dealer's right, other players must act before you do. The casino employee who does the actual dealing is often called the croupier. Unlike

Blackjack, the Hold 'em dealer never plays. He sits in one place and acts for everyone as the location of the dealer button, a round disk, moves clock-wise around the table, one place to the left with every hand. To me the actual physical location at the oval table was just as important. I like to sit to the right of the croupier, on the curve, where I have a better view of the other players. For a lot of players the game is spent calculating the odds of winning. They can never account for a bad beat. Seated on the curve I had more info to go on (even without tells and facial tics) and could play a looser, more aggressive hand. I felt myself relax as the logic and flow of the game came back to me and ended up with a tidy five hundred playing at an off-shore site.

I took a bath and a nap and called Chas when I woke up. There were a couple of questions about our predicament I was dying to ask. My guess was Love led Chas astray. I was right.

"He is such a Gemini! Impulsive and stubborn once he gets an idea in his head," Chas explained.

"And the idea was..." I finished the question in my head—lose a lot of money and put your life at risk?

"His idea was let's go be Lyle!"

"BE me? You're kidding, right?"

"What can I say? You're a legend in certain circles."

"And if a middle-aged woman can do it, so can a twenty-something hottie?" I asked acidly.

"Something like that," Chas sighed. "I didn't date him for his brains, I'm ashamed to say."

"And Love made you toss yours right out the window. No blame, Chas, merely an observation."

""You've been spending a lot of time with your aunts, haven't you." He really was quite clever.

"Don't change the subject. How could you lose so much?"

"I WAS DRUNK! How do you think?"

"And how did Max, or whoever the hell he is, keep lending you cash? It doesn't make sense."

"No idea. Maybe it was my boyish charm?"

"No, he doesn't play for your team." We pondered.

"Anyway, things go scary fast and little Mr. Smoochy disappeared," Chas said.

"Mr. Smoochy?"

"Don't tell me you're interested in his name, Lyle. Anyway, I was tapped out and in a panic. So I told Max about you, that you could probably front me the money. He seemed more interested in your skills. Max bought the pearls, by the way. They look great on you. Lyle, are you there?"

"I'm thinking. This whole set up feels weird. Something else is going on. I don't like it.

"Just be careful, OK?"

*

By 7:00 p.m. I was rested and ready to go, dressed conservatively in a black skirt and gray cashmere sweater with pearls. I did not wear the ring; the enormous ruby was too flashy for the image I wanted to convey. Poker is a far cry from James Bond in Monte Carlo, but it's not all baseball caps and hoodies like you see on TV. Not the high stakes tables, anyway.

It was quiet, but it was early in the evening. I needed the feel of playing with people at a table. At this hour, I'd likely be up against more tourists than serious gamblers, folks who were in a hurry to finish up and get to a show or dinner. People with other plans get distracted and make more mistakes. That was my hope.

At the first table, I had a seat two places to the croupier's left. Not the best position, but it gave me a chance to read people as the bet moved past me. I played tight but not as tight as the players who checked all the time. They irked me. If you're playing poker, bet or muck your cards, for crying out loud! Get out and wait for the next hand. Needless to say, I worked on my patience. That would have to be cultivated if I was to think clearly.

I came up to speed and time evaporated the way it does when you're working toward walking away with everyone else's chips. Players came and went, croupiers changed, and I found my sweet spot to the croupier's right.

Eight hours later, a guy bet his straight into my aces paired to a flush, thinking his hand was the winner. He was wrong. The river turned my fifth heart and I walked away with 20K. An amazing night, no matter how you cut it. I had the cashier wire the money to my usual account and then threaded my way through the endless banks of slot machines to the elevator.

There was a basket of fruit and a bottle of champagne waiting in my room, with a card commending my 'fine play.' I drank two glasses of water instead, stripped off my clothes, and fell into bed.

29

The second night started later and I jumped straight into faster play, hotter cards. I chose the Aria casino at the new City Center—well, new at the time. I was looking for hotshots and I found them. At one table I was surrounded by drinkers, tipping big. Me, I leaned toward dehydration; it meant less time away from the table. Thirst gave me an edge.

Most people think poker is slow. It's not. It takes maybe two minutes to finish a hand and there are no pauses. Texas no-limit hold 'em is fast, it's visual. Every hand is right in front of you. Everyone is dealt two "hole cards" with five more cards dealt face up on the table, revealed between rounds of betting, for everyone to see. You combine your hole cards with three of the community cards to make the winning hand. The best hole cards are pocket rockets, a pair of aces. After that a pair of kings or a pair of queens. *No-limit* means you can bet as many chips as you have, up to everything. At that point you're *all-in*. Everything is at risk and if you lose, you're out of the game.

I sank into a rhythm, not panicking when I lost. Inexperienced players will often get upset when they lose. Once that happens, they never get their focus back and they continue to lose. You have to be philosophical. A bad beat is a bad beat; shake it off and wait two minutes.

This one guy was a monster player, very sharp, very aggressive. He had me worried until he lost a hand. The man hated losing, really hated it. He didn't entirely lose his focus, but losing rattled him and brought him down to my skill level. I offered a prayer of thanks to the gods of poker.

Again and again, I was reminded of the elegant simplicity of poker. If you've got the best hand going, you've got the best chance of winning. That being said, Chance is a fickle beast—from the *flop* to the *river*. All you really know is the two cards you were dealt. The rest is calculation, speculation. And luck.

Observation helps, too. As it got later, I'd watch the other players at the table as the *flop* was dealt, the first three cards on the table. My rule of thumb is never to look at the *flop* as it is being dealt. It's a vulnerable moment. Most people, like the folks at my table that night, get so focused on those first cards, so filled with expectation, that they're bound to give something away. That I didn't want to miss. If I forgot the cards I held (which happened once in a while, later in the night), I could check them later. I was collecting micro-expressions—infinitesimal smiles, winces, even blinks. It was solid info that helped me through an intense two minutes.

Close to 3:00 a.m. it was down to me and a twitchy Indonesian woman with long red nails and shellacked hair. She'd been a flashy, impulsive player all night, but here she was, suddenly cool and watching me closely.

I had pocket jacks, not bad. Not great. There was no possibility of a flush in the cards on the table and no playable straight as far as I could tell. Interesting. The only card on the table higher than my jacks was a queen. She appeared on the *river*, right after everyone else folded. This was it.

Red Nails bet the pot, 5K, a huge bet. Was she bluffing? I didn't know this woman and here she was, quiet and watchful as a snake.

I faked a call, making the slightest gesture to my chips, and she lost it.

"What the hell was that?" she yelled at me. "You call or not? Hey, Grandma. You try to take my money? Not for hairdo, I bet! Ha Ha!"

At first, I was horrified that I'd made her so angry. But then I thought about her insult. She insulted my hair? Hers looked like it had been spray painted on. If she smoked, her hair would've caught fire.

Deciding she was desperate, I called. Red Nails turned over pocket tens. I turned over my jacks and she hissed at me as the dealer helped me haul in the pile of chips.

I was escorted to the cashier by management, who invited me to stay at the hotel. I was tempted to check out the Aria's reputation for ostentatious luxury, but I declined, opting for familiarity and habit. My first and biggest mistake of the night. The last thing I remember is being told my car was waiting for me. I couldn't remember if I had a car or not, I was that tired.

30

The first time I came to, I couldn't see anything. Wherever I was, it was pitch black. I was cold, groggy; my throat hurt and the ribs on my right side ached. Was I lying on the floor? I groaned and passed out, not fighting the pull taking me under.

Some time later, I awoke to a slant of light stabbing my eyes. I rolled over to get away from it, my ribs still aching, overcome with thirst, feeling dizzy and sick. Any part of me not covered by the coat was freezing. Even my hair felt cold. I squeezed an eye open and found that I was indeed lying on a floor. It was covered I dust, and so was I.

I sat up slowly holding on to my ribs, and squinted some more. Shafts of light fell almost vertically around me, coming through cracks and chinks in old wood. The place must have been and old barn or storage shed. Motes of dust drifted in the light, in total silence. I coughed drily, wincing at the sudden pain, which I explored with my left hand. It was the lower two ribs, sending me messages that I was breathing. Great.

I squirmed out of pools of light into shadows, the better to see where I was. The place felt abandoned, definitely hadn't been used in a while. Something blue winked at me over to my right. I crawled over to find a couple of water bottles. I twisted the cap off one and tried not to drink the whole thing. There were only two

and I wanted the water to last. Who knew how long I'd
be here.

I took inventory. No purse, which meant no phone,
no gun. No shoes, either. That was just mean. I hugged
my knees to my chin, trying to cover my freezing legs
with the coat. I was not bound or gagged, which told me
there was no one to hear me, nowhere to go. Maybe
whoever dumped me here was coming back. I got up
and staggered around, trying to bring some warmth back
to my numb feet.

All my instincts told me to get out, but how? No
windows. The timbered door felt braced on the other
side when I pounded on it. The wood was old. There
were beams overhead, maybe fifteen feet up—too high
to reach. Forget them.

I examined the walls, where the most light came in,
prying at seams between the boards. I thumped and
kicked and pulled at likely boards until my nails were
cracked and raw. Cursing in frustration, I resisted the
urge to kick a wall—not a good idea in bare feet.
Thinking of my feet made me mad. Yoga wasn't bad
enough? Now this? My feet were pissed off.

I threw myself against the wall, yelling, "Fuck you!"
three or four times. My ribs didn't like it, but the
exercise and the anger made me feel minimally warmer.
I heard a crack and stopped dead, praying it wasn't a rib.
The ribs were plenty unhappy, but they said they were
OK. The feet wanted to keep going.

Inspired by my feet, I lay down on the floor and
threw my coat over them to provide padding. Then my
feet and I pounded on the place we heard the cracking
sound. Gasping and panting, considerably warmer, I
scooted over for a closer look. A narrow section of board
had split from the rest of it. I stood up and yanked at the
now-loose section, eventually freeing it from its nail. It

came away in my hands and I used it as a lever to loosen the rest of the board, heedless of the scratches and splinters. I pulled and yanked and pushed and pounded, sweating and sore, until I had opened a space between two struts.

The sun was low in the sky and I didn't know how much time I had before it got dark. I drank the last of the water, threw my coat on the ground outside, and squeezed myself through the opening. Where I stood appeared to be a vacant, dusty yard. Avoiding prickly weeds where I could, I came to a rutted dirt road that curved around to a dilapidated barn with a sagging roof. The shed that held me was an appendage to the barn and sturdier than the original structure. Too bad, I could've saved some time if I'd been in the barn.

I followed the dirt road about a mile, to another dirt road. I stood there, listening, scanning the flat landscape in front of me. There might have been mountains to the east, but it also might have been clouds low on the horizon. I waited and watched, unwilling to walk for the sake of walking. My feet were in bad shape, but I knew things could get worse.

At this time of year, the sun sat in the south. I knew where west was, but which way was Las Vegas? Engine rumble to the north caught my attention, and I turned to see a livestock truck kick up a trail of dust and disappear. Nothing else in any direction made my choice easier. So I turned north.

Eventually making it to the pavement, I walked down the middle of the two-lane road to avoid shredding my feet on gravel. The sun dipped low behind me and I cast a long shadow out in front. I walked slowly to conserve energy, looking down at my aching feet, focusing on each step instead of the empty road ahead.

A pick-up with its lights on sped toward me and I stepped to the right to avoid getting run over. The truck honked and kept going. Possibly he hadn't seen me due to the glare of the setting sun. I held my aching ribs and kept walking.

From behind, I heard the rumble of a semi. It honked to signal its approach. I turned to the oncoming lights and waved my hands above my head, almost weeping when he downshifted and came to a stop.

"Lady, you OK?" the driver called down from his cab.

"Not really. Which way is Las Vegas?"

"You mean to say if I'm not heading in that direction you don't need a ride? You look pretty lost to me."

"You got that right." I looked at my feet and then up at his lined face. "Could you please give me a lift to wherever it is you're going?"

"Hop in."

It was more limping than hopping, but I managed to climb up into the cab.

"Here, put these on." The driver handed me a rolled up pair of socks. They felt so soft and warm I broke down and cried.

"Barefoot in the middle of nowhere. I can't wait to hear *that* story!" He grinned and handed me a bottle of water. That made me cry, too.

I told Leonard Hotchkiss—Enid, Oklahoma, semi driver and father of four, husband to Cathy, his high school sweetheart—that he wouldn't believe me, but I'd be pleased to invent a reasonable lie, if he wanted. Leonard insisted he'd heard tales on the road that strained human credulity, yet each proved to be true. Though I resist telling the truth under normal circumstances, I felt I owed Leonard, so I told him my tale of friendship, gambling, betrayal and abduction.

"No shit!" was his response.

Gentleman that he is, Leonard dropped me off at the Deliveries entrance to the Bellagio. Turns out he was passing through anyway, heading east. I was touched by his consideration.

"You know it was your shiny hair all on fire in the sun that made me see you back there. It glowed like a flashlight. Look here, this is my email, Lyle. You tell me how this all comes out. Good luck, girl!"

I pocketed Leonard's business card and limped inside. I was met by a security guard who refused to let me pass. Guests had to enter and exit via the main entrance.

"Just call the concierge, please. I'm sure it will be fine."

"I'm sorry, ma'am, we can't have you...it isn't allowed...what's that on your feet?"

"Socks."

"No, the red..."

"That would be blood. Maybe you better call the manager. If you call the police, he'll just get angry. And quite frankly, so will I."

The guard chose the path of wisdom and called the concierge, who appeared in person to escort me through staff passageways to my room, where he let me in, sat me down, opened the mini bar and poured me a scotch.

"I'll send a doctor to attend you, Lyle." He knew I hated being called Ms. Hudson or ma'am. "And, there is a person waiting for you in the lobby, quite some time, apparently." He described Chas to a T.

"If he's alone, please send him up. If he has an escort, I'm not back yet." The concierge left and I hobbled to the bathroom to wash my face, which was a mess, and soak my scratched and splintered hands, also a mess. The hotel doctor and Chas arrived together.

"No touching, no touching! Everything hurts," I told Chas. I sent him off for ice and assigned him the tasks of ordering food from room service, finding a bottle of scotch, and sending the coat out for dry cleaning.

With Chas out of the way, I didn't have to pretend I was fine. I handed myself over to the doctor. His assessment took some time. The feet needed to be soaked before the socks could be peeled off, and blisters and bruises treated. He sat me on the edge of the tub and phoned for medical supplies and an assistant to help with the splinters. The warm water felt wonderful.

"This is all going to hurt," he said. "Are you sure you won't take a sedative?"

I shook my head. "I'd just fall asleep."

Before he was through removing the first sock, I changed my mind. Sleep would be way better than this.

It was.

31

My eyes opened slowly and I smiled. I was in a real bed, I was safe, and Chas was beside me, green eyes facing mine. He brushed his hand through my hair and pushed it back, away form my face. I closed my eyes and sighed. I might be awake, but I was exhausted.

"Welcome back, sweetie," Chas whispered.

"Um." I drifted, not really wanting to wake up. My body was telling me various things I didn't want to know or remember.

"Wakey, wakey!" Chas said brightly.

"No."

"Open your eyes, Lyle. Time to wake up and greet the...afternoon. Coffee? Or, perhaps a lovely pot of tea? Let me help you sit up."

"Help me what?" I did open my eyes then. The covers felt like lead, my hands did not follow instruction, and my ribs hurt when I tried to sit up. "Oh, man..." I whined. "This sucks."

"Yes it does," Chas said soothingly. "Open." He popped a pill in my mouth and held out a glass of water, which I needed two hands to hold.

"Mittens?"

It all came back to me—the hands, the feet. I could only hope that one pill could cover all the varieties of ache I was feeling. Head to toe.

"Chas, what are you doing here?" We had explored my ravaged feet and put them back in bandages, unlike my hands, which were messy but insisted on remaining free. Snuggled in a white hotel robe, feet up on an ottoman, I sat back and regarded him.

"I escaped. Max probably wondered what took me so long."

"What do you mean?"

"He called while you were asleep. Asked if he could see you. He wants to know if you're OK."

"Yeah, right. He wants to stick me for disappearing and reneging on the deal. Rat bastard." Cursing always made me feel better.

"I think you should see him," Chas said.

"What? Why? I bet he had me kidnapped himself, slimy little…" I ran out of steam and had to put my head back and close my eyes. The medication, no doubt.

"He was very friendly on the phone, almost avuncular," Chas mused.

"Uncle Rat," I snickered.

"I'm curious, Lyle. He let me go. Didn't show up here. I have all my…" Chas wriggled his fingers at me.

"Show off." My hands would scare children. I wasn't sure I even had all my fingernails. I started to examine my fingers one by one, kissing them and telling them I loved them.

"Lyle, Lyle. Over here, sweetie." Chas snapped his fingers to get my attention. "Let's call him up, invite him over, find out what's up," Chas said.

"No. Not here." I didn't want the rodent in my personal space.

"Out, then. Where?"

"What are you, his secretary?" I grumped.

Chas lifted an eyebrow.

"Fine. It should only take a week to pull myself together and hobble out the door."

"It won't be that bad, you'll see," Chas replied. He called Max and made arrangements.

My coat had been cleaned, and in a black sweater and slacks, I'd be presentable. Shoes were the problem. I sat on the couch and stared at my feet.

"No shoes," my feet said. "We *will* kill you."

"Tough feet," I complimented them.

"You were warned."

It was going on four p.m., so I opened the drapes and turned the TV to the fountain music. The Bellagio fountains were dancing to Johnny Mathis singing *It's Beginning to Look a lot Like Christmas*. The feet made disparaging sounds, so I turned the sound down a bit. Johnny shifted to *Most Wonderful time of the Year* and I was siding with the feet, when Chas walked in the door.

"Oooh! I love Johnny Mathis!" Chas exclaimed, placing a shopping bag in front of me and going over to the window. "Pretty," Chas purred.

"He's making me ill," I complained.

"You just need food." He threw me an apple from the fruit basket and assembled a plate of pate, brie, and crackers.

"What's in the bag?" I asked, happily crunching and munching.

"It's for you. Open it." Chas handed me a glass of white wine and took a sip from his own.

"Himalayan Yak fur?" They were Ugg-like boots with shaggy white hairy stuff. Not shoes. They might work. The feet maintained a skeptical silence.

"That's sweet, Chas, but…"

"Thank you for going to the prom with me, Lyle." He kissed my cheek and sat back. "Is that a scar? Where did it come from? It's not recent, is it."

"Later. We have a date with Max, yes? One thing at a time."

"Fine. I charged the booties to your room. We'll settle up later."

"You're welcome." I kissed him back, also on the cheek. Madonna started singing *Santa Baby*, and we sang along with her as the fountain geysers exploded, launching water up to our eyes.

32

We met Max at 5:00 p.m. at the Lake Terrace at Wynn, a place I found peaceful and refreshing after a long night of poker. I loved the modernist sculpture of people all facing the 140-foot wall of water, each at a different depth in the blue lake. It was like a 3D Magritte that spoke to me of solitude instead of alienation.

The yak booties felt great, like walking in slippers. Chas and I were escorted to a table where Max sat waiting, my purse on the table, next to a cup of coffee.

"It suits you, you should keep it," I said to the little man, referring to the purse.

"Have a seat," Max said. "What are those—poodles?" He looked at my footwear as I sat down and crossed my legs.

"They were." I stuck my hands in my coat pockets and ordered a San Pellegrino from the waitress. Chas asked for Chardonnay.

When the waitress left, Max pushed the purse across the table to me. I let it sit there.

"What is with you?" Max asked, exasperated. "We were going to come get you, Lyle. All you had to do was wait. Sheesh!"

"Bullshit. I was—what—drugged? Dumped out in the boonies, no shoes, bruised ribs. As far as I knew I was in a lethal situation."

"Yeah, well, sorry about the ribs. Before you went under, you broke Mikey's nose. He might have been a bit rough with you. He's been reprimanded."

"Swell."

The waitress returned and we sat silently until she left.

"It felt like I was waiting for a bad end, Max. Why? What was up?"

"How the hell did you do that, tear the place apart? I almost had a heart attack when we couldn't find you."

"You had Chas. All you had to do was wait. Meanwhile, you took me out. All bets are off. Chas keeps his hand, I keep the money."

Max took a fake sip of coffee, smiling into his cup. "Gosh, I guess you're right."

"Tell." I was in no mood for games.

"There's this guy. Let's call him Mr. Y. Big deal guy, very competitive in my line of work. He was...never mind." Max waved away a lengthy historical explanation. "Anyway, long story short, somehow," Max raised his black eyebrows innocently, "he found out about a couple of high stakes games—somehow—and took an interest. He bet against you and lost big!" Max grinned.

"Against me?"

"No offense, Lyle, but look at you, gray hair and pearls and all." He chuckled unpleasantly, enjoying himself.

"That's stupid. I kicked ass. And it's silver, not gray."

"It is what it is," Max philosophized.

"What about your reputation?" I asked.

"Ha! My rep's just fine! Mr. Y is, shall we say out of the picture? My reputation shines, cutie pie."

"So, what did you do? You set me up? Then kidnapped me? Why?"

"He was boiling mad. It was a fluid situation for a while. I didn't want you to get hurt."

"Bullshit. You set Chas up in a condo. I get a drafty barn on the tundra?"

"Everybody knew all about Chas, including where he was. You had to be out of sight. Cripes, all you had to do was stay PUT!"

"I froze my ASS!"

"Yeah, well, all's well. No hard feelings. Open the purse."

"I reached for the purse and Max saw my hands.

"Holy shit," he said.

"Yeah, thanks." The .38, the phone, and a roll of Franklins. "What's this?" I closed the bag and looked at him.

"For your efforts…for the team." He smiled magnanimously.

"What! That's it?" I stood up furious I'd been played, resentful about my injuries.

Max looked up at me calmly.

Chas picked up the purse and grabbed my arm. "C'mon, sweetie. Let's go get a facial."

The next day, it was a facial and then some. We groomed, shopped, and dined our way through Max's wad. I called my aunts and ended up talking to Vern, which told me all was as usual in Lawrence. Except for Mac, who was still prickly.

"So, you found Chas," he said, summing up.

"Yes, which meant playing a lot of poker."

"OK. Now back up to the part about your hands. You were rock climbing? In December?"

"No, I said they *looked* that way. Feet, too."

"Why are you lying to me?"

"I'm not lying, I'm approximating, saying what they look *like*. I'll tell you the whole thing when I get back."

"What whole thing? When are you coming back?"

"Um, tomorrow or the next day."

Mac paused. I could hear him wondering why I wasn't on a plane right now. He was trying to be patient.

"Because..." He was waiting for a damn explanation.

"Because I am a grown up and that's what I decided."

"Fine, suit yourself."

"I am." We ended the call in silence and I studied my feet, which were sharing the couch with me.

"Bloody hell," I said.

"Men," they replied. Coming along nicely, the feet were in a philosophical mood.

Chas had gone out to a show and planned to hit the clubs after that. He wished me luck before he left and recommended I wear the pearls. I was way ahead of him.

I took a cab over to the Aria, site of my latest success, looking for flashy players with money to burn. The bigger the ego, the better. Most bad players have huge egos; they don't know they're bad. I loved that. They also make mistakes by hanging on to cards and calling when they should fold. It keeps them in the game, but they lose. The problem with bad choices like that is that bluffing isn't effective with them. They just don't get it. Still, it feels good to take their money.

Things looked good when I found a table with a seat to the dealer's right. I took my time and played cautiously at first, getting to know the players and reading their faces. I won small and let them think I was timid, with my silver hair and pearls. The yak boots were under the table—out of sight, out of mind.

The pot kept getting bigger as the night wore on and drinkers drank, egos blossoming. I watched the betting come around the table to me. It was time to step out and be bold. I had medium size connectors, the 8 and 9 of clubs, in my hand. Location was definitely a plus here.

No one folded. Everyone checked, including me. The *flop*, the first three community cards out on the table, were the six of hearts, seven of clubs, and king of clubs. Not bad. It gave me four out of the five clubs I needed for a flush, *and* an open-ended straight draw.

The *turn* card, next out, was the five of spades. I made my straight, but I wrinkled my eyebrows slightly to indicate concern.

Two players checked, which surprised me since the five looked so harmless. Did somebody have three of a kind? Was I being set up? I had to make a choice, fast. Do I make a small bet and try to draw them into betting more, or do I go all in and just not risk it?

Don't get greedy, Lyle. I reminded myself there was plenty of money in the pot as is. "All in," I declared, pushing all of my chips forward.

The *river* card, last one out on the table, was a ten of hearts. I had chosen wisely. The pot was mine, all 20K of it.

The last hand, which finished off the chips on the table, was anti-climactic. I called the other player's bluff with a pair of sixes and won. God, it was sweet! I tipped the dealer, made the usual arrangements for my winnings, and had the house call me a cab. This time I got back to the Bellagio without incident.

33

"Surprise!" A very loud voice yelled. I squeezed my eyes shut and pulled the covers over my head, or tied to. There was tugging and bouncing, and extremely irritating laughter.

"Go away! I need sleep!"

"C'mon, get up, Lyle. We got you a hat and everything!"

The covers were slipping from my hands. "Loretta? Who let you in? What are you doing here?" I groaned. "Chas! Get her off me!"

They started talking at the same time.

"I tried to explain, darling, but as you can see..."

"What kind of way is that to talk to your dear old auntie? Uppy, uppy!"

"What are you doing here?" I asked, hands over my eyes.

"Hell, we're all here! C'mon and look!" She whisked the covers away. "Whoa, better put some clothes on first. Vern is pretty impressionable," Loretta laughed.

As was my custom after a late night, I'd left my clothes on the floor and crawled into bed.

"I tried to tell them," Chas said, handing me a robe.

"Not your fault. It's Hudsons in tsunami mode. Four hours sleep. I feel like crap."

"OK! We're coming out!" Loretta called.

The suite was filled with Santas. One of them had a dark moustache. Another had four legs and a stubby white tail.

"Surprise!" they all shouted.

"What...?" Glory raced across the room and leaped into my arms, knocking me backwards into Chas. He led me to a couch to sit down. Chas looked unforgivably fresh and handsome. No fair, I thought, grumpily.

"This is a Santa intervention," Luce explained as the hubbub subsided. "We decided you needed to be rescued from—oh, not you, darling," she said, accepting a glass of orange juice from Chas who had slipped into hostess mode.

"From your evil habits and this pit of vice!" Loretta boomed gleefully. "You coulda knocked us over when your friend Max sent us all an invite and a private plane to come out here!"

I locked eyes with Chas at the mention of Max's name, but the golden boy merely shrugged and rolled his eyes. If I'd had the strength I'd have smacked him.

"So, here we are, all of us, and you are going to run with us in the Great Santa Race! We signed you up, got you a number, a hat—it'll be great! Oh, Max sent you a note. Here!"

Glory jumped off my lap and bounded off to the bedroom. I stood up slowly and turned to follow her, hoping I could sneak off and climb back into bed. I was a little unsteady on my feet.

"Lyle, wait." Mac came over and put his arms around me. He felt warm and smelled awfully good. I snuggled in and tried to go to sleep standing up.

"Chas told us about the *Prom*. You really did rescue him." He kissed my hair. "You crazy woman," he whispered. "Are you OK?"

I shook my head no against his red Santa chest and tried to snuggle in deeper.

"Oh, Loretta, look," Lenore tsk, tsk'd. "Glory has eaten her Santa hat."

"No problemo, sister mine. We'll get her some of those purple antlers! Hey, Lyle, we need to get going to be there when the race starts!"

Just then, Glory pranced out of the bedroom, flinging a hairy yak boot right and left.

"What the? Come here, you skinny bitch!" Loretta chased the dog around the room, finally prying the boot from the dog's mouth. She flopped Glory onto her side and started tickling her belly.

"This supposed to be footwear? Looks dead to me!"

"It's all I can stand to have on my feet right now." I explained what happened to my feet. "So, I won't be walking in the Santa Race today."

They all stood silently for a moment, looking at each other and communicating silently, eyeball to eyeball.

"I'll rent a bike," Mac suggested. "You can sit on the handlebars. Your furry boots will fit right in." He kissed me, causing Chas to put a hand on his heart and pat it, like he was having palpitations or something.

"OMG, that is just too sweet!" Chas looked to Lenore to share the sentiment with him.

"Aw, cut the mush!" Loretta ordered. "Put some clothes on, Lyle, and let's go!"

I stepped back from Mac's embrace and looked up at him. "Where's your Santa hat?" I asked.

"Where I come from, Santa wears a Stetson." He crinkled his eyes at me.

"This is Vegas. Sure, why not?" I stole a minute when I was getting dressed to pop a couple of pain pills and read Max's note. My hands were useless. Had to rip it open with my teeth.

No regrets, right, kiddo? Still, I feel bad about the mittens and the ugly footgear. You got pluck, Lyle. I got some people talking about how you play poker. Maybe we can work out an arrangement. Just kidding! You should be with family at Christmas.

Here they are. Merry Christmas!

PS: Give the deal some thought.

Max

The gang of us joined the red and white brigade pouring out onto the Strip. Mac had magically procured a bike, and between the two of them, he and Chas got me perched on the handlebars. I wasn't sure how long I'd stay on, but I gave it a try.

The Strip was a river of Santas, thousands of people, balloons and flags floating over their heads. The Great Santa Run is a fundraiser for Opportunity Village, a popular charity in Las Vegas, and every year thousands of people showed up to participate. There were Elvis Santas, Hawaiian Santas, ZZ Top Santas, bikini-clad Santas, clown Santas in rainbow wigs, Chihuahua Santas, bare-chested buff Santas, Santas with little Santas in strollers, as well as the one in the Stetson. Purple antlers abounded. Glory was SOL. Her antlers flopped like bunny ears. Each time she tried to rub them off on the legs of a passing Santa, Loretta made sure they stayed on Glory's head.

Luce and Lenore and Loretta walked arm in arm ahead of the bike, enjoying the scene. Chas and Vern were somewhere behind us, Vern animatedly waving his hands, explaining something to Chas, bass fishing possibly. I kept trying to peer over Mac's shoulder, trying to figure out what on earth they were talking about.

"You'll fall off, you keep twisting around like that," Mac said.

"Can we stop for a minute, Mac? This really is uncomfortable." My feet felt numb but I was sure they were OK. The meds were kicking in, full force. The rest of me felt like a pretzel, one with a fuzzy head.

"Sure." We pulled to the edges of the crowd to get out of people's way. A gap opened up around us. I stumbled off the bike and stood up, going for a stretch. Mac knelt to examine the bike's rear tire; he seemed to disappear as I looked at him.

In the momentary lull, the sudden gunshot sounded extremely loud and very close. People screamed and dropped to the pavement. On the other side of the street, a Santa in a ski mask pointed his gun straight at me. I was lucky he'd missed. I ducked, pulled the .38 from deep within my Santa costume, and jumped up.

The masked Santa was still there, his gun pointing right at me. I took a shot, swung around, grabbed the bike from Mac and jumped on, pressing the bike through the noisy, upset crowd, keeping my eyes on the black ski mask as the man ran down the sidewalk. I heard Mac shout behind me, but I was seeing red and pedaling hard.

The guy saw me following and gaining on him. He ducked into a nearby casino, one of the ones where the slots were practically out on the street. There were drops of blood on he sidewalk. Good, I hit him, which meant he'd have to slow down.

I rode the bike through the entrance and pulled out the .38, holding it ahead of me in both hands as I stopped, the red dot of the Crimson Trace jumping across the dimness of the casino. The demented dinging of slot machines grew louder. I swept the center aisle, looking left and right. No runaway Santa, nobody, period. The place was empty. Weird. Suddenly, I was surrounded by a ring of security guards wearing black ski masks, guns out, all pointed at me. The slot machines went silent, and everything went black.

34

"Ski masks! Guns! It was creepy. What happened? Am I under arrest?"

"You fainted," Mac said.

"In the casino?"

"You weren't in a casino, Lyle. You got off the bike and fainted right on the street."

"But a guy shot at me, a Santa in a ski mask!" I was confused and my head hurt.

"No ski mask. No shots were fired. There were a boatload of Santas, though. Maybe they, you know, affected your mind." He was trying hard not to laugh.

"Very funny."

"Lyle, listen to me. You fainted. Probably lack of food combined with your painkillers," he said reasonably.

"You're wrong, Mac. He shot at me and I shot back!"

"OK. Explain how you shoot someone without a gun. It was here in your room. " Mac pointed to the satchel sitting innocently in a chair.

"So, I passed out?" I was slow, but I was getting there. "Did I hit my head?"

"No head injuries involved, not a bump. The costume softened your fall." He sat on the bed next to me and patted my back.

"Shit. It was so real. I can't believe I dreamed it."

"More like a hallucination," Mac offered.

"Oh, that's helpful, thanks."

He shook an admonitory finger at me. "Don't do drugs."

I ignored him. "Where is everyone? What time is it? What's going on?" I picked up the glass of water on the bedside table and drank the whole thing.

"I believe Lenore and Loretta are downstairs, investigating the chocolate fountain."

"Thinking ahead to Valentine's Day, no doubt." My entrepreneurial aunts were constantly on the lookout for new opportunities. The thought of what they could do with a fountain of streaming chocolate in Lawrence was frightening.

"Chas has packed your things," Mac continued, "and Luce is conferring with the pilot."

"Pilot?"

"Charter flight Max set up," he explained. "Vern is walking Glory. Once everybody gets back, we're out of here." It seemed like Las Vegas was not Mac's beverage of choice.

"You all made plans behind my back, without consulting me?"

"It was more like conferring over your unconscious body, which voted to go home, by the way."

I glared at Mac, trying to work myself up to mad.

"Out cold. You raised your hand and voted. Scout's honor." How the man could keep a straight face I did not know.

I heaved a sigh. "The body wants what the body wants."

*

I don't remember much about getting back to Lawrence and home, having slept through most of it.

There are dim memories of Chas making everyone comfortable and then settling in for a chat with Luce—stock analysis or financial advice, no doubt. They had that in common. And Luce was no more impervious to Chas's charm than the rest of humanity. Chas had a talent for relationships. He wasn't manipulative or opportunistic; he genuinely liked people and found ways to make them like him, too. As in the case of the young man whose appeal to Chas's vanity led him to Max the Shark, it was a trait that could get him into trouble.

I don't know when he did it, but at some point Chas managed to turn Mac into a virtual uncle. At least that's how Mac put it.

"So, you're what—Uncle Mac, now?" I asked him later when my brain de-fuzzed.

"Well, he didn't come right out and say it," Mac chuckled, "it was implied. Chas can be a cute puppy when he wants to. You're important to him, Lyle."

"That makes me his *Aunt* Lyle?" I made a face that you'd see on a cat ready to heave a hairball.

Mac snorted and gave me one of those long, brown-eyed looks, the kind that come with a lazy smile. "I don't think it'd cross anyone's mind to think of you as *aunt* material, darlin'. That boy and I are friendlier, is all. I know he's gay, but I'm still keeping an eye on him."

Reassured at my exemption from Auntdom, I rewarded MacDonald George in a way he appreciated.

35

The warmth faded fast. Mac returned to pursuit mode, pressuring me to move in with him, to admit that I loved him and wanted to be with him. But Mac was just the tip of the iceberg. It seemed that everybody in Lawrence had a bone to pick with me. They all suddenly remembered they were mad. And if they weren't mad at me, they were AWOL—gone. Shore had disappeared again. How do you disappear with a giant schnauzer and an entire arsenal of semi-automatic weapons? Not a trace.

"Where did he go, Lyle?" Greta asked, jumping the line to be First Griper.

"How would I know? I've been out of town. Why are you here, Greta? What do you want?"

We were standing in the kitchen, both of us in socks. Greta had taken her boots off in the hall. Lawrence was experiencing unprecedented amounts of snow, and she made it a point to drop by and give me a piece of her mind.

"That man is a person of interest. What was he thinking, giving you a .38? The .22 was bad enough, now you got two guns? Give me a break. You show me the papers for that thing. What do I want? I want to know where he is! I want to know what your plans are. Just because you leave town doesn't mean that people forget what a pain in the ass you are, Carlyle Hudson. I got a civilian population to protect. What is that, a poodle?"

Greta left off her rant and squinted over my shoulder where Glory was contentedly chewing on a yak boot by the kitchen door.

"Glory, drop it!" I swung around and grabbed the shaggy piece of footwear, much to the dog's delight. We were going to have a tug! Awesome! She growled and yanked on the boot, dragging me half under the table.

"Oh my God. You're wearing it around the house? You planning on shooting the dog, she doesn't release the poodle?"

Wrestling with Glory had revealed the .38 on my hip to Greta's accusing glare.

"Boot. It's a boot, Greta."

Glory tugged the shaggy boot out of my hand and skittered away with her prize. I stood up and Greta and I faced off over the kitchen table, glare to glare. I took a deep breath.

"Officer Danielson, this gun is my legal property. I am trained in its use and handling. This domicile," I waved my hand expressively, "is my home, an I am entitled to, to…" I groped for words. "To wear a gun or walk around naked if I want to."

"Yeah, I heard about that." Greta shook her head. "Ms. Hudson, you are a danger to yourself and others, even without the guns. Just because we have Robin Breck's killer locked up doesn't mean you are free to assume…"

"Whoa! Back up! Who's *we*? Who is locked up? You made an arrest?"

"Don't sound so surprised. We are the Lawrence PD. Concentrated police work led to the arrest of the girl's boyfriend."

"What boyfriend? Which one?"

"That was the root of the problem, jealousy. The kid strangled her."

"What about the dead professor?"

"Addison? Unrelated. We're still working on it. Do not," she pointed a finger at my face, "take that gun out of this house."

"I…"

"Do not," she interrupted me, "tell me you have a permit. That is not my point. Which reminds me, why are you wearing the damn gun?"

"I don't feel safe, Greta. Intruder, remember? My windows get shot out again, I want to shoot back."

"No, no, no, no." Greta made a T with her hands, signaling time out.

"Hey, what's up?" Caitlin walked into the kitchen, small scraggly cat snuggled in her arms. Her eyes slid around the floor, into corners, under the table. Uh-oh.

"Caitlin?" I asked.

Greta swiveled back to me. "What?" she asked suspiciously.

"Not good," Caitlin muttered. "Here." She thrust an angry cat at me. "Try not to lose him." Caitlin went to the fridge and started to shove at it.

"Caitlin, did you see Glory with a…"

"No! I did not see the dog! I thought we were safe here!" Caitlin yelled at me and grabbed the cat. "Someone must've let her out, or taken her!"

"Hold on. Are you saying…"

"Yes! Brunhilde's gone!" Caitlin sobbed, totally freaking the cat, who yowled and leapt to the floor.

I went over to the upset girl and remembered just in time that she didn't like to be touched. I handed her a tissue and looked steadily into her eyes.

"She must be somewhere in the house, Caitlin," I said soothingly. "We'll find her, OK?"

"You're wearing a gun? You shoot Brunhilde and I'll fucking kill you!"

"Exactly what I'm saying. Lyle. Put the gun away." Greta used a soothing tone on me. I didn't like it any more than Caitlin did.

"Caitlin! I would not kill your boa; you know that! Rats, yes. Brunhilde no, OK?"

"A snake?" Greta's eyes started to slide around the floor and into corners.

"Boa. She's a boa constrictor; snakes are so juvenile." Caitlin rolled her eyes.

"Maybe she's hungry," I suggested, my eyes involuntarily sliding around the floor.

"Could be," Caitlin admitted, blowing her nose. "The rat's still in the cage."

"Really? Was the door open?" I asked.

"Rat?" Greta asked.

"No, it was closed," Caitlin said.

"Door to your room?" I continued.

"Also closed."

"So, she could have escaped? Somehow?"

"Possible," Caitlin reluctantly admitted.

"We'll find her," I said with a confidence I did not really feel.

"Find who?" Chas stood in the doorway, holding Caitlin's cat. "Hello, officer," Chas smiled at Greta.

"Hello, yourself," she smiled back at him.

"Who does this belong to and who are we looking for?" Chas inquired.

"Berg!" Caitlin took the cat and nuzzled its spiky fur.

"Berg? That's his name?" I asked.

"Short for Strindberg. He can get violent. You know, emotionally."

"Ah."

"We need to find, Caitlin's boa, Brunhilde," I explained to Chas.

"I've got to get going. Remember what I said!" Greta admonished me.

"Let me see you to the door," Chas offered.

"No need," Greta smiled.

"I insist," Chas smiled back.

What was that?" Caitlin asked me.

"He can't help himself," I explained.

36

"You're what?"

"I'm going to stay with Luce," Chas said. "She invited me, you know, and this missing boa thing..." Chas let the sentence trail off.

I stared at him.

"Luce said you might want some space. The tall man, etc., etc." He smiled.

"Do not. Smile at me. You coward."

"Can't help myself, sweetheart." He kissed me on the cheek. "How are the feet?"

I looked down at my socks. "Fine. Better. Thanks." I brooded about my feet under the best of circumstances. What I felt now was close to grief.

"Chin up." Chas lifted my chin, literally. "And do something about your hair. You look a wreck."

"Thanks. Have you seen Glory and my boot?"

"Mantelpiece." Chas pointed to the library. "It was the only safe place. She yakked up some yak hair, which I cleaned up—you're welcome very much." A horn sounded out front. "Oh, that must be Luce!"

"She's picking you up? You're already packed? That's snow out there, Chas. You hate snow."

"All I have to do is make it to the car." He grabbed his bag and opened the door. "Correction: truck. We're going shopping. Boots and jacket, then yoga. Bye!" He smiled a golden smile at me.

"Yoga?" I called after him.

"Love you!" Chas dashed to the yellow truck. Luce waved, shifted into first, and the truck rumbled off into the snow.

Muttering dark thoughts, I retrieved the yak boot from the mantel and put it on. Slightly damp around the edges, it now had a bald patch on the ankle and looked quite pathetic next to its fluffier white sister.

Boots on, I stomped into the hall and donned coat, cap and gloves, ready to wield a mighty shovel against the increasing snow. *Why not wait until it stops?* Asked a sane little vice at the back of my head.

"It'll never stop!" I yelled irrationally.

I hate shoveling snow. One of the perks of living in San Francisco is not having to deal with it. But if you need to work off excess energy, or just not think, it's an excellent activity. By the time I'd shoveled four inches of the stuff from the public sidewalk and cleared as path to the porch, I was sweating and at peace with the world. I shoveled the last bit of snow from the steps and stood there enjoying a sense of accomplishment, breathing steamy clouds into the cold air, watching the snow continue.

A snow-covered Volvo drove by, slowed down, the sped up, or tried to. Bald tires spun on the snowy street. Eventually it moved itself along. Someone's grandma venturing out for a quart of milk and cat food, no doubt. Why did it have to be an inept old person, I scolded myself. Anybody can be a bad driver in the snow. Something about the Volvo nagged at me, but I couldn't remember what it was. A senior moment, Lyle? I told myself to shut up.

Shovel in hand, I tromped through the house to the back door, where I resolved to continue my battle.

"You look like a yeti," Caitlin commented from the stairs. "You're making a mess, Lyle!"

"Sorry, mom! I'll clean it up later. Will you put Glory's coat on and send her out back? Thanks." I didn't wait for an answer. Caitlin loved animals and would do anything for them.

I stopped briefly at the kitchen sink and downed a glass of water, so thirsty that I ignored the fact that Kansas tap water tastes like crap.

Glory shot out the door and past me before I was half way down the steps. Caitlin threw a tennis ball across the yard in a high arc, laughing as she watched the dog pounce around in the snow looking for it. It was good to see her stop worrying about Brunhilde for a minute.

I cleared a path to the alley gate and another path into the bushes for Glory, who preferred a dry patch to do her business.

A clump of snow fell onto me from a tree branch, and I heard a peal of laughter from inside the house. Glory, tennis ball in mouth, ran circles around me, churning up snow. She tried to bark and hold the ball at the same time, which I always find hilarious. I took off a glove and dug snow from my neck.

Bending over to free snow from my collar probably saved my life. An angry buzzing sound followed by the crack of a gun sent me to the ground. All I could think of was protecting Glory. The dog thought I was wrestling; she nipped at my glove and licked my face.

By the time I'd disengaged and ran to the alley, the place was empty. I tracked a trail of prints from the side of the garage to the alley gate and off to the left where the alley met the street.

Glory's tracks crisscrossed mine as well as the other set of prints. Soon it would all be covered by more snow. I called Glory into the yard and closed the gate.

Caitlin stood at the kitchen door, waiting for me. I asked her to take Glory inside and then I searched for the bullet, which was easier said than done. I had to go back to where I was standing, guess at the direction of fire, and then crawl around in snow-laden lilac bushes near the corner of the house. Where was Shore when I needed him? It's like the man was a figment of my imagination.

More snow slipped down my back, creating cold, wet trickles. Eventually, I found a cracked branch and pushed past it to the foundation wall, where the round had imbedded itself. I sat for a moment and decided to leave it there.

Back in the kitchen, I dropped wet clothes in a pile on the floor. Caitlin handed me a towel and terry robe she'd brought from my room.

"You were gone so long," she said,

"Had some thinking to do." I gave her a weak smile. "Thanks for getting Glory dried off." The dog lay at her feet, wagging and smiling at me.

"No problem." Caitlin's eyes were serious.

"Caitlin, maybe you should stay somewhere else for a while."

"Not gonna happen." She raised her eyebrows, making the metal studs twinkle.

"But..."

"We find Brunhilde, I'll reconsider. But, no."

"OK, we'll search. It's not safe for you here." I looked around at the mess on the floor, idly wondering if it would make an attractive nest for the boa. Do boas like wet stuff?

"Put some clothes on, Lyle. You look like shit."

"Thanks, mom."

Caitlin snorted. Mom. That really cracked her up.

*

We started at the top of the house and worked our way downstairs, checking under beds, in closets, behind dressers, any dark spot a six-foot boa constrictor could squeeze into.

"Maybe you should try calling her," I suggested as we made our way through the second floor bedrooms, bathrooms, and linen closet.

"She's not a dog, Lyle."

"So, how do you communicate?" I stood up and brushed lint and dust from my jeans.

"It's different, you know? Time of year, feeding patterns, that kind of thing. Brunhilde is hard to read sometimes. She's been moody lately."

Great. A six-foot moody boa constrictor loose in the house. Happy holidays.

We entered Caitlin's room, where her cat sprang off the bed, going from sleep to attack mode in seconds. Glory backed out the door and looked up at me accusingly.

Caitlin thrust the angry cat into my arms. "Here. Scratch his chin. I want to check something out."

Caitlin unlatched the wire door to Brunhilde's living quarters and ducked inside. She rooted around the bottom of the cage, checking the joins. She stopped at a back corner and sat back in a crouch.

"Looks like she got out here." Caitlin pointed at a tear where the mesh met a 2X4 post.

We were interrupted from our meditation by a ringing doorbell and pounding on the front door, which precipitated loud barking. I handed the cat to Caitlin without incident and followed Glory down to the front door.

Crista was stamping snow off her boots on the porch and Blake was making a final sweep with the snow shovel, which the walk needed again. His beat up yard-decorating truck idled at the curb. Once the thing got going, Blake left it on as long as he could. Restarting the engine was problematic.

"Hi," I greeted them. "Why didn't you use your key, Crista?" They shed boots but kept the rest of the outerwear on.

"I must've left it at the shop. Sorry!" Crista's face was pink with happiness. She and Blake grinned at each other.

"So—what's up?" I asked.

"Blake and I are moving in together!"

"What? Here?"

"That is if it's alright with you," Blake offered.

"Oh. I guess. What the hell. Why not. Congratulations, I'm happy for you."

"You don't seem surprised," Crista said.

"No, I am. Really. I was just wondering about all those boxes upstairs."

"You went in my room?" Crista glared. "You were snooping?" She said the last words the way you'd say *poisoning babies?*

"Of course not. We were looking for...something that got lost. There are a lot of boxes. I was just surprised."

"Looking for what?" Crista asked accusingly. "You were away, remember?"

"Miss B." Caitlin stood behind me, holding Berg the cat. "She kind of got out."

Crista ignored her. "I can't believe you went into my room, Lyle! I am so out of here. Come on, Blake!" Crista pounded up the stairs, Blake trailing behind.

"You don't think the snake could've..." Blake said over one shoulder.

"Boa, Blake. No. Taped boxes, right? Brunhilde would need opposable thumbs. You're fine. Check under the bed again, will you? Just in case."

Cool," he said, uncertainly.

They were back down in an hour. Crista had calmed down a bit, but she still wasn't happy and announced that she and Blake would spend the night at her workroom, at Hyacinth.

"Crista, you and Blake will still be here for Christmas, right?"

"Yes," she said grudgingly. "You do know it's the day after tomorrow. Christmas Eve, anyway."

"Sure I do," I rushed past my lie and gave her a big hug.

I watched the ratty truck pull away from the curb, wheels spinning snow behind it. The path Blake had cleared was already dusted over. The yard was covered with at least a foot of snow.

"How about some cocoa?" I asked Caitlin. She thought I was being friendly. What I was really doing was delaying the search in the basement. Brunhilde, where are you? I do not want to go down there.

37

My mother had been a well-organized person, and that extended to the basement, as well. Wood shelving lined the walls, full of neatly organized items from canning jars, to medieval-looking, antique kitchen tools, to boxes of anything one could imagine—fabric, paper lanterns, seed packets, old hand puppets. I could almost hear her chiding me for not getting down here and giving the place a thorough dusting.

I hated the basement. It didn't matter to me, ever, how clean and bright and orderly it was. From the time I was a child, I felt certain that horrible creatures would pop out at me. The wardrobes down here would lead to a far worse place than Narnia. Stacked chairs, old beach umbrellas, battered steamer trunks, ancient lawn furniture, and assorted rakes and shovels all spoke to me of death and vampire visitations. It always seemed darker than the darkest place inside my head—pretty frightening when you think of it that way. Yet, here I was, toughing it out, helping Caitlin search for her damn snake.

"It's warm enough," Caitlin commented. "I could see her liking it down here."

"Shouldn't you put the cat in your room? Boas eat small cats, right?" A desperate plea from a desperate woman. "He could get lost down here."

"Berg? Nah, he's cool." The cat purred like a buzz saw, emphasizing the point.

"OK, I guess." My last chance at stalling, gone. We stood at the foot of the stairs, scouting out likely spots. The only sounds were the humming of the boiler and the demented purring of Strindberg the cat. My throat felt dry.

"Tell you, what. Why don't I go upstairs and get a couple of flashlights?"

"Why? There's plenty of light down here, and Miss B. is large enough we're likely to see her pretty easily."

"Good point." Did boa constrictors move quickly? I couldn't remember. My eyes slid around the floor. I examined the lawn furniture suspiciously.

Caitlin walked along the shelves, peeking in and under them, stopping to read the occasional label that caught her eye. I couldn't think of a good reason to leave the basement, so I stuck with her, random images of Abbott & Costello wandering through my head. I was definitely Costello.

Caitlin looked over her shoulder at me. "I already looked there. Why don't you look over by those closets?" She wanted me to check out the wardrobes? I felt my hands go clammy.

"Those are wardrobes, Caitlin. They haven't been opened in years."

"Miss B. doesn't know that. Check it out! You said we'd search together, right?" She turned back to crouching and peeking.

Shit. I wiped my hands on my jeans and reminded myself I was a grown-up. Two mahogany wardrobes stood off to the side, not too close to the foundation walls. They were up on cinderblocks and had boxes stacked on top that reached almost to the beams above. They were gorgeous pieces. I made a note to ask my aunts about them.

"Hey, Caitlin? I can't see underneath. I'm going to go upstairs and…"

"Tell Glory to give a sniff under there. She'll know."

"Oh, yeah. Good idea." I cursed under my breath and called the dog, who trotted over obligingly, dropped her nose between two cement blocks and stuck her white butt in the air, stubby tail wagging. Glory made a heavy breathing sound, then stepped back and let out a mighty sneeze. No snake. If Miss B. were under there, the dog would have let me know all about it.

One wardrobe was locked tight, its tiny metal key firmly in its lock. I gave the boa a pass on that one. No thumbs. The other was slightly ajar. I seemed to remember that the door was warped so that the latch and the lock wouldn't line up. If Brunhilde went in there, the door would have been open wider, I reassured myself. I opened the door and peered inside.

To the left, a couple of clothing bags hung side-by-side, zippered and inscrutable. To the right, a series of shelves held dusty shoeboxes. Given my aversion to the past, it's understandable I didn't want to look into them. No boa could fit in there! Ready to close the door and move on, I leaned over and examined the bottom-most shelf. It was larger than the others and dark with shadows. A big snake might fit in there. I sighed.

Glory poked her nose in and looked up at me. Then she looked around to see what Caitlin was up to and trotted away.

I bent over so that my head was level with my knees. Not fun. It was clear I hadn't done yoga in a while. There was a dim gleam at the back of the shelf. I reached in and pulled out a dusty snow globe. I sat down on the floor and took a breath, resisting sudden tears. I rubbed the dust off on my sweater. I made the snow fly and watched it settle slowly.

The globe sat on a stand of wood and fit comfortably into my two hands. Inside was Father Christmas in red robes with white trim, a crown of holly on his peaked red cap, a Christmas tree held like a scepter in his right hand, a brown bag of gifts on his back. A tiny trumpet and a French horn peeked out among the presents. He stood on gently mounded snow and had flowing white hair and beard, kind eyes, and a smile that lifted his cheeks. A bubble of air the size of a silver dollar sat at the top of the globe above his head, like a halo. He was so beautiful, and he made me so sad.

When my dad was around, he'd go on binges, get drunker and drunker. This behavior was pretty much year-round, but at Christmas it was particularly painful. He was a sarcastic, mean drunk. My mother's disappointment was palpable. It amazed me she waited as long as she did to divorce the bastard. When my aunts arrived with presents to put under the tree, they outnumbered him and he'd go off to do his drinking elsewhere. Odds were he'd drive off the road, total his car, and we'd have to go claim him at the hospital. Louise always went and got him. For so many years, Christmas morning meant a mean man with a hangover and a cane brooding over the unfairness of life. I totally agreed with him on that one.

I put the snow globe back in the wardrobe just as Glory let out a volley of sharp barks and tore up the stairs. A door slammed, followed by angry barking.

I beat Caitlin up the stairs. We stood at the locked door, pounding out fists on it and yelling. Glory yelped in pain.

"You hurt my dog, I'll kill you!" Silence. Did the footsteps go upstairs? Who was there?

I looked at Caitlin, pulled out my cell phone and called Mac, told him to get Greta, snow or no snow. He told me to stay put, and I bit my tongue, deciding not to bite his head off when I was calling him for help. The snow was pretty bad out at his place, but he'd get here eventually.

Greta Danielson opened the door and placed the chair that had been propped under the doorknob back at the kitchen table.

"At least you didn't try to shoot your way out," she grumped at me.

"Ha Ha. Caitlin?" Caitlin charged back down the steps.

"You go ahead," she called over her shoulder, "I've got to find Berg!" The cat must not have liked all that pounding and yelling. Maybe when she was looking for the cat, Caitlin would find the boa. It could happen, I reassured myself.

'Looks like they got in the kitchen door, used something on the latch," Greta said. "Could have been worse, no real damage."

"Shit! Where's Glory!"

The dog limped into the room. I knelt and ran my hands over her. Glory whimpered when I touched her front leg. Bruised but not broken. I rested my cheek on the dog's smooth head and did not object when she pulled back and licked my face. I was so relieved she was OK.

The house was intact, except for my bedroom, which had been tossed. I put the room to rights while Greta made notes and provided narrative commentary.

"Somebody looking for something, Lyle. What is it they think you have, I wonder." Greta hummed to herself, at ease with the situation, whereas I felt pissed off and edgy.

The doorbell rang and I went down to find MacDonald George brushing snow off the Stetson, his old Irish setter, Jesse, at his feet. He came inside, took his boots off and kissed me. I was so upset I barely noticed the tickle of his moustache.

"You OK?" Mac asked.

Glory shivered beside me, not budging from my side.

"What's wrong with her?"

"Somebody kicked her, I think." I glared through my tears.

Mac knelt as I had done earlier and examined the dog, speaking low, reassuring sounds to her. Jesse walked over and the dogs sniffed noses.

"Looks like a bruised shoulder. No broken bones," he observed.

"That's what I thought. I can't get her to lie down," I said.

"She'll only sit still when you do, she's pretty shaken." His brown eyes told me I probably was, too. I didn't listen to them.

Greta joined us, nodding to Mac. "So, we got what? A second intruder, or a second visit from the first one? Last time you were in town, someone shot the window out. Nothing happened here when you were away." She shook her head and narrowed her green eyes at me.

"She was shot at today, too!" Caitlin and Berg appeared, somewhat the worse for wear. "It was so intense!" she added.

Greta and Mac looked at each other and back to me.

"Maybe we should all sit down," Greta said. "This could take a while."

I told them the story, ending with the bullet still lodged in cement.

"Great," Greta said, going for irony. Her eyes stayed on her notes.

Mac furrowed his brow, frowning. "Obviously, somebody thinks you know something or have something, Lyle." He sat back in his chair, locking eyes with me. "Now that you're back, they're worried."

"Shooting, breaking into the house while you're here," Greta added, "looks desperate to me!"

"Or stupid," I said. "Who would kick a dog?" I held Glory on my lap, her bony haunches digging into me. I looked over at Jesse, lying with her head on Mac's foot. "Why is Jesse here?" I asked.

"I wasn't sure I'd get back in this snow, and I didn't want to leave her alone." Mac put his hand on Jesse's back.

"Which reminds me—I've got to get going." Greta closed her notes and stood to go. "If you can't talk any sense to her, just tie her up and stick her in a closet," she said to Mac.

We walked into the hall with Greta, the dogs trailing after us, Glory limping along.

"She just won't stay put," I complained, as Greta struggled into her boots and jacket.

"Now, who does that remind you of?" she asked me.

We said goodbye and turned to the sound of boots coming down the stairs. Caitlin was outfitted for Arctic winter, her eyes peeking out from a small gap between scarf and hat. She pulled the scarf down so she could speak.

"I'm heading out. Need fresh air, a change of vibes, you know?"

"In a blizzard?" I asked her. "Seriously?"

"It's only snow, Lyle."

"What about Berg?" I asked.

"Safe and warm," Caitlin said, pointing to her jacket. "Right here."

"What about Brunhilde?"

"You'll find her, I'll know."

"How?"

"I'll just know, OK? We have a psychic connection." Scarf in place, the young woman left the house.

"Who's Brunhilde?" MacDonald asked.

"Caitlin's boa constrictor. Not a big one, but still…" My eyes slid around the floor. She's around here somewhere."

38

"I'm sure she'll be OK," Mac said as we stood at the parlor window and watched Caitlin disappear into a curtain of snow. "She's pretty good at looking after herself, Lyle. Been on her own a long time." He put an arm around my shoulders.

"I guess." I sighed and looked over at the Christmas tree, the battered "Star of Davis" and Rainbow Serpent resting companionably at the top of the tree. What was wrong with me? Was this a mid-life crisis—rescuing Chas, worrying like a mom over Caitlin? Feeling all mushy around MacDonald George? I remembered the snow globe sitting in the dark wardrobe and felt tears welling up.

"Dammit! I'm turning into a sissy!"

Mac laughed, a loud noise that startled the dogs. "You are the only sissy I know who's been shot at, abducted, blackmailed, shot at some more. It takes courage to stand next to you, woman!"

"Caitlin has the right idea. I'm getting out of here!"

"How?

"In my car!"

"With those feet?" We took a moment and stared down at my socks, knowing what lurked inside.

"No fair picking on my feet. They're drivable." I was starting to sound sullen.

"If you say so. The streets are not drivable, however," Mac said equably. "Caitlin left on foot. She's probably heading down to the bookstore, if it's open. Where will you go?"

"I'll think of something," I muttered, walking away, pulling the gun out of its holster and opening the front door.

Mac came over and stood beside me. We watched the falling snow in silence. The day was darkening, a flat gray that had no shadows. Everything looked blurred around the edges.

"You can't shoot the snow, Lyle. That won't work." He took the gun from me and stuck it in his jacket pocket. Put the Stetson on his head and pulled on a pair of gloves. When did he put the jacket on?

"Where are you going?"

"You haven't had much to eat today, have you. And I'll bet there's no food in the fridge. I've got a bag of groceries in the car as well as kibble. Be right back."

I closed the door and heard the sound of the snow shovel on the sidewalk. The two dogs stood in the hall, looking at me expectantly. We all trooped upstairs together and the dogs watched as I pulled wrapped presents out of the closet. Christmas Eve was tomorrow, it was time to dig stuff out and put it under the tree.

The dogs were mildly interested in sniffing the boxes I set on the bed, but when Glory sniffed the air behind me, both she and Jesse made a beeline for the closet. Jesse sat politely and wagged her feathery tail. Glory, meanwhile, was practically climbing up the doorframe to get to the closet shelf. They had found the Bow Wow stocking.

I closed the door firmly. "Go find Brunhilde," I told them. The dogs raised their heads simultaneously and raced down the stairs. "I'll be damned, they listened!"

Putting an armload of gifts on one of the chintz chairs, I turned on the lights. Mac was still outside, shoveling around the Mustang. I'd need to put more water in the tree base, then I'd open the door for Mac. My feet were getting cold, despite the moving around. I sat down, pulled on the Yak boots and headed for the kitchen.

"You armed?" The voice was low and steady.

"What? NO! My gun is..." I really didn't want to tell Shore that the .38 was in Mac's pocket.

Martin Shore sat at the kitchen table, a shadowy presence in the gloom. He had closed the curtains and motioned me to stop when I reached for the light switch. Boots and an assault rifle stood by the back door, his jacket hung over the back of his chair. Gloves and a watch cap sat on the table next to a glass of water. He had Margot with him. All three dogs were lined up, regarding him attentively.

"What's up?" I asked, leaning against the doorjamb.

Shore leaned back and took a smartphone from his pocket and ran his thumb along its smooth surface. "Security has been breached," he said. "Can't go into my house until I've checked it out. Could be booby traps."

"Really? Why?"

"Anybody talk to you about my uncles yet, Lyle? Never mind. Let's just say the situation is classified. I need you to put Margot and me up for a day or two. Can you do that?"

"Sure, there's plenty of room."

Shore nodded his thanks.

"I'm turning on the lights. The curtains are closed, you'll be fine."

Shore nodded a second time. We watched the three dogs begin sniffing rituals. Glory was behaving herself. Schnauzer, setter, terrier.

"It's like the Westminster Dog Show in here."

Shore gave me a blank look. "You watch dog shows?"

"Well, yeah. I read the dogs, read the judges. It's a lot like playing poker. You don't bet on feelings or which dog you think should win, you go with what's in front of you."

"OK, I see that. You good at picking winners?"

"Pretty good. It's not something I keep track of."

MacDonald walked into the kitchen, a sack of groceries in one arm, a sack of kibble under the other. He nodded hello, noting the jacket over the back of the chair, the boots by the door, next to the semi-automatic rifle.

"Shore."

"Mac."

"That's some weapon. Is Lyle being difficult or is there a war in Lawrence I don't know about?"

Shore didn't answer and gestured Margot to his side. All dogs went to their people and looked up at us.

"Shore and Margot are going to visit...for a bit," I told Mac. "You can have Crista's room at the top of the house, Shore."

"Thanks, I owe you," he said, picking up his rifle, clothing, taking the dog, and removing every sign of his presence from the room.

"Keep an eye out for snakes, " Mac advised as Shore moved into the hall toward the stairs.

I explained about Brunhilde.

"The kid has a boa constrictor? Outstanding!" Shore grinned and headed upstairs.

Mac raised his eyebrows at me.

"Something you want to ask me, MacDonald?"

"Where do you want me to put the kibble?"

I pointed to the pantry and followed him in to the small space, putting his arms around me as he turned.

"I feel safer with Shore in the house, Mac. It's kind of like having my own army." I looked up at him, eyes about level with his chin.

He pulled me close, the man smelled good. Mac bent his head down and kissed my ear. "You're an exasperating woman, you know that, don't you?"

"Why, because of Shore?"

"Martin Shore is the least of it." He moved from my ear to my mouth. There was heavy breathing, clothing got rearranged, dry goods rattled on the shelves. The man seemed to enjoy being exasperated.

The remainder of the day passed quietly. No sign of the boa constrictor, no word from Caitlin or anyone else, no sound from Shore and Margot. I thought I heard the kitchen door at one point. Figuring it was Shore ducking out for a reconnaissance, I decided to let it be.

*

"I want my gun back." We were sitting in the library, watching the fire, dogs snoozing at our feet. Glory usually snuggled beside me, but she was getting along well with Jesse and was happy on the rug.

"You don't need a gun, Lyle. You want sex, just let me know." Mac grinned and I jabbed him with my elbow. "What about that personal army of yours? He's better than a gun, isn't he? And look at me, an unarmed man." He raised his hands to illustrate. "Why not just leave that revolver where it is?"

"Because...I just want it, OK?" I stood up and brushed unruly silver strands behind my ears, going for a serious look. I had a feeling that was making me anxious, personal army or not, but I'd be damned if I was going to tell MacDonald about it.

"OK, OK." Mac looked up at me from the leather couch. "Go get it and bring it in here. You can set it on the mantelpiece where you can see it. Go on." He shooed me away, all patient and manly. I wanted to smack him.

I stepped into the dark hallway, running my hand along the paneling, feeling for the light switch. I froze when the front door opened and a bulky figure stepped inside. Not Caitlin—she would have barged in and stomped her feet. Not Martin Shore—too short. I caught the gleam of a long barrel in the glow of Christmas tree lights in the parlor. A large gun, .45 probably, with a silencer. Mac's jacket hung on a peg half way between us. Shit.

"Step over here, please. Keep your hands where I can see them." A woman's voice.

I took a few steps forward, hands out to the side, open palms facing her.

"What are you doing creeping around in the dark? I can see you, you know." Even with a hooded jacket, ski mask, and night goggles, the voice was distinctive.

"I can see you, too," I said. "What are you doing in my house? Could you put the weapon down, please? We could talk. Ms. Mancuso, from the University, right?"

"It was you! You killed Ron, didn't you? He was mine you murderer! Now I have to kill you." She made a sound of disgust and then shouted, "NO!"

MacDonald had entered the hall in a rush and switched on the lights. We dived for his jacket at the same time. Domenica Mancuso tore the goggles off and fired a round into the ceiling. She had a solid stance and hardly reacted to the recoil at all. Even with the ski mask on, she looked angry, her dark eyes snapping.

"Don't be stupid," she hissed. "Into the room, please." She nodded towards the parlor. "One at a time.

Keep your distance." We followed her directions and took our seats in separate chintz chairs. I put my hands on my knees where she could see them. Mac did the same.

"How did you get in? Why are you here?" I kept my voice light, curious.

"Shut up and let me think!" She removed the ski mask, stuffing it in a pocket. Pointing the gun at us, she drew a pair of glasses from another pocket and put them on. Domenica Mancuso sighed distractedly. "Now this man," she gestured to Mac. "What a mess. I picked up a key on my last visit."

"That was you? What's going on?"

Glory and Jesse appeared at the entrance to the parlor and looked in at us.

"Make them go away or I'll shoot them too," she said.

"Shoot my dog and I'll strangle you!" Mac told me to calm down. "Oh yeah? The hell I will!" I stood up and took a step forward.

"Sit down," she said. "Don't be so dramatic. Just make them go away. Sheesh."

The dogs backed up a bit but would not leave. They sat and watched us anxiously.

"You're here because you think I did what?" I tried to regain my composure.

"Obviously I'm a bad shot or I wouldn't have to come in here, you murderer." Ms. Mancuso was put out with herself.

"That was you? Outside? The window, the drive by? Why are you trying to kill me?"

"Going. I'm going to kill you. Have to. You, too," she said to Mac. "Not a muscle. I can't miss, this close. Just shut up the both of you. I have to think."

I took a moment to think, myself, not wanting her to come up with a clear plan to dispose of Mac and me. One of us would have to get to Mac's jacket. Soon."

"It has to be Ron Addison," I said, thinking out loud. "You think I saw something or picked something up out at the corn maze. That's why you keep coming back to my house."

"Shut up! You don't know anything!"

"I must, mustn't I, or you wouldn't be here all desperate to kill me."

"You shot him, I can shoot you! And your boyfriend, too!" Her dark hair stood out, giving her a maniacal Einstein look. I wondered idly if Einstein wore glasses.

"He wouldn't listen, Ron. Thought he was such a ladies' man, worse than his asshole nemesis, Cassaday. I worshipped him. I'd have done anything for him. And I did. And then, THEN he tells me if I don't leave him alone, he'd post those horrible photos on the Internet. But the pictures weren't on him. Is that why you shot him? Because he made you pose for him too? You must have the camera. Give it to me!"

"OK," I said reasonably. "It's upstairs. I'll just go get it."

Just then a couple of things happened. I gave Mac a look, signaling that he should rush the mad Ms. Mancuso and grab her gun. Mancuso yelled at me to sit down, the dogs stood up and barked, and a small red dot appeared on Domenica's forehead as Mac tackled me and took me to the floor.

"Oh, my God! What is that? Stop or I'll shoot!" The woman sounded completely hysterical.

"You're already dead," Shore said as he entered the room. "Drop the gun."

Ms. Mancuso complied with the request and Shore entered the room, barefoot, in camo pants, Brunhilde draped around his shoulders.

"Get it away, get it away!" Domenica Mancuso cried.

Martin Shore grinned ferociously. "Guess she's afraid of snakes."

39

"Where is she?"

Caitlin entered the house and stamped her boots, dislodging cascades of snow from her head and shoulders, her face red with cold. Snow had drifted over the front steps and onto the porch. Wherever she had come from, it must've been quite a trek. The storm showed no signs of stopping.

I gestured up the stairs with the Crimson Trace, a glass of scotch in my left hand.

"Alcohol and guns don't mix, you know," she said solemnly. Caitlin piled the wet outerwear near the door, Strindberg the cat cradled in one arm. The young woman pushed damp bangs back from her glowing face, piercings a sparkle. She looked over my shoulder at MacDonald George who stood behind me, his own drink well in hand.

"What's going on?" Caitlin asked. "Miss B. OK?"

Mac pointed with his drink toward the parlor, where Domenica Mancuso sat exactly where Shore had left her—in one of the chintz chairs, hands in plastic manacles behind her back. She was disheveled and grim-faced, her eyes glittering. The woman glared silently, like a black hole in the middle of Christmas.

Caitlin took one look, said, "Later," and hurried up the stairs to check on her beloved boa. Glory and Jesse trailed after her. I assumed Margot was already up there with Shore as he tended to Brunhilde.

Mac and I stayed in the hall, sipping our drinks and leaning into each other. He had one arm around my shoulders. There was no argument about the Crimson Trace when I retrieved it from his jacket. We waited for the police to arrive, if they ever would, given the fierce weather.

Neither of us wanted to be in the same room with Ms. Mancuso, who hadn't said a word since her capture. Iago took the same tack after the death of Othello. She sat there, looking coiled and dangerous.

Mac kissed the top of my head and nuzzled my hair. I smiled into my glass and shook the ice cubes.

"Every time an ice cube clinks, another angel gets his wings," I sighed happily.

"You're so bad. Maybe I should take the gun for a while. It must be heavy holding it like that."

It was getting heavy, but I wasn't going to tell Mac that. The scotch glass was making my hand cold. My stomach was growling, the adrenaline subsiding, and I was getting a headache.

"No."

"C'mon, just for a minute."

"No."

Domenica Mancuso rolled her eyes. "Shut up! Just shoot me, already! You're making me crazy!"

"You're already crazy!" I yelled back. Maybe I should let Mac have the gun, I thought. I needed food.

Just before the lights went out, something small and fast raced across the hall into the parlor. Glory and Jesse sped down the stairs after it, barking their heads off.

Domenica yelled, "What the hell is that?" and the lights flickered and went out, the sudden darkness filled with the sound of barking dogs and a high-pitched screaming.

"Is it on me? Oh, my god, it's on me!" The woman shrieked and thrashed around. If she knocked the tree down I was definitely going to shoot her.

"Here, you better take this." I handed the gun to Mac, and before he could say, "Lyle, wait!" I charged into the dark room.

"Whoa!" I tripped over a growling dog and the scotch went flying. I heard the glass crash and shatter on the floor as I fell hard onto my left side, right onto the ribs I'd bruised in Vegas. The air whooshed out of me.

"Nobody move!" Mac said. "Jesse, heel!"

In the sudden silence I heard labored panting. It could have been Glory or Mancuso or me. I rolled onto my back and groaned.

"Ms. Mancuso, stay perfectly still." Mac's voice was calm, but the small red dot dancing around the room seemed a little jumpy.

"What, are you crazy? There's something in here! It attacked me!"

The lights flickered on and went off again. Not good. Caitlin's voice called into the room from the hall. "Everything OK in here? Who's got the gun?"

"Everything's fine, Caitlin. Stay back," Mac said.

"Somebody call the police! I can't take any more!" Domenica yelled in the darkness.

"We've already called them, Ms. Mancuso," Mac told her. "All we have to do is wait. Quietly."

"Great! Just great!" she complained.

"Um..." Caitlin said, hesitantly. "I've got a flashlight. Is it OK if I come in?"

"No, it's not OK!" I sat up and looked toward the doorway, where Caitlin stood pointing a beam of light at the floor. "The woman's insane!"

"Hey! My hands are tied behind my back, all right? Very uncomfortable, I might add."

"What is it, Caitlin?" Mac asked. The beam of light allowed us all a dim glimpse of the room. He moved closer to me.

"Where's Glory?" Usually, when I was on the floor the dog was all over me, slobbering on my face.

"That's your dog, the white one? It's over here, by my chair." Serious dog breathing came from the direction indicated.

"The rat? Brunhilde's dinner? It escaped. I'm pretty sure it's in here. Miss B. is so hungry. I wouldn't ask if it weren't important. Please?" Probably it was the gun that made Caitlin hesitate. She was fiercely protective of Brunhilde.

"A rat?" Domenica shrieked. "First a giant snake, now a rat? Get me outta here!"

"Relax, Caitlin. Mac has the gun, not me."

"I still don't think it's a good idea," Mac said.

"Come on in, Caitlin." My ribs hurt and I was feeling contrary.

She aimed the beam of light at the chair where Glory stood snuffling, butt in the air, head under the chair skirt. Above the dog, Domenica balanced on the cushion, hands behind her back, glasses askew, hair wild. The woman looked ready to bite the head off a chicken.

Caitlin got down on hands and knees next to Glory and placed the flashlight on the floor. Aiming the beam along the floor made the room darken. A small, black shape leapt out from under the Christmas tree and dived under the chair.

"Berg! No!"

The flashlight skittered into a corner. Glory barked hysterically, the cat hissed and spat and yowled, and there was that strange, squealing scream again. The heavy chintz chair rocked and bucked like a buffalo. I held tightly to Mac, the two of us giggling uncontrollably.

A gust of arctic air swept into the room, followed by a hooded figure with a powerful flashlight. From where I sat, it looked like a lighthouse with legs.

"Shoot me! Go ahead, I dare you!" Domenica Mancuso charged the lighthouse, slamming him or her into the wall. The woman ran out into the snow, screaming.

"Close the door!" I yelled.

The door closed, the hood was thrown back, and the light came on. Greta Danielson picked up her flashlight and switched it off.

"Lyle Hudson, get up off the floor, will you please? MacDonald, I thought you had better sense. Can't you people do anything right? All you had to do is guard the suspect until we got here. I hope you have candles or something because the power won't hold. We got power off all over. And what are you up to?" This last was addressed to Caitlin as she climbed out from behind the overturned chair, cat by the scruff of the neck in one hand, rat in the other. Glory was in play pose, waiting to see which one she'd get.

*

"This rat better be alive, Lyle, or you'll be so sorry!"

"Me! Me? I had nothing to do with your rat!"

"Just pray Miss B. will eat it, that's all I'm saying!"

Mac kept me on the floor until the angry girl left the room, then he helped me up. Moving hurt like hell.

"Shouldn't you be out apprehending the suspect?" I asked Greta.

"Are you crazy? She stays out there, she deserves what she gets."

A thump on the door made Greta's point. Domenica Mancuso stood there wet and bedraggled, hands still tied behind her, lavender suede boots sodden.

"I give up," she said. "Just, no rats or snakes, OK?"

"Looks like you're having a bad night," Greta said. "You planning on getting far in those boots?"

"Oh, yeah? Well, they're better than that!" Domenica sneered at my footwear.

"I'll have you know these are orthopedic," I said defensively.

"Orthopedic yak, of course they are," Greta said. "Domenica Mancuso, you are under arrest for the murder of Ron Addison. You have the right to remain silent…"

"What? I didn't kill him, she did!" Domenica pointed her chin at me and shuddered. "Can I have my coat, please?"

Greta laughed, "Lyle? Seriously?" She shook her head and spoke into her phone. I gathered up the ski mask and goggles, along with the .45. Mac shoveled a new path to the street. The wind was biting, the snow sharp as sand in my face, so I didn't see the vehicle right away.

"That your ride?" I asked as Mac stood back to allow Greta to escort Ms. Mancuso to the cab of the truck.

"Hell, yes! How else do you think I'd get over here?" She grinned and closed the door once she was inside. Officer Danielson had commandeered a snowplow.

40

"Where's Shore?" I asked Caitlin the next morning. We were sitting bleary-eyed over cups of cocoa and tea. Caitlin had a wicked sweet tooth. Her cup of cocoa had miniature marshmallows and a chunk of candy cane floating in it. I could hear Berg's manic purring from inside Caitlin's sweatshirt.

"Dunno." She lapped melted marshmallows like a cat, each lick revealing the silver stud in her tongue. I wondered if hot liquids were a problem but refrained from asking.

Shore had disappeared yet again, taking Margot and every trace with him. I wanted information, or even a good guess, but Caitlin wasn't curious at all, being a free spirit who came and went when she wanted. Shore's coming and going felt familiar to her. She admired him.

"Shore is so cool. He totally gets Brunhilde." She hooked the candy cane out of the cup and crunched it happily, sending wafts of chocolate and peppermint across the kitchen table.

"Where did he find her?" I asked.

"Didn't say. We were focused on Miss B., seeing she was OK. He fixed her cage in no time. Sorry about the rat," Caitlin added.

"No problem, it worked out fine," I laughed, remembering last night's hilarity. "Shore didn't say anything about where he was going?"

"Only that it was time, that the snow would cover his tracks." She paused, patting the cat-sized lump of her sweatshirt. "I have a feeling he's still around."

"Really? Why?"

"No reason." Caitlin shrugged. "See you later, OK?" She downed the rest of the cocoa and put her cup in the sink.

"You bet."

I washed the cups and went upstairs to get dressed. The power was back but the house felt cold. Gusts of wind buffeted the windows and shook frozen branches against the roof. The snow had abated over night, but the slate sky promised more. I bundled up, throwing one of my mother's old cardigans over jeans and a turtleneck. Olive green was not my favorite color, but if I wore black, I'd end up looking like something covered with sprinkles. Glory's white coat was impossible.

Downstairs, I found MacDonald in the parlor by the Christmas tree.

"What are you doing?"

"Checking for snakes," he answered, deadpan.

"No worries. Brunhilde is upstairs, sleeping off her rat."

"Good to know." Mac did that crinkly thing with his eyes, which as usual started to give me ideas, but before I could make my move, the cell buzzed in my pocket.

Crista and Blake had spent a long, cold night in the workroom at Hyacinth where the power was off. I invited them over and returned the cell to my pocket.

"You think they'll be able to get here?" I asked, brushing silver hair from my face and looking up at him.

"They're young, they'll manage," he said.

"Hey," I took his hand, "there's something I want to show you."

"And what might that be?" Mac asked, pulling me toward him.

"Etchings? Or, if you prefer, we could go in the pantry and admire the canned peaches." Canned peaches. Did I really say that?

*

"What are you doing?" I asked much later.

"I'm asking you about your plans. You know, looking ahead, the future, you and me. Trying to have the conversation," Mac said.

"Why would you do that? We're having a good time," I whined.

"Yes we are. And," he emphasized the word, "Grown ups make plans. It's what we do. Not a big deal."

"But, it's Christmas." It was all I had.

"Christmas will pass, the snow will pass. What are your plans? Pretty simple question, really," Mac said reasonably, tossing me a pillow.

We were dressed and he was helping me make the bed. Glory and Jesse sat by the door, watching us. Glory had a ball in her mouth, her mind on an entirely different subject. I smacked the pillow onto the bed in frustration.

"You're making me crazy!"

"You make yourself crazy, Lyle. I'll rephrase the question: What do you think you might be doing next? Time in Lawrence? Trips to Las Vegas? Take a few guesses. I'm looking for a heads-up, woman, not trying to change who you are."

I stared at him, speechless.

"Take your time. I'm going to let the dogs out."

Glory heard the words dog and out and raced down the stairs, Jesse and Mac following.

I sat on the bed and groaned. "What is wrong with me?"

Louise would have said I was in a swivet of wanting something I didn't want to want. Thanks, mom.

Later that evening, Luce pulled me aside into the library. We gravitated to the tall window by the leather couch and looked out. It was one of those winter evenings that made your eyes feel cold from looking at the deepening indigo.

"After the snow clears, I'm going to San Francisco," Luce said. "Oh, and Crista is here," she added, trying to distract me.

"San Francisco?"

"With Charles."

"Charles? Like in Chas?" The words were not fitting together in my head.

"I prefer Charles. Yes." Luce smiled calmly.

"Yes? You're going to San Francisco to stay with Chas?" What was going on?

"He thought I could stay next door, at your apartment. Charles is under the impression you won't be back for a while." Luce paused and looked at me. "Are you upset, Lyle?"

"Yes. No. I'm confused."

I hated the feeling that the compartments of my life were breaking down, that people were moving around like kaleidoscope pieces, changing the script, making decisions that left me outside. I've hated it since my parents divorced, back in the last ice age. I was the one who was supposed to come and go, change the game, up the ante. This was horrible! First Mac, now Luce with infuriating twinkles in her eyes.

MacDonald George chose that moment to enter the room, Chas right behind him. Chas spoke first.

"Oh, there you are puss-ums, can I get you a drink?" He handed a glass of wine to Luce, sipping from the one in his hand. "How about you, Mac? Merry Christmas, all!"

Mac declined the offer and asked me with his eyebrow if I wanted a scotch. I nodded and he went off on the appointed task, leaving Luce and Chas and me standing by the library fire. Luce and Chas raised their glasses in a silent toast and twinkled at each other, gray eyes and green eyes merry. I wanted to smack them.

"So. California," I nodded the way you would at a good idea. "Seeing the sights?" An awkward conversational opener, but I didn't know what the cards were. Yet.

"Charles and I have discovered that we have a great deal in common," Luce said.

"And, it would be lovely to have a live-in neighbor, darling. I have been so lonely." Chas brushed a non-existent stray blond hair, accentuating his profile, going all Garbo on me.

New friends for a New Year. Mazel tov." Mac put a drink in my hand. It went immediately into my mouth, ice clinking against my nose.

"New, my eye," Luce said, her twinkle turning into a dangerous glint. "It's as though we've known each other for ages, Lyle. We occasionally Skype, did you know?"

My mind reeled at the possible implications.

"Anyway," Chas interrupted soothingly, "While we were snowed in at Luce's house—impossible, snow, really, don't know how people live with it—we had this marvelous idea!

"That we're not quite ready to discuss," Luce interrupted back. "I'm merely going to San Francisco to explore some options for a start-up, assess the viability of the project." She and Chas shared a complicit smile.

" 'One may smile and smile and still be a villain,'" I muttered into my glass.

"Hamlet?" Luce laughed. "You hate Hamlet. No one's betraying you here, Lyle. Grow up.

"There, there," Chas patted Luce's hand. "She's just being dramatic. You Hudson women, so emotional."

"Are not!" Luce and I snapped in unison, causing Mac to pass scotch through his nose and sputter and cough.

We finished thumping on Mac's back, handed him tissues, calmed the dogs and discovered that there were three of them.

"Um, Lyle?" Crista poked her head in, looking for me. "There's a navy SEAL in the kitchen with a hunk of meat and a gun. Oh, and I answered your cell. The aunts are coming over a little early. Something about the church service ending ahead of schedule. I've got pita chips and Christmas veggie dip, if you're interested. And Blake made some tofu fritters!" Crista beamed and returned to the kitchen.

I turned to face Luce. "OK, where do you think Vern is?"

41

Christmas Eve dinner tends to be potluck. It used to be more formal, a back-to-back affair with the Christmas Day meal, involving planning and work for two days' worth of food. Formality and tradition still apply to the latter, but Christmas Eve dining has evolved into a more free form, Twelfth Night kind of production. Those who went to church attended the 5:30 children's pageant, alternating between Alban's Episcopal, where Loretta attended, and the congregational church, where Lenore remained loyal to Pastor White.

"I get the appeal of Midnight Mass and all— candles, *Silent Night*, the whole enchilada," Lenore would say, "But I just can't stay up that late!"

The L&L's shared an appreciation for the children's service that mystified me. Not wanting to provoke my aunts, fearing they'd drag me off to "see for myself," I once asked Vern why they went. "I think it's the possibility that mayhem and pandemonium may break out at any moment," he'd explained. "That's what keeps me going." Vern laughed, a deep chuckle rising in his chest.

"Just think about it," he continued. "All those angels and magi, and shepherds and lambs. Not to mention a real live baby Jesus in a stroller. One year, somebody volunteered a donkey for the production. Cute little critter, but turns out the organist had some hitherto unknown allergy to donkey dander. Her face swole up and got all red. The choir was a capella for a while, until someone jabbed her with an EpiPen and the antihistamine kicked in."

"You're kidding me."

"God's truth, Lyle. I wouldn't miss it for the world."

This year was no exception, three feet of snow or not.

*

"Vern's not with them?" Luce asked.

"Usually it's Vern who calls while the L&L's help with the clean up, right? It's not like them to break with tradition," I said.

"Hm. Interesting. I wonder what happened this time."

"Darling," Chas tapped Luce on the shoulder with his wine glass, "Was that cranberry sorbet for tonight or tomorrow? I can't remember. All this familial commotion—so distracting."

"Dar—ling," I snorted into my ice cubes.

Before I could make any more trouble, Mac took my arm and steered me out of the room. "Let's see if we can't contribute in the food department, make some popcorn or something," he said mildly.

"Hey, I can cook, you know," I complained.

Mac shook the ice in his glass, holding it before me like a carrot.

"Scotch?" I followed willingly.

In the kitchen, every surface was in use, including the top of the refrigerator, as a staging, storing, or preparation area for the meal to come. Crista was sitting on Blake's lap, across the table from Shore, who was doing something ninja-like with a knife and a piece of raw meat. All three dogs sat at his feet, looking up at Shore adoringly.

Crista and Blake raised their beers in a toast as we walked in.

"Shore was just explaining the difference between steak tartar and carpaccio," Crista informed us.

"Dude," Blake said admiringly.

Shore kept his eyes on the steak, cutting it so thin that you could see the blade through the slice of meat.

"Invented at Harry's Bar, in Venice," he said. Shore was obviously continuing a lecture, educating vegetarians in carnivore lore.

"Why? Go figure. Some countess, I think. It was named carpaccio by Giuseppe Cipriani, who owned Harry's Bar. Got it?" So why call it 'Harry's', I wondered.

Blake and Crista nodded. Shore kept slicing, gently laying each fragile slice on a large, white plate. Mac and I were mesmerized, as were the dogs.

"This was an homage to Vittore Carpaccio. Cipriani said the colors of the meat reminded him of the guy's paintings. I looked him up—Carpaccio. He was Renaissance, mostly religious stuff: St. Augustine, Lamentation of Christ, really sad."

"Dude." Blake nodded. He could totally see it.

"I like his St. George, though," Shore concluded, wiping the knife and placing it in the sink. "Guy definitely liked reds and grays—meaty colors. There."

The plate looked like a rose window of meat. Shore spooned capers onto the center of the arrangement, and drizzled a mustard sauce around the outer edge. He wrapped the remaining slab and put it in the fridge.

"We should eat this now," he said. "It's not the kind of thing you want to leave sitting around."

I explained the situation with the latecomers and Shore nodded. We took the carpaccio, a baguette, the veggies and fritters to the parlor, dragging along Luce and Chas as we went. Caitlin and Berg joined us as we camped out on the floor and chairs. Small plates were passed around, and Caitlin made a kitchen run for napkins and forks.

"Here." She dumped the angry fur ball in my lap." "No food. Just hold him until I get back."

I held out a bite of tofu fritter and Berg sniffed it, curious. The cat decided he was not interested and proceeded to bat at the plate in my lap.

"Oh, man, that's so good!" Blake was purring and chewing at the same time.

"You ate that? You ate meat?" Crista stared at Blake, incredulous.

"Mmm." Blake continued purring and chewing.

"Lips that touch meat shall never touch mine," she said primly.

"Oh, baby, don't be like that."

Crista fled the room and Blake followed, but not before snagging another slice of carpaccio.

"Crista, come on…"

"You had more, didn't you? That's disgusting."

Their voices retreated down the hall. Caitlin returned, passed out supplies and retrieved her cat.

"What's with them?" she asked.

"Blake ate meat," Chas whispered loudly.

"Serious breach of ethics," Caitlin said, popping raw meat into her mouth and chewing with gusto.

Lenore and Loretta arrived, amid the clumping of boots and happy dog greetings. The two hung up their coats on pegs in the hall and commenced hugging and greeting people.

"You started without us?" Loretta complained, grabbing some bread and cheese.

"We were hungry!" I protested.

"Where's Vern?" Luce asked.

The L&L's eyeballed each other. "I'm sure he'll be along soon, dear," Lenore said.

"The snow's stopped," Loretta volunteered. "And the roads aren't too bad!"

"Are you stonewalling us?" I asked.

"Hey! I need some Christmas cheer! Any beer in this place? Hello, Shore, good to see you!"

"Loretta." Shore nodded, smiling. "Can I interest you in some carpaccio? This plate's empty, but there's more."

"Raw meat? You bet! Let's go!"

They headed off to the kitchen, and Lenore greeted everyone, her cheeks pink from the cold, eyes shining, and white hair glowing. If ever there was a Christmas angel, she was it.

"Let me just hang up this scarf, she said, unwinding about two yards of red fuzzy stuff that had probably been knitted by her sister. "Did you put the tandoori chicken in the oven, Luce?"

"Along with the nan, Lenore. It should be good to go," Luce replied.

"I have died and gone to heaven," Chas said. "Or I've fallen into a gourmet, gypsy Christmas, which amounts to the same thing."

"Totally," Caitlin agreed.

Mac brought in a couple of chairs from the dining room for the L&L's. Loretta and Shore returned, platter of carpaccio in hand, Loretta happily purring and chewing. Mac offered her a chair next to Lenore's.

"Hell, no! I'll sit on the floor. You can haul me up later. Save that chair for Vern."

Everyone laughed and Loretta settled in next to Caitlin. A place at the coffee table was cleared, followed by a hum of admiration over the arrival of the tandoori chicken. Crista arrived with a plate of hummus and veggies, Blake right behind her.

"Merry Christmas, everyone!" Crista said. Obviously, something angelic had occurred in the kitchen.

42

"You what?"

"I said I'd appreciate it if you gave me a minute to finish my beer before you unleashed the women on me," Vern said.

"No. Before that." I dumped the ice in the sink and poured some water from a bottle on the table. Looking at Vern, I felt the need to sober up. A little. "The part about the eye patch."

Vern looked like Pirate Santa, the black eye patch framed by one curly, white eyebrow. Ernest Hemingway would have looked just like him if he's poked himself in the eye with that shotgun instead of blowing his head off.

" It's a scratched cornea, nothing serious," he explained.

"Self-inflicted?" I asked. The thought made him chuckle. "What happened? Where? Do the L&L's know?"

"Hold on, hold on, Lyle. I'm just going to tell this once." He took a sip of his beer and picked up a tandoori chicken leg from a plate on the kitchen table. "Pardon me while I eat. I only have seconds. I can feel the Hudson antennae reaching out already."

Vern had snuck in the back door so quietly the dogs hadn't heard him. They were still in the parlor hoping for treats. His parka hung across the back of a kitchen chair. The man shook his head when I walked in the kitchen, as if to say he just couldn't catch a break. A gentle man, resigned to the ways of Hudson women, he sat back and waited for my barrage of questions. The eye that wasn't covered by a patch looked weary.

"Think I might forgo the Christmas pageant next year," He told me. "There more of this chicken?"

Before I could answer, a tide of Hudson women, dogs, and assorted others flowed into the room.

"I told you I heard his voice!" Loretta said. "Where you been, Vern? You said you were right behind us. Like the eyewear, hon. My kind of Santa!" Loretta cracked herself up.

"Peace, woman!" Vern responded. "Off!" This was directed at Glory, who was jumping and licking, dancing around Vern, pinning him to the chair.

"Glory! Out!" I commanded the dog. No dice. Glory dived under the table, out of reach.

"What happened, Vern?" Lenore asked. "I thought things had quieted down before we left."

"Quieted down? " I asked.

"Melee," Loretta said. "The usual goings on. Place was almost empty when we left."

"Can we move to another room, please? I'm feeling hemmed in. I could use a more comfortable chair. This could take a while."

We trooped back to the parlor, rearranged chairs and plates and waited for Vern to speak. As people settled in, I counted dog noses. We were down to two. I looked over at Caitlin.

"Yeah," she said, reading my question. "Shore left. Has a date with some uncles. Said to say thanks for dinner." She paused, scratching Berg's spiky head, thinking about it. "He's not used to all the camaraderie," she said. "Takes getting used to."

"Indeed it does, " Mac agreed.

"OK," Loretta said. "Last Lenore and I knew, there was a shepherd and a lamb getting into it. Shepherd boy poked the lamb with his thingamajig—the crook—and the lamb got pissed off. Must've been all of four. She stood up, took the crook away and clobbered the shepherd. The magi bumped into each other, and the angels, little bitty ones, started crying. Lamby Pie ran into the pews, and parents started complaining about whose fault it was. Then a couple of exe's had opinions to share and a questionable hand gesture was met with a punch. That about right, Lenore?"

"Yes, I'm afraid so. But you weren't involved in any of that Vern." Lenore said, clearly looking for information.

"No, I wasn't," Vern agreed. "Wasn't near the choir, either. The organist took the opportunity to scold one of the sopranos for being off key, and the woman says 'That's it, I'm outta here.' Threw her hymnal. Organist ducked, book hit a grandmother in the first pew and things kind of escalated from there," Vern recalled.

"One of the altos accused a soprano of 'being such a stone bitch' and a choral exodus ensued," Loretta added.

"Father Edwin was at wits end," Lenore said."

"Everyone calls him Ed. Man hates it," Loretta chuckled. He was in a pickle, alright!"

"May I?" Vern asked.

"Go right ahead," Loretta said. "We're just providing color commentary!" The two sisters laughed and then settled down, waiting for Vern to proceed with his story.

"Right. The man didn't know what to do, so he started calling Merry Christmas to everyone, trying to sneak in a plea for grown-ups to come back at 10:30 for Lessons and Carols and such."

"Yeah, that's gonna happen!" Loretta interjected.

"It might, dear. People are curious, word gets around. Some might show up just to see if Ed Hodge got a black eye," she added philosophically.

"The church cleared out pretty fast," Vern continued. "You two went on ahead, and I stayed to pick things up a bit. Thought the least I could do was pick up candles. I was out in the pews, collecting candles in an usher's basket, when I heard voices up by the altar. It was Father Edwin and his wife, having words. Started out quiet enough, but then she pointed a finger in the man's face, he said something down his nose at her, and the conversation turned ugly. What's her name?"

"Kirsty," the L&L's said in unison.

"So Kirsty there picks up the advent wreath and starts whaling on him. Like a fool, I go up to keep them from bodily harm. 'Bastard!' she yells, 'I saw you with your hand…'

"I say something pacifying, like 'Whoa there,' and she whirls on me and slaps me in the face with the damned wreath. Beg your pardon, Lenore. Anyway, there was holly in there, caught me in the eye and I went down, just to get away from her. She turns back, has one more go at Father Ed, and storms out of the sanctuary, madder than a wet cat." Vern touched the eye patch briefly. "Hurt like hell. Father Ed, though, looks like he was attacked by wasps. Lumps and scratches all over his face. He got me to the emergency room, where they rinsed my eye, put something tingly on my eyeball, and gave me this patch. So, that's the event after the event. Elvis, what's for dessert?"

My aunts fussed over Vern and life in the busy kitchen seemed to move around me as I reflected on the scene between the rector and his angry wife. I recalled the hissed accusations overheard at the Faire and how the good reverend might have been involved with Robin Breck, the murdered coed. It struck me as odd—the way life can be odd—that some people were killed for infidelity and others got away with it indefinitely. Remembering events at the Faire took me to the dead professor in the corn maze. He, too, was murdered by misplaced love. If jealousy can be called love. So much rage at rejection. Maybe it was loneliness, or fear of being alone that led to the attacks. Not Christmassy thoughts.

I shook myself out of my reverie and stood up from the table. I wanted to have MacDonald's dark eyes in front of me, his warmth and sanity. I passed Crista and Blake in the hall, bringing dishes to the kitchen. In the parlor, Caitlin was curled up in one of the big chairs with her little cat, teasing him with a piece of ribbon. No MacDonald George. I checked upstairs, only to find empty rooms. My mother's house felt lived in, in a way I hadn't expected. No longer a monument to the past, the house had developed a new character, becoming a place of friendly togetherness. Listen to me, going all mushy. Maybe I was changing, too. The voice in my head sounded just like Louise. Perish the thought.

I found Mac downstairs in the library in one of the leather chairs, feet up on the ottoman, Jesse lying on her side by the fire. Mac turned his gaze from the fire to me, and I smiled at the sight of him, dark eyes, moustache, long legs crossed at the ankles. He did not smile back.

The room was a quiet counterpoint to the laughter and bustle going on in the kitchen. No plates clattered here. The quiet grew as Mac silently regarded me and I looked back. He was so solid, so masculine. Men are such different creatures, I thought. But Mac was more. He seemed so comfortable in his own skin. I envied his solidity and strength. I entered the room and walked toward the fire, turning to face the man in the chair.

"I was thinking of getting some fresh air. Care to join me?"

Mac took his feet from the ottoman and sat forward, looking at the fire. He took a deep breath and nodded. "Sure." He stood up and put his hands in his pockets.

"Hiding something from me?"

He shook his head. "You don't want to know."

"Mysterious."

"Some things are. You want to keep asking questions or are we going outside?"

I told the crowd in the kitchen we were going outside.

Luce called out as we headed toward the front door," Don't be long! You know what's next." I rolled my eyes, even though she couldn't see me. I really needed some fresh air; round two was going to be an event.

"Don't do anything I wouldn't do!" Chas added, waving over Luce's shoulder.

Mac and I left the porch and walked out to the snowy street where tires had worn ruts into the deep snow, proving the street drivable for the brave of heart and anyone with a truck. I turned and looked at the lighted windows of the house. My house. It looked like a movie set for one of those warm, ensemble movies, like "Love Actually," only Midwestern. The thought made me laugh.

I looked up at Mac to find he was watching me closely, thinking about something.

"A penny for your thoughts?" My grandmother used to say that all the time. I'd have to watch it; I was starting to sound Kansan.

He grimaced and looked up at the night sky. I looked up, too, at the stars in the inky darkness. I breathed in the sharp air and waited for Mac to say something. When he didn't, I laughed nervously.

"My aunts, they take Christmas to a whole other level. It can be a bit much." Mac looked at me, still not talking. I made small circle on the snow packed street, crunching ridges or tire ruts with my shaggy yak boots.

"How are the feet?" Mac asked.

"Fine. A little frisky, even." I made a little hop, hinting.

"Good." Mac paused. "Jesse and I should go back to the house, check on things out there."

"But tomorrow's Christmas Day."

"It is."

"But..."

"The sky's clear," he said. "I should go."

Talk about a shoe on the other foot. I didn't like how it felt. "I guess I just assumed that you'd stay." My voice trailed off and my throat felt tight.

"You have family around, things going on. Right?"

We stood there facing each other in the middle of the road and I heard the words that weren't being said. The elephant in the room was in the street with us.

"Oh." I put my hands in my coat pockets. "I see."

"Hey, you two!" Loretta called from the porch. "Come on in! Show's getting started!"

"Show?" Mac asked.

"You have to see it to believe it," I said. "If you tried to leave now, they'd only track you down and haul your ass back in there." I shook my head. "I know. I've tried."

Mac laughed quietly and followed me back into the house.

43

The action had moved from the front parlor to the library where there were more options for comfortable seating. Besides, Vern said, we wouldn't want to insult the real presents; this could get ugly. I pointed out that the library was closer to the drinks, for the faint of heart. Crista and Blake and Caitlin all looked confused. Mac leaned against the doorjamb looking philosophical, or maybe he was figuring out his getaway. Luce and Chas sat side by side on the leather couch, glasses of wine in hand. Chas's head was inclined toward Luce, who was probably explaining the tribal event about to occur.

"Come in and sit down, MacDonald," Luce said, shifting her attention from the blond loveliness of Chas. "Set a good example for the children."

Mac complied, taking a seat next to Luce on the couch. When I asked if he wanted a drink, Mac shook his head, the barest hint of a smile flickering on his lips. I'd have missed it if I hadn't been looking closely at the man. His silence made me feel guilty, which was irritating. I hadn't done anything, dammit.

I left the room intending to get a scotch but returned with a glass of water. If we were going to end up fighting, I wanted a clear head. The habitual grousing about other people's expectations began inside my head. I resisted the urge to frown and put on my poker face.

"If that's your poker face, Lyle, you just forget about it!" Loretta commanded. "We want to see chagrin and humiliation, just like the rest of us!" The older folks laughed, and Lenore explained.

"The way a white elephant works around here is that people bring in hideous stuff and inflict it on others. No tasteful book & bottle exchanges. You might encounter a bottle of Pepto-Bismol cleverly hidden inside a gift box for Chanel No. 5, for example."

"Or a pair of left handed toe clippers!" Loretta jumped in. "We are adhering to the basic principle," she continued, "but instead of making everyone go out and find horrible crap, we just did it for you!" Lenore patted her sister's arm and asked if she could continue. "Just sayin," Loretta grumbled.

"We weren't sure how many people would be here, so we collected an assortment of odd and amusing items. Loretta wrapped half and I wrapped the rest. That way neither of us knows exactly what's what. The surprise is the fun part," she smiled. "You tell everybody the rules, Vernon."

My uncle stood up from arranging the jumble of wrapped packages on top of and beside the ottoman, which was moved closer to the fireplace to accommodate foot room. Vern smiled, his face rosy from bending over. He really did look like Santa in an eye patch. Vern received a round of applause; his one eye sparkled.

"The number you pick from the bowl determines who goes first. Just take a number and pass the bowl to the next person." Vern handed a cereal bowl filled with bits of paper to his wife, Loretta. "When it's your turn, you choose a present and open it. Loretta hates going first, because that poor soul doesn't have a chance to swap."

"Swap?" Blake asked.

"OK, your turn comes, you can take another person's white elephant and give them your ticket. That person takes your turn. Pretty basic. If you've had a bit to drink and get confused, just ask a Hudson woman. Hudson women love rules," he grinned. Vern got a chorus of boos for that one.

"All right, then! Who has number one?" Loretta couldn't wait to get started.

"I do." Caitlin waved her little white slip.

Eyebrow piercings gleaming in the firelight, Caitlin circled the pile of loot, her face bright with happiness. A long-time couch surfer and habitual outsider, the young woman suddenly found herself in the middle of family games, included as one of us. She chose a package about the size of a shoebox and held it up, glancing back and forth between the L&L's, looking for a sign. My twin aunts simply grinned at her, waiting for Caitlin to open the present.

"It's a…pig!" Caitlin said, wide-eyed. A hot water bottle, to be exact, dressed in a pink, fuzzy pig suit, with a round little snout, googly eyes, and pointy, black felt trotters. "Cool!" she declared, "Brunhilde will love it!" Caitlin gave the nearest L&L a big hug and sat down beaming. If anyone tried to swap that pig, I'd hit them.

A variety of white elephants appeared and traded hands to gales of laughter and applause, derisive hoots, and the occasional pout. Chas was not pleased at all when Blake claimed a lime green blanket with sleeves.

"Sorry, dude," Blake apologized, "but I just have to have it."

There was a giant jar of mango facial mask that ended up with Vern, a volcano-shaped bottle of bourbon, two kazoos and a bag of confetti—for New Year's Eve, Lenore explained—a goldfish in a baggie, which was immediately transferred to the cereal bowl for safe keeping, a laughing carp on a plaque, a pair of knee sox guaranteed to help pesky circulation problems, a Pilates instruction book, a guest pass to Deirdre's yoga studio—courtesy of Luce—a box of bullet-shaped erasers—obviously intended for Shore—and a tin of anatomically correct chocolates.

"Wait," I protested, trying to disqualify the candies. "Those things are a year old, at least! They're not safe to eat!"

"Hell, they are, too!" Loretta said, popping a tiny pink breast into her mouth. "Practically immortal, like Twinkies!"

I mentally checked out while the L&L's teased and provoked each other. A couple of questions kept nagging me. If Domenica Mancuso didn't kill Addison, who did? I reviewed details of the scene in the corn maze, the dark feeling of being watched hanging over it like a cloud.

Lenore shook her head at her sister. "Now, Loretta, I thought we agreed to throw those out when we dissolved the business."

"You agreed, sister mine! I like to keep 'em around, just to watch people's faces. Those little penises really get to folks!"

I chuckled along with everyone, still asking questions in my heads that contrasted with the hilarity. The Power Point threat at Angel Bride, the vandalism of my Benz...personal attack? Or had somebody paid for it, to study how I'd respond?

"You can trade the candies for the yoga pass, Lyle, Luce suggested with a sly smile.

"What?" I shook myself out of my dark mood and came up to speed fast, lightning poker moves kicking in. Deflect and deceive. "No, thanks. You're starting to sound like Chas, you know that? Change the Lyle to a Darling and it's totally him. You two cut that out!" I demanded.

"Cut what out?" they murmured, eyes wide and innocent.

"That!" I got up and started shoving wrapping paper into a plastic trash bag.

Mac took the bag from me. "Here, let me help with that." His eyes said it was time for him to go. Everyone in the room heard his eyes say it. The sudden quiet was pretty loud.

"Hey Luce?" Caitlin said, breaking the spell. "I'll take care of the goldfish for you. For a while, I mean. He won't have to change environments so much." Her love of creatures allowed Caitlin to ignore the complicated emotional atmosphere in the room.

"Thank you, Caitlin, that's a great idea," Luce said.

"That fish is cat food," Chas whispered in Luce's ear.

"Don't be an asshole, Chas," Caitlin said, standing up, cat in one hand, cereal bowl with small orange fish in the other. "I can look after the fish just fine!"

Chas held up his hands, ducking his head before Luce could smack it. "Of course you can," he said to the glaring young woman. "That was a clever remark gone bad. I apologize." Caitlin continued to glare at him. "Truly. Merry Christmas," Chas smiled endearingly. No one could resist Chas when he turned on the charm.

Caitlin shrugged. "OK. Merry Christmas." Détente was achieved. Caitlin left the library and headed upstairs.

Mac and I stood there awkwardly, avoiding each other's eyes, focused on the bag of used wrapping paper. Chas decided further diversion was called for.

"Fox trot, anyone? A little cozy dance or two among friends?"

"What's a fox trot?" Blake asked, wrapping Crista in his lime green arms.

"It's too late to take on the child's education," Loretta groaned. "Folks, it's time to leave. Come on, Vern! Let's go wait for Santa!"

General departure ensued, with Merry Christmases, hugs, bundling into coats and boots, everyone piling into vehicles and driving away. Crista and Blake retreated upstairs to research fox trot videos on computer. Mac and I remained in the hall by the front door, Jesse and Glory wagging tails expectantly.

MacDonald reached for his shearling jacket, draping the scarf around his neck, not taking his eyes off me. Jacket on, he lifted the Stetson from the hall table and took a step toward me. I moved into his arms and looked up. No words passed between us. It was a complicated kiss, tender and full of questions.

I stepped back and Mac put his hat on, took car keys and gloves from his pockets. He opened the door, letting in cold night air, and gestured Jesse out the door. I told Glory to stay.

"Good night, Lyle. Merry Christmas."

"Night. Merry Christmas." My voice felt thin and faint.

Standing at the door, I heard the solid chunk of the Mustang's door, watched the headlights go on, listened to the V-8 growl into life. Mac let the engine warm up a bit and then drove off, unhurried and deliberate. I closed the door and locked it, freezing in my bare feet. Glory sniffed around the door and then my knees, looking for clues.

"This sucks," I informed my curious dog. "It totally sucks."

44

"Bloody hell."

So much for impulse. I'd bundled Glory into her blue coat, bundled myself up, and headed to the Benz. I could have noticed that the snow in the back yard was up to my knees, but I didn't. I got an inkling in the alley, when the dog followed behind me instead of bounding ahead, but I trudged to the garage anyway. Staring at the garage door did it. A drift of snow climbed halfway up the door, a sheet of white glowing in the darkness. Even if I could shovel the door clear, I couldn't shovel the entire alley. There was no way the Benz would make it out to the street, much less to Mac's place outside of town. What was I thinking?

The I'll-show-him attitude evaporated in the cold air, along with visions of reconciliation sex, the feel of Mac's moustache on my face, his arms around me. I wanted to kick something. Snow was not satisfying in that regard.

"This wouldn't happen in Vegas," I told the dog as we retraced our steps. "It doesn't snow in Vegas." I stomped up the stairs, slammed the kitchen door, and clunked my boots around until I got them off.

"Lyle? You OK down there?" Caitlin called.

"Fine! Sorry about the noise."

"Everything's fine," she called up to Crista and Blake. Two doors closed.

"Fine. Right, Little Miss?" I got a lick as I helped Glory out of her coat. I felt so not fine.

With Glory at my heels, I checked that the doors were locked and walked through rooms, checking for things to pick up and put away. Everything was orderly and quiet. There was nothing to do, which left me to my restless self, who was feeling moody. I wandered to the front parlor and surveyed the tree with its Rainbow Serpent and jumble of presents waiting for tomorrow. I remembered broken glass, the bullets in the walls, the excitement of just a few weeks ago that now felt so distant in time. MacDonald was here, too. I sighed and left the room.

Upstairs, I turned on all the lights in my room and changed into an old pair of pajama bottoms and a long-sleeved t-shirt. On top of that I wore one of Louise's old sweaters, the kind that was a magnet for stray dog hair. Glory stretched out at the foot of the bed, plopped onto her side, and promptly fell asleep. It was late.

Avoiding the bed, I pulled out my old deck of cards from the dresser and moved to one of the chairs in the sitting area. Not that I ever sat here, but it was something to do with the extra space in the room. I moved a small table in front of my chair and looked around the room. No signs of Christmas here. I relaxed, fractionally. But the room felt too bright. I made adjustments and sat back down, noting the extent of my restlessness. It would be a long night.

I took the cards from their battered box and held them, shuffling slowly. My 'thinking' cards, so softened by use and time, curled and flapped like glove leather. Here I was again, turning to this deck when I needed to puzzle through a situation and examine how people and events fit together. I was looking for clues, as I studied the faces and aces. Nines and tens called attention to obstacles and complications.

I thumbed through the deck until I found the queen of diamonds. I placed her on the table. The thing about being a grown-up is that after a while you get it that the central problem of your life is you. So there, I was, front and center. "Hello, Lyle. Long time no see."

"Whose fault is that?" the queen archly replied. "Get on with it."

I hated the experience of looking at myself, but I knew I could avoid it only so long. Avoidance led to loss of sleep, bad poker, drinking to much, and ill-advised forms of acting out. Glory sighed in her sleep. Minutes passed.

Next card was the king of hearts. Usually, I made Mac the king of clubs because of his dark hair and his strength. Tonight I needed to be honest about the issue, painful as it was. In this deck, the king looked right out at you. I placed him next to the queen and stood up and walked away from the table to the bathroom.

I brushed my teeth, not meeting my eyes in the mirror. What I was doing with the cards made me feel so vulnerable I couldn't bear to look at myself. I knew my hair was silver as I brushed it, knew the lines around my mouth and eyes were there as I washed my face.

"Let's not forget to moisturize," Chas's voice admonished me. My eyes teared up. I missed him so much. I didn't mind his friendship with Luce, really; I just felt left out.

Back at the table, I examined the faces of the king and queen in the lamp light—no other faces necessary. What was the problem? Gambling? I put the ace of diamonds near the queen. No, MacDonald said he was OK with it. I left the card there, anyway, a reminder of importance. I placed all four tens beneath the king, indicating expectations. I picked them up again, recognizing that I was being unfair. Sorting through the deck once more, I took the two of hearts and placed it above the king and queen.

"There it is," I said aloud. The hair on my arms stood on end. I was creeping myself out.

"What's the problem?" the red queen asked. "You love him, don't you?" I put on my poker face and thought about it.

"Well, don't you?" Insistent bitch. "What is it with you?" she squinted up at me with a critical eye.

Did I love MacDonald George? Could I answer that question honestly? I was certainly unhappy when he left, when the snow kept me from going after him. How much of that was vanity? I was the one who did the leaving. It was part of my charm. I placed all four nines below the queen of diamonds. Complications, barriers I erected around myself.

The queen was getting impatient with me. "Quit stalling, stop the psychobabble and get to the point.

"Do I love him?"

"Duh!" she rolled her eyes at me.

"Yes. I do. But I'm not sure I want to love him."

I turned the queen face down before she could scold me. I turned the king over, too, with his charming, unchanging expression.

"It changes too much!" I raked my fingers through my hair, stood up and sat down again. I stared at the backs of the cards, fancying I could hear papery muttering as the queen and king shared complaints about me. I was afraid and they knew it. I was afraid that loving Mac would mean losing my independence, my self-sufficiency. I was afraid I'd get trapped and tangled up in having to explain myself and be answerable all the time. I was afraid I'd screw it up. I felt the fears as I thought about them. I turned the Nines over so they, too, were face down, then I turned over the aces. All the cards looked exactly the same—blank. It was not a reassuring picture. Nothing ventured, nothing gained. Great. Now my dead mother was putting in her two cents.

I remembered a conversation from childhood, when I'd asked Louise what it felt like to fall in love, and how would I know. We were in the back yard, in coats and boots, and she was cutting forsythia switches to bring indoors and force into early bloom. The tiny flowers would look like yellow stars in a gray world.

"Oh, you'll know," she said. "There is nothing else that feels anything like it. Love can be sudden, or it can sneak up on you. It's an amazing thing, Lyle." She bent down and brought her face close to mine, eyes bright. And then she whispered, "It's so scary and so sweet! It's kisses just for you!" My mother grabbed my face and started kissing me all over—on my eyelids and my nose and my chin. I squirmed, trying to get away but not really, the two of us wrestling and giggling in the forsythia bush.

I was focusing on the scary and forgetting the sweet. Muffled assent from the mind reading playing cards. I picked them up and returned them to the tattered box, giving the queen one last look.

"I'm working on it," I told her.

"Just don't be a jerk," she snapped. Queens.

45

"Mac?" I was in bed with the cell phone, Glory snoring softly at my feet. It was later than late. I ignored the time, not letting myself get cold feet.

"What is it? Are you OK?" His voice was hoarse with sleep.

"I was thinking about what you said earlier. About making choices, about being honest with myself and not being such an ass."

"I never said that," Mac said, humor tingeing his voice. "I'm quite sure I never called you an ass," he said. "Tightly wrapped, maybe, but not an ass."

"Thanks."

"You're welcome." A small silence presented itself, stretched and rolled around between us.

I cleared my throat. "I tried to follow you tonight."

"How far did you get?"

"To the garage. There was a drift against the door."

"I'm glad."

"You are?" I tried not to sound disappointed.

"You'd never have made it. Jesse and I had to hike in almost a mile from the road. Thought I'd killed my dog at one point."

"You could have come back here," I said, lamely. No. We both knew he was stuck with the snow at the time.

"Why are you calling, Lyle?"

"I'm calling because I love you, MacDonald, and thought you should know. It seemed important to tell you." The pause stretched and rolled over. I thought I was going to throw up.

"I know."

"You know I love you?"

"Yes, I do..."

"Wait!" I interrupted whatever he was going to say. "How could you know that without me telling you?" Hell, I didn't even know it until the interview with the queen.

"People know. Don't get your feathers ruffled. You knew I loved you, right?"

"Loved? It's over?"

Mac laughed. "You know I love you. That's not the issue. What I need to know, and you need to know, Lyle, is whether you and I can build a life out of that love. I think we can. Do you?" I scratched the pause on its tummy.

"Oh, yeah. We can. I'm a believer."

We snuggled as best we could on the phone, saying mushy things to each other and cursing the snow. I felt like that Wallenda guy who walked a tightrope across Niagara Falls. But he used a safety harness. I did not. I was excited and exhausted and needed sleep bad.

"I'll see you tomorrow," Mac said.

"Yes you will. And I'll see you, too." I smiled and turned off the phone.

46

I woke up to a single, sharp bark from Glory at the foot of the bed. The sudden lurch into consciousness startled me, and it took a minute to adjust to being awake. I sat up and looked at the dog, who was standing on alert, facing the bedroom door. She looked over her shoulder at me, then back at the door. Glory usually liked to sleep in; I wondered what was up.

Glory jumped down and stretched into a perfect downward facing dog pose, reminding me that so many yoga poses were named after the natural movements of animals. Nothing like a totally random thought for your first thought of the day, Lyle.

I rubbed my eyes and squinted at the clock. Seven a.m. "Way too early," I complained to the dog. I'd had, what, three hours sleep? I replayed last night's conversation with Mac in my head while Glory stood there looking at me. It felt good, no regrets, no second thoughts or anxiety. I hardly recognized myself. I smiled and got out of bed and scouted around for a robe. Not finding one, I opted for Louise's hairball sweater and pulled it over the t-shirt. It would do.

"You're going out and then it's right back to bed, OK?" Glory parked herself by the bedroom door and waited.

Stumbling around the room, looking for slippers I couldn't find, I came across the .38, sitting on the dresser without its holster. Damn. Scolding myself for carelessness, I stuck the gun in a sweater pocket. The weight of it dragged the old sweater to my knees. This was ridiculous. Muttering and wrestling with the gun and the stretchy sweater, I stumbled to the foot of the stairs, Glory scrambling ahead of me. I managed to get the yak boots onto my cold feet with one hand, groaning and hopping around, wisps of silver hair plastering themselves to my eyes. Glory growled. Had she spotted an escaped rat? I turned toward the dog and glanced past her, down the hall to the kitchen, where Andressa Keach sat at the kitchen table, pointing a gun at me.

To be exact, she was aiming past Blake, who was sitting very still across the table from an angry woman with an angry face. Glory barked, and I bent over, ostensibly to quiet the dog, but I was fumbling madly with the gun in the folds of the sweater. Glory quieted, but only just. Andressa gestured with the gun, directing me to join her in the kitchen.

"You OK, Blake?"

The young man nodded tensely.

"No talking!" Andressa ordered, waving the gun around. Was she drunk?

I stood in the entrance to the kitchen, bunching wads of sweater, hoping I looked tangled and helpless.

"That's my gun, Andressa," I said conversationally.

"Careless of you to leave it lying about." She narrowed her eyes at me.

I stood very still and waited her out.

"You are dangerously stupid, Lyle. I thought you figured out I'd killed him, that you were playing me. So I tried to get close to you to find out." She shook her head. "Stupid." Andressa leaned her elbows on the table, bracing the gun, steadying her aim, somewhere around my mid-section.

She glanced briefly out the window, where the day was slowly brightening. Blake shifted in his seat. Andressa cocked an eyebrow as if to say too bad about the boy.

"If he'd just done it my way, I wouldn't have had to shoot him. It was over but he wouldn't go away, Ron. Tried to threaten me, to show Carl the pictures. Stupid man. Carl didn't care. Ron shouldn't have threatened me, though. The corn maze was perfect! It could've taken weeks to find him. Except for you."

"Andressa …"

"Shut up! You came back to Lawrence. Again. I almost had a chance with Mac. Except for you." She said the word 'you' the way someone would turn over pocket aces, convinced they had the winning hand.

Andressa laughed at the shock on my face when she mentioned Mac. "Yes! I almost got him. He and Carl hate each other. It must have been tempting. Then you ruined it!" She shouted at me and rose from the kitchen chair, gun in both hands, her face red with rage.

It seemed to happen in slow motion, but it was over in seconds. I yelled at Blake to grab Glory, and as he ducked down, I reached my arms in front of me and shot Andressa through the stretchy wool of the sweater, flinging myself over the table at her. She shrieked, rocked back in the chair and fired as she went down.

Ears ringing, I scrambled off the table and bent over the woman writhing on the floor. She was bleeding and groaning, clutching her side. I told Blake to take Glory out of the room, grab a phone, and dial 911, which he promptly did. I took two dishtowels and folded them tightly, kneeling down to apply pressure to Andressa's wound.

She lay on her back now, bloody hands grabbing her side, face contorted, breathing in shallow gasps. I thought my hands were shaking as I held the wad of towels, but it was my whole body, overloaded with adrenaline. It looked like Andressa was going to die on my kitchen floor, and I could do nothing to keep that from happening. That's what happens when you shoot a hole in someone—they die. Shore would have told me that was the point. He'd have said I'd done good. Nothing about the situation felt good to me right then.

The police and EMT's arrived. Somebody helped me stand up. I washed the blood off my hands at the kitchen sink. I felt wired and shaky and I couldn't think. The smell of blood made me retch. My hands felt numb as I grabbed onto the sink.

A young policeman I didn't know helped me from the room. We went into the library, which felt cool and quiet after the chaos in the kitchen.

"Anything I can get you, ma'am? Glass of water?"

My mouth felt dry as ashes. I nodded and brushed the tangled hair from my face. Alone for a moment, I gazed around the familiar room. I had always felt so comfortable in this house, secure. Now there were bullet holes in the walls, blood on the kitchen floor. I'd shot a woman I thought was my friend at close range, in my own house. Suddenly, my brain switched gears. What was she doing here? Why? How did she get in? It was crazy, surreal.

The cop handed me a glass of water, and my hand shook as I took it from him. I drank the water and took a deep breath.

"Just tell me what happened, ma'am, and I'll stop and ask questions as I need to. No rush, all right?"

"You bet." I hated being called ma'am, and the irritation made me feel more myself. The interview did not take long, the story of coming downstairs and shooting Andressa Keach was minimal.

Recounting the whole thing helped me regain some perspective. The woman was out of control, and I'd had the bad luck to be in the path of her storm of jealous rage. I just had to stop blaming myself for the disaster.

"Any idea why she came here?" the young cop asked.

"She thought I had Addison's pictures of her." Why are some women so stupid, I wondered, showing their bony bare asses to a camera at their age? "When she found out I didn't have them, she became enraged. Is her husband OK? Did she kill him, too?"

"We're looking into that, ma'am."

"Lyle. Call me Lyle. I don't like to be ma'amed."

"Right," he nodded. "Anything else?"

"About her logic? Well..." I stopped and tried to put myself in Andressa's place. But I couldn't do it, and shook my head. "Not a clue. I thought she was my friend ..." The thought of all that hate silenced me.

The young man started to get up and make polite comments about staying in touch. I stood up, too wrapping the ratty sweater tightly around me.

He gave me a patient, understanding nod and checked his watch. Time to go, lady, his attitude said. My attitude wanted to smack him. I was starting to feel better.

Another officer came in and told my guy the EMT's were taking Andressa to the hospital, that she was stable now. They conferred quietly and I shifted my attention to Glory, who paced beside me.

"Excuse me, but my dog needs to go out. Can we go through the kitchen?"

"No, ma'am—Lyle—'fraid the kitchen is a crime scene."

"Oh," I said in a small voice. "I'll just—take her out front, then..."

I let Glory out front and came back in to find Crista, Blake, Caitlin and Berg the cat sitting on the stairs.

"Hey," I greeted them. They hey'd me back. "Are you OK, Blake?" I felt terrible about the danger he'd been in.

"Hell no!" he laughed reaching out to pat Glory, who had squeezed past Crista to get to him. "I almost OD'd on adrenaline, man! It was all, like, slow motion yet very fast. I'm going down, grabbing Glory, thinking shit! I'm gonna get shot! Then, BAM! You nailed her! Kickass Lyle, going over the top, shooting! I thought I was going to be deaf, you know? It was awesome!"

Blake's excitement and enthusiasm broke the tension that had engulfed us all, and we felt closer, safer for it.

"Still," I said, "you could have been hurt. I'm so sorry, Blake."

Narrowly avoiding a group hug, I suggested we decamp and go impose ourselves on the L&Ls, who likely had a wealth of sticky buns. And no blood on the kitchen floor.

47

"You shot her? Outstanding!"

We were at work digging out the garage door and clearing a narrow path from the alley to the street, when Martin Shore joined us, one of those ergonomic snow shovels slung over his shoulder. Jacketless despite the cold, sidearm strapped to his belt, dark stubble outlining his jaw, Shore emanated a lethal, wolf-like grace, nothing Santa-like about him at all.

The three young people clamored around him, all telling bits of the story at once. Margot and Glory bounced around in the snow, chasing snowballs that Crista lobbed up the alley. Blake got to the part about flying through the air, shooting through my sweater and Shore laughed out loud and pulled me to him.

"Well done, Lyle," he growled in my ear, then kissed me, hard on the cheek.

"Hey. Thanks." I could do lame like nobody's business. Shore got the message and stepped back.

"Mad, bad, and dangerous to know," I muttered, idly wondering if Lord Byron liked to play with guns.

Caitlin pushed forward and threw her arms around Shore. Bless the man, he didn't shrug her off but gave her a big hug and asked about Brunhilde.

"She's great, Shore, awesome! When we come back later, after the cops are gone, you can see for yourself."

Shore glanced at the house briefly, a hard glint in his eye. He stuck a smile on his face and said it sounded like a plan.

"Let's put these shovels to work and get you out of here," he said.

I invited Shore to join us at the L&L's, but he politely declined, promising he'd stop by later as planned. If what I suspected was true, he was probably checking up on his crazy uncles again, keeping the family war from going nuclear. Christmas can have a destructive power, I thought.

Bags of presents in the trunk, we got the Benz onto the street without mishap and negotiated roads that were mostly drivable, to the rambling house that belonged to Loretta and Vern, but we called it the L&L's house because the twins sisters were inseparable. Vern always said that apart from Loretta's habit of bickering, it was a place of peace and harmony. He also went fishing fairly often.

I followed the tracks of Luce's truck up the snowy driveway, glad they were there so we wouldn't have to walk in from the street. The bright yellow of the truck glowed against the white of the snow. That Luce was here meant that I'd face a full Hudson court of inquiry. Maybe I could use Christmas as a get-out-of-jail-free card. My three young friends would be a buffer. Hudsons could be clannish about their business. I'd have to wait and see.

Leaving coats and boots in the mudroom, we headed into the house. I hung back and let the others go ahead. I pulled my cell out and texted Mac. I'd let too much time pass before contacting him. Some believer I was. Lyle and the endless pile of new leaves. I sent the text inviting Mac to join us and then changed my mind and decided to call.

"Just got your text. What's up? Merry Christmas, by the way."

"I thought you deserved a human-voice apology for not calling sooner. I'm sorry, Mac. Merry Christmas."

There was a significant pause. "What did you do?"

My turn to pause. Just saying I'm sorry was hard enough.

Mac broke into the silence. "You didn't have time to do anything, Lyle. We talked on the phone half the night. It's still early in the day. You couldn't get anywhere because of the snow." He was thinking it through. "You didn't shoot anyone did you? Not Crista, Blake, Caitlin. Shore? Did you shoot Martin Shore?" The man was stymied.

"Yes. I did shoot someone, but it's not what you think!" My lower lip trembled and my eyes started to leak. For reasons unknown to me, I was feeling fairly emotional. "It was Andressa ..."

"WHO?" I could hear his eyeballs bugging out. "That's impossible!"

I took the phone away from my ear and then put it back. I was now officially mad. "Oh, yeah? Well, she shot Ron Addison, she broke into my house, she held Blake hostage, and I shot her! Don't believe me. Come over and ask anyone. We're at the L&L's. Goodbye!" I ended the call and threw a yak boot against the wall.

"That make you feel better, sweetheart?" Pirate Santa was standing in the doorway. I went over to Vern and wrapped my arms around his neck, proceeding to sniffle into his Christmas vest.

"Oh, Vern, I can't do it. I can't face them."

"Come on, hon. It'll be alright. The kids told the story while you were out here on the phone. Those girls are concerned about you, more concerned than angry, Lyle. Come on inside."

The kitchen smelled of coffee and cinnamon. A pan of sticky buns was being passed around, for a second time, evidently. It was all but empty. Lenore reassured me that another pan would come out of the oven shortly. I was pointed to a seat at the kitchen table and the entire circle of family and friends stood up and arranged themselves around me.

"She doesn't look that bad!" Loretta announced. "Maybe a touch peckish, but we've seen worse!"

"True," Luce agreed. "I think it's lack of proper sleep," she added, gesturing with her mug. "Look at the circles under her eyes. At 'a certain age' one must look after oneself."

"Brilliant, absolutely brilliant," Chas said, giving Luce a hug. "But I think she needs to be commended, both for aim and courage, don't you agree?"

"Here, here!" People raised various beverage containers in my direction. I ducked my head and started to laugh.

"Here," Loretta shoved a champagne glass at me, "This will help with your ontological insecurity. It'll pass, always does!" The bells on her felt antlers chimed as she nodded her head.

"Champagne?" I accepted the glass.

"No caffeine for Femme Nikita," Chas admonished.

"We know you dislike eggnog, dear," Lenore said, "and orange juice just spoils the wine."

"Beer kinda clashes with breakfast pastry," Vern chimed in.

"So we all voted for champagne," Crista said from her permanent roost on Blake's lap.

I raised my glass to them. "I love you all. Merry Christmas."

Oh—Good King Wenceslas looked out, on the feast of Stephen!" Loretta boomed and marched around the kitchen, antlers jingling, wisps of curly white hair bouncing like demented angel fluff. She exited the room, her voice echoing back to us, strange and marvelous syllables embellishing the phrase 'figgy pudding.'

"Did she say freaking pudding?" I asked.

"Froggy pudding, more like," Vern said, shaking his head. "You never know. If she gives it up before February, I'll be a happy man."

"Think I'll go lie down," Luce said, carefully placing her champagne glass by the sink.

"Door on the left," Vern said.

"I know where I am, Vernon."

"Yes, ma'am." My uncle knew the futility of sparring with Hudson women. But he forgot the injunction against ma'aming. Fortunately, Luce chose to ignore the offensive word and went to put her feet up.

I found Chas in the living room, putting a throw over Loretta, who had dived onto the couch. He turned to me, hands on hips, and sighed.

"Really," Chas said, "I feel rather like Dorothy, only I can't tell if I'm in Oz or Kansas."

"Oh, it's Kansas, alright," I assured him.

"I begin to understand your reluctance to return."

"How so?"

Chas flapped his arms. "It's just so intense! Lovely people. Mesmerizing, actually—but, darling, it's like doing drugs!"

"You don't do drugs, Chas," I reminded him.

"It's what doing drugs would feel like if I did do drugs, Miss Picky." Chas paused and scrutinized my attire.

White cashmere turtleneck, black jeans, totally acceptable. If he said a word, I'd smack him.

"You're not," he waved a hand at me, "wearing a gun, are you?"

"Chas!" I yelled at him, fairly certain my silver hair was standing on end.

"Just checking," he said.

"Is this a private fight, or can anyone join in?" MacDonald George stood at the door, Jesse beside him. He grinned, which was irritating, but I forgave him because he looked so good. Chas quietly left the room.

The hello-hug-and-kiss was very nice, but I became suspicious at how much time Mac's hands were spending at my hips.

"I. Am not. Carrying," I said through clenched teeth.

"Never crossed my mind." He kissed me.

"Liar." Kissed again. I could so play this game.

"How are you, really?" Mac asked.

"Much better," I sighed.

Mac looked over at the supine Loretta and back at me, his eyes asking if we should leave the room.

"Nah, she's OK." I looked up at the tall man, deeply glad to see him. "Let's sit over here." We took the couch facing Loretta's and spoke in whispers.

"You got here OK?" I started to say.

"Shh," Mac shushed me. "I'm not here to talk about the weather."

"No?" I was disappointed. Guns. Had to be guns he wanted to discuss.

"Not here about the shooting, either, Lyle," Mac said. "Greta confirmed Andressa did kill Addison. Took me by surprise."

I looked at Mac.

"Hey, she was married. I'm not that guy, Lyle. By the way Greta Danielson says to stay out of her way. If I were you, I'd do it."

"I need some water. How about you?"

"Just sit here for a minute. Please."

I settled back into the couch. "Mac?"

"Um hm."

"That's a box."

"Good. You know what it is. Open it. Please."

"But..."

"You're a believer, you said so yourself."

"I did." Oddly enough, I think I still was.

"I'll explain when you open it."

"OK." I opened the box and, yes, it held a ring, a delicate circle of silvery leaves.

"What kind of leaves are they?"

"Don't know. Leaf-leaves. A complication of leaves."

"Complication. I like that. What does it mean?"

"I thought you'd like it. Take a guess."

"That I'm complicated? We're complicated? More than friends? Like that?" I said quietly.

"Exactly like that. The ring says so."

"Well said, ring."

Mac took the ring and put it on my left hand. "Lyle Hudson, I am asking you to enter complicated territory with me."

"But I don't have a ring for you," I stalled.

"I took the liberty of acquiring one on your behalf."

Mac took another box from his pocked and opened it. Same leaves, only larger. He handed me the ring.

"Thanks!" I smiled. "You're very clever, you know that?"

"I do. Know that."

"MacDonald George, will you get complicated with me?"

"With all my heart."

I contemplated the rings, side by side. "They look like something from Andressa's store."

"They are. It's a long story."

"Andressa?"

"Life is complicated."

"What the hell, I'm all in." Complication never felt so good.

Elisabeth Lee earned a Ph.D. in Victorian Literature from the University of Colorado at Boulder. A retired private school teacher and sometime administrator, she lives in Denver, Colorado. It figures prominently in her work, along with San Francisco, Lawrence, Kansas and New York City where she has also lived.